Totally Bound Publishing books by MJ Klipfel

Crossed Souls

Blood Promotion

Blood Coronation

Crossed Souls

BLOOD CORONATION

MJ KLIPFEL

Blood Coronation
ISBN # 978-1-80250-547-4

Interior text design by Claire Siemaszkiewicz
Totally Bound Publishing

Published in 2023 by Totally Bound Publishing, United Kingdom.

Totally Bound Publishing is an imprint of Totally Entwined Group Limited.

BLOOD CORONATION

Dedication

Mom and Dad—thank you for being epic. Natalia—
thank you for reading *that* scene three hundred times.
Nikki—you're my badass angel. Anna.
Readers—enjoy the ride.
Coffee. So much coffee.

Chapter One

In the dead of January, there were only two reasons for a person to move to upstate New York. One—they had an unhealthy obsession with snowmobiling. Two—they were hiding from someone…or thing.

From the over-stuffed canvas sack tossed over his shoulder to his brisk pace, signs pointed to the new neighbor's residency edging toward reason number two. Hiding. Which had my curiosity on overdrive and my worry on full alert.

For the past three months, the only renters at the secluded property housing a shed and three decrepit log cabins had been me and my best friend, Ben. We were also residents for reason number two, and I was pretty sure that if the landlord knew their tenants were a werewolf and a country-music-loving reporter, they'd let it slide to keep the rent coming in.

Tilting my head, I studied the neighbor. He sure knew his way around the winter elements. At his clip, the average person would've faceplanted. My right glute throbbed in memory of my most recent ice encounter. Not average or human, I still was a klutz all the same.

Well…he looks human.

As I cracked the window, frigid air bit my fingertips, and my sharp inhale had the hairs of my nostrils sticking together. Rubbing the freeze from my nose, I sniffed. Past the exhaust from his rundown vehicle, the scent of leather and sweat carried to me.

Smells human.

Still… I closed my eyes. Buffering one sense intensified the others. Beneath the sweat, a faint tartness of lemon and fresh-cut grass drifted from the neighbor. *Bingo.* He ticked a box on the nonhuman checklist. Monsters had a distinct base scent. No amount of perfume or body spray could mask it. Sure, the neighbor passed as human, but all it took was a drop of blood or a full moon to lose the act. From my brief introduction to the monster world, *good* nonhumans were nonexistent.

Myself included.

Unless the neighbor was a half-blood. I'd never had a chance to sniff one. An unsuspecting human with watered-down genes from a long-dead nonhuman race. An instant death sentence if they crossed a vampire.

Shit. Of all the damn days to move in, he picked today.

I opened my eyes to meet the man's dark narrowed gaze. With no way to duck out of view, I offered a wave. "Why don't you just go on and leave," I gritted through my tight smile.

He tilted his chin in greeting, then headed up the steps to his cabin.

"Don't get too comfortable," I grumbled at his closing door.

Taking a step away from the window, I knocked my heel against a box filled with Ben's comic book collection. All that we owned fit inside that box and an overnight bag. On the optimistic side, it made packing up easy-peasy. On the flip side, a life with dozens of throw blankets and candles wasn't in our future.

I sighed at the box. Once more, the collection waited to be shoved into the trunk of Ben's rust-bucket. He had a valid reason. Last night a vampire had left his calling card on our doorstep. Well, more like a debt-collection notice. I owed the bloodsucker a favor. However, I had freed his ass from the former Queen Bloodsucker. In my opinion, that was the favor of all favors.

Memories fought to the surface of my mind, setting my heart beating wildly against my ribs. To keep from being dragged into the depths of my subconscious, I focused on the afternoon sun highlighting the comics. The plan was for us to head to Georgia's Blue Ridge Mountains within the next hour. Was—keyword. In good conscience, I couldn't let the neighbor become the bloodsucker's dinner.

Grabbing my phone, I sent a text to Ben.

On a run.

Instantly, my phone vibrated with his response.

No. I'm fifteen minutes out. We are leaving.

Guilt slunk around my brain as I left my phone on the desk and tugged on my windbreaker. Before the neighbor's unfortunate appearance, I had been gearing up for my daily run. Physical fatigue kept the wolf under my skin content-ish. With a two-day road trip ahead, stuck in a car with Ben yodeling to country music, I'd need to run a freaking marathon. Dropping a stick of cinnamon gum into my pocket, I headed for the door.

Outside, a snow squall offered me a greeting of pelting ice crystals and blistering wind. I tucked my head and, with great caution, trotted down the steps. *Fifteen minutes.* Plenty of time to break a sweat and scare the shit out of the neighbor.

* * * *

Deep in the evergreen forest, I forced myself to continue trudging through the new foot-worth of powder snow. In the distance, snowmobiles whizzed by on the trail. Although my thighs and lungs burned, pleading with me to take the path of least resistance, I didn't want to end up as roadkill, so I kept on my trailblazing course toward the cliff's jetty.

Soon, all that mattered was paying respect to my past transgressions. Not the vampire and his stupid favor. Not the neighbor and his lemongrass scent. Not Ben and his country music remixes. Just my regrets. Two very big, handsome…monster mistakes. Plenty enough to distract me from the elements by setting my blood boiling and mind spinning.

Minutes later, dripping in sweat, I made it to the clearing. Thankfully, no one had ventured off the snowmobile trail, leaving the patch of land unmarred by humans. In the center stood a massive evergreen. *Yep. Some fine human world esthetics.* The scenic view belonged as a backdrop to a holiday card…not as a gravesite.

Every day, I made a pilgrimage to the boulder leaning against the evergreen's trunk. Tears prickled my eyes while I brushed away a blanket of snow, revealing dozens of frozen gum wrappers clinging to the stone façade. Pausing, I folded my arms around myself.

"Nathaniel found us," I whispered to Andrea's makeshift grave. "I thought we were safe." A gust of wind screamed against my ears, triggering memories of the Vampire Queen's lips painted with Andrea's blood. I gasped. "I'm sorry. I promise—"

Snow dusted the crown of my head and I snapped my attention upward to a large crow perching on a branch. Under the judgment of the bird's beady eyes, my ears warmed with the heat of embarrassment.

"Nothing to see here." I glared at the crow. "Shoo. Go."

The bird blinked its creepy third eyelids at me.

"You know, I've never eaten crow before." Raising my lips off my teeth, I let a growl rumble from my chest.

Unamused at my threat, the bird ruffled its feathers.

"Fine. Freeze your beak off." Fishing the stick of gum out of my pocket, I settled to my knees and placed my offering on top of the boulder. With my focus locked on Andrea's grave, I strained my ears, willing to hear her snarky advice. As always, silence answered.

"I promise, I'll keep Ben safe," I said. "I'll keep them *all* safe."

Mere seconds passed before frostbite gnawed at my knees. Shivering, I rose to my feet. "You better not eat that gum." I jabbed my finger at the empty branch. Turning, I scanned the vacant surroundings. *Weird.* When I glanced back at the tree, glaring sunlight reflected off its ice-coated bark. The crow wasn't the only thing that had vanished. At least a half-hour had flown by.

Tearing down my path, I prayed that no humans caught a glimpse of me hauling ass through the three-foot-deep snow, and if they did, they'd chalk it up to their day drinking. *Hopefully.*

When I rounded the forest edge, I skidded to a halt. Only the neighbor's car sat in the snow-covered driveway. Smoke, drifting from the neighbor's chimney, hinted at his whereabouts.

Perfect.

I circled to the back of the cabin. Inside, footsteps milled around to the beat of seventies rock music. *Nice.* Lengthening my claws, I locked my attention on the woodpile stacked alongside the backdoor while formulating a plan to send the neighbor packing.

Step one—I used the woodpile as a ramp to propel myself onto the roof. To keep from sliding off, I dug my claws against the shingles. Once I hoisted myself upright, I tore off my windbreaker, then stuffed it down the chimney. With a hip slide, I exited the roof, falling into a snowdrift.

Step two—I hauled ass back to my cabin.

While I rounded the side of the building, a grin spread across my face. Still no sign of Ben's rust bucket, and now the neighbor would be good and gone before we left for Georgia. With a little victory dance, I climbed the steps to my cabin. "Nathaniel can suck on our exhaust fumes—" I froze mid-fist-pump.

The neighbor stood at my front door.

Chapter Two

Fighting the urge to brush the snow from my running tights and T-shirt, I checked my surprise and walked up the rest of the steps. The wind caught the stray salt-and-pepper hairs framing the neighbor's ageless face of sculpted angles. Maybe it was the hypothermia setting in. One moment he looked fifty, the next, twenty.

"Hi." My voice trembled from the cold. "Can I—"

He turned his head toward the side of my cabin. "Your window is open."

"Oh." I kept my focus on him while the fine hairs along my arms stood on end. Like a vampire, the man stood motionless. Unlike a bloodsucker, his heart beat slow and steady. "I better go shut it." Hoping my words would move him, but no luck, he kept rooted in front of my door. "Nice to meet you…"

"Corbus," he answered.

He made no move to shake my hand.

Nor did I.

"If you don't mind stepping aside, Corbus." I ticked my chin at the door. "I'd like to shut the window before my roommate gets back."

His gaze drew to my bare arms. "Where is your coat?"

"Inside. Less wind resistance without a jacket." Confident with my half-truth, I nodded to myself. "I run. Lots."

Corbus tipped his chin at the sky. "Bad storm coming."

No shit, meteorologist. Gritting my teeth, I kept my snark hidden. "Looks it."

Snow blew across the driveway. Not unlike Ben to run late. When it stormed, he drove like an eighty-year-old. The wind blasting against the back of my kneecaps sparked an idea.

"Smell that?" My nose tingled from the neighbor's scent. Scrunching my face, I played up the reaction to the chimney fire that I'd started. "Stinks like...burnt plastic."

Corbus spared a glance at his cabin where black smoke billowed out of the chimney. His mouth drew into a flat line. As he hustled past me, energy blazed across my skin.

Definitely not human.

Releasing my breath, I plucked the key from my frozen tights and shoved it into the lock. Once inside, I sighed in delight from the dry heat pelting my face. Still, my teeth chattered so violently that I almost missed my phone signaling a text message. The only person with my number was Ben. Forcing my stiff limbs into movement, I grabbed my cell.

Four missed messages.

Running late.

The main road's blocked by a tree.

I cut my attention to the neighbor's cabin. Smoke floated out of the front door and the canvas sack now sat disregarded on the porch. Grinning, I glanced at my phone.

Went the back way.

Blocked by a tree too.

Corbus emerged from the cabin. When he looked at my window, I plastered my back against the wall, hoping to avoid him spotting me.

My phone buzzed, making me about jump through my skin.

"Hey," I said.

"Where the hell have you been?" Ben asked.

"I went running."

"The wind is dropping trees left and right." His exaggerated breath hit the receiver. "You could have been crushed."

"I'm fine. So. Listen, we have a problem." I turned just long enough to shut the window, then re-plastered myself against the wall. "We have a neighbor."

"Had." Ben's voice took on a stern tone. "As in past tense. We are leaving. They can—"

"I handled it. He'll be leaving soon."

"What did you do?"

"Set a chimney fire."

A string of curses flowed into my eardrum.

"Relax, it's only some smoke." I chanced a look. "Wow. A lot of smoke."

"I can't leave you alone for a minute." Ben groaned. "Shit. Another tree down. It'll be damn near dusk by the time I get back. *Wait.* I'm five miles away on Black River Road. Can you catch a ride with this person?"

"That's a big nope. I'm not getting into a car with him." I ran my fingers along the yellowed cord to the blinds. "He's not human."

A brief pause preceded Ben's tentative question, "Is he a werewolf?"

"No."

"How do you know?"

"He doesn't act like one. No glowing eyeballs or trying to drag me to his pack."

"Then what is he?"

"I don't know. Maybe a half-blood? He has a smell, and his energy did this snap thing against me."

"You got that up close and personal?"

"He was at the door when I came back from my run. Caught me off guard."

"What if he knows about you not being…"

I glanced at my bare shoulder, semi-optimistic that Corbus had bought the missing jacket story. I kicked my gaze to my wet sneakers. *Shit.* My attention darted to the size-eight-snow-prints leading away from Corbus' smoke-filled cabin and up to my front doorstep. "Umm. Nahhh."

"Yeah, I'm not happy with that answer," Ben muttered. "You know what? We're wasting time. Turn into a wolf and run your ass over here."

"I can't…control." I sighed. "I'm not going to—"

"You won't eat me."

"Do you *not* remember last month?"

"That's because you refuse to practice. And I got up the tree in time."

"Barely." I pressed the heel of my hand against my forehead. "Never. Ever. Again. Will I Change around you."

"It was my fault. I should have warned you I was outside. Now, I'm letting you know. I'm safe. I'll be in the—"

"Werewolves can destroy cars."

"Then shift before you get to the crossroad. You can't miss the down tree. That's where I'll wait for you, *inside* my car. I have an extra coat in the trunk. We can buy you clothes in the next town."

"No." I dragged my fingers down my face. "Both ways into town are blocked. I'm going to give the neighbor directions to the snowmobile lodge before he ends up as vampire cuisine."

"There's two hours and eleven minutes before sunset. The more time you—"

Knuckles rapped against the front door.

"Shh," I hushed Ben. "He's here. I'll keep you on the phone."

"Tess—"

I shoved the phone into the waistband of my tights. Tucking the damp strands of wayward hair behind my ears, I straightened my spine and slapped on a blank expression.

As I cracked the door, snow flurries hit my face. A near whiteout engulfed Corbus bracing against the wind. The canvas sack resting against his thigh kicked my panic into gear. *Oh no, is his car dead? Crap.* Corbus' attention latched onto my chin. Come to think of it, never had he looked into my eyes. I stole a peek at the floorboards. A layer of snow masked my footprints. *Phew.* I returned my focus to Corbus.

"The smoke needs time to clear out." With his unasked question, Corbus' gaze shifted over my shoulder toward my kitchen.

"Look. You seem like a nice guy, but I don't know you." I swallowed. "Before it gets worse, you should take a left out of here. Seven miles down the road there's a snowmobile lodge. I'm sure they could take you in until the smoke clears."

Corbus' gaze narrowed. "I don't trust men."

Same. Hell, the whole human race minus Ben. Oh, I'd toss in every bloodsucker and werewolf, too. I owned my trust issues. They had kept me alive. So far.

Corbus lifted his arms, exposing his open palms. "I bring no harm."

The foreign gesture set my teeth to worry at my lip. "I—"

The shrill of a car horn sounded from my phone.

"Excuse me." With my focus still on Corbus' hands, I fumbled for my phone. "Ben? Ben!"

The horn stopped.

"Don't..." Static crackled between Ben's words. "Let...him...in."

"Not planning on it."

"Tess? I can't...hear—"

The line went dead.

"Shit," I muttered under my breath. Corbus' focus lingered on the phone shaking in my hand. "I'm sorry about your cabin. But you need to go. Now."

Corbus lowered his hands, then turned to walk down the steps.

Overhead, the streetlight flickered on, sending my pulse to tick at my temples. Vampires were dead until sunset. Except for Nathaniel. His special ass was undead and bitchy at any hour. Thankfully, the sun still burned him to a crunchy crisp. Yet with the cloak of the snowstorm, there was a possibility that the bloodsucker could make an early arrival.

Shit. Shit. Shit... I bounced on the balls of my feet. A foot away, the abandoned canvas sack gathered snow on its weathered surface. "Wait. You left your stuff."

Corbus slowly turned. When his gaze rose to mine, calmness flooded my nervous system. I tried to shake the sensation, but my bones hummed with the urge to trust him. He moved back up the steps. "You need it more than me." He crouched over the sack and unknotted the drawstring, then pulled out a puffy jacket which he extended to me.

Different than the burnt plastic smell from the chimney fire, a woodsy smoke scent drifted from the fabric. "Thank—"

"No need to thank me."

"Um, okay, but I have a coat."

"Now you have another." He gave a nod before descending the steps again.

Shaking my head, I held the coat to my chest while my pale ego screamed, *You're a freaking werewolf. He tries anything, he'll be sorry. Or dinner. No. No eating the neighbor.*

"Wait," I said.

Corbus paused.

"Come inside, until the storm passes." Bone marrow frozen, I shrugged into the nylon coat. As Corbus passed me, I added, "Afterward, you'll head to the landlord's office and ask for a refund."

When he dipped his head and crossed the threshold, I took that as an agreement. Resting my back against the closed door, I kept my eyes on Corbus as I dialed Ben. Tentative, Corbus circled the kitchen table. His lips moved in silent mutterings. Not that the place was a complete mess, but I'd probably say a prayer or two if I were trapped in a cottage with fist-sized dust bunnies and sun-bleached flooring.

"Can you hear me?" Ben's voice crackled through the phone. "Tess?"

"Hi," I answered, too peppy, like a kid leading their parents into the valid reason why their prized vase lay smashed on the floor. "So. I. We have a guest."

"You let him in," Ben snapped. "You won't get in a car with him, but you let him in the damn house?"

"Only until the storm passes."

"This whiteout will last through nightfall." He sighed. "I'm serious. You need to leave. Go out through the bathroom window—"

"No." I brushed past Corbus, dropping my voice into a harsh whisper as I ducked into my bedroom. "The last time I escaped through a bathroom window, people died."

"Fine." The muffled sound of a car door slamming echoed through my ear. "Then I'm going to walk my way back."

I plopped onto my bed, keeping a clear view of Corbus pacing the kitchen. "Don't be an idiot."

"Like you're being?" Ben paused. "Please, Tess. I can't lose you…too."

"You won't." My voice hitched with the probable lie. "Nathaniel needs me. He won't kill me."

"Bullshit. He said—"

"I owe him a favor. *He said* he would collect it before he killed me." I cut my eyes to Corbus. He stood still at the kitchen sink. "I gotta get back to our…guest. I'll keep the phone on."

"So, I can hear you being killed by that bloodsucker or the energy-buzzing-not-human-neighbor?"

"The neighbor's name is Corbus."

"Corbus? That's different."

"Since we're in the middle of a snowstorm, maybe you could go to the café, find some reliable Wi-Fi and use your reporting skills to look up anything on a six-foot-tall man, between the ages of twenty and fifty with that name?"

"Twenty to fifty? What kind of age range is that?"

"I haven't gotten around to checking his ID or gawking at his face." I shrugged. "Now, get back in your car. I can hear your teeth chattering."

The car door slammed again, and the engine sputtered to life. "Keep the phone on speaker. I have some words for this Corbus."

I shoved to my feet and emerged from the bedroom. Corbus kept his focus out of the window.

"Hey." Ben cleared his throat. "Corbus. I'm—"

"Her roommate," Corbus answered.

"Yes. And—"

Corbus ticked his chin at the window. "Then who is that?"

Chapter Three

Feet away from the window, a figure stood unfazed against the raging snowstorm. When the waif-like monster caught sight of me, he flashed his fangs and offered a wave.

"Go to the bedroom," I muttered under my breath to Corbus.

"He's there," Ben said.

"Close the door." I kept speaking to Corbus.

"Grab the gun," Ben ordered.

Transfixed, Corbus kept staring at the vampire.

"Shit." Dropping the phone, I grabbed Corbus by the shoulders. When I shoved him away from the windows, intense energy stabbed my fingertips, then clawed its way up my arms.

"You're not human," he said, grasping my forearms. Not a hint of fear, but only calm came from Corbus' stare. Probably from the confidence that he could incinerate me with his touch at any moment.

"Look who's talking." I groaned around the pain. "Now, go to the bedroom. Leave through the window."

"Tess," Ben screamed from the phone. "Answer me!"

A knock hit against the front door.

"Please," I whispered to Corbus. "Go."

"I can help," he said.

"No." The pain morphed my voice into a growl. "He'll kill you."

"I know his kind." Corbus squeezed my arms and the clawing pain ceased. "He does not know mine."

Nathaniel's persistent knocking matched the frantic rhythm of my heartbeat.

"I will stay out of sight." Corbus released me with a warning, "Do not take the jacket off."

I nodded. Corbus returned the gesture before exiting for the bedroom.

"Answer me." Ben's voice came from underneath a kitchen chair. "What's going on?"

I scooped up the phone. Eyes to the door, I reached under the table where Ben had crafted a nook to hold the pistol. Not that it would kill the bloodsucker, but a bullet would slow him down. I disengaged the safety.

The knocking ceased.

"Come now." The door muffled Nathaniel's mocking tone. "Is the firearm necessary?"

I aimed the gun. "Yep."

"Don't talk to him," Ben screamed.

"Silence, Benjamin," Nathaniel said. "His whining is insufferable."

I bit my tongue, refusing to give Nathaniel the upper hand. He was undoubtedly tracking my movements. Which meant the bloodsucker had a point. Wincing, I pressed the volume button down to mute and shoved the phone into the waistband of my tights.

"Tell me, she-beast. In the past three months, have you finally learned the art of silence?" Nathaniel dragged in an inhale. "You still stink."

As Nathaniel heckled, I crept around the kitchen table toward the door, then flattened my back against the wall. I had a clear view of the bedroom. True to his word, Corbus stayed out of sight. My best guess was that, similar to my position, his back was hugging a wall, too.

"I'm not here to kill you," Nathaniel said. Energy crackled around me. On the opposite side of the kitchen table, Nathaniel appeared. "You owe me a favor first."

On instinct, I pulled the trigger. He took the shot to the shoulder. Before I could load another bullet, he reappeared in front of me and tore the gun from my hand. The metal crumbled in his grasp. Nathaniel's thin lips pulled into a half-grin as he dropped the useless gun to the floor. Then he stuck his bony index finger into the bullet wound. A wet sucking sound filled the silence between us while he dug around the blood and flesh.

My stomach turned. No matter how much bloodsucker gore I'd witnessed, it still made me sick. In essence, a miracle—I still clutched onto a ghost of my former human self.

Withdrawing the bullet, he rolled it between his blood-slick fingers, grumbling, "This dampens our reunion. Now, I'm going to need to feed. Where is Benjamin?"

"Safe from you."

Nathaniel slid his tongue across his fangs. "What about the neighbor? It appears that they had a chimney fire. No one was home. Still, their vehicle is present. I could have sworn I saw someone here with you." His upturned nose wrinkled. "Yet I only smell Benjamin and wet dog."

Behind Nathaniel, the bedroom sat still. Corbus took hiding seriously. I flared my nostrils, dragging in Nathaniel's fresh-turned dirt scent. "All I smell is earthworms."

He smirked, flicking the bullet to the floor. His gaze lingered on the wound to his shoulder. "These garments are ruined."

In our last encounter, Nathaniel had worn an ensemble straight from the regency era. Now, with his blond hair tucked underneath a ski cap, fitted peacoat, skinny jeans and suede boots, he passed as a tourist who'd taken a few wrong turns.

"You're lucky. I gave you a warning shot," I said.

He waved his hands in mock fear, then gestured again to his clothes. "I thought I'd blend in with the local…food."

"Before I blew a hole in you? Nope. More Aspen than Adirondacks."

Nathaniel's eyes pinched. "Still better than the nylon-nightmare clothing you're in."

"It's called mountain chic." In the moment of bantering, I'd almost let my guard down. At any millisecond, the bloodsucker could attack. However, his shoulders loosened with each verbal blow. A faint smile tugged at his thin lips. The amusement stopped at his fangs. His hollowed cheeks and ashen flesh spoke of unease. Hunger.

Freedom did not look well on Nathaniel.

A thread of trepidation curled around my spine. Even more of a contrast to his current appearance was the void at Nathaniel's side. His companion, Derek. The vampire who had dragged me into the monster world. In the depths of my subconscious, Derek still hunted me. Every dream…nightmare revolved around his chase, which always ended with me restrained by his hands and a prisoner to his kiss.

The hiss of Nathaniel's breath jarred me from my thoughts. "You still think of him."

"No. I…" My words caught at the roof of my mouth while guilt warmed my cheeks.

"Tragic fools," Nathaniel muttered.

"Fools?" My stupid heart hiccupped. "He survived?"

"The state in which Derek exists is not survival." Nathaniel's ice-blue glare pinned me to the wall. "You condemned him to Hell."

"I freed him."

Nathaniel jabbed a bloodstained finger at me. "Before I tear your foolish head from your body, I've come to collect on the favor."

"I freed you. I chose"—I gestured at my shivering body—"this…life. Leaving you to live happily undead with Derek. I say we are more than even—"

"Not *even* close." In a movement too fast to follow, Nathaniel clamped his hands around my arms and the puffy coat buffered some of the bone-breaking pressure. Suddenly, the acridity of burnt flesh filled the ozone. Nathaniel retracted his smoldering hands while the blackness of his pupils swallowed the blue of his irises.

Corbus loomed inside the bedroom threshold. Wide-eyed, I popped my mouth open. Before I could warn Corbus to run, Nathaniel pivoted. In a blur, the bloodsucker spun, grabbing ahold of my arm. My stomach somersaulted as Nathaniel drew the shadows around us, readying to pull his disappearing act. Then silence. Nothing. We remained inside the kitchen.

Nathaniel slashed his claws at the jacket. "What magic have you let in?"

Behind Nathaniel, a glowing ring encircled the kitchen. Corbus' stare caught mine. I snaked my foot around Nathaniel's leg, tipping him off balance and through the ring.

Nathaniel corrected himself and raced after me. As he attempted to pass through the glowing ring, he was repelled backward. He charged again and met the same resistance. He tried to disappear and reappeared right where he stood. His fangs pushed from his bloody gums. "Idiot she-beast. What did you give up for the fae's aid?"

I returned my attention to Corbus, who remained silent and unmoving.

"I know the touch of your magic," Nathaniel snapped over his shoulder at Corbus. Slowly, Nathaniel returned his focus to me. "Trolls, wolves, vampires and now the winged folk. Watch yourself, she-beast, there is only one reason for their kind to visit your home."

I cut my attention to Corbus. "What's the re—"

"Never ask them a question," Nathaniel interrupted. "You'll owe them for the answer." He turned to face Corbus. "She owes me *my* favor first."

"I asked for shelter. She provided." Corbus' gaze returned to mine. "I am at your service."

"That's really not necessary." My focus bounced between the two. "You—"

"She accepts your service," Nathaniel answered, shrugging his uninjured shoulder. "Keep your enemies close."

My eyes narrowed at Nathaniel. He spoke the truth. Otherwise, his tongue would have burst into flames. Vampires could not lie. Sure, they were masters at twisting words, but a straight-out lie and they lost the appendage until their next feeding.

"How long did you give him shelter for?" Nathaniel asked.

"Until the storm passes."

Nathaniel smirked. "Can you manage to live that long?"

"Umm…" I cut a look at Corbus. He nodded. I glanced back at Nathaniel sizing up Corbus. "Yeah?"

"I suppose that will do." Nathaniel set his full attention on me. "Tell him, that by blood, you bound your word to me. You owe me a favor, she-beast."

I kept my eyes on the bloodsucker's blank face. "I did."

A curt nod bobbed Nathaniel's head. "Do not converse at all with him. When the storm passes, you announce that you are revoking your invitation. Understood?"

I just blinked.

"My favor before you collect yours." Nathaniel pivoted to face Corbus. "By *Neach Neamhshaolta* Law, you must fulfill these agreements."

"By what law?" I asked.

Nathaniel glanced over his shoulder at me. "You have some time to fill with researching the translation." Returning his attention to Corbus, Nathaniel pointed a claw at the floor. A circle of what appeared to be dirt mirrored the floating ring of light that trapped Nathaniel. "Remove your soil."

Corbus looked at me. "What is this favor you owe?"

Nathaniel chuckled. "She hasn't a clue."

"I will not release you," Corbus said, "until you tell her."

My phone buzzed at my hip. At some point, I must have lost connection with Ben. Fishing into my waistband, I answered the call, raising the volume just enough to hear Ben's scolding. "Hold on," I muttered to Ben, then lowered the phone to my side. "What's the favor?"

"Tonight." Nathaniel's lips twitched. "You're going to rescue Derek."

Before I could protest or run, the air swirled around the kitchen, disturbing the ring of dirt on the floor. Instantly, the glowing circle vanished. The tips of Nathaniel's fangs peeked from his thin smile as he stepped over the scattered dirt.

"No." I pressed my back against the wall. "I can't. I won't—"

"You don't have a choice. You agreed. By blood. By the way." Nathaniel paused, wiggling his claw at me while speaking to Corbus. "Her footprints cover the roof of your cabin. She set the fire."

"Whoa. Sorry, but I did it—" Before I finished my mashup of an apology and reasoning, Nathaniel disappeared.

Chapter Four

"I can't believe you let him go," I snapped at Corbus.

"It was the agreement." Corbus tipped his chin at my phone. "He's silent."

I fumbled to get the phone to my ear. "Ben?" The faint pelt of his breath hit the receiver. "I can hear you. Please, say something."

"Who's Derek?" Ben asked.

Corbus seemed pretty interested in the answer, too. Thinking it better to get both men in the loop, I hit speaker mode and said, "Another bloodsucker, is all."

"Bullshit. What about...you know what? Forget it." Ben's voice sharpened. "Why? Why didn't you tell me about this *Derek*?"

"I didn't think I'd ever deal with him again."

"Well, now you do. You did some blood thing and must rescue *Derek*. From what?"

"I don't know."

"If that half-blood vampire needs you, it's bad."

Panic raised my eyebrows. Corbus showed no change in emotion from learning the truth about

Nathaniel. From what I knew about bloodsuckers, all half-blood vampires were destroyed. They were too powerful. Uncontrollable. So far, Nathaniel had gotten away with his undead life by serving the now-permanently-deceased Vampire Queen. Some sick thread of worry caused me to pause the conversation. "Do not kill Nathaniel," I whispered to Corbus.

"I heard that," Ben grumbled. "Speaker works both ways, Tess."

"No more death," I said. "I'm done with it. Hear *that*?"

"Yeah. And it's not done with you. We discussed this. If we ever felt threatened—"

"What did you do?" Dread raced through my blood. "Tell me."

"I heard you fire the gun. I heard the struggle."

"Damn it, Ben." Tears glazed my eyes. "Please tell me you didn't call…Sam."

Ben's silence was his answer. He'd called the alpha. Soon, a pack of werewolves would be at my door ready to haul me away and lock me up.

"I had it under control," I snapped.

"You did not."

I shot my attention at the window. Beyond the reflection of my now glowing eyes, the snowstorm battered the landscape. There was still time to escape. "I *did*—"

Ben screamed.

I spun around, almost knocking into Corbus blocking the door. When he refused to move, the wolf below my flesh rose to the challenge and the Change prickled along my spine. "Move it, Corbus."

A swirling opacity consumed Corbus' eyes. When he blinked, his eyes returned to their normal dark brown. "It is Nathaniel."

Rigid, I jammed the phone to my lips. "Nathaniel, you so much as hurt a hair on his head and I will kill you."

Nathaniel tsked me. "You said you were done with killing."

"Let me talk to Ben."

"He is...resting." The thump of a body hit a floor. "Can you blame me for securing collateral? Next time don't answer the phone. In Benjamin's state of fear, he gave me perfect directions to his location. You should thank me. What if the wolves found him first?"

"Have you seen any?" I asked.

"Only you."

I let go of my breath.

"You are the Wolf Born?" Corbus asked.

With no need to prolong the inevitable reveal, I nodded and fixated back on Nathaniel's ramblings. Turning my hearing solely to the background, I listened for any sounds to tip off the bloodsucker's location. Country music drifted through the background until some sort of collision overshadowed the twang of a guitar riff. Voices cheered. Knowing where Ben was, I shifted my attention to Nathaniel's words.

"Ben will slumber the night away," he said. "*After* I collect my favor, you can have him. That's if you live. Now, you have five minutes. Dress in...fur." Nathaniel ended the call.

I snapped my attention to Corbus. "You said you are in my service."

He nodded.

"Can you—" I stopped the question on the tip of my tongue. "Save Ben. He's at the bowling alley. Shit. There is a tree blocking the road."

"The tree is not an issue," Corbus said.

Right, because he's a scary winged folk. "Here." I scrolled through my phone, hitting on the most current photo of Ben, clad with a goofy face, shoving his fist inside the Christmas turkey's ass. "This is Ben. Go before Nathaniel comes back."

Corbus opened the door. "Do not take the jacket off."

"You don't have to say that twice." I curled my fingers around the sleeve openings. "Hope it works on werewolves."

"Those who seek to harm you will harm themselves."

"Thank—"

"Do not thank an Otherworldly Creature, *Neach Neamhshaolta*, you will owe them." He started down the steps. "You have much to learn, Wolf Born."

"My name is Tessa," I said.

Corbus stopped in his tracks. "Trust no one, Wolf Born." And with that warning, he got in his car.

I shut the door, then race-stumbled, kicking off my soggy sneakers. Plopping into a kitchen chair, I tugged on and laced up my winter boots. Then I tore through the junk drawer. A pencil had once aided me, momentarily, from Derek. I tucked two sharpened number twos into the sleeves of the coat. Hopefully, Nathaniel wouldn't frisk me, and Derek had forgotten about the past pencil staking.

As I took up pacing the kitchen, I caught a glance at my reflection in the window, and damn me, if I didn't stop and fix my dilapidated ponytail. A shuttered breath left me in a curse as I jabbed a finger at my reflection. "No. Feelings."

Energy crackled around me, announcing the bloodsucker's return. Across the room, a shadow pulled away from the wall, morphing into Nathaniel. "I said fur."

"Unless you want me to tear you apart, I stay human."

"Nonhuman."

"Otherworldly."

"When did you have time to research *and* play with your hair?" He quirked an eyebrow. "Are you blushing?"

"The favor," I said flatly. "After I rescue Derek, Ben is returned to me, safe."

"*If* you live."

My heart did a terror-induced jig. "You mean *if* Derek doesn't kill me."

"Yes, I believe his last words to you were—"

"Stay safe, my wol—"

"No." Nathaniel's face soured. "I missed that. Blessedly. The part before, she-beast, where he said, 'Nothing will keep you from me'." As if sniffing the sweetest rose, Nathaniel drew in a breath. "The scent of fear drifting from your flesh warms my heart."

Instead of denying it, which would make the fear ooze more from my pores, I steered the conversation forward. "Who has Derek?"

Nathaniel's expression settled into blank bloodsucker mode. "Vampires. After the Gathering, the late queen's legion imprisoned Derek. Tonight, you will be the distraction—the bait—while I send Derek's captors to their final death."

"You want me to run around and get attacked?"

"Do you have a better plan?"

I pursed my lips. "Nope. Why do I need to go wolf?"

"Your scent is stronger in that form." He narrowed his eyes. "You are harder to kill. Faster."

I stiffened. All those facts were news to me. I did anything and everything to remain human.

"How many times have you made the Change?"

"Only during the full moon."

"Three times." He cursed in French. "Only three?"

"Yes."

"I gave you three months to practice gaining control over your beast. Waited for the new moon where"—Nathaniel jabbed his finger at me—"this form should be dominant. You have avoided bettering your chance of survival. Having Derek end your life…you should thank me for the favor. Truly, I'm granting your death wish."

"You think I'll let him?"

"No." Nathaniel stepped closer. "You will fail at protecting yourself."

"If I die, you leave Ben alone."

He chuckled.

"Promise me." I lowered my hands to my sides. Rolling my shoulder blades down my back, I lifted my chin and added order to my voice. "I do this favor, and you are gone from our lives. Forever."

Nathaniel gave me the vampire blank stare. "Come. Take off that thing."

"Coat stays. It will not hurt you if you don't hurt me. So Corbus says."

"The longer you use an enchanted relic, the harder it is for you to remove the item. It draws from you as well, like a parasite. I assume by the increase of your heartbeat, Corbus did not inform you of this. Where is he?" Nathaniel's eyes shifted to vampire-blackhole. "Magic works both ways. I can find him, too. Good, he's occupying the police. Someone set fire to the bowling alley."

I glared at the vampire.

"Learn from a skilled pyro, she-beast. A perplexed Benjamin is in custody. Corbus is soon to join him. You may keep the jacket until we are at the location. Then you lose it." Nathaniel offered his hand to me. "Before the wolves come."

Clenching my jaw, I slapped my hand in his. Weightlessness and darkness surrounded me as Nathaniel gathered me to his chest. The metallic ting of blood clung to his garments. Sealing my eyes, I steered my mind away from the images of the Monday bowling league drained of their blood.

When we retook our solid forms, frozen air raced through my lungs while my boots sunk into a foot's worth of snow. Nathaniel pried himself from my death-grip. Blinking against the pelting snow, I spotted the bloodsucker heading toward an abandoned utility van on the side of a single-lane country road.

"Get in." Nathaniel hopped into the driver's side and slammed the door shut.

I trudged through the snow around to the passenger side. As I opened the door, the reek of blood overwhelmed my frozen nostrils. I cut my attention to the vampire gripping the steering wheel.

"Relax," he said. "I have been practicing."

"Hijacking and murder?" I scrambled into the seat and secured the grease-stained seatbelt.

"Driving." He flashed a grin. "I don't always kill my dinner. Leftovers, I believe you call them."

I shot my worry over my shoulder. Scattered fast food containers and power tools set my mind to ease. No dead bodies. The quasi-comfort shattered when Nathaniel shifted the van into drive. Tucked in the back corner, a massive coil of chains rattled about.

"Chains?" The tremor in my voice had nothing to do with the subzero temperatures outside. I had once found myself a prisoner to a similar coil. As I dug my nails against the silver burn scar on my palm, my breath rushed past my chapped lips.

"The state of Derek's mind is unknown. He may need restraint."

"Compulsion works."

Nathaniel grunted. "In most cases. I err on the side of caution with Derek."

I nodded.

The van fishtailed on a patch of ice and I braced my hands against the dashboard. "Why not use the shadows to get us there?"

"It depletes strength, and the vampires will sense the energy. We drive and then we walk. Once we are a mile out, you will Change. In the meantime...." He fidgeted with the radio until he found an eighties station. "The Prince."

"Prince," I corrected, tucking my chin to my chest and grinning. Never would I admit to the bloodsucker that the eighties were my jam.

He stole a glance at me. "You tremble."

"It is cold and I'm still alive."

"Ah." He reached for the vents and blasted stale cigarette-smoke air at my face.

Wrinkling my nose, I asked, "How long of a drive?"

"An hour."

"You *are* being cautious."

"You don't get to see four hundred years by beauty alone."

Cocky and rightfully so. Nathaniel possessed an angelic murderous beauty. One which artists would willingly open their veins for to paint his portrait. If he paired his looks with his wit, Nathaniel could rule the world. Instead, he was risking his undead life for Derek. Then again, there I sat right along with Nathaniel, abandoning Ben and Corbus. Perhaps being taken into custody would buy them safety from the werewolves. Like the bloodsuckers, wolves, too, had a life-or-death rule for staying off the human radar.

Pressure drummed at my temple as Nathaniel slipped into my thoughts. *"Your mind. Must it chatter so?"*

"Stay out of it," I answered out loud.

"If you want to keep them safe, you need to accept your curse." He flicked his attention at me. "Or else, you die. Ben dies. And *all* the wolves die."

"Your happily ever after." My sigh fogged the windshield. "How did you find me?"

"Quite easy. That insidious blog. Who writes about fake monsters in upstate New York?"

I quirked an eyebrow. "So, you're a tech-savvy pyro vampire."

"Indeed." He chuckled. "Oh, but I found your cabin through Benjamin's blood."

As I grabbed Nathaniel by the ear, the van yanked to the side of the road. "When?"

"Nights ago, he was at the market browsing the sweets section." Nathaniel flashed his cocky smile. "I was too."

"You ever, *ever*"—I tugged his earlobe, eliciting a wince from the bloodsucker—"touch Ben again, and I will tear your fangs off." I shoved my palm against Nathaniel's cheek and pushed him to his side of the vehicle.

We stayed silent for the next forty-nine minutes until he pulled off the side of the road. Deep in mountain territory, we shuffled through miles of snow. Lungs burning, toes numb, I was one snowdrift away from calling a timeout when Nathaniel stopped. He ducked behind a pine tree and retrieved a backpack.

"This is where you Change." He tugged a pair of dress pants from the bag, then began to peel off his clothes.

"Whoa. Could you wait?"

He turned over his bare shoulder as he tugged his jeans off. "It will be nightfall in fifteen minutes."

I huffed, spinning my heels away from the naked vampire. "That just happened." Rounding a bush, I fought with the zipper of the jacket. It wouldn't budge.

"I don't hear wolf sounds," Nathaniel muttered.

"I need help. The zipper is jammed."

In a déjà vu nightmare, Nathaniel turned the corner in his three-piece suit. He grumbled under his breath as he tentatively tried the zipper. "I warned you."

I shrugged.

His claws lengthened as his eyes locked with mine. "Don't move." He slid a claw up my torso, freeing me of the zipper. The sleeves sucked to my arms. Nathaniel moved to my back. As I struggled forward, he pried the jacket off.

Instantly, energy rushed through me. "Whoa."

"I told you."

I wiped the sweat from my brow. Overhead, the snowstorm lost steam. Flakes drifted lazily across the blood-red sky. "If you want me to do this, you need to leave."

He knocked his shoulder against a tree. "Nothing I have not seen before."

"Nothing you will see again."

He rolled his eyes, then shifted his back to me. I marched around another tree and fumbled out of my frozen boots and clothes. Hesitant to part with the pencils, I buried them in the snow by my clothing, somewhat confident I'd find my belongings again. While we made our way to the stopping point, I'd marked our trail by slashing discreet notches into trees with my claws.

As I willed the Change, energy enveloped me. When the light dimmed, I rose in my wolf form. The urge to hunt did not cross my mind. Nathaniel was right. Under the new moon, I truly was more in control.

Smartly, Nathaniel cleared his throat, giving me a cue for his slow approach. With the last sun rays dancing across the snow, he hovered amongst the tree cover. His gaze roamed over my wolf form, cautious not to look me in the eyes. *"Can you understand me?"*

"Yes," I spoke to his mind.

"Good. Follow me."

Chapter Five

My soft pants rose in plumes of frozen breath above my head to the night sky. Even in my wolf form, the weather was unmerciful. Shaking out the snow from my coat, I waited for Nathaniel's return. He had left me at the edge of the woods to scout the property.

As I took a step closer, energy hummed along my body. A compulsion forcefield of sorts. Vampires used it to hide their location from humans. To anyone passing by, if they traveled through the miles of winter wasteland, they'd see only a barren field. What truly lay ahead was a twelve-foot-tall brick wall, dressed in barbed wire, that surrounded a three-story fortress.

Nathaniel's voice slipped inside my mind. *"Two come your way."*

I stretched and flexed my claws. *"How many in all?"*

"Forty or so."

I didn't have time to protest. Fur rose at my haunches with the approach of the two bloodsuckers.

My vision blurred as I allowed the wolf more control. Seamlessly, she flowed through my limbs.

Muttering in a foreign language, the oblivious bloodsuckers drew closer. I stepped into their path and Nathaniel crept from behind. His claws sliced through one of their necks, dusting the vampire into oblivion. The other bloodsucker lunged at me. I rolled to my side in time for Nathaniel to impale the vampire from behind.

Nathaniel tucked a coil of bloodstained hair behind his ear. *"This will be easier than I presumed."*

To keep the wolf within me from attacking Nathaniel, I dug my claws against the frozen earth.

"Harness that beast." He sneered then turned his back on me. *"Circle around the fortress. I will pick the rest off."*

"Leave Nathaniel alone," I sent to the being sharing my body. It didn't like the message. The world went dark as the wolf completely took over. Helpless, from the depths of my mind, I watched on as the huntress bounded through the snow, heading straight for Nathaniel.

Nathaniel disappeared. With no way to stop the wolf, she continued toward the wall, digging claws against the bricks and using the momentum to vault over the barbed wire. The effortless landing ended in front of a group of charging vampires. The wolf, in control of my body, tore toward the incoming threats.

Yards away from the fortress, Nathaniel reappeared, blocking the wolf. *"Control the beast,"* he screamed in my mind.

"I can't."

Nathaniel crouched, bringing his stare in line with the wolf. "Give Tessa control," he bellowed, sending compulsion with his words.

The wolf tumbled to a stop. Instantly, I was back in control, but the time spent had cost us. Bodies piled on top of me. Claws dug. Hands grabbed. Feet kicked. The crushing weight of the pile suffocated me.

"I'll keep him safe." My promise to Andrea echoed through my mind. I couldn't protect Ben if I died. Running on instinct and despair, I opened the link that connected me to every werewolf. Energy coursed through my being. Now, there would be no escaping the werewolves. The link acted like a beacon to my race. If there were any werewolves nearby, they'd find me.

I heaved upward, tossing the bloodsuckers off me. The vampires dispersed long enough for me to draw a single breath. Again, they descended. I braced for the incoming attacks until someone grabbed me by the scruff of my neck, then threw me.

I crashed against the fortress' stone wall. Blood splattered from my snout while I gathered my legs beneath me. Yards away, a cloud of ash surrounded Nathaniel where he fought the hoard of vampires. Tiny explosions joined the dust vortex. *Bullets.* Vampires shot at Nathaniel from the third floor.

Inches from my head, a bullet ricocheted against the building. One bloodsucker got smart and started firing down at me. Being flush to the wall, I lost the benefit of a running start. I tried to climb, but my claws lost traction. Another bullet whizzed by my ear. Just when I went to retreat, a vampire crashed through a window to my right. Seeing the opportunity for an entrance, I dodged his attack, jumping through the window.

Inside, a bloodsucker welcomed me by firing his pistol.

The crack of the bullet shoved me backward. Searing pain exploded in my shoulder. *Silver.* I attacked the bloodsucker who was loading another round. As I crushed his arm between my jaws, blood splashed down my throat. The combination of agony and hunger stirred the wolf below. My vision blurred while she fought for control. Shaking my head, I pushed her back.

During my inner struggle, Nathaniel appeared behind the bloodsucker, then tore off the man's head. Before the vampire's ashes flew into the air, Nathaniel screamed at my mind, *"Derek is below ground."* Nathaniel jabbed a claw toward a staircase. *"Go."*

I turned tail and raced down three flights of stairs. As my paws left the last step, the edges of my vision darkened while a fever tore through me. I needed to make the Change back to human. The longer the silver bullet remained lodged in my flesh, the more damage to my body…even death. However, the thought of rescuing Derek in my human form, naked and unarmed, dumped adrenaline into my veins.

I pressed onward. Ahead, the narrow hallway plunged into darkness, and the close-range shots left a high-pitched screech blasting through my ears, forcing me to rely solely on my snout to lead the way. The reek of mildew and death filled the air until the undertone of a dark aroma raised the fur at the back of my neck. I picked up my pace, chasing the familiar scent.

A sharp right turn led me down another corridor where a single overhead light illuminated my destination. Energy quivered through my body, urging me toward a massive steel door guarding the end of the hallway.

Nathaniel appeared next to me with a key pinched between his bloody fingers. *"Hurry. Change and unlock the door. I'll hold off the remaining vampires."*

He disappeared.

I willed the Change. With the silver lodged in my shoulder, there was no fluid transition. I screamed as my limbs and tendons tore in unison. Unconsciousness flirted with me while I lay gasping on the floor, until the sizzling of my flesh roused me enough to move.

Biting my lip, I dug into the wound. When my fingers burned against the embedded silver bullet, I tore it free, then flung it across the hall. Tears blurred my vision. I didn't have the time to rub them away. Footfalls pounded the steps behind me. I snatched the key from the ground and clambered to my feet.

Blood and sweat coated my hands as I fumbled with the lock. The handle gave way and I shoved open the door. Cold fluorescent lights momentarily blinded me while tendrils of energy caressed my arms and legs. Although he was out of sight, I knew Derek was somewhere inside. Bloody, shivering and naked, I tried to prepare myself for the reunion, until a palm struck between my shoulder blades. Tumbling through the entrance, I smacked my elbows and knees onto the concrete floor.

Nathaniel slammed the door shut.

I pummeled my fists against the steel door, leaving deep bloody dents.

"Turn around," Nathaniel said to my mind.

I peered over my shoulder. In the center of the dungeon, on top of a stone altar, lay a corpse. Recognizing the dust-covered garments from the last time I'd seen Derek, my heart slammed into my throat. This wasn't the fighting-for-my-life reunion I'd envisioned. No. Strangely, the scene in front of me terrified me more. "What did they do to him?" I whispered.

"They?" Nathaniel chose to still speak to my mind. *"You."*

"Me?"

"Go to him."

I glanced at the blood rolling down my arm. "No."

"He can close your wound."

"Or he could kill me."

"You are seconds away from upholding your favor."

"Look. You have him. He's saved."

"Does he look saved? Feed Derek."

"No." I spun around, yelling at the door. "You keep changing the rules."

"There are no rules."

"I did not agree to this."

"You did."

"I hate you."

"The feeling is mutual. Now, Derek needs fresh blood. Best get to opening a vein or I will leave you to the wolves."

"Don't." As I turned back to the altar, terror racked my body. "You can't."

"You're an idiot for opening the link," Nathaniel continued. *"There are at least twenty wolves within miles from here. I can hear them…"*

Derek's mummified face became my focal point, from his pearl-white fangs jutting out of the hole of his once sinful mouth to the sunken skin hooding his eyes that had left me breathless. *How could Nathaniel think I did this? Could do this?*

Anger propelled me over to the stone slab. I ripped my gaze from Derek's face to glance at the rest of his remains. At his heart, the white of his dress shirt peeked through a jagged hole of his tux where he, or someone else, had torn off the queen's emblem. When my attention drifted to his bony hands laced over his chest, I sucked in a breath. The glint of diamonds and hunter-green satin shone between the cracks of his fingers. Derek held a piece of the headband I'd worn the night of the Gathering.

"Revive him." Nathaniel paused, letting the silence dance around the cell. *"Derek will be free. Ben will be unharmed. Just a single, small cut, she-beast."*

I scored a claw against my index finger. While blood rolled from my fingertip, I clenched every muscle and bone in my body. One crimson droplet escaped, splattering onto Derek's lip.

Nothing happened. At first. Another droplet fell and a buzzing sensation raced up my spine. Before I could react, a heady shot of euphoria coursed through my mind. I snapped my eyes shut to compose myself. The last thing I needed was to give in to the warm and fuzzies wreaking havoc through my body. Taking a deep breath, I slanted my eyes open to meet Derek's.

"Do not move," Nathaniel ordered.

Derek grabbed my forearm, dragging me over his body, then sank his fangs into my wrist. His ravenous pulls at my veins drove me deeper into a euphoric state. While I braced my free hand against his chest, his body transformed from corpse-like to the powerful version that ruled my dreams. Damn me, my body responded, molding itself against his. A pleasure-laced scream edged toward my sealed lips until he withdrew his fangs.

"Is this the afterlife?" Derek chased his words with his tongue, sliding it across his bite, sealing my wound. With his breath running hot along my tender flesh, he pressed a kiss at my pulse.

Every one of my nerve endings hummed in his presence, aching in anticipation for his next move. He captured the back of my neck, tangling his fingers in my hair as he lowered my face to his. My breath left in a rush and his lips were there to steal it.

Dreams clashed with reality. Urgency drove our kiss deeper. Forbidden. Dangerous. My self-control faded with each second. Before it slipped completely from my grasp, I eased away. "This" —my voice hitched— "is not the afterlife."

Derek's gaze lifted to mine. Not wanting to be captured by his compulsion, I shifted my focus to his mouth. The way my blood painted his lips shot desire through me. A groan rumbled from Derek's throat and once more my gaze lifted to his. My want was mirrored within his eyes. We both stilled as the familiar surge of what should have been the severed blood-bond raged like an inferno between us. I scrambled from Derek's loosening grasp, dropping to the floor.

"Let me out." I choked on my carnal-laced fear as I crawled to the door. "I did your damn favor."

"Not yet," Nathaniel responded to my mind.

"I saved him."

"Not yet."

"What do you mean?" I scurried to the side of the door, pressing my back against the brick wall as I curled over to hide my nakedness. "The vampires are dead. He's free."

"The blood-bond is still intact. Until it is broken, Derek is not free."

"How do I break it?"

"A ceremonial dance. A precious jewel. No. There is no breaking." Nathaniel cut the lights and darkness swallowed the dungeon. "I'm taking a brief leave. The wolves come."

The click of Derek's boots hitting the concrete floor, speared fear through me. Skimming my fingers along the wall, I stumbled around the room. If I stayed in the same place, he could track my blood. I hoped if I kept moving, I could distract him. Easier thought than done. Exhausted from the blood loss, I knocked against the wall while my bruised ribs kept me from dragging in enough air to fuel my oxygen-deprived body.

"Tessa…" Derek's rich voice caressed my feverish skin. "You are driving us both into madness."

I reversed my direction and the air stirred at my temples with our near-collision.

"Your heartbeat echoes through my blood." Derek stopped. "It grows weak—"

Instantly, my wrists were tugged over my head and pinned against the wall. Derek hoisted me to my tiptoes. I tried to struggle free, but he pressed himself against my shivering body. Caged by his taut frame and the freezing bricks digging against my knuckles and ass, I glared into the darkness.

"Have you forgotten?" His breath rushed across my tear-streaked cheek. "I will always find you, my wolf."

As he trailed his lips along my jawline, a cry caught in my throat. The rich scent of his blood washed through my senses. Fearing the taste would be my death, I tensed, clenching my teeth shut. Yet he continued his travels down to my injured shoulder. When he lapped at my wound, pain and pleasure flowed through my being. Muting my gasps, I bit my tongue.

Slowly, he lowered me to the ground. The pressure at my wrists loosened and he removed his lips from my flesh. And damn me, I whimpered.

His sharp inhalation triggered my toes to curl.

"Do not move." His voice quivered with restraint. "If you give chase, I will hunt you."

The pain was no longer a burning sensation, but still my shoulder throbbed from the shot. Blood drooled from the wound, sliding between my breast and armpit. Whatever Derek had done with his blood and lips had lessened the damage caused by the silver, but something was still wrong with the wound. I kept my concern to myself…or so I thought.

"The silver poisons your blood," he said.

"Stay out of my head."

"I cannot read your thoughts. I feel them. You burn with fever. Do not attempt to make the Change. It could be your death."

To test that theory, I tried to draw energy for the Change. Needles of pain attacked my temples and I groaned.

"I cautioned you."

My heart thundered in my throat as I braced against the wall. "If I stay human, I'll freeze to death."

Clothing whispered in the darkness.

"Hold out your hand," he ordered.

Hesitant, I reached out. His tux coat and shirt dropped into my sweaty palm. Forcing my limbs into action, I slipped into his dusty shirt, then balled the coat up, holding it against my chest, hoping to mask the erratic beating of my heart.

"Remember. Slow movements." Derek's voice grew distant as he traveled to the other side of the room. "What is this favor?"

"For me to save you."

"You are a fool."

"Yep." Needing to conserve my strength, I slid my back down the wall, tucking the shirt underneath my bottom. I bunched up the coat, making a pillow for my chin to rest on my knees. "I am."

His sigh bounced off the walls. "How will you flee this time?"

"Have any ideas?"

"Plenty." Derek's voice deepened. "None of which end with your escape. I warned you."

"So. This is it." I hugged the balled-up coat to my chest. "You kill me. Even after I just saved you—"

"You did not."

"Really? Five minutes ago—"

"Your lips were mine."

I knocked my head against the wall. "You were a corpse."

"Better than my current predicament."

Silence.

"How?" I asked.

"Here, in this physical entrapment, dreams were my salvation. No hunger. No pain. No loss. All I ever wanted was in my arms."

A shiver raised the fine hairs at the nape of my neck. "What were these dreams about?"

"What, in this life, will never be." His voice drifted to my level, signaling he had taken a seat on the floor. "So, no, my wolf, you did not free me. You have imprisoned me."

"Nathaniel left me no choice. He had Ben. If I knew—"

"You still would have opened your vein." Derek shifted against the wall. "You love Ben."

"Like a brother. He's the only family I have." I glared into the pitch-blackness. "And you're right. I would have taken the risk—"

"What about that *wolf* you *risked* your life for?"

"Wolves. That night I chose—"

"I am well acquainted with your choice."

"Since I am here, and not chained up being guarded by werewolves, then you know, I didn't choose him either." I dug my fingers into the coat. "Stop being an ass."

"I am no fool."

"There's that ego." The adrenaline rush dwindled from my system while fatigue washed over me with each heartbeat. Derek stayed on his side of the cell. He'd offered me some of his clothing. Perhaps he didn't want to kill me. Or he was biding his time. I had to test the waters. No better way than a dose of snark. "Oh wise vampire, bestow upon me your knowledge on how to get the hell outta here."

His chuckle sent flicks of fire to my core. "I prefer to sit a bit longer."

"You can sit all you want *after* I escape."

"It is not safe for you to leave." Derek's voice grew serious. "Nathaniel spoke of wolves coming for you."

"Yep." I continued, "So if you could find it in your heart to give me a death-pass by getting me out of here, that would be great."

"Why do you think I am here?"

"Nathaniel said the queen's leftover bloodsuckers imprisoned you—" Anger buzzed across the blood-bond. "Hey. Tone down the rage over there."

As if Derek had put up a magical buffer, the sensation lessened. "Never. Trust. Nathaniel."

Warning bells blared through my skull. Nathaniel was proficient in the craft of turning words to save his tongue from bursting into flames. "You're here because the blood-bond is still intact."

"Yes. Your Change did not sever the blood-bond." Derek's voice drifted into a gravel. Most would pair that tone with desire, but after being around monsters, I knew the undertone matched a different want. Hunger. "I can only block your tether, sparing you from the madness of denying the bond. While I…I will not burden you with my trials."

"Try me," I muttered.

"Momentarily sating the bond requires excessive feeding of both blood and carnal—"

"Got it." I shook my head from the images of Derek doing all of the above and then some. "So doing…those things turned you into a mummy?"

"No, your absence continued to spiral me into insanity. Until one night, I discovered a loophole…when I entered *your* dreams."

"No." The room tilted. Embarrassment burned hotter than the silver bullet. "You invaded my dreams?"

"There was no force." He paused, and I could have sworn I heard a smile fill his voice. "You were a willing participant."

"I thought that I was dreaming."

"You were." He paused again before murdering me with the truth. "You always left satisfied."

"I can't believe this." I slapped my hands over my face. "Okay. My dreams were your outlet. No more. Got it? You can't. It's wrong."

Silence.

The sudden stillness set my nerves to unease. I tugged on his coat, then hugged myself. My mind raced to bring words to my mouth before we went down another life-or-death rabbit hole. "I'm sorry that you ended up here."

Silence.

"I *wanted* to be here. I compelled the queen's vampires to guard me as I invited the slumber death to protect you. I would have had them execute me, but I feared—"

"I would die, too."

"Yes." His voice traveled upward, signaling he was done with sitting. "So, in essence, I gave you a death-pass. Coming here, you revoked it."

I lengthened my claws, readying if he came near. "If you mummified yourself to protect me, then why did your guards shoot me with silver?"

"Nathaniel." Derek raised his voice. "Why were the rounds exchanged?"

From the other side of the door, Nathaniel answered, "I refuse to watch you rot while she frolics around."

"I ordered you to—"

"Keep her safe. Et cetera. Or else. Blah blah," Nathaniel snipped. "You forget, I'm free and grossly more powerful than you, Derek. Besides, it was not a kill shot but a catalyst to end this torture once and for all. Feel the burn, she-beast?" Nathaniel asked. "Liquid silver poisons your body. Meaning, you'll be dead by sunrise."

Derek slammed against the door.

Nathaniel raised his voice. "Or, Derek, you can turn her. Better get to it because the wolves will be here within minutes."

"You cannot turn a werewolf." Derek growled.

"The blood-bond should have been destroyed when she shifted into the beast," Nathaniel countered. "But lo and behold, it still is present. Maybe she will be lucky and survive the turning, or not, and then she can die like the animal she is."

"Nathaniel." Derek stilled, and the clarity of his words cut through the three-foot-thick metal door. "I will send you to your eternal night."

Floors above, glass shattered, then a howl echoed through the dungeon.

"They are here," Nathaniel warned. "Now or never, Derek."

Chapter Six

I scrambled to my hands and knees, willing the Change, and again I was denied. True to Derek's words and actions, he found me hiding behind the stone altar. The air stirred with his movements as he crouched to my level. Tensing, I pleaded that the pitch-black room would hinder his judgment and he'd miss grabbing me.

The metal door swung open. Light from the hallway cloaked Derek in shadows. Thankfully. The combination of silver poisoning and blood loss didn't need gawking to join my stupor party.

Nathaniel appeared between us. "We need to—"

Derek lunged upward, attacking Nathaniel.

While they fought, I belly-crawled to the entrance. Snarls and howls stilled my advancement. Peeking around the frame, I froze. A wolf stood at the end of the hallway. Its eyes locked with mine.

Someone grabbed my waist, tugging me back into the dungeon. My stomach somersaulted, then my knees crashed against a wood floor. Nathaniel had disappeared us into another dark room. Feet ahead, shattered glass and a dust pile of a vampire's remains graced the floorboards. A gust of wind brushed across the crown of my head, and I darted my attention toward the busted window across the small room. Nathaniel slapped his hand on my shoulder, holding me in place. "We are three stories up. You would die from the fall."

"They come." Derek braced against the door.

Nathaniel ran to the window. Pressing himself against the wall, he looked outside. "There are too many. I will take her by shadows. There is a van—"

"No," Derek growled. "You will *never* touch her again."

"Talk some sense into him," Nathaniel spoke to me.

Thinking it better to talk to Nathaniel's mind, I asked, *"How many are out there?"*

Nathaniel moved enough to allow me access to the window. I stumbled my way over and stole a glance outside. Twelve wolves lined the length of the fortress. Three men scaled the wall, then joined the wolves.

One of the men had a swagger I'd recognize anywhere. The second thorn in my heart. The night had gone to a full-blown shitstorm real fast. Sam, the alpha, lifted his attention to the window. Before his eyes met mine, I popped my face back inside and promptly set my focus on Derek's back.

"Give us the Wolf Born," Sam called out.

I bit my tongue at the coldness of his demand. It was my fault. To save Sam's life, I'd had his memories erased. Sam would never remember our friendship…relationship. For the better. I had enough repressed steam with Derek.

Nathaniel moved in front of the window. "Not by the hair of my chinny chin—"

His body jerked. Nathaniel turned toward me with an arrow lodged in the middle of his sternum. "Well. They have weapons." He snapped the rod off and leaned against the wall.

"There are two outside the room," Derek said.

I shot my attention at Nathaniel. "You had to have had a backup plan. How do you remove liquid silver?"

He chuckled. "You don't."

I glared at him as I shrugged off the coat.

"Getting naked for the alpha?" Nathaniel wiggled his bloody eyebrows.

Ignoring him, I held the coat out of the window, waving it like a surrender flag before I let it fall. I'd hoped to earn some sympathy, that after smelling my blood, the wolves would go easy on us.

A wolf sniffed at the door. Our only barrier against a werewolf attack would be splitters in a matter of minutes.

"Don't shoot," I yelled at the window. A heartbeat passed and I chanced a glance outside. Sam stood front and center. One of his men trotted over to him, handing Sam the coat. He gave it a sniff, then glared his glowing eyeballs right up at me. His mouth popped open, and I spoke over him, "Tell the wolves, outside the room, to, umm…" I looked at Nathaniel and muttered, "What do you say?"

Nathaniel rolled his eyes. "Stand down."

"Tell them to stand down," I repeated to Sam. Catching myself, from trying to look away from Sam, I kept my stare on his. "I was shot with liquid silver. The only way I'll survive is with the aid of a vampire. I need a safe passage for Derek."

Nathaniel gasped. "You little bitch."

"No," Sam answered.

"Then I die."

"Use the link. You can drain our energy to keep yourself alive."

"And kill a few of you doing so? No."

"For the good of the pack," the two men flanking Sam said in unison.

"Then I will stay here, and you all can die with me."

A growl erupted on the other side of the door.

"Caution with your words," Derek warned.

"Fine." Sam's voice lowered. "One vampire stays behind. We'll let the other escort you outside."

"What now?" I asked the vampires.

"This." Nathaniel pointed at the partial arrow still embedded in his chest. "Until it is completely removed, I cannot use the shadows."

"Then we go by foot," Derek answered.

"Can you command the wolves?" Nathaniel asked me.

I bunched my fists to keep from smacking him. "You mean, can I keep them from attacking like I did the last time we were trapped in a bloodsucker hellhole? No. I would have done so already but a selfish vampire had me shot with liquid silver. I can't use any of my…."

"Power," Nathaniel finished.

"Wolf Born," Sam called out. "We will enter if you do not come willingly."

Derek turned over his shoulder and I nodded at him. While Nathaniel shook his head, Derek opened the door.

Two wolves loomed at the threshold. Their lips pulled away from their jowls. Derek raised his hands in front of himself and took a few steps back toward me.

The wolves followed. When Nathaniel lengthened his claws, I shoved off the wall and stumbled in front of the vampires. Glaring into each of the wolves' eyes, I ordered, "Lead me to your alpha."

Their lips lay over their teeth. The larger wolf stepped to the side while the other turned toward the hall. He made a throaty growl over his shoulder as he started walking. The other turned to guard Nathaniel.

Holding Nathaniel's stare, I switched to talking to his mind. "*We live through this, and so help me, I'm going to kick your ass.*"

"*Unlikely, but on the off chance you survive, I welcome the opportunity to beat you senseless.*"

I spun on my heels and the floor rose to meet me. Derek intercepted by grabbing my forearm, then helped me to my feet. I spared a glance at his face. "I don't think I'm going to…."

He gathered me tight against the length of his body. The blood-bond stirred, sending energy pounding through me. I pulled away and even in the darkness, the contours of Derek's face sharpened. His skin stretched tight over his bones.

"Don't," I whispered, "do that again."

Derek swept me off my feet and I allowed it. Even with that dose of energy, my strength faded with each breath. Folding my arms around his neck, I rested my chin on Derek's shoulder and peered back at Nathaniel. The scowl on his face would make the Devil cower. For me, I pulled my trembling lips into a grin and flipped Nathaniel the bird.

Minutes passed like hours as Derek carried me down flights of stairs and through narrow hallways littered with vampire ash. Outside, the storm returned with a vengeance. Numbness consumed me and my grip involuntarily loosened around Derek's neck. I rested my temple against his shoulder. Eyelids grew heavy. Breath slowed. Even his hands cupping my bare thighs did nothing to rouse me.

"Stay awake." His voice vibrated against my chest. "Or I'll haunt you for eternity."

"Promise?" *Ooh, I shouldn't have said that.* Close to death, my commonsense filter was MIA, allowing my failing heart to hijack my mouth.

"With every fiber of my being," he answered.

To clear my vision from the fall of tears, I batted my eyelashes. Sam came into view. "Don't let them take me," I whispered against Derek's ear.

Derek's hold tightened. He uttered something in a foreign language and the words rolling from his tongue lulled the sobs wracking my body.

"That is far enough, vampire," Sam said. "Release her."

"She is unable to stand," Derek said.

"Beta, take her." Sam stepped to the side to make room for a man to walk past.

Derek backstepped, and the wolf who escorted us growled. Mechanical clicks overshadowed the growling. Three men, each holding crossbows, flanked Sam. The beta guy moved back behind the group.

"Don't hurt Derek," I mumbled at the men.

"He has you under his compulsion," Sam said. "Once you are safe—"

"I'm not going with you."

Sam's lips flattened and a flash of hurt crossed his expression. "Not your decision." He flicked a glance at the man to his right. One thing Sam had taught me was to always keep your eyes on your opponent's hands. My attention went to Sam's fist at his side. He ticked a finger against his thigh. The man raised the crossbow toward Derek's head and fired.

I screamed.

A fist appeared, grabbing the flying missile inches from Derek's eye. My mind raced to catch up with the action. Corbus stepped to the side of us. As he lifted his free hand, energy hummed around him as the wind raced past us, pelleting snow at Sam's group.

The wolf still at our side growled.

"Quiet," Corbus spoke with power toward the wolf and it took a seat on the ground. Then Corbus turned his attention to me. "I told you not to remove the jacket."

"I…" That was the last word to pass my lips. Agony strangled my throat.

"We must leave." Corbus dropped the arrow to the ground. "Give me your hand, Wolf Born. I grant you and this vampire safe passage."

Derek protested, but I brushed my fingertips against Corbus' outreaching hand. Another wave of white-hot pain tore through me while Corbus grabbed my forearm, shoving the shirt up to my elbow. Beneath his hand, my veins turned black. Beads of silver oozed from my pores, hitting the snow with a hiss as they burned through to the barren ground. When Corbus released me, darkness swallowed my vision.

Chapter Seven

"He should be here." My father's voice echoed through my subconsciousness.

"He will come," my mom answered.

I snapped open my eyes. I sat crouching on the stairs of my childhood home, peering down at the living room illuminated by moonlight. I went to slap a hand on my mouth but stopped mid-motion. A full-length mirror hung across from the stairway. I gawked at my reflection of a wide-eyed eight-year-old with frizzy hair and pink PJs.

A kid-sized hand rested on my shoulder. "Who are they talking about, Tess?"

I flinched at the sweetness of Drew's little voice. Slowly, I turned to look over my shoulder. The dusting of freckles stood out against my brother's pale skin. His hair smashed to the side of his face paired with a line of drool hanging from the corner of his mouth.

"Am I dreaming?" I mumbled.

"No." Concern pinched his brows. "Then I would be too."

The warmth from my brother's hand, the horrid PJs, the citrus scent of the wax polish on the banister… All were too real. I dug my nails against my palms, hoping I'd wake from the dream. Or maybe, I too, was dead. Swallowing the lump in my throat, I averted my focus toward my parents' voices coming from the kitchen.

"We should leave," Dad said.

"He'll find us," Mom responded.

Energy prickled along my skin, and at the same instant, my brother shivered. I slapped a hand over his and pressed a finger to my lips.

Drew nodded absently.

A shimmering glow illuminated the kitchen. Overhead, ripples of golden light reflected off the ceiling. Drew leaned over me, whispering to my ear, "I hear seagulls."

In the distance, birds screeched while the thunder of waves crashed against a nonexistent shore. Acknowledging the oddness, I nodded. We lived miles from the ocean.

"Dylan," an unfamiliar man's voice boomed from the kitchen. "It has been too long."

My dad didn't respond to his name. Nor did my mom.

"I see there is still some adversity on your part," the stranger said as he made his way into the living room. More like he floated. The man stood twelve feet tall with his iridescent skin glowing in the moonlight. When he turned, an unseen current rippled through his sea-moss-colored hair and matching toga. The stranger stopped in the center of the room next to our piano while his piercing gaze roamed across the living room. "What a common place you have. I – "

"After decades," my dad cut the man off, "you choose now."

A thread of fear ran up my spine. Unable to wake, I huddled with Drew.

"The guard stirs," the stranger said.

"You come with kindling for poetry. A rumor." The creases on Dad's forehead deepened. "Still they sleep. As they will for centuries more."

"This is not a season of rest but one of anticipation."

"Not our concern." Dad shifted his attention to Mom. "I denounced myself."

"About that." The stranger turned his focus to the piano where our family portrait sat on top of its lacquered hood. He ran a needle-like finger over the gold-plated frame. "You decided to breed. Your offspring must denounce themselves before they – "

"They will be given a choice," Mom interjected. Anger glinted in her eyes as she stood at the kitchen threshold. "It is the law."

The stranger ignored Mom and kept talking to Dad. "I'd hate for you to feel the pain of loss."

Dad fisted his hands at his sides. His lips pulled into a sneer. Never had I witnessed this side of him. Drew pressed his fingers tighter against my shoulder.

"You threaten my family." Dad's voice shook.

The phantom seagulls screamed overhead while malice filled the stranger's voice. "I give warning. Your spawn will denounce themselves." He turned the picture upside down. "Free will or not, you bring your spawn to me, or else they will be exterminated."

"I revoke my invite," Dad snapped. "Leave."

As he tipped his chin at my dad, the stranger locked his eyes with mine. A grin stretched his lips, revealing rows of serrated teeth.

* * * *

I bolted awake. In my room. *Great.* In my bed, trapped underneath someone's bare arm. *Bad.* I glanced over my naked shoulder at Ben, fast asleep with a trail of drool running down his chin.

Gripping the sheet to my body, I scrambled my naked ass out of the bed. "What the fuck?"

Ben startled awake. His mouth worked like a fish gasping for water while he shoved his glasses into place over the bridge of his nose. "Wait." He tossed up his hands. "Corbus—"

I whirled around to the closed bedroom door and the room kept on spinning until the back of my legs bumped against the bed. "Where is he?"

"I don't know," Ben answered with a franticness that matched mine. "I just woke up."

"Why are you in my bed?" My gaze landed on his thighs. "Wearing nothing but your boxers?"

Ben tossed a pillow over his lap. "Corbus said that you needed skin-to-skin contact with someone you wouldn't kill when you woke up." A puff of air popped from Ben's mouth. "Shit. I didn't think he meant literally."

I chewed my lip instead of hitting Ben with a snarky comment as we were both equally mortified.

"Tess, you were convulsing. Burning up. Hallucinating. He told me to get undressed and to hug you. So, I did. As hard as I could. I didn't let you go." Ben's voice thinned. "I thought you were going to die."

My brain tried to form an apology. Guilt overshadowed me. Ben was as human as a human came. How selfish for me to have dragged him into the world of monsters.

"Don't give me that look." He huffed.

"What look?"

"Staring at me while your eyebrows do that scrunch thing." Ben tilted his head, studying my expression. "Now, you're doing the plotting-on-running-away look."

"No." I scrubbed my face with my free hand. "Just dealing with the fact that I woke up next to you naked—" The memory of last night's nude lip-lock flashed across my mind. "Derek."

"There's that name." Ben propped his back against the wall.

I dropped my hand as a replay of the night sped forward. "Oh no. Sam."

Ben whistled. "Wow, you *really* had a reunion last night."

"Get up," I grumbled. "Get dressed. We are leaving." I peered out of the window. The van Nathaniel had hijacked sat feet away from the cabin.

Ben answered my unasked question. "Corbus drove you back here in that thing."

"Was there anyone else with him?"

"The infamous Derek."

I scanned the afternoon sky. "When did he leave?"

"He didn't. Derek's currently in the crawlspace under the kitchen table."

I shuffled over to the closet. "Anyone else come here?"

"No."

"Anyone in town die last night?"

"Die? What? Just—" Ben grabbed his head, grimacing. "What the… I can't remember…"

"Compulsion. Nathaniel must have erased your memories."

"I remember some." Ben stared at his toes. "I woke up in the cellar of the bowling alley where I was being arrested for breaking and entering *and* setting the place on fire. Corbus showed up, then there was this flash of light, and poof, the cops disappeared. Corbus seems like a decent nonhuman."

"Do not get friendly with Corbus." Narrowing my eyes, I pinned Ben to the wall with my warning. "Don't thank him or ask him questions. If you do, you'll owe him."

"Well." Ben's eyes bugged. "That would have been helpful information last night. I'm a damn reporter. All I did was drill him with questions as he drove us back here. Then he said he had to leave, and I fell asleep. I woke up when he brought you back. What the hell is going on with my brain? Why can't I remember? I thought only vampires did the mind scramble thing."

The front door opened and closed.

My nose tingled with Corbus' scent. I tripped over to my dresser, dug around the top drawer and grabbed a tube of lipstick. I scribbled a note on the mirror.

Out the window in ten.

Ben shook his head.

I gave him an aggressive nod.

He rolled his eyes and kicked his legs over the bed.

My breath dropped to the floor. I lunged for Ben. Clasping the sides of his face, I turned his head. Two angry puncture marks marred Ben's neck.

"What the hell." He tugged free and stumbled toward the mirror. Ben gasped, probing the wounds with his shaking fingers. "Who bit me?"

"Nathaniel. He'll find us through your blood," I whispered, smudging the lipstick message with my fingers. The words ran together, taking on the appearance of blood dripping down the mirror. I had promised to keep Ben safe. Currently, the nonhuman moseying around our kitchen was the only chance against Nathaniel. Numb, defeated, I grabbed some random clothes and got dressed.

"Smell that?" Ben asked.

The aroma of fresh-brewed coffee slipped under the door, tempting my salivary glands. "Let me do the talking," I warned as I glanced at Ben, tucking in his wrinkled shirt. Rolling my shoulders, I opened the door.

Corbus had made himself right at home in front of our fridge, grabbing the creamer. I tore my glare away, setting it on the floor. A new circle of dirt surrounded the kitchen table.

"The undead cannot cross soil from a grave," Corbus said.

Ben squeezed past me and walked over to the coffeemaker.

"Don't drink that," I said.

"If he wanted us dead, he'd have let you die last night." Ben set to making our cups.

Corbus took a seat at the table. He nursed his coffee while watching me shuffle into the kitchen. Lowering the mug, he glanced at the empty seat across from him.

I took Corbus' cue and sat.

"We need to discuss your lack of a court," Corbus said to me.

I blinked.

Ben cleared his throat. "Like royalty?"

A giggle escaped me and when no one joined in, I covered my hysterics with a fake yawn.

"You have much to learn." Corbus stared at me. "All Otherworldly leaders have courts."

"Do you have a court?" Ben asked Corbus.

I glared at Ben. "I told you not to ask him questions."

"He is human. Our laws do not apply to him." Corbus passed Ben a glance. "No, I do not."

"Good to both those answers," I mumbled.

"Indeed." Corbus took another sip of coffee. "Ben must hold a position within your court."

I shook my head.

"Yes," they said in unison.

"You don't know anything about the monster world," I snapped at Ben.

"Correct." He set a mug in front of me and proceeded to sit his ass in the chair next to mine. "Do you?"

He had a point. That slap of reality woke me up more than the caffeine fumes tickling my nose. "No. I don't."

"You both will learn," Corbus said. "Being human, Ben has certain immunities. He does not have to follow or uphold our laws. As a member of your court, he can speak for you in times of negotiations, without fear of certain ramifications."

"Negotiating for Tess. That's nothing new for me." Ben took a sip of his coffee. "Instead of deflecting your bosses, it'll just be—"

"It's not just vampires and werewolves." I ticked my chin at Corbus. "There's a lot more scarier things."

Over the bridge of his glasses, Ben gave me a stare-down. "And they can't touch me."

"They should not," Corbus corrected.

I shot my attention at Corbus. "I'm not putting Ben in danger."

"His life *is* threatened without a title. Your enemies will use him against you," Corbus said. "Like Nathaniel did."

"Fine." I huffed. "This is only temporary. Until there are no more people. Things. Others. Trying to kill us."

"So, you're saying this is forever." Ben flashed me a grin, then looked at Corbus. "What does she need to do?"

Corbus kept his focus on me while he pulled a pocketknife from his jeans. "Prick your fingers and then press them together. When you feel his heartbeat, say Ben's full name and give him the title of Steward."

"If there are werewolves around here, they'll smell my blood," I said to Ben. "They could find me. Us."

"Prove that you no longer fear them," Corbus said.

"But I do—"

"Pretend," Ben blurted. The puncture marks on his neck vibrated with his strained voice. "Please. For me."

I looked him square in the face while I grabbed the knife from Corbus. I nicked my finger. Ben winced when I pricked his. Awkward as a first kiss, I pressed my bloody finger to Ben's. True to Corbus' account, Ben's heartbeat pulsed against my finger. "Benjamin Wright." The words flowed from my lips like some deep-rooted instinct. "I name you Steward of my pack. May no harm come to you as you deliver my voice." Once the last word left my lips, I took back my finger. Thankfully, there were no blood droplets and the nick had already mended. I went to retrieve the pocketknife but Corbus beat me to it.

He gave me a wink, then stuffed the weapon into his jeans.

Ben inspected his finger. "Holy shit. The cut's healed. How?"

"Magic," Corbus said, reaching down toward his hip. I glanced under the table. The canvas sack sat against Corbus' leg. He rummaged around inside, then set a black ring on the table. "This will also protect Ben."

I slapped my hand on Ben's arm. "That coat you pulled out of your magical sack almost killed me."

"It kept you from harm."

"Yeah, at the cost of my energy."

Corbus gave a slight nod. "The ring is a gift. No repayment is needed. No harm to you, Ben."

Slowly, I released Ben. He chewed the inside of his cheek before taking the ring and slipping it on his finger. Nothing happened. We let out a collective breath.

Ben set his attention on Corbus. "Your laws do not apply to me so I can ask questions without owing you anything." He used caution in making a statement versus a question.

Corbus nodded.

Ben grinned, folding his arms across his chest. "Why are you here?"

"Three months ago, a power vibrated through the earth. I followed its call." Corbus looked at me. "To the Wolf Born."

"Three months ago, I made the Change." I added for Ben, "I became a full-blown werewolf."

"I felt the power from your Change," Corbus said. "It amplified what *first* stirred me days before."

I fought the urge to run my fingers against the side of my neck. Before the werewolf had taken a chunk out of me, Derek had taken a bite first. That night, energy had passed between Derek and me. I kept from sharing that tidbit with the men at the table. Yeah, Corbus had saved my life, but I did not trust him.

"Just as I searched for the source, others will too." Corbus' gaze settled on mine. "To control you."

"And you didn't come here to control her?" Ben asked.

"I came to destroy or aid." Corbus finished his coffee, setting the mug down with a clink. "I choose to aid."

"What made your decision?" Ben asked.

"The Wolf Born is neutral."

Ben served another question, "What do you mean?"

"Werewolves are the side of Light. Vampires are the side of Darkness. Her power comes from both. She exists in balance."

"You're not a vampire," Ben said to me.

"Nope."

"You share a blood-bond with the vampire." Corbus leveled his attention at my face. "It was formed before you made your Change."

Ben tapped his ring against the table. "What's a blood-bond?"

Corbus kept his focus on me as he answered Ben. "One of the methods for turning a human into a vampire."

I brushed my toe against the floorboards hiding Derek. "I only know of the blood-bond way."

"There are two." Corbus shifted his gaze to Ben rubbing his neck. "The common method is for a vampire to share the dark gift through blood exchanges. The process is slow. Painful. Once the human dies, they turn. When the transformation is complete, there are no ties between the vampires. Whereas with the blood-bond, it is not just blood exchanging." Corbus paused, returning his attention to me. "Souls are shared."

"The blood-bond is my connection to the darkness." Fear needled up my spine. "Werewolves cannot be turned."

"No," Corbus affirmed. "The wolf within you will not allow you to be turned, therefore the blood-bond will become a craving with no end."

"I need to destroy it," I said.

Corbus sat in silence. His eyes grew distant for a moment before he returned his intense focus to me. "There are some bonds which neither Heaven nor Hell can sever. This is one."

"Then I'll fight it," I said.

"The bond will consume you both." Corbus dropped his attention to the table. "Your loss of control will drive the werewolves into madness. When this happens, I will be forced to end your life." Corbus stood and so help me, if he leaned down and grabbed something to kill me right then and there from his magical sack… Thankfully, he went to pour himself more coffee.

"You said you chose to aid her." Ben grabbed my forearm, signaling me to let him continue. "So help us. There's gotta be a buffer of some sort."

"What is set to happen, will." Corbus tilted his head and a ghost of a grin touched his lips. "However, there is no *set* time."

"Exactly." I slipped loose of Ben's grip. "This monster life has taught me there are exceptions to every rule. I'll find one to this blood-bond without killing off the entire werewolf population."

"The blood-bond is also why you need a court," Corbus said. "Through the link, you may draw on their energy to fight the craving."

"So, I'm a parasitic werewolf now." I turned to Ben, whose eyes were bugging out of his skull. "Can you ask Corbus how many are supposed to be in this court?"

Corbus did not wait for Ben to ask him. "There is no set number. However, each title must be selected with utmost care. The implications of a weak court can birth corruption and war." Corbus locked his attention on me. "Ultimately, the fall of the kingdom."

"Great," Ben mumbled under his breath. "Way to just go and dump that all on her."

"You are part of her court," Corbus said to Ben. "You share her burden."

As I recapped my predicaments, I rubbed my temples. "I'm neutral. For now. Corbus won't kill me if I battle the blood-bond by sucking the energy out of members of my monster court. And Ben is—"

"Your steward," Ben answered. "Who will keep your ass alive. Along with this guy."

We both aimed our attention at Corbus.

"To keep this world safe, I offer my aid to you, Wolf Born, as long as I am able." Corbus paused, staring at me, through me, to the pit of my soul. "Until the others come."

Others. My mind flicked back to my dream of the saw-toothed, toga-wearing stranger. To mask the shaking of my hands, I grabbed the coffee mug in front of me. "Then we better get searching for a loophole to the blood-bond because I'm not comfy with the parasitic lifestyle."

"Later," Corbus said. "The alpha will be here soon."

My heart dropped to the bottom of my ribcage.

"You need protection," Ben said. A bead of sweat ran down the side of his temple while he drummed his fingers against the table.

"You are in on this?"

"He has a pack." Ben paused. "Sam was our friend."

"*Was.*" I set my frustration at Corbus. "You were there last night. *You* stopped the freaking arrow."

"Not aimed for you," Corbus countered. "The alpha *is* your ally."

"I'm not sure about that." I dropped my voice to keep my fear in check. "I owe Nathaniel the favor because I had him erase Sam's memories of me."

"She did that to save Sam's life," Ben said to Corbus.

"Yes." I swallowed. "But then I left Sam at the Gathering to die."

"You had no choice," Ben said. "If you didn't escape, every werewolf would be dead."

Silence filled the kitchen. Briefly.

"Hey." Ben cupped my hands holding the lukewarm mug. "We will meet Sam together."

"Thanks," I whispered.

Ben squeezed my hands. "After we are done with Sam, we'll find the loophole to your vampire boyfriend—"

"He's not my boyfriend," I grumbled.

"Yeah. We'll have that talk later." Ben quirked his lips into a half-grin. "For now, you need to shower while I research my new title."

Chapter Eight

Problem number thirty-three for having the tiniest water heater – procrastination came with uncomfortable consequences. Twelve minutes into my shower and the water was running like ice daggers down my spine. Still, I stayed under the spray, not ready or willing to deal with the impending visitor.

The bathroom door opened for the tenth time.

"You gotta move it," Ben said, tossing a towel over the curtain rod. "We need to talk strategy before Sam shows up. I set your clothes out for you."

The door shut and I peeked around the curtain. Piled neatly on the counter sat a pair of black slacks, a green sweater and a satin bow on top of a matching bra and panties. Shivering, I reluctantly left the shower.

Outside the door, Ben paced.

While I tossed on the undergarments, I said, "So we are going for the business buddies and not sworn enemies look today."

Ben chuckled. "You can trade in for your sports bra and leggings afterward."

"I may need to run, better have the appropriate garments."

"Be glad you don't own a dress." Ben's voice drifted away from the door. "Hurry. Corbus wants to go over my role during the meeting."

On the floor, Ben had even set out the pair of flats he'd bought a month ago when he'd bribed me for a night out. I'd abandoned the human world too, only venturing out for food and laundry. That night filled with laughter, bowling and tacos had been one for the records. If we made it through this meeting, there would be a repeat of that outing.

I wiped the steam from the mirrored vanity and cringed. My hair hung like seaweed, giving me the appearance of a swamp thing instead of a werewolf. *Fitting*. Before last night, my last encounter with Sam had been of me drenched in the swamp remains of a troll that had skewered himself on my claws. Interesting fact, when a troll died, they liquefied into a blob of exploding swamp water. *Gross*. However, the troll had tried to take over the human world and he had stabbed me, so he'd gotten his comeuppance.

I peeled a lock of hair away from my shoulder. "Isn't that a bitch," I muttered at the shiny new star-shaped scar grazing my shoulder. Wolf bite. Silver burn. Silver bullet. If I lived another three months, who knew how many more scars would canvas my flesh?

Shaking my head, I pulled out the hairdryer and set to work. The heat and noise took me out of my thoughts so that I almost missed the truck engine purring down the driveway. Uncomfortable conversation number three of the day waited beyond the bathroom door.

I went to toss on the sweater, stopping mid-grab. A piece of cinnamon gum sat on the folded garment. "Thanks, Ben," I whispered to myself, unwrapping the gum. Popping the stick in my mouth, I closed my eyes and played the memory of when Andrea had given me a pep talk for my bartender interview with Sam. *"Smile and give him hell,"* she had said. *"You'll have Sam wrapped around your pinky."*

Forcing my trembling fingers still, I painted my lips with some gloss, then nodded at my pale reflection. "Smile and give him hell. I can do that."

Before I lost my nerves, I slipped into the flats, channeled my inner Andrea badassness and exited the bathroom. Ben and Corbus stopped their conversation to stare at me. While I had showered, they had both made wardrobe changes. Corbus wore a pair of jeans and a thick flannel shirt. His once free-flowing ebony hair was now pulled into a tight braid that reached down his back. He still wore his boots. *Smart guy.* No doubt, they were worn for if he needed to run. Ben sported a pair of khakis and a crisp white dress shirt topped off with a burgundy bowtie. The man usually refused ties. His footwear was his standard loafers. Making a mental note, after the meeting, I needed to have the appropriate monster-world-footwear conversation with Ben.

I glanced out of the kitchen window. A full-sized truck sat idling in the snow-covered driveway. Four figures waited inside.

"Come." Corbus motioned for me to have a seat at the table.

I should have felt relieved to have a few minutes with my team before talking to Sam. But the stall sent my heart slamming against my ribs. Practically diving into the chair to hide my trembling body, I gave Ben a forced smile while I twisted the damp sleeves of my sweater under the table.

Corbus stood by the sink. He spoke at me but kept his attention on the truck. "Speak only to your steward. He will then relay to the alpha."

"Sam," I corrected.

Corbus shook his head. "In political and public meetings, you will use titles. The use of names gives your opponent power over you. Names are reserved for private encounters." Corbus looked at Ben. "Meaning, any time you are out of this space, you address her as Wolf Born."

"What—crap." I winced at the almost slip for asking Corbus a question. I looked at Ben. "Can you ask Corbus, what should we address him as?"

Corbus blinked and a rush of emotions passed through his eyes before he allowed stillness to consume them once more. "Witness. I take no sides."

"We will not mention the blood-bond. Or vampires." Ben shot a look between me and Corbus. "We will stick to the sole objective of this meeting."

"Get the alpha and his pack to protect me."

"By..." Ben hesitated.

"By?" I prompted.

"We need Sam, I mean the alpha, to join your court. He needs a title." Ben raised his hand to keep me from protesting. "He'd be like a bouncer. You know, like how he was in your human life. If he agrees, then all is good."

"If he does not?" I asked.

"Then Corbus—" Ben cringed. "Sorry. The witness will remove Sam."

"You're not killing Sam," I told Corbus.

Corbus raised an eyebrow in my direction. "Not all endings resort to death, Wolf Born."

"Well, I haven't met an end that didn't."

The truck engine turned off and a heavy silence filled the cabin. Unable to just sit there and wait all nice and calm, I tapped my foot against the floor. Thankfully, Derek was dead to the world, or else he'd have one heck of a headache from my nervous tic.

Outside, four doors opened and closed. Ben moved to stand at my right side. He tucked the corners of his mouth between his teeth, trying to hide the trembling of his jaw. Corbus moved to the door. He gave us both an emotionless glance. His focus lowered to the table which vibrated with my foot tapping. I crossed my ankles, ceasing the table's jitter dance. Corbus turned his attention to the footsteps approaching the cabin.

A solid knock announced the four men breathing on the opposite side of the door.

"Stay seated"—Ben rested his hand on my shoulder—"until they leave."

Keeping my attention on the door, I nodded.

The rush of frigid air pelted me in the face until two massive bodies moved into the small kitchen. The other two traveling companions turned their backs and blocked the front door. I set my attention on the man accompanying Sam.

Freaking Chippendales had nothing on werewolves. He folded his muscular arms across his broad chest and stood in front of the closed door. Below his chestnut locks, a deep scar ran down from his forehead to the right side of his chin. When my gaze traveled to his gunmetal-gray eyes, he lowered his attention to the table. His lips drew into a flat line, triggering my vague memory from the past night. Sam had called him beta.

Sam cleared his throat. Time stilled as I sucked all the courage into my clenched lungs and leveled my eyes to his. Where there had once been playfulness, an uneasiness stared back at me. His temples pulsed and he grimaced. Anger replaced the uncertainty in his gaze.

With perfect timing, Corbus moved to stand to the left, careful to remain at an equal distance between Sam and me. "Thank you, Alpha, for meeting today. Your beta is welcome to stay."

Sam dragged his attention from me to Corbus, then he inhaled. Wrinkling his nose, Sam directed his glare at Ben. "How do I address the fae?"

"Witness," Ben answered.

Sam gave an abrupt nod then returned to stare at me. "You asked for my aid."

I went to answer, but Ben squeezed my shoulder. Then he said, "You will address her by her title."

Sam's nostrils flared as he made a show of dragging in Ben's scent. "Why is there a human answering for the Wolf Born?"

"I am the Wolf Born's Steward."

"That's ballsy." Sam smirked. "Smart. But risky. There are loopholes to everything, Wolf Born." He spoke at Ben, but his attention landed on me. "What aid is needed?"

"Witness?" Ben asked.

"The balance of this world is in jeopardy." Corbus shifted his focus to me. "You need to prepare the werewolves for who is coming."

"Wh—"

"Who?" Ben finished my question.

Corbus nodded at Ben's impeccable response time. "One of the Light."

"Light means good, right?" Ben asked.

"Light means Light," Corbus answered. "Just as Dark means Dark."

The sweet scent of fear wafted from the guy hanging out by the front door.

"Beta." Sam cut a glare at the man. The link stirred between the two and the beta's aroma of terror thinned. Sam turned his focus back to me. "Our race stays out of the affairs of fae court endeavors, Wolf Born."

"No longer," Corbus said. "Her power will continue to draw the Otherworldly Creatures' attention. They will pursue her. They seek to control her."

The corner of Sam's lips hooked into a grin. "From what I *can* remember and saw last night, she is not some meek thing to be possessed."

"Regardless," Corbus said. "She is the last of her bloodline. The power of your race runs solely through the Wolf Born's veins. This puts the werewolves in grave danger of eradication or enslavement. Either outcome will tip the balance of the world."

"Vampires have tried and failed at destroying us." Sam narrowed his eyes at Corbus. "If you think threatening our race will have me submitting to the fae's bidding, you're fucking wrong."

Corbus gave a hesitant nod. "That is why she will choose you."

"That's not how she acted last night." Sam cut his attention back to me. "Or today."

Ben's hand tightened against my shoulder. "If we could—"

"No. I've heard and seen all that I need. We're through." Sam dipped his head at me, then turned to the door.

The beta guy shifted to let Sam pass.

"Wait," I whispered.

Sam turned around. I bit my lip and gripped my knees. *No. Give him hell.* Composing myself, I lifted my chin, then tossed all my confidence into my voice. "We're *not* done."

Sam's eyes flashed. "Is that so?"

Energy buzzed up my spine, then pulsed outward, latching onto Ben's hand against my shoulder. As the current reverted back into me, he sucked in a breath. *Shit.* I was inadvertently draining Ben. I tossed up a mental barrier between us. Instantly, the energy exchange ceased. I refocused on the alpha eyeballing me while Ben's energy raced through me like a double-shot espresso topped with sunshine. "You'll stay," I said to Sam. "Until I tell you to leave."

Without lowering his gaze from mine, Sam stepped up to the table. His nostrils flared. "Even your scent holds power."

"Just as it calls your wolf, her power calls to the fae. She cannot fight them alone," Corbus said. "She needs to establish her court."

"And she'll choose me to protect—" Sam's jaw ticked. Fury blazed in the glare he targeted Ben with. "Does she know?"

As Ben's eyes grew wide, warning signs flashed within my skull. "Know what, Steward?"

Corbus cleared his throat, and I shot my attention to his emotionless face. "The Wolf Born will title the alpha 'Guardian of My Body'. She must continue her bloodline."

"You said the title was for protection." I glared at Ben whose attention darted around the kitchen. "Like a bouncer. Not a…mate—"

"I accept," Sam said.

I whipped my head around. Sam failed at hiding the heat burning in his eyes. No. He chose not to. His gaze locked with mine, refusing to look away. The room tilted. Black spots ate at my vision. Cold sweat poured from my body.

"Wolf Born." Corbus' voice rose, dragging me from the throes of my panic. "The werewolves must be unified."

"As your guardian, all packs will follow the alpha," Ben added. He flicked his attention between me and Sam, hinting at the unsaid truth. I was only their leader by blood. Loyalty ran Y-chromosome deep in the werewolf world.

"Blindsiding does not pair with unity," I gritted through my teeth.

"We will talk afterward," Corbus said. "Titles can be given and taken. If this alpha is not an appropriate choice, you may choose another, but you need an alpha to be the guardian of your body, now."

Silence filled the tiny kitchen closing around me while my tears splattered onto the table. *Tap. Tap. Tap.*

"I know compulsion was used on me," Sam spoke in his signature soft tone meant to calm, yet his words sent flicks of pain through my heart. "I can't remember my recent past. But dammit, I know we had something. I feel it, Wolf Born. I promise to respect and protect you."

"Alpha, I need to cut your finger," Corbus said, opening his pocketknife.

Sam nodded.

Corbus took the blade to the tip of the alpha's ready and waiting finger. Then Corbus looked at me and tipped his chin. *Smart.* Not that I'd stab anyone, but impaling the table with the stupid knife was definitely a thought. I tore my hand from my shaking knee, then shoved my index finger at Corbus.

As he nicked me, Corbus said, "When you feel his heartbeat, give the alpha the title 'Guardian of My Body'."

I flicked my blurry gaze to the beta guy. The scar tugged his lip away from his teeth. He narrowed his eyes at Corbus. At least someone else was physically upset too. I took up tapping my foot against the floor concealing Derek's body. *Oh no!* A sob almost cracked from my throat. In a few hours, I'd have to face Derek.

"This title will protect the alpha," Corbus said. "Nathaniel will come tonight. We need to be prepared."

"Fine." I forced myself to look at Sam. A bit aggressive on my part, I pressed my finger to his. At the first hit of his heartbeat, I whispered, "Samuel Lyncourt, I name you Guardian of My Body. May you protect me and my blood with your last breath." I pulled away and snapped my attention to Ben. "Can they leave now?"

"I will stay outside." Sam nodded to me, then motioned for his beta to leave as well. A millisecond after Sam closed the front door, I scrambled to my feet, then bolted to my bedroom.

Chapter Nine

Once in my room, I tore off the business clothes. On the other side of the door, Ben and Corbus continued conversing. They could have all the political talks they wanted without me. I was done. I was…naked. *Shit.* I stormed over to my drawers then dressed in hiking gear. Dropping to my knees, I shoved my hand under my bed, feeling around for my boots. Gone.

A growl vibrated my chest. They were buried in the tundra of that vampire fortress. However, my sneakers sat by the front door. I straightened my spine, planning my next steps. I'd walk by them, grab my sneakers then deal with the fucking posse of werewolf guards popping a squat on the porch. *They must be freezing.* I shook off my concern and welcomed the angry tears coating my cheeks.

Like my boots, my freedom was gone. Blood roared at my temples, fanning my madness. All I needed was the wolf within me to join the rage party. Strangely, she appeared to be sleeping. Dormant. For sure, my temper was a siren call to her. Yet nothing. I pursed my lips. At least I was in control of my body, for now. My stomach clenched. *A kid? Me? With Sam? No. No. Just no.*

I swung open the door and met Sam's chest. Dressed head to toe in winter gear, he belonged on a billboard for some rustic outdoor fashion line. Not here. His boot lodged between the door and frame, blocking my dramatic retreat. He dangled my boots by their laces as an offering. "I found these last night—"

I snagged them and he removed his foot. When he smiled, I slammed the door.

"Can we talk?" he asked.

"Nope." I shoved my feet into the warm boots. He'd left them in the truck, keeping them toasty. *How nice.*

"Can we—"

"Nope."

"Can you at least listen?"

"Nope. And the answer to the next question is hell nope." I knotted the boots and tugged on a coat.

His sigh pelted the door, yet his crisp pine scent slipped underneath, drifting its way to my flared nostrils. I shoved my back against the door. Movement outside the window became my focal point. The beta guy paced back and forth. He paused his patrolling, then tipped his chin at me in acknowledgment—or warning—before he continued his track.

"Your men are cold," I mumbled, shoving on my gloves.

"They have had it worse. More are on the way. They'll trade out."

"This beta guy is like your best bro?"

"Yes." The floorboards creaked as Sam shifted his weight. "He's the second in command to our pack."

"What's his name?"

"We use titles—" Sam paused. "Nolan."

"Well, Nolan's ears are going to get frostbite."

Energy prickled along my spine. Nolan stopped in front of the window and tugged a knit cap on his head. The energy continued humming across my body, singing with the familiarity of Sam's alpha link. I pinched the bridge of my nose. "Are you just going to stand there?"

"Yes."

"Don't you have alpha things to do?"

"They will wait." He paused. "You're my priority."

Gritting my teeth, I spun to face the door and flung it open. "That's a great mindset to land you dead, Alpha."

His eyebrows rose at my challenge. "You gave me the title—"

"You." I jabbed a finger at him. "Do not touch me. Got it?"

His jaw ticked.

"Answer me, Alpha."

"If there is a threat, and I need to move you, I will." He folded his arms across his chest. "Other than that, you're hands-off."

I leveled my glare at his honey-brown eyes. "Good."

The corner of his lip pulled into a grin and his sexy-as-hell dimple made an appearance. "There's a couple of hours before sundown," he said. "Where would you like to go?"

I froze, leery that he was tricking me into some alone time. Unlike bloodsuckers, werewolves could lie. Devil-skilled crafters of tales. I'd fallen for a sweet lie from Sam's lips one too many times. On the other side of Sam's perfect body, silent spectators, Ben and Corbus, sat at the kitchen table.

Snapping my attention to Sam's face, I said, "A hike."

He nodded.

Outside, two more trucks pulled up.

"One group of men will follow behind us," Sam said.

I rolled my eyes but was secretly happy that I'd not be out in the woods alone with Sam. Instantly, my focus and worry fell underneath the kitchen table. *Derek. The blood-bond. How can Sam's guardian title be addressed without someone dying?* I chewed my lip. *Are my feelings for Derek even my own? Do I have feelings?*

"Wolf Born," Corbus said, "be back before the sun touches the treetops. We need to discuss the other's return." Corbus stared at the table, hinting at the 'other.'

I looked Sam dead in the eyes. "You and your pack—"

"*Your* pack, Wolf Born," he corrected. "You rule over the entire race. Your word over mine."

"Sure." The last Wolf Born hadn't held a voice among the Y chromosomes. The same fate waited for me given the right opportunity. Until then, I'd make damn sure I'd fight them tooth and claw on everything. "No one or thing is to harm Derek. The vampire your man almost shot last night."

Anger flashed across Sam's features. Before he said something to raise the rage in me, I continued, "Also, no one kills Nathaniel, the annoying blond vampire. We need him. I think. So, until I think otherwise, he is not dusted."

Corbus nodded. A spark of approval slipped into his eyes which he cast to his coffee mug. All the same, I caught it. On the other side of the table, Ben shook his head but kept his mouth shut. He had soaked up the whole monster-title thing, so I added, "Go tell everyone that, Steward."

As I headed out of the door, the wind howled against us, knocking me backward into Sam. I squinted against the pelting snowflakes. "How is it still storming?"

Sam leaned over to speak at my ear. His warm breath stirred the ghost of my human self who'd lost speech and brain cells when he was near. "Would a drive be better?"

"No." I started down the steps. Sam signaled toward the eight men grouped by the trucks. Five took up behind us. At the end of the driveway, three wolves waited.

I nodded at the werewolves and added another predicament to my growing list of worries. Wolves didn't live in these mountains. Nearly half the size of the males in my wolf form, I kept to the deep woods when I was forced to make the Change, miles from humans. If a person were to see me, hopefully, they'd think I was just a huge coyote. There would be no mistaking one of these men as anything but lupine.

"Where are we heading?" Sam asked.

"To the cliff. A mile east."

The link stirred between Sam and the group of wolves, then they turned and bounded ahead of us. Huddled inside my coat, I dipped my head toward the ground and trudged on. Since we were stuck in the winter wonderland for who knew how long, I'd be damned if I didn't make my daily appointment with Andrea's grave.

During the hike, Sam respected my want and need for silence. When we neared the cliff, the storm turned into a dancing flurry, allowing the afternoon sun to shimmer off the snow-covered ground. I stopped to enjoy the view. Sam shot a look over his shoulder, sending the link at the men following, and they hung farther back. Overhead, the evergreen branches groaned under the weight of snow, dropping a dusting now and then. When I tipped my chin upward, a stray ray of sunlight warmed my face. I sighed.

Sam came to a stop a mere foot away from me. "Fucking gorgeous."

I flicked my attention to Sam admiring the trees. A breeze stirred the fine hairs at his temples, snapping to life the memory of me running my fingers through his blood-soaked locks. Forcing the vision from my brain, I drew my focus lower. The afternoon sunshine kissed his lips, which tugged into a grin. *Shit.* I had taken way too long strolling down nightmare lane.

"Yeah, trees are pretty." I cringed.

"I was talking about you." His stare lingered on mine a second too long, so I looked away. "Can I ask you some questions?"

"You can." I kicked the snow off my boots. "Can't say I'll answer them."

"What were we?"

"Friends."

"Bullshit."

"I'm not lying." I shrugged. "You can smell if I am lying. Hear my heartbeat change."

"You're playing your words."

In a mock bow, I tipped my chin. "Learned from the best."

"Me?"

"No. Nathaniel."

"Ouch." Playfully, Sam slapped the side of his neck. This was a game we'd played in our past life. I'd burn him, and he'd act like he had been stung. His smile flattened and the playfulness stopped. "What?"

"Sa—Alpha."

"We are alone." Sam faced me. His voice dropped into a deep satin drawl, "Say my name."

I bit my lip. "I prefer to keep this formal."

"All right, Wolf Born." A challenge laced his grin. "Your heart is thumping against those ribs."

"We're hiking through three-foot-deep snow."

"For the past five minutes, we've been standing still." When he took a step closer, our frozen breath swirled and tangled together in the wind. I matched his game, taking a step past him, leaving just a sliver of space between our bodies.

A growl vibrated from his chest. "If we're exercising formality, you need to brush up on werewolf etiquette. Turning your back on me is a challenge."

"I'm not challenging." I kept heading toward the cliff. "I'm teasing."

In two powerful strides, he was at my side. "There is no playing in formality."

I gave him the side-eye. "Who made this monster rulebook? I have some serious beef with them."

"Ha. Join the club."

"Do this. Not that," I grumbled. "Damn *Neach Neamhshaolta* laws."

"Whoa. Haven't heard that term in ages. You some history buff?"

"No. The annoying vampire, Nathaniel, tossed an Otherworldly Creatures law at Corbus." I stopped. "Crap. I mean, the witness."

"Last night, your Steward told me the fae's name over the phone." Sam's attention drifted to the clearing ahead. "How'd you get caught up with this fae?"

"I tried to burn his cabin down." I raised my hand. "Before I knew he was some powerful nonhuman. Then Nathaniel showed up. To keep Corbus safe, I offered him shelter until the storm passed."

Sam tilted his head to the falling snow. "As soon as the last flake falls—"

"I revoke my invitation."

He nodded. "You need to practice caution around the witness. He says he's all for world kumbaya, but there's no neutrality for the fae. They are Light or Dark. Both sides are nasty. Things of nightmares." Sam cut his eyes to mine. "A fae is as trustworthy as a bloodsucker."

I turned fully to face Sam. "What if Corbus is not fae?"

"What the hell would he be with all that power buzzing around him? Not to sell us short, but"—Sam lifted his gloved hands, making a triangle—"the base is humans. Then, in the middle, are werewolves and bloodsuckers. At the peak, that's where the fae are on the power scale."

"The witness said he wants balance." I pondered Sam's diagram. Not thinking of formality and titles, I placed my hands on his and mashed down the peak, making more of an oval shape with his hands. "If Corbus is fae, why would he give up the power?"

Sam shifted his focus from our hands to my face. "I don't know."

I shot my attention to the tree and Andrea's rock covered with snow. I let go of Sam's hands, then pretended to brush snow off my coat. "Can you tell them to give me some room?"

The link rose between Sam and the wolves. While I hiked the last few yards to the stone, the wolves darted between the trees, giving me space.

Settling to my knees, I brushed away the foot's worth of new snow, unburying the frozen gum sticks. "Hey. It kinda got batshit crazy."

Silence.

"Okay, more like mammoth-size-shit crazy," I muttered, biting the frozen glove at my index finger, then tugging it off. When I shoved my hand into my empty pocket, a curse passed by my chattering teeth.

"What is it?" Sam asked.

"You don't have a stick of gum on you?"

"No." Sam loomed over me. His eyes locked onto the scattering of gum and wrappers. He winced. "Why is this triggering the compulsion?"

"Let's go." I rose to my feet, keeping my stare glued to the stone.

"This looks like some sort of a monument."

"It is." I turned to face Sam. Confusion, rage and grief cycled through his eyes blurring with Nathaniel's compulsion.

"Who were they?" Sam fisted his hands. "I want a name. Her name. I see a woman. Short."

Tears burned the surface of my eyes. No one should have to suffer their best friend's death, twice. For the second time, I told Sam, "Andrea."

He recoiled. His hands clawed at the side of his skull as he fought against the compulsion. "When I find the bloodsucker who fucked with my mind, I'm going to kill them. No." Fury cut his voice. "I'll make them suffer. Make them beg for their death."

There. At that moment. I'd the chance to come clean. To lay it all out. My confession. I had thought I'd saved Sam's life, having Nathaniel strip Sam of any memories of me. How wrong. What I had done was anything but merciful. The suffering in Sam's voice. Eyes. The agony. What I had done was selfish. Cruel. Evil.

"Shit." Sam lowered his hands. "I didn't mean to scare you."

If he only knew….

I bit my tongue and took a back step, tripping over Andrea's grave. As I fumbled to recover my balance, I braced my bare palm against the jagged edges of the rock.

Sam went to grab for me, then stopped. "Don't move. You're bleeding."

I opened my scuffed-up palm. "I'm fine."

Sam kneeled, plucking my glove off the ground. He shifted his attention to the wolves standing at the tree line. "Put the glove on."

I cut my gaze to the blood sliding between my fingers.

As I grabbed for the glove, my blood speckled the snow. Crackling and sizzling drew my attention to the droplets melting through to the earth.

"What the hell?" Sam squinted at my blood, then flicked his glowing stare to my face.

I didn't have a chance to share my equal concern. The ground trembled and a wave of pressure crashed against us, knocking the wind from our lungs. Mirroring my distress, Sam dug at his throat. As an invisible force constricted around my body, a power buzzed through me. Not the link. Not the blood-bond. Wild and chaotic, the power raced outward to challenge the phantom force restraining us.

Instantly, we were released. I crashed to my knees at the lack of resistance. As I choked in a breath, the frigid wind brushed my ear, carrying a voice. *"I found you."*

I turned over my shoulder. Formed out of wind and snow, the stranger from my dream stood feet away.

"Sam," I whispered.

"I see him," Sam gritted.

Chapter Ten

The ice stranger stood by as the wind formed an impenetrable barrier of spinning snow and ice to trap Sam and me. One of the wolves tried to dive through the vortex, but on contact, he went airborne. The other two wolves held back next to their fallen companion. The five men who had followed us stood at the forest line with their claws out ready to fight, yet an invisible force froze them in place.

"I can't send the link through this," Sam screamed over the wind. "Can you reach the witness?"

"How?"

"How did he find you last night?"

"I don't know. I had his coat. Maybe that?"

"There is no way he got to you that fast by tracking your scent."

There wasn't time to explain that the coat was magical. An idea hit. Back at the cabin, Corbus' energy had touched mine. Perhaps he had found me when I'd used the link. Running on that hypothesis, I attempted to summon the energy. Nothing happened. *What the hell?* I tried again and pain split through my temples, knocking me off balance.

Sam righted me, then froze. We didn't have time for another escape attempt. The ice stranger passed through the vortex. I grabbed Sam's forearm, keeping him at my side instead of attacking. The stranger stopped at Andrea's grave. He dragged his needle-like finger across my blood smearing the stone. Raising his bloody finger, he parted his serrated teeth. When his tongue skimmed across his fingertip, the stranger recoiled.

He jabbed his finger at me. "Thief."

"Don't look at his eyes," Sam growled. "Do not speak."

I kept my attention on the stranger's pointed chin.

He stayed by the rock, turning his head toward Sam. "I have no quarrel with you, Alpha."

"You harmed one of my wolves," Sam answered.

"On the beast's account, it injured itself." The stranger angled his chin in my direction. "You have stolen from me."

Sam tensed. "She—"

"She has a voice," the stranger interrupted. "I am eager to listen. Does she respond like father or mother? Come, child, let me hear the dead speak."

I tried. I really did. To stay poised. Silent. "I have *nothing* of yours."

"Pity. I'd hope to hear the blind optimism of your father." A grin cinched the corners of the stranger's mouth. "Instead, you inherited your mother's ignorance. I foresee a similar demise for you. Alas, I am in no position to offer mercy, for you stole from me, and I require repayment."

Sam's arm flexed under my hand.

The stranger waited, probably, hoping one of us would slip and ask a question. After a few hellish moments, he continued, "You killed the last korrigan."

"I remember that." Sam growled under his breath. "That thing almost *killed* you."

I raised my voice at the stranger. "In self-defense."

"He belonged to me," the stranger said. "The korrigan's blood laces yours. His power lives on."

Bile tickled my throat at the memory of McKay exploding into swamp water. My hand drifted to where he'd driven his sword through my side. My exposed wound had encountered his remains. Like an amoeba, the troll had slithered his power into my body. *Gross to the tenth power.*

The stranger tipped his head, no doubt studying the array of emotions slipping from my face. "In three nights," he said, "you will return what you have stolen."

Replaying the troll's last minutes in my mind, searching for a loophole, and be damned, I landed on one. Literally. Schooling my face into a mask of blankness, taking a breath, I let the confidence bubble in my chest. "The korrigan *willingly* impaled his heart on my claws. I owe you nothing."

"That was not his to give." The wind constricted around us with the stranger's words. He raised an accusing finger at me. "I rule all that are Light."

"Apparently not," I said.

"Wolf Born," Sam whispered.

"I shall relish the pain you will eagerly ask for." The stranger retracted his trembling finger. "When you beg for the agony to end, I will not be kind."

My widening eyes elicited screeching laughter from the stranger. If I lived, I needed to lock down the stone-cold monster façade. Splitting my attention between the stranger and the thinning vortex, I muttered to Sam, "Look."

"I see." Sam's muscles bulged, readying an attack. "I trust you. Be careful."

My attention faltered. In the past, Sam would have tricked me into letting him save me. Here, he let me take the lead. I gave him a hesitant nod and took a step forward. "You're looking a little transparent," I said to the stranger.

"I grow tired of your disobedient nature." He sneered. "You are a disgrace to the bloodlines."

"I get that a lot." Well, the disgrace part. The plural bloodlines part was fresh. However, I'd not let the stranger in on my lack of Otherworldly Creatures' knowledge. "You are no different than the monsters I faced before you," I said, ticking off the similarities on my gloveless hand. "Bitter. Uptight. Proud. Stupid clothing—"

He took a step forward. With the flick of his wrist, energy snapped against my flesh. I wavered in my footing, biting the sides of my cheeks to keep from gasping. Sam returned to my side, leaving enough space between us in case he needed to grab or toss me out of the stranger's way.

The stranger stopped his advancement. "May this dull your tongue, Wolf Born." He rushed his words which took on an airy tone as if, dare I hoped, his loss of control weakened his magic. An orb of ice formed between his hands which he then rolled toward my feet. Inside the sphere, swirling light formed an image.

My breath left in a rush as I struggled with Sam to get closer to the orb. Mirroring my horror, a pair of light-green eyes stared back at me. A bloody gash marred the dusting of freckles over a nose that I'd thought no longer graced the living world. My brother struggled against the chains binding him to a stone wall. Blood oozed from his swollen lip as he mouthed, "Tess."

"You have three days." The stranger snapped his fingers and the orb shattered. "If you do not return what you stole, I will take your brother's heart as repayment."

The air popped with pressure. Silence crashed around us. Then stillness. The vortex and stranger disappeared. I spun to face Sam. "He has Drew."

Sam said nothing. He didn't need to. A range of emotions crossed his eyes. The resolution of his feelings ended with a lowered gaze and flattened lips.

"No." Shaking my head, I snapped, "You can try to stop me—"

"We need to get back to the witness." Sam raised his stare to mine. "He's our best bet to find where this fae is."

"Wait. What?" I blinked. "You're not going to stop me?"

"From what I remember and what I have seen, there is no stopping you." He took a step closer, making me tilt my chin to keep direct eye contact. "Now. I *am* against you putting yourself in danger. I'll be damned if you go alone."

His stare was unwavering, his heartbeat strong and steady. My gut instinct hummed with certainty that Sam spoke the truth. He would help me. I turned away with my mind abuzz.

Drew is alive.

My focus connected with the unconscious wolf. *Oh no.* I hauled myself through the snow, then dropped to my knees, placing my bloody hand on his neck. The wolf's ragged breaths hitched against my palm.

Sam crashed down next to me, then pressed both his hands on the wolf. "I'm going to use the link." He raised his voice so the advancing pack members could hear. "Stop moving."

I braced against the ground, preparing for the link's surge. Energy pulsed from Sam, rocketing against me, knocking the breath from my lungs. Then nothing. Instead of drawing on my power, the link continued onward toward the surrounding werewolves. As the men fell to their knees, light spilled from Sam's hands to encase the wolf. When its breathing leveled, Sam pulled back the link and the glowing cloak disappeared.

It took a few cycles of breaths for me to string words together. "What is the wolf's name?" I asked Sam.

"He…" Sam said between swallowed breaths, "is a delta."

"I asked for a name." I cut my stare to Sam's glowing eyes.

"Jimmy," Sam answered.

"Hold on, Jimmy," I said to the wolf.

Jimmy cracked open an eye. A groan slipped from his muzzle.

To Sam's right, a man bent over, sucking in a breath. Besides Sam, he seemed the surest footed of the men. "You, with the nice hair, carry Jimmy—"

The man flashed a brilliant smile. "Max," he said.

Sam raised his eyebrow at Max.

"Sorry." Max dipped his head. "In case she wanted to know my name too."

"I'll want to know everyone's names," I said to Sam. "When fighting for your life, it takes less time to call out a name than thinking about titles or screaming a warning to, 'the dude with nice hair'."

Max's face lit. "Oh, I like her."

Sam glared at Max. "Show respect and restraint toward the Wolf Born."

In the distance, snowmobiles screamed through the forest.

"They're pack." Max picked up Jimmy. "I called in reinforcements."

Sam extended his hand to me and with minor effort, he plucked me off the ground. Unable to gather my balance, I tipped forward and he encircled my waist in his free arm, tugging me against the length of his body. As I got my feet under me, Sam made no move to let me go. Instead, his hold tightened the slightest. *Damn him.* As his faint sigh brushed against the crown of my head, his deep voice vibrated down to my toes. "I got you."

Hook. Line. Sinker.

"Thanks." Bracing my hands on his chest, I fought the urge to gaze into Sam's eyes. "I'm good now."

Instantly, cold air raced between our parting bodies.

"I honor your hands-off order"—the rumble of Sam's voice sent fire through my veins—"so, indulge me in a challenge."

"A challenge?" I folded my arms around myself, masking my body shivers as a byproduct of the cold and not a reaction to the way his heated stare tracked my movements. "Go on."

"By tomorrow"—he paused, and his wicked dimple made an appearance—"you will ask me to touch you."

My traitor heart jumped into my throat. It took a second for me to remember how to form words. "You're going to lose. Bad."

Sam grinned, then turned to follow Max. As the pack members' attentions burned hot on the back of my head, I grumbled over my shoulder at them, "He will."

Chapter Eleven

Thanks to the snowmobiles, we made it back to the cabin within minutes. Ben was pacing on the porch. When he saw us, he skidded down the steps. Nolan wasn't far behind. He narrowed his gray eyes at Sam. As soon as the snowmobiles came to a stop, I let go of Sam and hopped off.

"Set him in front of the fire," I said to Max as he effortlessly tossed Jimmy over his shoulder.

"Whoa." Ben eyed the unconscious wolf while Max raced toward the cabin. "He's freaking huge."

"Yes – "

Ben grabbed my arm, dragging me toward the cabin. "What happened?"

I cut my attention to Sam and Nolan standing next to the snowmobiles, deep in conversation. Stopping in my tracks, I pulled Ben closer. They could hear us, but I wanted to be as private as possible. "My brother is alive."

Ben went dead still. "The accident. You saw your family…"

Shivering, I focused on the slush covering my boots. "Let's get inside. I'll explain everything."

Ben hesitated.

"What?" I asked.

"So, to fill *you* in, while you were gone, the witness showed me this book about Otherworldly Creature laws. This thing is as thick as an encyclopedia. Anyhow, he told me to read about being a steward, and then boom, he froze. His eyes did this thing."

"The complete opaque look?"

"Yes." Ben dropped his voice, "He stayed like that for at least fifteen minutes."

"Interesting," I mumbled. That had been about the length of our encounter with the stranger.

"Then he snapped awake, and I swear what looked like a third eyelid came down, and poof, his eyes were back to normal. About that time, a few of the guys hauled ass out of here on snowmobiles. Then the beta ordered me to stay indoors. Can he do that?"

I shrugged. "I know jack about all these titles. Did the witness say anything after he came to?"

"Yeah. *He found her.*" Ben peered at me. "Who found you?"

"A twelve-foot-tall, toga-wearing ice fae."

"The Lord of Light." Corbus stood inside the cabin door threshold. "Ruler of the Light Realm."

"Realm?" I muttered at Ben.

"Like in my comics." Ben cut his attention to Corbus.

I swallowed. "So this ice-asshole rules over some kinda universe?"

"Yeah," Ben answered.

"Wonderful." I tugged Ben up the porch. "Ask the witness if he knows this ice-asshole."

Before Ben asked, Corbus nodded and moved to the side, letting us through the door.

Dry heat hit my numb face and the aroma of fresh coffee tickled my nose. I groaned against the protest of my stiff muscles refusing to loosen. When my attention landed on the ring of dirt, I came to a full-out stop. Soon, Derek would wake. A mixture of panic and anticipation revved my heartbeat, and before some nosy werewolf caught on, I dragged my focus and feet past the kitchen.

In the living room, Max arranged blankets and couch cushions around Jimmy where he lay by the hearth.

"Can I help?" I asked.

Max sat, placing his splayed hand across the wolf's shoulder. "He needs the touch of his pack to heal."

I took a seat on a cushion opposite Max. While resting my hip against Jimmy's rump, I kicked off my boots and yanked the remaining glove free. As I rested my palm on the wolf's hip, he relaxed into my touch.

Max's ebony eyes met mine. "Thank you."

If I were still a bartender, I'd have triple-checked his ID. *What alpha asshole stole Max's human life?*

Corbus entered the room. He took up a spot next to the fireplace, careful not to block the heat from the three of us on the floor. Ben hung back by the kitchen. His foggy glasses pointed toward the massive wolf taking up most of the floor space.

"You can come in," I said to Ben. "You're safe."

"There's more room out here." He took off his glasses and rubbed the lenses against his sweater. "I'll make some coffee."

Corbus perked up.

Ben looked at Max. "Uh, you want some?"

"Have any tea?" Max asked.

"Finally." An actual smile graced Ben's face. "Someone with tastebuds."

Max chuckled. "I take it with honey and milk if you have any."

"I have both." Ben kept gawking at Max.

"Ben." I used his name on purpose, in case the two wanted to converse informally. "This is, what is your title, Max?"

"Delta," Max said with his smile on full display.

Corbus interrupted my matchmaking convo. "You're injured."

"Already healed." Flipping over my palm, I showed him that only a red welt remained. I used my damp glove as a washcloth, cleaning away the remaining blood.

Max eyed the glove. "You'll want to toss that. Your blood sets off the wolf in us."

And with that warning, we returned to the monster world, ceasing the pleasantries of tea and honey. Ben made himself busy in the kitchen while I chucked the glove into the fireplace.

Sam and Nolan crowded into the living room, bringing a blast of tension with them. Most days, the space was perfectly cozy for Ben and me, but add four werewolves and Corbus and we were out of elbow room. As sweat beaded along my brow, I tugged off my coat, almost knocking my arm against Nolan's leg.

The beta stiffened, then set his annoyance on Max. "We need another patroller down the road. Delta—"

"Is about to discuss what happened to us with the witness," I said. Max still had snow on his shoulders and his lips were tinted blue. A few minutes more warming up would do him good. "He had a viewpoint that no one else within this room had."

Nolan looked at Sam, who nodded at me. Sam then cut his attention to Max. "What did you see?"

Max bounced his attention between me and Sam. "We were at the tree line when this wolf tried to enter that vortex of ice and snow. After he was tossed twenty feet back, this giant being, also made of snow and ice, appeared, looked at us, flicked his wrists and whatever he did froze us in place. Then the iceman walked through the vortex."

"The fae acted alone?" Sam asked.

"Yes. But we weren't the only spectators," Max said. "This crow landed—"

"You're birdwatching," Nolan grumbled. "While our alpha was—"

"Beta," Sam warned. "Go on, Delta."

While Nolan straightened and clenched his jaw, Max continued, "After the ice forcefield crashed, the crow vanished." A blush crept up his neck. "It didn't fly off. I mean, gone. Like magic."

"That was a third eyelid," Ben said. The tray, stacked with hot beverages, rattled in his grasp while he flicked his wide eyes to mine. "The crow was the witness."

"That *thing* could have killed her," Sam growled at Corbus. "And you did nothing."

"You both needed the experience," Corbus answered. He lowered his gaze to me. "That was only a fraction of his power."

While my jacked-up heartbeat crashed against my ears, I kept staring into Corbus' eyes. The nonhuman—with the slow and steady heart rate—had proved that I needed his aid more than ever. Forcing my voice neutral, I asked a question masked as a statement. "You said you would leave when the *others* showed up."

"That was only an illusion. The Lord of Light gave you three days for a reason."

"Travel time," I muttered.

"Yes." Corbus paused. "Your brother—"

"Drew is alive."

"He is being used as a lure," Corbus said.

"Well, it worked," I snapped. "I'm saving my brother. The fae can have the korrigan's blood."

"What's a korrigan?" Ben asked me.

"A troll." I leveled my gaze at Ben. "*That* troll."

Ben's eyes grew wide. "McKay."

"When he stabbed me, he stuffed his magical blood inside me."

Ben grimaced.

"Yep. My thoughts exactly." I looked at Corbus. "My brother for the troll blood is a win-win."

"If you play into the Lord of Light's trap, you put bloodlines at risk."

"That thing said something about bloodlines," Sam said to Corbus.

"In the Wolf Born's blood, she carries the power of korrigan, wolf and vampire."

Nolan spun, making a shield of muscle in front of Sam. "Vampire. How?"

On its own accord, my attention raced to the floorboards underneath the kitchen table. "Before your deceased alpha took a chomp out of me, I was bitten by a vampire and he—"

"Fed her his blood," Ben interrupted while giving me the stare-down to zip it.

"She's contaminated," Nolan growled.

"I wasn't given a choice." I glared right back at Nolan's sneer. "Not with the troll. Or the vampire. And definitely not with the alpha. They all took a bite *without* my permission."

The room fell into a silence punctuated with cracks and pops from the fire. Ben took the momentary pause as a cue to pass out the beverages. Perhaps to keep our hands busy instead of wringing each other's necks.

"I'm sorry," Max said to me. "I didn't have a choice either."

"Most do not," Sam added.

"Regardless." Nolan turned to face Sam. "She is contaminated."

"She *is* the Wolf Born." Sam's gaze returned fully to mine. "What she asks for or needs, our pack will provide without hesitation."

"What about the other packs?" Nolan asked. "When they find out she opened her mouth for a vampire—"

"Enough." Sam raised his voice, setting his attention between Max and Nolan. "Only the wolves in this room know. Word gets out, the punishment will be death. Understood?"

Max scrambled to his feet, then brought his right fist to his heart and bowed to me. "My life for yours."

Nolan followed the fist-to-heart motion. "My life for my pack."

"She *is* your pack." Sam curled his lips away from his elongating fangs.

"No." Nolan swung his attention at me. "Not until she bears your mark."

"What mark?" I asked Sam.

"A scarring bite." He paused to drag in some air. When he sucked in a lungful of the sticky-sweet fear pouring off me, his eyes darkened. "Marks are exchanged during sex, joining the mates until death."

"Your title was made known to the packs," Nolan said to Sam. "The alphas are coming to inspect the marks. To validate your union."

Sam kept his attention solely on me. "Let them challenge."

"They will." Nolan glared at me. "When they see you do not bear his mark, there will be a bloodbath."

"If I take your mark…" The mug shaking in my hands splashed coffee onto my lap while I gazed up at Sam. He loomed closer. No desire pooled within his eyes. No witty banter fell from his mouth. Nothing. He'd locked down his emotions. I followed suit. My voice grew distant…cold. "Then the alphas would not challenge you. They would follow you."

"You," Sam said. Heated determination returned through his gaze and words. "I follow *you*."

"The Lord of Light is not a mere fae." Corbus moved away from the fire. "Even with the packs united, you lack numbers and power to challenge him. You need support from the vampires as well."

"Bloodsuckers killed my family," Nolan snapped. "I am not—"

"You will." Sam's energy flooded the room, bringing Nolan crashing to his knees. "Or you can leave this pack."

"You are sending us to our death." Nolan groaned through his teeth.

"Choose," Sam ordered.

Nolan's eyes glowed. "I stay for *my* brothers."

"Alpha." I looked at Sam. "Release him."

Sam's energy retracted and Nolan rose to his feet. Observing how the two stared at each other, I superimposed Nathaniel and Derek in their places. The room closed in around me. *I destroyed another relationship.*

"When will the other alphas get here?" I asked.

With his focus still on Nolan, Sam answered, "Tomorrow night."

Unable to move or think, I surveyed the others occupying the room. Ben leaned against the wall with the empty tray shaking in his white knuckles. Jimmy still slept, oblivious to all. Max stared off into the fire while Corbus stood silent with his attention fully on me.

"Wolf Born." Sam's voice tightened. "I will not—"

"Tell the alphas to bring their packs." I lifted my gaze to Sam. "I'll take your mark before morning." I climbed to my feet, then added, "I'm going to my room. Alone."

Chapter Twelve

Outside my bedroom window, the sky lit crimson against the snowfall. Shortly, I'd add the vampires into the mix of my epic tragedy. I bunched my knees to my chest, resting my back against the cold wall. The fading scent of Ben's body wash clung to the mattress. I'd never guessed that waking up naked next to my best friend would've been the *least* unpleasant experience of the day. Sighing, I stared at the door, focusing on the activities outside of the bedroom.

Max left once Jimmy woke. Currently in Ben's bedroom, Jimmy underwent shifting into his human form. Ben and Corbus moved to the kitchen where Ben busied himself banging pans together, probably to drown out the groans and fleshy pops coming from his bedroom. Outside, Nolan paced the porch, stopping at my window occasionally while Sam sat on the other side of my bedroom door, texting away, more than likely, to his pack and the other alphas.

The aroma of grilled cheese and tomato soup flooded my senses. My stomach quivered. I hadn't eaten all day. Usually, my inner wolf would have protested, yet she stayed asleep. "This got too screwed up for you?" I muttered to her as I settled my chin on my knees. "Tough. You gotta deal with this, too."

A soft knock hit my door.

"Can I come in?" Ben asked.

"Yep."

He opened the door and slipped in, but not before I caught a glimpse of Sam's shoulder. I ticked my chin at Sam. "He needs to eat."

Ben shut the door. "He has food in the kitchen. He refuses to leave."

"Alpha," I called out. "Please eat. I'm not going anywhere."

With that, Sam's footsteps moved toward the kitchen. Thankfully, his phone rang. While Sam grumbled a heated conversation, he left the cabin. For the moment, Ben and I were free to talk.

I unfolded my legs and patted the bed next to me. "Here, give me the food." I grabbed the tray from Ben.

Ben settled next to me with a sigh. "Shit, Tess. What are we going to do?"

To give myself some time to answer, I shoved a wedge of grilled cheese into my mouth.

"Pure genius." Ben pointed at my bread-filled cheeks. "A carb-induced coma. Let me join you." He picked up a grilled cheese wedge.

"You haven't eaten?" I grumbled.

"How can I?" he asked around a bite. "All these brawny men."

I snorted. "You think these fellows are lookers, wait until you see—"

"Oh, I saw Derek." Ben fanned himself.

I raised my eyebrows in agreement and toasted with a grilled cheese wedge. Ben grabbed another piece and tapped it against mine. We munched in silence while I claimed the last wedge, dipping it into the soup.

"What are you going to say to him?" Ben asked.

"I don't know. Maybe…" I kept dabbing the soggy grilled cheese into the soup. "While you were day-dead, I made Sam the Guardian of My Body and I have to sleep with him, by tomorrow, to stop a werewolf bloodbath. Also, I pissed off the Lord of Light. Oh, my brother is alive, and I need your help to rescue him."

Ben sat with his mouth gaping while the half-eaten sandwich wobbled in his fingertips. To stifle the sob brewing in my throat, I stopped playing with my food and folded the soggy mess into my mouth.

"Well, shit." Ben dropped the wedge onto the plate. "I don't think that would go over too well. At least the Sam parts. Maybe leave those out until tomorrow night?"

"Why wait?" I batted a tear away with my knuckle. "Better to just get it over with."

"Tess…" Ben grabbed my hand. When his eyes locked with mine, his heartbeat skipped and fluttered. "I *knew* it."

I snatched back my hand. "Knew what?"

"Does Derek know? Do *you* know?" Ben fought back his smile. "That you love—"

"I don't." Panic buzzed through my body. "I *can't.*"

"I'm sorry." Ben schooled his face, nixing any expression. "I shouldn't have."

"Correct and never again. Got it?" A tear rolled down my cheek. Another followed. "You're right. I'll tell Derek after I...you know. Because I need werewolves *and* vampires to save my brother."

"About the vampires..." Ben paused until I looked at him. "There's a plan for tonight. You—"

The front door opened. Sam had returned, cursing at the storm under his breath. He paused, no doubt trying to eavesdrop. After a few moments, Ben went over to my dresser. He came back with a pen and a book I'd been reading. Sitting next to me, he started to scribble on the inside cover.

When Derek wakes, you both leave with Nathaniel. Corbus will handle the wolves.

I went to speak, but Ben gave me a death stare while he continued to write.

You need to secure a vampire allegiance. BY TONIGHT.

He wrote the last part in caps and added some urgent underlines too. After he raised his eyebrow at me and I nodded, he closed the book, then placed it on my nightstand.

The streetlight flickered, capturing our attention. Within minutes, Derek would wake. While I rubbed the last of my tears from my eyes, Ben grabbed the tray.

"You got some cheese on your shirt." He glanced at a pile of clothes on my dresser, then back at me. "I'll meet you in the kitchen...*after* you brush your teeth."

Cringing, I grabbed Ben by the arm and helped him out through the door. Sam wasn't a dummy. He'd pick up on Ben's theatrics.

In record time, I changed into jeans and my favorite hunter-green sweater while tracking Sam's location. He was in the kitchen listening to Ben chatter about bowling. With a decent amount of space between us, I bolted to the bathroom

After raking the tangles out of my snow-damp hair, I tossed the mess into a ponytail and took up the mantra—*No feelings*—repeating it over and over to my brain and body. While I was mid-brushing my teeth, a crash vibrated through the cabin. I yanked on the doorknob, but someone held the door closed. The heady pine scent outed the door blocker as Sam.

I twisted the doorknob. "Let me out."

"A head's up about the bloodsucker under the kitchen table would've been nice," Sam muttered. "How did we not smell it?"

"Magic," I answered.

"I told you not to trust the witness."

"Derek can't hurt you. There's grave dirt keeping him in the kitchen. Look at the floor. See that ring? Bet there is a floating circle aglow too."

Slowly, the door cracked. Sam's body shielded me from a direct view of the kitchen. "Anything else I should know before someone ends up dead?" he asked.

"Nathaniel will come for Derek," I answered. "You promised not to harm them. Remind the pack, again." The alpha link raced across my skin. "Thank you. Now, move out of my way."

Sam angled his body enough to give me a peek into the kitchen.

We could kiss our security deposit goodbye. Torn-up floorboards lay scattered in every direction while the table rested on its side, creating a hidey-hole for Ben. Besides the look of terror on his face, he appeared unharmed and did a great job of staying off Derek's radar. It was up to me to keep it that way.

I should have marched myself right up to that glowing ring, but I just stood dumbstruck next to Sam, transfixed by Derek's seamless gait and lack of a shirt. Sheer Gothic poetry in motion paced inside the dirt circle. When Derek pivoted toward the front door, I ran my gaze down to the dusty pants covering his ass. *No.* I snapped my attention to the back of his head. *Feelings.*

At most, mere seconds passed. Too many for Sam. When he moved to shield me, my ungraceful dodge caught Derek's attention. His eyes locked with mine and time screeched to a halt. The way he fixated on me. The way my reaction mirrored his. Dangerous. Dark. Perfect.

Sam grabbed my arm and Derek unsheathed his fangs.

"He's using compulsion on you," Sam warned.

"Compulsion can't pass through the circle, Nathaniel tried—"

The cruelty of fate.

"Are you serious? You feel..." Sam's jaw ticked. Hurt blazed in his eyes. "For him. A bloodsucker?"

Unable to admit or deny, I glanced at Sam's hand holding me in place, restraining me. *Wait.* Corbus said nothing could break the blood-bond, even his magic, meaning the mind-buzzing attraction toward Derek was a side effect of the bond. I pinned that affirmation to my heart.

"Let me go," I said to Sam.

"I promised not to *harm* him. But the way he's—you..." Sam paused to drag in a breath. His shoulders trembled. He shook his head. "Anything you two need to discuss, you can do so standing right here."

"He can't leave the circle, and you crowding me is setting him off." I rested my hand on Sam's fingers where he clenched my arm. My touch stole his attention from Derek. Sam's gaze locked with mine. "You heard the witness. We need the vampires. For my brother, please. Trust me."

"Bloodsucker." Sam returned his focus to Derek. "I'll tear your fangs out if you hurt her."

When Sam's grip slipped from my forearm, I stepped away, turning my attention to Corbus. He stood in the living room with energy pulsing around him, creating some sort of invisible barrier that kept Jimmy inside Ben's room.

I glanced over my shoulder at Sam. "Send the link to the pack. Let them know we are safe."

Sam did and Jimmy's eyes bugged out of his skull.

"Safe my ass," Jimmy said to Sam. "There's a bloodsucker in the motherfucking kitchen."

I recognized Jimmy's human form—he was the sharpshooter who had almost put an arrow through Derek's eye. Probably the one who had shot Nathaniel too. I forced my anger away. Jimmy was doing what was natural for a werewolf. *Follow your alpha and kill all the vampires.*

I walked around a busted kitchen chair, stopping at the edge of the ring. Derek's focus pinpointed on mine. He gestured to the dirt circle, giving me a devilish grin. "Save me once more, my wolf."

Corbus moved behind me. When his fingertips brushed against mine, I glanced down. He placed a black feather in my sweaty palm. "This talisman warns you of magical attacks. It will protect you. Cross the circle. Go."

Grasping the feather, I stepped over the dirt ring.

Sam raced forward. When the magic kept him from piercing through the ring, terror filled his wild eyes.

Even his screams couldn't slip past the magic. There wasn't time for me to quell the raging werewolf. Another monster demanded my attention.

Derek hooked an arm around my shoulders, then snaked his free hand around my hips, pressing our bodies flush. I shivered. Not from creditable fear but with morbid anticipation. Derek grazed his cheek against mine and inhaled deeply. "You have cried."

"Yes," I whispered. "A lot."

"Who?" The harnessed violence in his voice sent my heart rocketing against my breasts. "Give me their name."

"Not a *who*." I spun in his hold to face him. "But a *why*."

Derek cupped my face. His brows creased as he ran his thumbs along the dried trail of my tears. Damn me, I pressed into his touch. Derek swept a hand down to my clenched fist, then he raised my knuckles to his chilled lips. "Give me the why and I shall tear it asunder."

My nails bit into my palm while I scrunched the concealed feather. "Later."

"As you wish." A wisp of Derek's raven locks slipped in front of his piercing gaze as he teased a kiss against my knuckles. He flipped my wrist and my pulse beat against his parting lips. "You denied me your dreams."

"I was busy—"

He dragged a fang across my flesh. "Your blood sings to me."

Forcing the last of my restraint into my voice, I whispered, "It's *just* the blood-bond."

"How wrong you are." His eyes drifted shut and he released me. "I am suppressing the bond." To prove the point, he let it stir to life.

As raw lust tore through me, white-hot embers nibbled at my fingertips. Concentrating on the feather burning my palm, I fought the craving to straddle Derek in front of the kitchen filling with werewolves. Suddenly, Derek closed off the blood-bond and the feather ceased to burn. I shoved it in my back pocket while rethinking the whole ask the vampires for aid idea.

"No blood-bond." Derek gasped between his desire-laced breaths. "Simply you. *You* are my rapture."

"I'm sorry," I whispered.

"No, you are not," Derek called me right out while he closed the sliver of space between us. "Nor am I."

As if by answer to a dilapidated prayer, Nathaniel appeared at the front door. The other cabin occupants froze while Sam squared off with Nathaniel.

Derek shifted in front of me with his claws drawn.

"Kill him later," I said. "We need to leave with Nathaniel. Right now." I dragged my foot across the dirt line and the magic fell.

Nathaniel reappeared next to us, snagging my arm in one hand and grabbing Derek with the other. Pulling the shadows around our group, Nathaniel disappeared us away from the cabin.

Chapter Thirteen

Fluttering my eyes open, I gasped. We stood in the center of a penthouse twice the size of my once humble, now werewolf-filled cabin. In front of me, a wall of windows showcased an awe-inspiring view of snow-covered mountains. The lack of compulsion buzzing around us hinted our location wasn't some secret vampire fortress.

Studying the mountains' peaks, I swallowed. I was pretty sure my cabin sat miles on the opposite side of the ridge. Maybe Nathaniel had vampire Wheaties for dinner because it took tremendous energy for him to move three bodies.

Closing my eyes, I attuned my hearing beyond the room. A ding of an elevator. People mumbling. A floor below, a couple enjoyed each other's company. Excitedly. When I focused on my sniffer, cleaning sprays and stale coffee hit my nose. No foreign nonhuman scents. With my conclusion about our whereabouts, I popped open my eyes. Only one luxury hotel overlooked the mountains—the Stone Casino.

"Vampires and gambling," I said to Nathaniel. "What a perfect match."

"Far enough away from your flea condo where I could still keep track of you. These past months I've suffered here. The food is…bland and depressing. The entertainment wooden," Nathaniel grumbled. As he smoothed the wrinkles out of his suit jacket, he came into contact with a stray piece of my hair. Pinching the strand between his fingertips, he let it drift to the floor. "Disgusting. You're shedding."

Derek loomed over my shoulder. "May I dispose of him?"

"Are you not inches from her throat?" Nathaniel scowled. "No alpha to contend with. You're welcome, Derek. She's yours."

"First, I'm no one's." I stepped away from Derek and turned to face the vampires. "Second, my brother is alive. Third, what is the probability you two can help me persuade the Vampire Council to join with the werewolves in rescuing him from the Lord of Light? By tonight."

Derek swore in four different languages.

Nathaniel cackled wildly. Hunched over, he gestured at me. "I stand corrected. I'd thought you would try batting your eyes and begging for aid."

I froze. "How did you know?"

"I have had orchestra seats to the goings-on of today." Nathaniel grinned.

"Ben," I muttered, shoving the new vampire fact into my brain. Not only could the bloodsucker track Ben, but Nathaniel also had a telepathy link to my best friend. I turned to Derek. "How long can a vampire control someone after drinking their blood?"

"For a mere vampire, at most, a night." Derek kept his attention on Nathaniel. "He is not mere."

My eyes flashed.

"Oh, yes." Nathaniel smirked, switching to mock me within my mind. *"I know all, she-beast. You have until sunrise to inform Derek of the alpha's title. You are not going to cower your way out of that conversation."*

"In the presence of others"—Derek pinned Nathaniel with a glare—"it is rude to use mind speech."

"We haven't the time for politeness." Nathaniel set his hands on his hips. "We have a meeting in less than an hour. She-beast, the bedroom is behind those doors. There are garments for you on the bed. Derek, in minutes, your refreshments will be here. Afterward, there is a lavatory down the hall. Shower and dress."

"Who are we meeting?" I asked.

"It's a surprise. Now, shoo." Nathaniel flicked his wrist at me. "While Derek feeds, I will update him on the day's events. Once everyone is dressed, we will proceed to the next course of action."

"Why are you helping me?" I asked.

"Let me be clear, my involvement is self-serving." A sneer eclipsed Nathaniel's face. "Since the moment your existence was known to me, I've waited eagerly for your ruin." He flashed his unburning tongue at me, further proving his truth.

However, I caught a slight shift. For the first time, ever, Nathaniel didn't say he wished for my death. To keep from revealing my grin, I spun on my heels and headed to the bedroom.

Closing the doors behind me, I groaned. The heated vampire grumblings and cusses in multiple dialects paired great with the ensemble draped across the massive bed. Eyeballing the skimpy, floor-length cocktail number, I shuffled over to the bed. I pinched the royal-blue fabric between my fingers. When I lifted the dress, a pair of nude-colored ankle-breakers peeked out from underneath the dress' hem.

Vampires suck.

A knock sounded on the main room door, followed by a woman's sultry voice and obnoxious perfume slinking into the room. "You're not kidding." She whistled a catcall. "Hello, Daddy—"

Nathaniel's compulsion flew through the penthouse. "You will not remember this encounter."

The vampires' *refreshment* sighed. Moaned. Gasped. When the telltale metallic tang layered through the air, I sat on the edge of the bed, clenching the goose-down comforter between my fingers, bracing for the wolf within me to demand her share of blood. Unbelievable. She was still playing hooky.

"Where are you?" I muttered to my missing wolf. How finicky the mind. For the past three months, I had prayed for the return of my human life. Dreaded the full moon. Refused to walk down the meat section in the grocery store. Cursed my glowing eyeballs when my feelings consumed me. Now, I sat coaxing the monster to come out and play. Raspberrying a breath past my lips, I kicked my focus to the ceiling and jerked in startlement. My reflection peered down at me from a full-sized mirror hanging on the ceiling.

"Cheeky bastard." I smirked.

"Next," Nathaniel called out.

While I wrangled into the dress, the feeding event replayed three times over. Still, with my wolf on a hiatus, and all the humans remaining breathing, so far, the night had behaved better than the day.

Almost.

I turned in front of the full-length mirror facing the bed. The gown clung to my curves and its side slit ran practically to my waist. One puff of air and I'd be flashing more than a thigh. Eyeing the shoes that I'd shoved under the bed, I fought with the zipper at the back of the dress, unable to get it closed over my bottom. *Freaking cleavage.* When the main room fell silent and a shower turned on, I emerged from the bedroom.

Nathaniel dragged an unconscious woman toward a wall graced in shadows. A drop of blood accentuated his lips hooking into a grin. "I missed a true calling in my mortal life."

"BDSM?"

"Ha. A tailor. I had to make some alterations."

"Wow," was all I said. I'd roll over dead before paying him a compliment. "A little tight in the back."

"You bind your bosom. I thought you were less endowed. Suck in your breath. I will return after I dispose of the refreshments." He disappeared with the woman.

I turned to the window. "Damn it—"

A rush of air swept the stray wisps from my ponytail against the back of my neck.

"Stunning." Derek stood behind me, smelling like a carnal delight.

"Vampire speed showering?" Instead of turning, I kept staring at the snowscape while plastering the image of my brother into my mind. "I thought it took you hours to get ready."

"I'd not waste an opportunity to see you alone."

I swallowed. "Can you help me with the zip—"

Derek skirted his fingers against the small of my back. The chill of the day still lingered in my bones and soul. Relishing in the warmth of his hand from the shower, I fluttered my eyes shut.

"The Devil tempts me," Derek whispered against my ear. "This dress is the forbidden fruit to my Garden of Eden."

Goosebumps screamed across my flesh begging to be touched. With each heartbeat, my reservation slipped away. Unable to handle another lust-filled standoff, I wetted my lips. "Take your bite."

He hooked a finger under the dress seam, tracing the swell of my bottom as his lips captured my earlobe. "Don't move." He nipped the sensitive flesh while his free hand swept across my collarbone to cage my throat.

My heart throttled against my ribs as desire tightened my belly. He could snap my neck, yet his fingers caressed ever so delicately over my pulse. A moan escaped from my lips.

"Oh, what music your body plays at my fingertips." He grazed his mouth along my jawbone, mere inches from where his lips would touch mine. I arched my spine and torturously, he held me in place.

"Kiss me," I growled.

A dark chuckle rumbled from his chest which molded to my shoulder blades. "I waited centuries for you." Derek swept his free hand to my hip where he slipped his fingers into the thigh-high slit and traced to my bare thigh. He palmed my quivering muscles and tightened his hold at my throat, hinting at the restraint he'd issue if I struggled to claim his lips again. "Now, *you* must be patient."

Energy prickled inside the room. As Nathaniel stepped away from the wall, Derek released me. Then, like a gentleman, Derek zipped up the dress with trembling fingers.

Nathaniel, none the wiser, or turning a blind eye willingly, tilted his head, studying me collecting my nerves. "Come now. It is not that tight," he said. "Get the shoes. Our guest waits."

On wobbly legs, I shimmied into the bedroom. As I strapped into the heels, the stack of my clothes sitting on the nightstand became my focal point, particularly the crumbled feather peeking out from the jean pocket. Mentally slapping myself for forgetting the talisman in the first place, I scanned my body for a spot to tuck in the feather. *Nada.* A skintight dress and strappy heels were a no-go for secret compartments.

"What am I going to do with you?" When I picked up the feather, a light flashed between my knuckles. Opening my fist, I blinked at a white-gold feather pendant. "That works," I mumbled, clasping its delicate chain around my neck. The hum of Corbus' energy brushed my skin before the necklace went cold. I tugged my hair out of the ponytail, giving myself one last glance over in the mirror before rejoining the vampires.

They'd donned jackets to complete their spiffy three-piece suits.

"Do I get a coat?" I asked.

"To hide my craftsmanship?" Nathaniel scoffed. "No. You can freeze."

Derek hooked his arm. "May I have the honors?"

I slipped my arm through his. "Did Nathaniel tell you who we are meeting?"

"Yes." Derek escorted me behind the blond bloodsucker sashaying down the hall toward the elevators. "A council member."

Excitement with a healthy dash of dread spiraled me to the image of my brother chained and bloodied. *I'm coming, Drew. Hold on for me.*

Nathaniel popped his head out of an elevator. "Hurry."

Derek narrowed his eyes at Nathaniel. "And of all the members—"

"Oh. The thrill that awaits." Nathaniel's blue eyes brightened as he shifted to make room for us to enter the elevator. He tapped the close button, sealing the door. "She-beast, do you remember how to address a council member?"

"Let them greet me how they see fit." Flinching, I focused on the bronze panel where the floor number buttons illuminated our countdown.

"Nathaniel will do the conversing." Derek's free hand caught my elbow, guiding me to face him. "I lost my title when you bested the queen. I may not be allowed to escort you past this elevator."

"What?" I slipped from his arms.

"Derek needs a title," Nathaniel said.

"All these damn titles." I looked at them both. "Can I give him one?"

"Derek is a vampire," Nathaniel answered. "He cannot hold a position in your *wolf* court."

"However"—Derek gave me a killer grin—"you did draw the Vampire Queen's blood."

"True." Nathaniel pressed a finger to his thin lips. "She bested the queen. She-beast outranks all vampires, except council members, therefore, by our laws, as her escort, the pooch could title you."

"What title?" I asked.

"Hunter," Nathaniel responded. "Your death dealer."

"Protector," Derek added.

I scrubbed the replay of Sam's *protection* titling and rolled my shoulders. *This is for Drew.* "All right," I said to Derek.

Nathaniel hit the elevator's emergency brake button. "We perform a ceremony when issuing our titles."

"Fine," I grumbled. "Tell me what to do."

"Do nothing." Bitterness peeked from the edges of Nathaniel's ill-fitted mask of emotionlessness. "Derek."

"Brace yourself." Derek crowded me, forcing my back to bump against the wall. He lifted my hand to his lips. "I take your blood, then you give me the title."

I stupidly nodded.

He slipped the tip of my index finger into his mouth, pricking it against a fang. As he imbibed at the wound, a wave of pleasure crashed into me. With each pull of my blood, the intensity increased. *Now*, I understood the 'brace yourself' part. The foreshadowing release fuzzed my mind and I sucked my lip into my mouth, riding the current of bliss so close to taking me over the edge.

Deliberate and abrupt, Derek released my finger from his mouth. All pleasure ceased and the denial snapped my senses into overdrive. When his scent enveloped me, my rapid heartbeat echoed through the elevator while the damn dress scratched against my hypersensitive flesh. I clenched my jaw to stifle my growl.

As desire blazed within Derek's stare, I froze while he ran his tongue over my fingertip, healing the nick. "Now, repeat after me." He clasped my hands in his, easing me away from the wall. "Within my blood, I seal you as my hunter.'"

I held his gaze as the words transformed into sacred vows. "Within my blood, I seal you as my hunter."

He lifted my hands, turning them to reveal the undersides of my wrists where he pressed a kiss to each. Heart-stealing intensity burned in his eyes as he whispered to my very soul, "My blood for your blood, until my eternal night."

The elevator dinged.

No one moved.

"If that was not vomit-inducing…" Nathaniel growled. "No more talking, she-beast."

Chapter Fourteen

The elevator opened to an elegant hallway. Dim overhead lighting sent an orange cast to the lacquered wood panel walls and marble floors. I wrinkled my nose at the rank scent of vampire drifting through the stagnant air. The night made quick work of overtaking the gold star of terror from the day.

"Speak only to my mind until I tell you to use your voice," Nathaniel said inside my skull.

I nodded.

A set of double doors sat at the end of the hall. Derek kept his attention forward while he tightened his arm around mine. Reading the sign listing the room reservation for 'the Roberson wedding,' I muttered a well-wish that the council member used their compulsion to keep the wedding guests away versus a fast-forward to the 'death does us part.' Nathaniel shimmied in front of us, giving a tap to the frosted-glass panes.

The doors opened from the inside.

A tux-wearing, cut-to-shreds-and-then-some bloodsucker moved to block our entrance. "You"—he ticked his square jaw at Derek—"leave."

"I think not." Even though Nathaniel's height left him eyeballing the bloodsucker's puffed-out chest, his curt voice gained the guard's attention. "He holds the title of Hunter." Nathaniel gestured at me. "This is the Wolf Born, as you already know, and she has been given the invitation to meet with your patrician, as you also know. Now put the three parts together, and let us pass."

The bloodsucker roamed his seedy gaze down the length of me. The glint of gold at his shoulder caught my attention, and my throat clenched. The pendant of two snakes intertwining signaled the council member we were meeting.

"Are you freaking kidding me? Count Transylvania?" I sent to Nathaniel. *"The violet-eyed, sex-in-satin council member? Out of the twenty-seven left you couldn't have found another?"*

"Oh, this buffoon spoiled the surprise."

Square-Jaw took a step toward me. "I'll escort the bitch."

Derek flashed his vampire-black eyes at the bloodsucker. "Let me remove this insubordinate from your view."

Nathaniel cursed under his breath. *"Nod at Derek. Then close your eyes."*

I nodded and didn't close my eyes.

In a blur, Derek raced at the vampire. Square-Jaw's mouth snapped open, giving a perfect target to Derek's wrath. The wet pop of flesh and bone echoed through the room as Derek tore the guard's jawbone from his face.

"Hold out your hand," Derek ordered.

Obediently, the bloodsucker obliged and Derek plopped the mangled heap of flesh into the guard's waiting hand. A merry-go-round of terror spun the room around me as the jawless bloodsucker stood to attention, then Derek swept his leg around the man's calf, knocking him to his knees. As quickly as Derek had removed the jawbone, he stood behind the kneeling man, fisting the bloodsucker's blood-tangled hair, driving his face down. The hollow smack against the floor rang through my skull.

Nathaniel threaded his arm through mine, keeping me righted. *"Nod to Derek."*

Clenching my body, I refused to show the tremors of my limbs as I nodded at Derek. In a similar fashion to how the werewolves showed respect, Derek pressed his bloody fist to his heart and bowed to me.

Nathaniel escorted me around the keeled-over bloodsucker. The crunch of a molar underneath Nathaniel's shoe snapped my attention forward. Ahead, the abandoned venue, overkill on the posh and white theme, stretched before us. We passed a fountain sputtering champagne and clusters of empty tables to stop in the center of the room. A tapestry of white rose petals fashioned a path across the marble floor leading to a booth cloaked in darkness.

"I miss the art form of a skilled hunter," a velvet-rich voice rumbled from the booth.

Nathaniel's grip tightened the slightest amount.

The flick of a match illuminated the face of sin. Hector. As a flame spun around the rolled cigarette between his lips, he sucked in a slow inhale. His gaze roamed over me while he exhaled a ribbon of smoke. Without so much as a flinch, Hector pinched out the flame of the match. He draped his arms over the leather headrest of the booth. The white silk shirt he half-wore bunched upward as a pair of lacquered nails reached up from underneath the table. A cascade of blonde curls rose from his lap. Hector locked his violet eyes with mine, then ran his nails over his chest. As crimson droplets beaded from the self-inflicted lacerations, the woman ravaged him, worshiping his chest with her tongue.

"Do all council members have to be this extra?" I sent to Nathaniel.

A dark chuckle erupted from Hector. His power caressed my skull as he spoke to my mind. *"I miss your humor."*

Instantly, the talisman around my neck heated, snapping my libido sober. *"Out of my head, council member."*

Taking a final drag of his cigarette, he then smashed it against a crystal snifter resting on the table. Hector sat up, whispering in a foreign language at the woman. She spun around and hissed through her bloodstained fangs at me. Hector grabbed her by the throat and growled the same order. When he released her, the woman shimmied her naked self away from the booth, then strutted across the floor and through another set of doors.

Hector curled his finger at me. "Come, Wolf Born, you owe me a dance."

I nailed the image of my brother to my mind, biting the inside of my cheeks to stop the curses from bubbling past my lips. To keep from falling victim to Hector's compulsion, I slipped my attention to the hollow of his throat.

Nathaniel ushered me forward while Derek moved to my left shoulder.

"Striking," Hector breathed. "Grace exudes from you since your first Change."

Too close for my comfort, we stopped feet from the booth.

Hector patted the seat next to his hip. "Shall we first negotiate or dance?"

"Negotiate," Nathaniel answered. "May the greeting proceed?"

"Forgive me." Hector appeared in front of us. "I am too eager to indulge in pleasantries. My formality betrays me."

Vampire hospitality required the host to greet their guest before killing or dancing could commence. A breath of silence stirred between us while I focused on the pale flesh of his bobbing throat.

"Wolf Born," Nathaniel said, releasing my arm, "This is council member Hector. The new king of *all* vampires."

Flipping fantastic. Horny Hector had taken the queen's vacancy. Oh, and I caught the influx and the weight that 'all' carried in Nathaniel's greeting. My only shot at getting the vampires on my side was currently running the tip of his tongue across his upper lip.

"Look into my eyes, Wolf Born." Hector laced his words with a warning. "Our time is short."

As I lifted my stare to Hector's, he closed the distance between us. He reached for my hand. Tensing, I waited for his greeting, praying that a kiss to the wrist would serve versus a peck to the jugular.

Mother of all miracles, he raised my wrist to his lips, pressing a chaste kiss. At his deep inhale over my skin, goosebumps raced along my arm. "You smell of a May night." Hector shifted his attention to Derek. "Jasmine, warmth and secrets."

My eyes widened.

"Shall we share drinks and spill truths?" The tips of Hector's fangs appeared with his smile while the grip on my wrist tightened. "Or do we set the streets aflame with passion?"

The whites of Nathaniel's eyes flashed. "She—"

"The drinks and truths option," I sent to Hector.

"Clever. Answering with mind speech. No more, unless you wish to end our night prematurely." He paused, before speaking out loud. "You have the makings of a fine leader, seeing past distraction." Hector winked. As quickly as the nonsexual personality slipped through his eyes, it left. Once more, white-hot desire filled his gaze, which he swept between me and Derek. "Some advice, little ruler. The deadliest threat comes not from an enemy's sword, but by the risk you take for love."

Fear struck like a bullet to my brain. Hector's words spoke the truth. Unwisely, I had hopped into an elevator with two vampires. Given my blood to Derek. Now the Vampire King rubbed his thumb along my wrist, all done for an image inside a snow globe wielded by the Lord of Light. I shook my head, firming my reasoning. Drew was alive.

"For my brother," I said. "I need—"

"Forgive her," Nathaniel interjected. "She is still learning her place."

"Let this vampire do your bidding." Hector swept his free hand to my shoulder where he curled a strand of my hair around his finger. "I would hate to see blood upon these locks."

When I nodded, Hector released me. Derek moved to my side, keeping his hands free and his attention between Hector and Nathaniel.

"We shall proceed with the gift." Nathaniel stepped to my right side, and spoke under his breath at me, "It is our custom to offer a gift at these meetings. You were the honored guest at the Gathering. Here, you are asking for aid. You do not have protection as you did then. To keep your head, just nod."

When I had been the honored guest, the queen had attempted to enslave the werewolves, kill me and eradicate the Vampire Council. My mind ran wild with the possibilities of horrors that came with no protection during a meeting with a council member.

"Wolf Born." Nathaniel glared at me. "This is where you nod."

Biting my tongue, I nodded.

Hector folded his arms behind his back. "Proceed with the gift."

Nathaniel bowed his head. A sign of respect? A quick prayer? No clue. When he rose from his genuflection, he spoke to Hector, "The Wolf Born will gift you with information. She will share who bested the queen—"

"It was *me*," Hector answered. "I found the queen bloody and chained to her throne. *I* took her blood. Now *I* am king." Hector turned to me, then ran his curled fingers across his face, mimicking how I had scored my claws against the vile queen's before leaving her to burn in the sun. His gesture proved that he knew it was me who had bested the bitch…first. "You have my utmost gratitude for your part, Wolf Born." He paused. "I *also* respect your creativity by titling Derek. In case these opportunists did not explain to you, only a *vampire* who bested a council member can give titles. You, little ruler, are not a vampire, therefore, the title is void." Hector raised his index finger. "Derek, you are my guest, please remain."

My mind reeled. Opportunists indeed. Nathaniel knew vampire law inside out and upside down. He relished shoving it in my face. The gleam in his eye and the matching one in Derek's spoke that the two had conspired to set me up to title Derek. They knew I could. The revealing of the loophole as to *how* would have to wait as Hector once more pinned me with his undivided attention.

"I will consider the gift of information by the question of my choice," Hector said.

Nathaniel nodded at me, then said, "Agreed."

"Why does the Lord of Light hold interest in the Wolf Born?" Hector reached for an empty wine glass from the nearest table. "I grow thirsty."

Nathaniel turned to me. "Hector can view the past through consuming a vampire's blood."

"Time walking," Hector added. "Gained the gift from the fourth council member I bested. Better to see the truth than rely on a turn of words this one is so skilled at."

Nathaniel shrugged out of his jacket and proceeded to roll up his sleeve.

"No," Hector said. "Derek."

Nathaniel stilled. "He only knows what I have told him—"

"You love Derek." The frankness in Hector's words hit like a punch to the solar plexus. No doubt Hector had used Nathaniel's affection obsession for Derek as a ruse for one of us to break vampire etiquette. I clenched my hands into fists. Hector continued goading

Nathaniel. "You should heed the advice I gave the Wolf Born, fugitive. You came to me on hands and knees, begging for this meeting. For that demonstration of careless abandon, I'm certain you told Derek everything that I desire to know."

As Derek reached for the wine glass, Nathaniel grabbed his arm. A look passed between them.

Hector tapped his finger to his temple. "I hear the mind-chatter. You will speak with voices if I am to continue this arrangement, or the Wolf Born and I will resume in my private quarters."

Nathaniel let go of Derek's arm. As Derek discarded his jacket on the table and rolled his sleeve up, Nathaniel angled the glass underneath Derek's exposed wrist.

"The king will ask Derek's blood the question." Nathaniel glared at me. "You must agree to the question. Nod only." Nathaniel cut his attention to Hector. "For the gift of information, Your Majesty, you may ask Derek's blood the question, 'what does the Lord of Light want from the Wolf Born?'"

When no one spoke, I took that as my cue and nodded.

"I accept the gift," Hector answered.

Derek scored a claw across his wrist, splattering blood into the glass. When Hector nodded, Derek handed it over.

Hector's eyes flashed vampire-black as he lifted the glass to his lips. "Show me what the Lord of Light wants from the Wolf Born." With a thick gulp, he snapped his eyes shut. Ecstasy flooded his expression. Abruptly, his eyes flicked open. "Korrigan blood." Hector's intense stare lowered to my neck as he spoke. "You have my utmost intrigue."

Nathaniel wasted no time to move the meeting forward, "With the acceptance of the gift, the Wolf Born requests to discuss a temporary alliance between werewolves and vampires as she negotiates with the Lord of Light."

Hector rubbed his chin while a smirk crossed his lips.

Nathaniel cut his attention back to me. "Wolf Born, nod."

I did.

Nathaniel turned to Hector. "What do you request in return?"

Hector set his focus on me. "Both our kingdoms could be annihilated in attempting a meeting with the fae. However, the rewards from a successful negotiation are ripe with such possibilities." He paused and my heart hitched. "An alliance forged between our kingdoms henceforth, until the failing of the meeting, or upon successful negotiation with the Lord of Light, at which I will give one hour before dissolving the alliance. Now, Wolf Born, think carefully on these words. Agree, and I will add my request."

Nathaniel gave a nod while Derek stayed indifferent.

I nodded at Hector and his wicked grin.

"Perfect." He offered his hand to me. "Shall we dance?"

Nathaniel cleared his throat and raised both eyebrows, motioning this wasn't an offer I could refuse.

When I placed my hand in Hector's, he gathered me close. Compulsion hummed against my body, sending my pulse to hammer at my ears. While his gaze captured mine, the talisman heated against my skin. His attention slipped to the chain and its glowing reflection filled his violet eyes. As he retracted his compulsion, the glow dimmed and the talisman rested cold around my neck.

"What an entrancing trinket," Hector said. "Old magic. I desire to know its origins. Later, of course." He draped my arms around his neck, then caressed his fingers down the length of my arms. I tensed as he lingered at the sensitive skin of my underarms before he advanced down my sides, cupping my hips. While he pressed his cheek against mine, he started to sway us. "I could dance to your heartbeat the night through. Sadly, I must remember we are rivals with a similar…cause."

I stilled and his grip tightened at my hips.

"Do not leave my embrace," Hector warned while he continued the dance. "I would have to kill you. Understood?"

While dizziness from the swaying paired with my rising fear, I once more nodded my compliance.

"I need you to finish what the late queen started," Hector whispered against my cheek. "The Vampire Council must fall." He inhaled. "Your terror is exquisite. Please, speak."

"I have no love for the council, but I won't kil—"

He brought us to a stop. "The old laws must *die*. This human world is a hairpin away from destroying itself. It is time for the Otherworldly Creatures to intervene. Let our kingdoms be seen…feared." He brought a finger to rest under my chin, forcing me to look into his eyes as he spoke. "*Your* wolves will send the council members to their final death. Then, *you and I* will infiltrate the human world. Those are my conditions to aid in your endeavor. Your answer?"

Nathaniel stood next to us and nodded. Derek loomed behind Hector.

Laminating the image of my brother to my mind, I willed air into my lungs. "Yes," I whispered.

"The rawness in your voice…" Hector brushed his thumb across my lips.

"Both parties accept the conditions?" Nathaniel asked Hector.

"I bind my word. A temporary alliance is forged between our kingdoms. Should you be successful in your meeting with the Lord of Light, your wolves will then eradicate the Vampire Council and *you* will join my endeavor into the human world." Hector released me and took a step backward. "To show my devotion to you, I will provide thirty vampires for your protection during the meeting."

"Thirty?" I asked. "We need them all."

Hector grinned. "You agreed to an alliance, not an army." He turned his back on me and headed toward the same door that his blonde lap-mate had exited.

"Wait." I rushed after Hector but Nathaniel blocked me.

"Be silent," Nathaniel growled.

"My brother." I raised my voice. "I need help rescuing—"

Faster than a strike of lightning, Hector cleared the length of the room. In one arm, he snagged me around the waist then fisted his other hand in my hair, tugging my chin upward, baring my neck to his lips. "Little ruler, you were warned."

Out of the corner of my eye, Derek dropped to his knees. "Your Majesty, let me take her punishment."

Hector angled his head, brushing the stubble of his chin against my jugular. His breath ran cold over my perspiring skin as he whispered to me, "I am at your throat, yet notice how your trinket rests silently around your neck. Remember my warning regarding love? Enjoy the lesson." Suddenly, Hector released me.

As I caught my balance, Nathaniel returned to my right side, refusing to look at me while Hector appeared in front of Derek, who was kneeling.

"Name the punishment," Nathaniel said.

"I lost my hunter at the Gathering to a pack of wolves. I require a replacement," Hector answered.

I drew in a breath to protest.

Nathaniel snapped at me, "Do not speak."

Derek kept his focus on Hector's dress shoes.

"How long will Derek's servitude last?" Nathaniel asked.

"A hundred years." Hector directed his attention to me.

"Wolf Born." Nathaniel paused. "Only say agree."

Terror spliced through me. I had no right to trade Derek's freedom for my stupidity. I shook my head.

"The terms have changed," Hector said. "Five hundred years of servitude for the hunter."

"I agree," Derek said. He turned to look at me. "The next change in terms will be a blood payment."

Remembering the Vampire Queen tearing the limbs away from the werewolves serving as blood payments, my lungs tightened. "I…"

"Please," Derek said.

Hector sighed. "The terms—"

"I agree," I whispered.

"Both sides agree to the punishment," Nathaniel said.

"Derek is yours until after you meet with the Lord of Light." Hector gave me a deep bow then disappeared, yet his voice still filled the room, "Hunter, on your way out, take care of that bloody mess of a guard."

Chapter Fifteen

Derek stood, and before I could say or do something stupid, he had me in his arms. Pressing his forehead against mine, he shuddered out a breath. "Hector better thank his gods I did not tear him off you."

"For the record." Nathaniel circled us. "I did not beg. I simply…" Around and around Nathaniel paced while his chattering ran mute against the fierceness in Derek's stare.

All rationality and instinct screamed for me to pull away, yet selfishness, dressed as desire, had me twisting his shirt between my fingers. Anger blazed through me, catching my heart on fire. Within hours, I'd be in another's arms. I let my fury burn through my voice. "You have to stop throwing your freedom away. Lowering yourself—"

Derek stole my words with his lips. Urgent and dominating, he consumed me. Shattering the barrier of frustration between us, I matched Derek's ferocity, caging his face between my hands. As I held his mouth captive against mine, he groaned into my possessiveness, running his tongue across my teeth while he shoved our bodies flush. When I gasped, he was there to steal my breath, dragging it into his eager mouth. With his skilled manipulation, Derek took me to the edge of consciousness before he broke the kiss.

While I regained control of my breath and body, he traced a finger along my jaw, staring into the pit of my soul. "For you, I fall to my knees. Willingly. I—"

"I cannot bear this," Nathaniel grumbled "I'm not risking my immortality to chauffeur two infatuated beings."

I pulled back from Derek to track Nathaniel's whereabouts. He stood behind me. A film of dust covered Nathaniel's suit. He shook his jacket, flicking a cloud of ash at us. My attention raced to where the bloodsucker guard had faceplanted. Gone. In his place was a humanoid-shaped pile of dust. Panic danced up my spine and I affirmed to myself, no more kissing Derek. The track record for our lip-locks ending with death was a sobering one hundred percent. I dragged my hands down my face and sighed. "Did you have to dust him?"

"Ashes are easier to clean than blood," Nathaniel answered. "No need to place compulsion on the humans who will be here soon. All in love. Cheerful. Happy ever after." Nathaniel's eyes narrowed at me. *"I am so close to spoiling your big news."*

"No. I need to be the one." My attention cut to Derek, preoccupied with a napkin, wiping away the blood-turned-ash remnant of the bloodsucker's jawbone. *"I owe him that."*

Derek's stare caught mine. "Your heart beats faster."

"Yep." *You can't hide anything from monsters.* I hiked a shoulder. "Lots to freak out about. You took on my punishment."

"Protecting you is my duty." Derek discarded the napkin onto a nearby table. "I am your hunter."

"About that title—"

"Wait." Nathaniel pressed a finger to his lips, silencing us as his eyes shifted to vampire-black. After a moment, his finger lowered, and his eyes returned to their icy blue. "Hector has left the area. Proceed with caution. He most certainly has spies."

"The title loophole." Lowering my voice, I focused on both vampires. "I know there is one."

Nathaniel's famous scowl accompanied his words, "What part of 'he has spies' did you not understand? This is not a conversation—"

"She needs to know." Once more, Derek stood inches from me, sternness creasing his brow. He tapped his temple then cut his gaze to Nathaniel. "Listen for threats."

"I always do." A burst of air flared Nathaniel's nostrils. "Be quick."

Derek rose to his full height, making me lift my chin to keep my stare on his. "The loophole is the mystery of our blood-bond. When you first made the Change, it forever sealed the bond between us..." When I just blinked at him, Derek continued, "Because you suspended your vampire transformation—"

"Wait. At the Gathering..." I touched my side where the troll had run his sword through me. "Did I die?"

"Yes." Derek's voice dropped just above a whisper, forcing me to focus intently on his words. "A single missed heartbeat starts the transformation. You are—"

"An unturned vampire," Nathaniel chimed in. "Therefore, you could title."

"Um. Whoa." My focus returned to Derek. "You think you should have told me this sooner?"

"I was not privy to this until last night."

Nathaniel leaned over my shoulder, whispering at my ear. "When you opened your vein to Derek and he tasted your tainted blood." Nathaniel withdrew with a smirk. "Surprise. You're even more of a disaster."

Derek squeezed my arms, snapping my focus back to him and away from Nathaniel's spoiler alert. "Tonight, events escalated, leaving us no time to…" Derek's gaze roamed to my lips. "Talk."

"The great news is that you can still die," Nathaniel chirped. "That being said, you possess minimal attributes from the dark gift. Nothing awe-inspiring. The basics."

My eye roll carried my attention to Nathaniel. "That's why I can still talk to your mind? Because I'm a kinda-vampire?"

"Perhaps," Nathaniel said. "Your speed, as well, is not entirely wolfen."

"Why can't I hear your thoughts?" I asked Derek.

"He's lucky," Nathaniel grumbled. "Not as powerful and all-knowing as I."

Derek tsked.

A lopsided grin tugged at Nathaniel's lips. In response, Derek returned his signature smirk. Within that moment, a truce and healing happened between the vampires. If only the drama of life would give us a breather for the remainder of the evening.

But nope.

Nathaniel's face returned to blankness. "Tonight, if Hector challenged Derek's right to stay, we would have had to reveal your…condition, sooner. Thankfully, he did not. This will work to our benefit in the future."

"Does my *condition* get Derek out of the punishment?" I asked.

"No," Derek answered. "You must honor the agreement."

"Or else Derek is executed," Nathaniel said. He tilted his head toward the entrance. "Come. The humans are here and we have places to go."

"No." I stepped away from the vampires. "We need to get back to Corbus and plan on how I'm—we're—going to save my brother. How we'll get Derek out of becoming Hector's servant."

"She is a fool." Nathaniel pinched the bridge of his nose, peering at Derek. "You two *are* perfect for each other."

Echoes of laughter filled the hallway outside the reception hall. As the doors opened, Nathaniel grabbed us by the arms and disappeared our group away.

When we solidified, cheap perfume and cigarette smoke attacked my nose. I snapped open my eyes to an introvert's horror show. People. Everywhere. Derek's voice bounced around the packed room while his compulsion raced across my skin, setting the talisman to heat against my neck.

Ahead, dozens of people in compulsion-filled dazes left the massive viewing room. While their heartbeats and breathing hammered in my ears, panic rolled through my stomach. If I didn't chill out, I'd vomit all over the sweaty mob. Shoving my back against a stone wall, I set my focus on the two-story fountain in the center of the room.

The structure belonged at the entrance of a Roman coliseum. Overhead, a glass ceiling showcased the crescent moon peeking through the storm clouds, spotlighting two massive sculptures of toga-clad men wielding tritons in front of the fountain's marble archway.

A foot away, Nathaniel propped himself against the wall, folding his arms over his chest. "You don't listen. It must be your breed's default." He tipped his chin at the necklace. "Taking gifts from the fae. Guaranteed, the witness has been watching us. No need to scurry back to him."

In the hopes of getting out of dodge, I scanned the room for an exit, besides the one Derek blocked. Through the fountain archway, on the other side of the room, sat a pair of sealed double doors. A bronze sign overhead read *High Limit Room.*

A phone chirped.

Nathaniel fished around in his pant pocket, retrieving the ringing cell phone.

I raised an eyebrow at the flip phone.

"You prefer a carrier pigeon?" Nathaniel grumbled, lifting the phone to his ear. "We are here." He disconnected before the caller even spoke a word.

"Who was that?"

"You'll see." He pulled off the wall to aid Derek in closing the doors leading to the room that we stood inside. Upon the sealing of the doors, the thundering of the fountain's water amplified. An uneasiness washed over me, triggering goosebumps to march along my skin. As I rubbed my arms, I peered at the two battling sculptures. Lifelike indeed. The way the water moved at their backs gave the illusion that they were breathing.

Derek walked into my line of vision, but his glare landed on Nathaniel. "This was not discussed with me."

"In case of a faux pas, which is a given with she-beast, I formulated a backup plan. One we now need to face the fae, and free you from Hector." Nathaniel mock-bowed at Derek. "You're welcome."

"Hey." I folded my arms. "If you would fill me in on your plans, I wouldn't mess things up."

They both gave me a look.

"Fine." I huffed. "I *might* not mess things up."

The doors to the High Limit Room opened, and all the blood drained from my face. Ben, dressed in a tux, gave a hesitant wave as he walked over to us.

"Take him back," I snapped at Nathaniel. "Right now."

"No. He is required." Nathaniel grinned and batted his eyelashes at me as his voice slipped into my head, *"Oh, the look on the alpha's face when I popped in to snatch Benjamin was... Well, let's say, you have your paws full."*

Derek moved to my side, speaking under his breath at Nathaniel, "Why do we require her steward?"

"He holds immunity to where we are going." Nathaniel's attention swept to Ben. In a fraction of a second, Nathaniel's eyes softened.

Oh. Fuck. No.

I gritted my teeth and fisted my hands. I'd move Hell itself to keep Ben from Nathaniel's affections. His infatuation with Derek set cities afire. Had almost ended in my death countless times. I'd be damn sure Ben wouldn't be swept into Nathaniel's murderous obsession.

"Tes—Wolf Born," Ben said, pulling me from my daydream of kicking Nathaniel's ass. The snark fought to the surface of Ben's smile. "You look…nice."

"As do you, Steward." I bit my lip, keeping my sarcasm harnessed. Since it appeared we were onto formal and title talks, I motioned to Derek. "This is my hunter."

Ben shoved his glasses up the bridge of his nose. His eyes narrowed at Derek. "There is no title, Hunter, used in—"

"A complicated story," Nathaniel said. "Later, I will bring you abreast. Now, the coins." He held out his hand to Ben.

Ben dug three quarters from his pocket. Instead of transferring them to Nathaniel's awaiting palm, Ben kept them in his hand. "You asked for only three coins. Who is not going?"

"We all are." Nathaniel gave a smug grin. "Derek has a coin already."

Ben handed me a quarter then gave one to Nathaniel.

"What are these for?" I asked.

"A toll." Nathaniel walked over to the fountain. "I wish to speak to the Keeper," he said, flipping the quarter into the fountain.

Magic brushed across my skin and the talisman heated. Ben shivered next to me. The ring Corbus had given Ben glowed. We each looked at our illuminating jewelry.

"Now." Nathaniel faced us. "In turn, you all will say, 'I wish to speak to the Keeper,' and then toss your coin into the fountain."

Ben followed Nathaniel's instructions.

"Hunter." Nathaniel gestured to Derek.

Derek's eyes narrowed at Nathaniel. "I have no coin."

"You do." Nathaniel tented his fingers under his chin. "That worn one you keep."

Derek reached inside his breast pocket, retrieving a coin. As he moved toward the fountain, copper shone between his fingertips. A flip of a worn penny catapulted me into the monster world. Attacked by Derek. Bitten by a werewolf. Andrea's murder. At each event, that coin, that omen of death, had played a part. Nothing good would come from tossing it into the fountain.

"No—" With my monster speed, I intercepted Derek, grabbing his arm to steady myself because the stupid heels had busted. "We'll find another coin."

"Hunter." Nathaniel growled. "Toss the penny."

"No," I repeated. "It's bad luck—"

"Not for me." Derek tugged me closer. For an eternity. A heartbeat. Who knew? Time held no meaning or merit when staring into his eyes.

Nathaniel snapped his fingers. "Hunter—"

Magic prickled along my arms and legs and before I could move away, an energetic current flowed from me, then rolled into Derek. His eyes widened.

"Fool," Nathaniel spat at me. "You insulted them. Steward, front and center, now."

The thundering of the fountain ceased. Over Derek's shoulder, the lack of movement caught my attention. Suspended in the air, the waterfall framed the archway, revealing a marble podium where in its center, water bubbled upward and took a human form.

Ben stopped by my side. "Holy—"

The screech of rock grinding against stone had me cringing. In the reflection of Ben's glasses, the two statues turned their heads toward us. Their vacant eye sockets illuminated with a bluish glow. In unison, they angled their weapons at us.

Grabbing Ben by the lapels of his tux, I spun and tossed him toward the wall while I let my momentum crash me to my knees. Derek joined me floor-side just as a triton flew overhead, impaling the wall a fraction from Ben's shoulder.

From Corbus' ring, a translucent ball of light surrounded Ben. The glowing sphere expanded and absorbed the triton, liquefying the weapon which rolled down the wall and puddled on the floor next to Ben's shivering hip.

"Stay by your steward," Derek ordered. "The magic will protect you."

He took off to join Nathaniel. The two vampires tore around the room, keeping the focus of the statues off me. Freeing myself of the busted shoes, I grabbed one of the broken heels, wielding it as a makeshift weapon.

Nathaniel landed in a heap next to me. "They are stone," he gritted. "A toothpick is not a weapon."

"Then what the heck is?"

"You are not to fight," he growled.

"What am I supposed to do?" I palmed my weapon and crouched, readying for the statue rounding the fountain. "Let them kill you—"

The remaining triton nearly missed Nathaniel's head. He grabbed me by the arm and disappeared us against the wall. Magic buzzed against my shoulder from the orb encircling Ben. When he reached out for me, I dodged his hand.

"You can't fight," Ben warned. "You have to follow the rules."

"Well, the rules suck." A searing burn encircled my neck from the talisman, warning me of the evident danger in the room, so I ripped it off, tossing it onto Ben's lap.

Nathaniel took off to shield Derek, who was recovering from one of the stone man's blows. While the two continued fighting the thing, they didn't notice that the other statue had retrieved the triton.

I tore after the statue, then jumped onto its back, hooking my legs around the thing's neck. The statue dropped the triton and attempted to pry me off. I missed its grabs but my toes slid against the statue's glossy stone. A violent shake of its head sent me sprawling onto my back, knocking the wind out of me. While I struggled to breathe, the statue's eyes lowered to the triton laying a foot away from me. *Oh no, you don't.*

As I grabbed the weapon, something inside me stirred. Not my wolf. *Nope.* Energy hummed through my bones. Different than the link or the blood-bond anchoring me to a person, the strange energy sought to escape. As it raced through my arms, the triton's three gold prongs illuminated. *What the –*

The statue loomed over me, pinning me between its legs. Using my speed, I slipped the triton between my armpit and side. Another quick alteration and I tucked my knees toward my chest, heaving the triton upward and wedging it between the statue's chin and neck. Before the statue pulled back, I slammed my heels onto the staff and with a hollow pop, the statue's head crashed against the floor. Inches from my nose, the blue slits of its eyes dimmed and all movement ceased from the stone man. I grabbed the still glowing triton, then wiggled out from between the feet of the lifeless statue.

"Go for the" – my squashed lungs struggled to fuel my voice – "head."

I heaved the triton onto my shoulder and stumbled after the remaining statue holding Derek by the throat. My height left me at a vertical disadvantage. With no time to adjust my point of attack, I drove the glowing prongs against the statue's leg. The force of the blow bounced me backward, smacking my tailbone against the floor.

The statue released Derek. *Great.*

The thing spun and lunged at me. *Bad.*

I rolled to the side, missing its foot stomp. However, the triton didn't. The non-glowing weapon matched the state of my disregarded shoes. As the statue raised its foot toward my head, Derek grabbed me by the ankles and swung me across the floor.

When I crash-stopped against the fountain pool, Nathaniel tugged me to my feet. He jabbed a claw at Ben. "Get to – "

The stone man caught Nathaniel's arm, yanking him away from me. When Nathaniel attempted to escape, the statue threw him to the floor, then crushed its foot against Nathaniel's ankle. A blood-curdling scream burst from Nathaniel.

Once again, the strange energy vibrated through me and I flicked my attention to my pulsing fingers. They were freaking glowing. When the stone man raised his free foot toward Nathaniel's head, I shoved my hands outward and the energy tore from my fingertips, hitting the statue. A glowing spiderweb of cracks covered its body.

"Strike once more," a feminine voice said.

I spun around to face the water figure standing on the podium. The thing pointed in the direction of the statue. When I turned around, Derek took the opportunity to rescue Nathaniel. Once they cleared the middle of the room, I released another blast of energy against the statue. The force of its explosion hurled me backward into the fountain.

Fragments of rock peppered the water as I surfaced from the three-foot-deep pool. Gasping for breath, I gripped the edge of the fountain.

Something brushed my knuckles and I frantically retreated. While the frigid water splashed around me, Derek hopped into the fountain and pulled me to my feet. As I fought with my hair hanging in my face, my panic and fear rushed to Ben's previous location. Through the dust settling, I spotted him helping Nathaniel to his good foot while the other hung at an unnatural angle.

Nathaniel allowed Ben to hobble them over to the fountain edge. When Ben cleared his throat, he tipped his chin toward the water figure standing on the podium.

Once more, Derek retrieved the damn penny from his pocket. "I wish to speak to the Keeper." He flipped the coin into the fountain, then moved to my left side, placing a quarter in my hand. "Your turn."

I sloshed through the pool to face the archway framed by the suspended waterfall. In the center, the figure stood motionless on the podium. "I wish to speak to the Keeper." Glaring at what I assumed would be its face, I dropped the quarter into the fountain.

The water figure angled its body toward Nathaniel. Its feminine voice echoed through the room. "Betrayer of Kin."

Nathaniel bowed.

The water figure turned to address me. "Wolf Born, and her court."

Ben and Derek bowed.

"Wolf Born," Ben whispered. "You tip your head, in greeting."

Keeping my eyes on the figure, I dipped my chin.

In a flash of light, the water figure materialized into a seven-foot-tall woman clad in ancient armor. A gold crown of olive leaves encircled her head of curly ebony hair. As she peered down at me, a mischievous smile lit her face. "I honor your wishes. May your past trespass heed a warning. Raise no hand nor harm within my kingdom or you shall suffer a chosen consequence."

Chapter Sixteen

With the wave of the Keeper's hand, the fountain pool divided, revealing a makeshift path of glittering coins that led to a staircase running up to the archway.

"No questions, she-beast," Nathaniel warned. He disappeared his way over to us then snapped his fingers, signaling Ben to join our group. "Only speak to your steward."

"Should you stay?" Ben asked Nathaniel.

Nathaniel glanced at his busted ankle. "Tis a minor inconvenience."

The Keeper's hazel eyes tracked our awkward movements as Nathaniel ushered us into the correct positioning. Derek was at my back. Ben flanked my left. Nathaniel was a body length in front and off to my right.

"Enter of your free will," the Keeper said. Then she turned and walked through the archway, vanishing.

"We are about to enter the Fae Kingdom of the Naiads," Nathaniel said.

"Naiads?" I whispered to Ben.

"Water Nymphs," Ben answered. "Guardians of fountains. Granters of wishes. Tricksters. Merry-makers."

"Rubbish." Nathaniel gestured at the destruction around us. "That book you stuff your nose in needs a proper edit. Murderers, warlords, the lot of them."

"Yet you agreed to a meeting," Derek grumbled.

"I've survived worse fae encounters. Do not touch anything." Nathaniel's warning and glare zeroed in on me. "Or blow up anything with korrigan magic."

My fingertips had returned to their non-glowing, in need of a manicure state. "I don't know how I did that."

Behind me, Derek rested his wet hand on my shoulder. "Let them think you do."

Ben nodded.

"Come," Nathaniel said. "Before she animates more sculptures." He disappeared on his way to the archway. When Nathaniel crossed the threshold, he too vanished.

"Remember, I am your hunter." Derek slipped his hand from my shoulder. "On the other side of that archway, do not look or speak to me unless you request for me to kill. Any other reason for you to communicate with me is seen as disrespectful. As atonement, the fae would have the right to kill anyone in your court."

Shivering, I lifted the sopping gown to my ankles and climbed the steps. Ben kept glancing over at me. So many questions raced through my mind. I could only imagine what was going through his. Together, we crossed under the archway. Magic brushed against my skin, causing the hairs along my arms to stand.

On the other side, a liquid haziness cloaked the room. Our movement became buoyant as if we were moving through water. When the doors to the High Limit Room opened, Ben grabbed my arm. Nathaniel gave us a peripheral glare before he entered the room.

Immediately, Ben let me go and took up fidgeting with the cufflinks of his shirt. Once we were inside, two stone statues, identical to the ones I had destroyed, closed the doors. Hopefully, they were oblivious to what had gone down with their counterparts.

In the center of the room, the Keeper settled into a horseshoe-shaped booth. Like her prior form, a water figure flowed across the room, offering her a crystal flute.

She raised the glass toward our group. "I offer you a drink, Wolf Born."

"No." Ben rushed to speak. "The Wolf Born graciously declines." He gave me the side-eye as an apology. "No accepting gifts from the fae."

The Keeper smirked and took a sip. "Her steward is sharp."

"Fortunately," Nathaniel added.

She wiped her mouth across her knuckles while studying me as I dripped water all over the marble floor. "You wish aid from me and mine, states the Betrayer of Kin."

Oh, how I wanted to know why Nathaniel held that title. Both times she had used it, he had cringed. Ben's attention wavered between Nathaniel and the Keeper. Derek stood motionless at my back. A shadow waiting to attack if needed. An occasional pelt of his breath hit my bare shoulder.

"What say you?" the Keeper asked me.

Ben spoke at me as he glanced at Nathaniel. "Let him do the talking. He'll then turn it over to me. You will be able to speak freely with me."

Sure. As freely as a room filled with water beings and animate sculptures allowed.

Nathaniel clasped his hands behind his back. "The Lord of Li—"

The Keeper raised a finger, silencing Nathaniel. "Speak not his title in my kingdom. Refer to him as his kind—sprite."

"The sprite," Nathaniel continued, "demands the Wolf Born meet him in three days."

"Simple solution." She took another sip. "Do not. He cannot cross over to the Human realm without invitation."

"The sprite holds her brother captive," Nathaniel said.

"Bait for the Wolf Born to relinquish the korrigan's blood," the Keeper said. "Where there is a fountain, I have eyes. I viewed the Vampire King's meeting." Her gaze locked with mine. "My spies confirmed. The sprite keeps a male half-blood prisoner. Red hair. Green-eyed."

With that confirmation, relief crashed into my heart. There would be no more questioning or trying to pacify me. Drew was alive.

Flashing me a brief view of his profile, Nathaniel nodded—a subtle cue for me to focus on the conversation. He continued, "If she does not meet with the sprite, he will kill her brother."

"That he will." The Keeper lowered her glass to the table.

I shook my head. Behind me, Derek cleared his throat as a warning for me to keep silent.

"You entertain me, Wolf Born," she said. "It has been centuries since I have witnessed an aristocrat bear arms."

My mouth popped open and I clamped it shut. *Aristocrat my ass.* I was a pawn. That, at least, I knew.

"Alas." The Keeper traced her finger along the edge of her glass. "I believe you have the soul of a warrior versus a ruler. The sprite is a ruler. Cunning. Meet on his terms, you will lose more than your brother and blood."

"She gained an alliance with the vampires," Nathaniel stated.

"Korrigan's blood and a modicum of vampires to support her endeavor." Her gaze locked on mine. "She needs an army."

"Her wolves are ready to fight," Nathaniel added.

"Hoplites killed in minutes." The Keeper's body shimmered, revealing her water form before solidifying. "Have you not thought that this is the sprite's intention? Numerous races have fallen to his cunning. They were enslaved or slain. That will be the fate of all your wolves. Best to honor your brother's sacrifice."

I opened my mouth and Nathaniel spun around faster than an atom. "Zip it." He set his attention back to the Keeper. "You could join us."

She tipped her head back with laughter.

Nathaniel spoke over the Keeper's chuckles. "This is a chance for you to restore the naiads' position amongst the fae. Permit your return to the Light realm."

As dissipating giggles tremored through her body, the Keeper spoke to me. "I dream of redemption. Though time has given me experience, I will not move my people to their deaths for a faded promise of revenge."

"My pardon." Ben straightened himself. "Have you not thought this is the sprite's intention, for you to sit idle?"

"Careful, human, with your question." Her eyes flickered. "You may be safe physically, but the Betrayer of Kin can take your punishment."

When one of the statues moved forward, she raised her hand, keeping the sculpture from advancing. Ben's throat bobbed with his dry swallow. I wanted to squeeze his hand, reassuring him that, no matter if the Keeper had a stone army on standby to crush us, debating was Ben's combat of choice. His forte. A bead of sweat trickled down his temple. Yet he looked her square in the eyes as he spoke. "The sprite relies on your passivity."

She angled her thick brows in a sharp crease. "Is that so?"

"Yes." Ben's voice hitched. "The last time one of the Otherworldly Creatures went against the sprite was…"

"The fall of Atlantis," Nathaniel muttered.

"Wow." Ben went rigid. His face drained of color. "Ancient Greece."

The Keeper leaned forward. "He gained much that day."

"Yet he fears her." Ben pointed at me. "A single, inexperienced, reckless, not fully courted ruler."

"Steward," Nathaniel warned. "This is not the—"

"You have my ear," the Keeper said to Ben. "Use your words wisely."

Ben turned to me, his eyes shining with pride. "The Wolf Born negotiated for two feuding races to form an alliance. She has saved my life countless times. She attacked two of your guards to rescue a member of her court. Unlike any other Otherworldly Creature, the

Wolf Born's actions are not ploys to gain power or wealth and *that* is what troubles the sprite." Ben paused, allowing his words to sink into the inquisitive minds of the room.

Sitting back in her booth, the Keeper folded her muscled arms across her chest. "I propose a question for a favor."

Nathaniel took over. "Ask a question."

"Silence." The Keeper kept her focus on Ben. "I negotiate with the human."

With a ghost of a smile and a glimmer in his eye, Ben said, "Proceed."

"What is the motivation for the Wolf Born's actions which sparks fear within the sprite?"

"For the answer, the Wolf Born requests the naiads' support and arms when meeting with the sprite."

Trying to stop the words from reaching the Keeper's ears, Nathaniel raised his hands. "No—"

"Agreed," she said.

"Your steward forfeited an opportunity to free Derek," Nathaniel sent to me.

I didn't respond. My entire focus was on my best friend binding the fae to her favor.

"The Otherworldly Creatures book has taught me that the fae have an affliction for love. A great fear." Ben stared at me. "The motivation for the Wolf Born's actions is *love.*"

As the room fell silent, Derek's breath ran against my shoulder, tempting me to turn, but I forced my attention to remain on the Keeper peering at me.

When she lifted her finger, the water figure next to the Keeper divided multiple times. As the copies surrounded our group, a cluster of weapon-wielding statues filtered into the room. All the while, Nathaniel and Ben bickered and Derek moved to my side. Between the barrier of water and stone bodies, I caught a glimpse of the Keeper. She dissolved into a silvery pool. The liquid undulated and rolled its way toward us. Effortlessly, it maneuvered through the barrier. Feet from me, the pool reformed into the seven-foot-tall Keeper.

"Tell your hunter to step away or I'll have him crushed," she warned.

As I nodded, Derek took a single step back.

With her gaze running over my waterlogged gown, the Keeper shortened the distance to tower over me. "I cannot enter the human realm in this form. I must take another. I will reach into your mind and pull an image. Best not someone you see daily as that can complicate things. Also, I wish to stay strong. Female. Easy on the eye if I am to be mortal for the next few days."

My mind raced to find someone to meet the unrealistic expectations of the Keeper. Before I could shut off the thought, a blinding light filled the room. When it dimmed, I had to drastically lower my gaze to the person standing in front of me.

My brain fired off a series of basic survival messages to keep me breathing and standing while I gawked at the strongest human I had ever known. Andrea.

A perfectly arched eyebrow lifted with her signature grin. She turned in a slow circle, wearing the outfit I'd last seen her alive in, holey fishnet stockings, a boob-crushing corset and a pleated miniskirt. "Not bad, Wolf Born."

Hearing Andrea's voice, I flinched.

Wide-eyed, Ben just stood there. After a few blinks, he brought a trembling knuckle to his lips. Tears glazed his eyes. "She even smells like her."

The Keeper brought the crook of her arm to her nose and sniffed. "Spicy." Her eyes brightened. "Oh! Cinnamon—"

Nathaniel interjected, "The treaty is struck."

"Yes." With the flick of the Keeper's wrists, the sculptures retreated, and the water figures joined into a single form standing behind the Keeper.

Nathaniel spoke at me, "Once we cross into the human realm, the Keeper will become mortal. She is your guest. You will protect her as you would your friend. If mortal death falls upon her—"

"Mine will rise from every water fountain and drown yours." Imitating another signature Andrea idiom, she bounced on her tiptoes.

Sheer panic flooded Ben's face. "She will have no magic to protect her?"

"Nope." She accentuated the 'P.' Her fingers danced over her vocal cords. "I already adore this human form."

To keep from throttling the fae posing as Andrea, I fisted my hands.

"Yes, no more fitting form for you to possess," Nathaniel said. "When confronting the Vampire Queen, this human, Andrea, looked into the queen's eyes, brandished the middle finger, and said, 'piss off, fang head'."

The Keeper stilled. Unnervingly, she gave me one of Andrea's sincere looks. "Then this human was a warrior. I will wear her form well, Wolf Born."

Nathaniel's gaze dropped to the bone jetting out from his ankle. "Shall we?"

The Keeper turned to face the water figure. "Speak not of my leave. I will return when it is time." She pressed her forehead to the water figure's. After a moment, she withdrew, then spun around to address our group. “I’m ready.”

Chapter Seventeen

Since the Keeper had left her magic behind when we had taken our leave of the Naiad Kingdom, we were met by a wall of water crashing around us. Thankfully, we stood under the fountain's archway, avoiding a direct blast. With the coin stairway no longer present, the only way down was a two-story plunge into the shallow pool.

The Keeper tipped her chin at Ben's ring and yelled, "Can that do anything besides protect you?"

Ben shrugged. "So far, no."

"I can move you one at a time," Nathaniel said. "Hunter."

The two vampires disappeared, leaving me with Ben and the Keeper.

"Before I have to kill someone," the Keeper said, "let me disclose a few rules. One, you need to call me by her name. You give away my identity and—" She drew a black lacquered nail across her throat. "Two, no using magic, links, whatever otherworldly things you have hidden, Wolf Born, to harm me. Three, I need seaweed."

Giving me a we-are-going-to-die look, Ben asked the Keeper, "Is the seaweed for you to eat?"

"Ha." She wrinkled her nose. "I'm not a mermaid. I like it with my tea."

"And if we cannot find a store open that sells seaweed?" he asked.

"I have killed for much fewer trivialities. Once, I sunk a great city over a peach." She smiled. "I'm not fond of humans tossing their leftovers into my fountains."

Nathaniel reappeared. Dark circles rimmed his sunken eyes as he held a shaking hand out to me. "Come."

I stepped out of his way. "Take my steward."

Nathaniel grabbed Ben and disappeared.

"Interesting." Tilting her head, the Keeper rested her hands on her hips. "He never was one to take orders without complaint."

I was pretty sure the combination of energy drain and busted ankle had quieted Nathaniel's sarcasm. Not that I'd share the observation with the Keeper. Instead, I switched topics with a statement. "Since you are human, I can ask you questions."

"Yes. Doesn't mean I'll answer. Or tell the whole truth."

"You'll fit in perfect with the crew."

A twisted blend of amusement and mischief shone through her eyes. "Crew?"

"The group I temporarily live with."

"You mean your court." She cocked her head. "They are permanent until death takes them."

Remembering Corbus' words, I said, "I was told I can change court members."

"True. To do so brings them dishonor. They will be killed." Her attention roamed to the waterfall before us. "A ruler who frequently switches members of their court is seen as unfit. Unstable. Weak. A true ruler treats their court as kin."

Anger warmed my blood. Because of my ignorance, Derek, Sam and Ben were forever chained to me until their final breaths. I'd be damn sure not to court another single soul.

She rubbed the goosebumps along her arms. "What is taking him so long?"

"Not sure." The waterfall acted as a barrier, debilitating my heightened senses. "Why did you give up your magic?"

"Our magic and blood attract Otherworldly Creatures." She paused. "How did they find you?"

"Blood." The realization smacked me upside the head. "That's how he found me. Today, at Andrea's grave, I cut myself. When my blood hit the snow, the sprite appeared."

"Interesting. But I'm not talking about him." She pointed at my bare neck. "The one who gifted you the talisman. How did *they* find you?"

Fear prickled my skin. She knew there was another Otherworldly Creature aiding us. Was that the reason she had chosen to help us? To get to Corbus? *Shit.* Pain splintered my temples as another issue surfaced. Corbus had warned that once a Light or Dark fae crossed to our realm, he would leave. Could we hide the Keeper's identity long enough for him to aid us? I sure hoped so.

The Keeper lasered her focus on me. "I'm waiting."

"You're gonna be."

"Fine." A wicked grin curled her lips. "I'll use my acquired assets to get one of the wolves to give me the answer."

"No and nope. That is not going to happen." I dragged my numb fingers down my face, scrubbing the image of her shoving her boobs, Andrea's breasts, into Nolan's line of vision. "The first time I Changed, the magic attracted them."

She winked. "Good Wolf Queen."

"I'm *not* a queen."

"You want to save your brother?"

"Yes."

"Keep the wolves and vampires on this side of the realm?"

"Yes."

"Then"—the Keeper paused, and I would swear, Andrea's mind, body and soul stood before me—"you better learn to own *your* title."

"I do."

Calling my bluff, she shook her head. "With rulers, the battle begins with a challenge of wit. Act as if I am the sprite, standing here, ready to destroy all you love. Say your title."

I dropped my hands to my sides and straightened my spine. My mouth opened, yet the words clung to my throat. When I took a sharp breath to dislodge them, they released in the form of a pale whisper. "I'm the Wolf Born."

"Yeah." She smirked. "Not buying what you're selling. You mentally and physically had to prepare to say that. If someone challenges your title, you take their head. Better practice both skills." The Keeper mistook my silence for confusion, and clarified with, "Become proficient in the taking of heads, and owning your title."

Nathaniel reappeared. Bent over with his hands braced against his knees, he struggled to raise his gaze past the hem of my dress. "We have a problem."

In unison, the Keeper and I responded, "What?"

"Time passes differently in the fae kingdoms," he answered.

My heart stopped. "Like how?"

"Our time moves slower," the Keeper answered.

I gritted my teeth against the panic burning the back of my throat. "What time is it?"

"Two hours to sunrise." Struggling to catch his breath, Nathaniel raised his gaze. "That is part one of our predicament."

"You can tell me the rest at the bottom." I hiked the dress to my thighs and crouched. "Andrea," I said to the Keeper, "climb on and hold tight." Without hesitation, she leaped onto my back, hooking her legs around my torso and arms around my shoulders.

"The fall is too..." He panted. "Just give me a bloody second."

"I've jumped off a couple of roofs since my Change. I can handle this drop."

My stomach flipped as we plunged into the pool below. The force of my landing and the Keeper shifting her weight countered my balance, tipping us backward to splash into the water. Shoving my hair away from my face, I locked my attention on the man standing in front of the fountain. The urge to sink deeper into the pool won over a graceful stand.

One of the busted heels hung by its ankle strap from Sam's index finger. His scent, a blend of pine and sweat, drifted toward my cowering form. I raised my eyes to meet his—mostly—neutral expression. The undertone of hurt and betrayal had my attention darting around the room. Ben and Max were off to the right, paused mid-convo, ping-ponging looks between Sam and me. Derek was nowhere in sight. *Thankfully.*

The Keeper slapped a hand on my shoulder. "Gotta work on those landings, too."

The heel clattered against the floor. Sam gripped the sides of his head. When his eyes locked with the Keeper, he crumbled to his knees.

I raced to Sam. As his eyes rolled back into their sockets, his body convulsed. I tugged his head into my lap. Even with the skin-to-skin contact, the link refused to stir between us.

Nathaniel appeared at my side. He, too, crumbled to the floor. "He is fighting my compulsion. It will kill him. Command him. Call his wolf."

"Alpha, I command—" Only my voice called out. My wolf was silent. "I can't. Something is wrong."

Ben rushed to Nathaniel's side while Max joined me with Sam. The Keeper made her way to our group. She fidgeted with the hem of her skirt. Restraint to offer her support was evident on her tight lips, but she was firm in her human role. Max's eyes glowed as the link stirred between him and his alpha, yet it did not pass to me.

"I'll stabilize him as best as I can," Max said. "But we need your link, Wolf Born."

Nathaniel's glare scaled upward. "Hunter, is there a reason her wolf is unable to join us?"

I cranked over my shoulder. "What is he talking about?"

Derek scowled at Sam's writhing body. "I gave you the freedom to choose."

Pressing my palms against Sam's thundering chest, I screamed at Derek, "What did you do?"

"When you awakened me from the sleeping death," Derek paused, holding me prisoner in the depths of his eyes, "I bound your wolf to me."

"Fool," Nathaniel growled.

"Why?" I gritted.

"So, you can think for yourself. You can decide"—anger lowered Derek's voice—"not as the animal, who desires *him*."

Max went to stand.

"Stay with your alpha," I ordered.

Max stilled.

"Hunter." No matter how his betrayal burned me alive, I needed to remain as calm as possible. "Let her go. We will talk after this."

Instantly, a rush of energy hit me. When the reflection of my glowing eyes shone in Ben's glasses, I shoved my attention to Sam. "Alpha, I command your wolf to still." Below my palms, his heart rate slowed, and his breathing eased. Closing my eyes, I forced my wolf back into my subconscious.

"Max—" I mentally scolded myself for using his name instead of his title. Hopefully, I'd get a pass due to Sam's near-death experience. "Sorry, Delta, can you carry the alpha?" I asked.

"Yes," he answered.

"I have Nathaniel," Ben said.

Derek's footsteps triggered my eyes to flash open. When he extended a hand to me, the room filled with tension. Mustering a would-be-ruler reaction, I slipped my hand into his. Any weakness in our court would be a prime target to attack. I hadn't wholeheartedly aligned the Keeper with our team. Our bickering might be a deciding factor for her to jump ship and go rub elbows with the Lord of Light. Derek eased me to my feet. As soon as I found my footing, I took back my hand.

"I need..." Nathaniel's heavy-lidded eyes drifted shut with his words. "Get to the room. Now."

"I have the key." Ben pointed toward the High Limit room. "There's an elevator that takes you directly to the suites."

No one hesitated. With an unconscious Sam slung over his shoulder, Max kicked down the doors. We raced through the room. Eerily, it was a replica of the one within the Keeper's realm. Even though all furniture and sculptures remained inanimate, anticipation tightened my limbs. Ben and Nathaniel made it to the elevator first. When Ben hit the door panel, Nathaniel almost crumbled to the floor. With ninja reflexes, Ben used his body to sandwich Nathaniel between the wall. Their eyes met, lips close enough to touch. At that moment, I lost my best friend to the vampire.

Miracles of miracles, before they got too comfortable, the elevator dinged. The door slid open, revealing an impossible fit for seven people. The Keeper slipped inside. Max, carrying Sam, the hobbling Nathaniel and Ben followed. Seeing the metal box was packed, and an opportunity to drag answers from Derek, I took a backstep. "We'll catch the next one."

The door slid shut on a bunch of protests. Overhead, the floor numbers illuminated with the elevator's slow climb. While water crawled down my spine, I stared at the door holding our contorted reflections. "Outta the two ways to turn a human, why did you choose the blood-bond?"

"For you to bring forth such a ridiculous question proves that my actions and words have failed." Derek's voice heated as he fastened his attention to me. "There was *never* a choice."

I refused to look at him. "Bullshit."

"My tongue does not burn."

"You're just twisting words." I gave him the side-eye. "Now you have my wolf on a leash too."

"No longer."

"You thought I couldn't control her." I seethed. "What do you think I've been doing all these months?"

"Hiding." A half-grin tugged his lips. "And a fair amount of vivid dreaming."

I clenched my jaw. I'd not let my mouth run me into more trouble.

"Does your heart race from reminiscing?" Derek leaned closer, brushing his soaking jacket against the side of my arm. "Or is it the anticipation of seeing the alpha?"

The door dinged while my anger reached its zenith. Inside, I moved to the farthest corner away from Derek. The stupid elevator sported mirrored walls and ceiling. *Wonderful.* Derek in all his hotness taunted me everywhere I looked. Even the back of his freaking head was sexy.

Frustration merged with anger, layering my voice. "I'm not some weak thing that turns into a puddle at his feet."

"You did when you were held captive."

"This is different."

"Is it?" Derek's chuckle went straight to my core. "Are you not under his watchful eye during the day?"

"Along with the entire pack. We will never be alone." The lie bit at my heart. I'd a few hours, at most, to sleep with Sam and take his mark, or else lose the packs' loyalties.

Derek's eyes darkened. "Like us?"

He had a point. At no time would *we* be alone. In two days, Derek would be on his way to serve Hector. "Yes. Like us. You'll be gone. I'll be—"

Derek flicked the emergency brake of the elevator. "I will *always* find you." The tips of his fangs flashed against his crimson lips as he closed the distance between us. "I believe, my wolf, you don't understand the gravity of certainty. What the cost is to you."

I jammed my chin up to keep looking him square in the eyes. Challenging Derek stirred something dark and feral within me. "Then tell me, hunter. What's *my* price?"

With his speed, Derek caged me between his arms, bracing his hands against the wall by the sides of my head. The glass groaned under the pressure of his fading restraint. As adrenaline roared through my limbs, anticipation dragged me to the edge of no return. One move, his or mine, would decide if we dove off or clung to the jagged rocks of our self-imposed purgatory.

"This is madness," I uttered.

"That *is* the cost." He slipped a hand around my throat, caressing his thumb over my throbbing pulse. "Your curiosity. Your desire. Your soul pulls you as violently to me as mine does to you."

"No," I whispered.

"Your heartbeat betrays you." He ran his thumb from my pulse to trace along my collarbone. "Why lie?"

"Because…" I couldn't tell him about Sam. Through burning tears, I pushed at Derek's firm chest. "Let me go—"

He slid his thigh between my legs, parting the dress and pinning me against the wall. "I will *never* let you go."

"You have to." I braced my hands against his chest. Below my sweaty palms rested his un-beating heart, reaffirming why we could never be together. We stood on opposite sides of the monster world. I forced courage into my voice. "All these fucking Otherworldly laws. We don't get a choice."

Underneath his hand, still braced by my head, the glass wall cracked. "Wrong."

"No." I paused, making sure he listened and understood. "Not with us, and you know it too."

He pulled his hand away from the wall.

I released a breath.

Derek's gaze darted to my lips. "Screw the laws." He shoved forward, brushing his thigh up against my core while he growled against my ear. "Let our races fight through eternity. Let the fae wage war upon us." He cupped my face, holding my lust-filled eyes with his. "No matter what fate rules, I will always *choose* you."

He kissed me, hard and unforgiving. In a series of rough adjustments, he grabbed the backs of my thighs, hoisting me up. The movements bunched the soaking dress past my abdomen. Drastically aware that only his pants separated us, I locked my legs around his hips, pressing myself against his hardness.

"I'll take you here," he growled against my mouth. "Claim you as mine."

He trailed his tongue from my bottom lip to my breasts. When his fangs dragged across the wet fabric covering my nipples, a moan tore from my throat. He responded by tightening his grip against my thighs, grinding himself against me. As his breath raced across my skin, I tipped back my head to the mirrored ceiling. My glowing eyes locked onto a masterpiece of passion. One Michelangelo would have refused to recreate, fearing ultimate failure in the undertaking of capturing a pixel in this moment. A passion so tragic, forbidden and solely ours.

Above, the elevator's gears hummed and clicked. Once more, it started its upward climb. Derek lowered me to my feet then settled my dress back into place. "I will kill whoever bypassed the emergency brake."

Not trusting my voice or body, I blinked my agreement.

"Soon." He raised the underside of my wrists to his lips, pressing a kiss to each. "I'll have you screaming to the angels."

Pressure built inside me and my flesh burned for release. One flick of his tongue, a caress of his breath, and I would *soar* with the angels. Instead, he stepped away. Tears caught on my eyelashes as the denial prickled along every nerve ending.

"I am trying to honor your modesty." Derek's voice shook. "You can't be seen in a compromised position with me…yet."

Yet. That word—promise—did me in. I bit my lip and clenched my thighs as the door opened.

Chapter Eighteen

Derek shifted in front of me, blocking the spectator from witnessing my ruin.

"You okay in there?" The Keeper peeked around Derek's arm.

Derek countered her move, shielding me once more. It was too late. The knowing gleam in her eye spoke a whole conversation. She knew. The million-dollar question—would she use it against us?

I stumbled out of the elevator, side-stepping past Derek and the Keeper. Somehow, I made it down the private hallway to the suite where two men stood. By their scent, I knew they were werewolves. They schooled their expressions as I approached, barefooted and shivering in a soaking wet dress.

I sucked in a breath and my heart jumped. My arousal lingered in the air around me. *Shit.* I glanced over my shoulder. The Keeper and Derek stood by the elevator in hushed conversation. Derek's attention rested on mine. How easy for me to spin on my heel and race back to that metal box. To Derek. Instead, I turned to face the werewolves.

"Wolf Born," the man on the right said, tipping his head and placing his fist to his heart.

I nodded at him.

"Wolf Born," the man on the left grumbled. He lifted his fist, haphazardly hitting his heart.

Fifty-fifty fighting odds were better than I'd had before. Still. Not great. A deep rift ran between the pack. Running on a hunch, one side was me and my lack of werewolf credentials while the other was a rightfully concerned beta, Nolan.

The Keeper scurried to my side. Her focus landed on the guy with the half-assed fist to his heart. She tilted her chin at the man. "You better handle that."

The man's lips curled. "Humans don't—"

With my speed, I rushed the dude, fisting the front of his shirt and dragging him down to my eye level. Glaring at him, I let my wolf slip through my eyes. My fangs pulsed from my gums. My nails lengthened. "This is Andrea. She is a sister to me. You treat and respect her as such." I released him. "Now, open the door."

"Yes, Wolf Born." The man gave a brisk nod and obliged.

Glee filled the Keeper's wide eyes. She linked her arm with mine, tugging me down so she could whisper in my ear. "That's what I am talking about. Although, you should have taken his head." She pulled at the hem of her skirt. "This garment rides up with every step. Speaking of riding…" She snorted. "The hunter took leave. No worries. He'll be *riding* back soon enough."

The dry tears stretched my skin as I harnessed a laugh. "It's like you're…you know."

She arched her eyebrow, acknowledging my unsaid words. Each second, she became more like Andrea. "So, while you were…*riding* up here, the alpha recovered."

Shit. "Great," I said loud and clear for the werewolves.

"Anyhow," the Keeper said, "he took the other elevator and is downstairs with some of the pack."

When we slipped inside the suite, the aroma of fresh blood hit my nose. My vision tunneled onto the source—Nathaniel sprawled and groaning on the sofa. Leaning over Nathaniel's ankle, Ben tossed a blood-soaked towel to the floor. My now fully-present wolf stirred. In the hopes of countering the hunger for blood, I shoved the crook of my free arm to my nose, dragging in Derek's scent. Instead of simmering her down, she surged through me. Swaying, I let go of the Keeper to steady myself.

"I'm *undead,*" Nathaniel snapped at Ben. "Not dead."

"Then hold still." Ben poked at Nathaniel's swollen ankle. "I have to make sure I reset it."

Nathaniel propped himself on his elbows, glancing at Ben's handiwork. "Not bad."

I clenched my fists at the tender grin on Nathaniel's bratty face, then settled my focus on the pink flesh covering the once-broken limb.

Out of the corner of my eyes, I caught sight of sharpshooter Jimmy walking out of the bedroom while Max paced the length of the bed, talking on a phone. Closing my eyes, I eavesdropped.

"They need more time," Max whispered.

"*He* is out of time," Nolan responded with heat. "She takes his mark, or the pack leaves. I'm not losing our alpha to a vampire's whore."

I flashed my eyes open and stormed into the bedroom. Max cut his attention to me. Panic filled his expression.

"Hello, Delta." I raised my voice to carry to Nolan's ears. "Beta."

Max ended the call. "Wolf Born." He dropped to his knees, placed his fist to his heart and bared his neck. Vaguely, I remembered Sam, in his wolf form, similarly exposing his neck. At that time, Derek had walked me through what to do. Slowly, I placed my hand on Max's exposed neck.

He snapped his gaze to mine. "The beta doesn't mean… He worries about—"

"The beta can answer for himself." When I looked into Max's eyes, sorrow frayed the anger burning through me. What a cruel world to rob Max of so many human adventures. He should've been out dating and singing bad karaoke, *anything* but genuflecting to me. I settled to my knees in front of Max, then rested a hand on his massive shoulder.

"Wolf Born." Max's eyes widened. "You should not be on your knees."

"I concur," the Keeper muttered over my shoulder. "Get up."

"No," I snapped. "The sooner the pack learns that I'm not some doll meant to sit on a shelf and collect dust, the better."

"Please," Max said. "You not following the rules is why some of the wolves are frustrated."

"Half the pack," I added.

"At least." The sweet scent of fear drifted from Max's pores. "They believe you are reckless. That you act as a lone wolf. Come morning, we may lose our alpha."

I tightened my grip on Max's shoulder. "I will keep us *all* safe by any means that I can. That includes *our* alpha." The familiar scent of pine wrapped around me. I turned over my shoulder to lock eyes with Sam. "My life for the pack."

Sam stood in the doorway with his fist pressed to his heart. "My life for you." When I rose, Sam lowered his fist to his side. His attention landed on Max. "Leave us, Delta." Sam turned his focus to the Keeper. "You too."

"Not unless she says so," the Keeper snipped.

I nodded.

"Come on, Delta." She huffed. "I'm hungry. Let's order the shit out of room service."

Once they left, Sam moved to the door. "May we speak in privacy?"

Not trusting my vocal cords, I nodded.

Sam closed the doors. "Would you like to change?"

On top of the nightstand, I eyed longingly at the pile of my clothes. *Crap.* I'd be out of the dress soon enough. Trembling, I rubbed my arms. "No, I'm good."

"You're freezing."

"I'm fine," I insisted, then flipped the convo to his state. "You look better. Standing. How are you feeling?"

"Besides getting zapped in the head every time I see Andrea, I'm fine."

I forced my face into a blank mask. "Did you get your memory back?"

"No." He paused, taking a moment to study my expression. "Relieved?"

I swallowed. "Yes."

His lips tugged to the side of his mouth. "Thanks for the honesty."

"Sure." I lowered my gaze to the bed and panic twisted my gut.

"What the—"

I flicked my attention back to Sam, whose focus was pinned on the mirror over the bed. His throat bobbed. "This night just keeps getting—" A breath rushed from Sam's chest while he composed himself. "Your steward said Andrea's been in hiding since the Gathering and when she heard you were in trouble, she sought you out." Sam's narrowed gaze leveled to my face. "What type of friend would let you think they're dead?"

I hugged myself, focusing on keeping my heart inside my ribcage. "People do weird things when they're scared."

"True." Sam's gaze lowered to my chest. He tightened his jaw and directed his attention once more to my face. "I don't trust her."

Safe assumption. "She's under my protection."

"*Our* protection."

Okay. Good. He accepts her…for now. "Thanks."

"Speaking of protection…" Sam cocked his head at me. "Why are there thirty bloodsuckers downstairs, claiming to be *your* protectors?"

Stay cool. I loosened the death-grip around my ribs. "We have an alliance with the vampires until after the fae meeting—"

"After which time, you'll send the packs to take out the Vampire Council," Sam added, tipping his chin at the closed doors. "The blond bloodsucker told us. I didn't trust him with his truth-splitting proficiency. I wanted to hear it from you." Sam's dimple popped with his grin. "The Bloodsucker King's an idiot. That's been our mission for centuries. He's gained nothing."

"Killing is like breathing to monsters." I raised an eyebrow at Sam. "I plan to change that for our pack."

"Good. I'll be right there helping you." Sam's grin deepened. "After all the bloodsuckers are dust."

I dug my toes against the wet floorboards. "Did Nathaniel inform you about the second part of the trade where we expose ourselves to the humans?"

"There won't be a part two." Sam's grin stayed in place. "This *king* is a council member. Didn't he say, after *all* the members are given a final death?"

Relief loosened my chest and I let out my breath. "Oh, shit. A loophole."

Sam cut his attention to the puddle of water at my feet. "No one explained why you all were behind the fountain."

Fidgeting with one of the dress' straps, I crafted a half-truth that would keep us alive. "Nathaniel is not like other vampires."

"Yeah," Sam grumbled. "The fucker teleports. Never seen one do that."

"Well, he has connections with a group of water fae. We visited them to see if they would join us when we meet the Lord of Light."

"Do we have them?"

"The jury's out."

Silence pressed into the room.

"We need to head back," Sam said. "And the bloodsuckers downstairs are required to come with us."

"How?" I forced my stiff limbs to the window. Outside, flurries dotted the deep-purple sky. "They go corpse mode in an hour. We won't be able to move them."

"We have vans. That bloodsucker, Derek, is coordinating the transports."

So that's where he went. My exhale frosted against the window. "Where are we going to put them all?"

"We agreed to have two stay in the empty cabin on your rental property, guarded by the pack. The rest will occupy the town's bowling alley. The building is out of commission due to a fire and it has a cellar."

"They'll need to feed." I turned to face Sam. "They can't eat the citizens."

"There's a blood donation center not far from here. I sent a group of men and one of those bloodsuckers to get access."

"Thanks for jumping on this."

"Of course." Sam moved deeper into the room. "That will hold them for tomorrow but the next day—"

"Nathaniel will be better. He can handle feeding arrangements before we meet with the Lord of Light."

Sam chewed the inside of his cheek. "You're still wanting to go through with it?"

"I am saving my brother."

"You die, we die." Sam cleared the last feet between us. "Have you forgotten that?"

"No." I pinned him with a glare while I dumped confidence into my words. "I'll find a way to keep everyone alive."

"How are you so…"

"Stubborn? Naïve? Reckless—"

"I was going to say fearless."

"Guess I've built up a terror tolerance." When his mug stayed in serious mode, I sighed. "Sam—"

"It sounds damn good hearing you say my name." A war of emotions passed through Sam's eyes. "You'll call pack members by their names, yet you cringe when you use mine. How did I fuck up so bad with you?"

Since his reintroduction, Sam had been nothing but honest and patient. He deserved both in return. I swallowed past the lump in my throat. "You thought I couldn't fight the Vampire Queen and live, so you tried to stop me."

His narrowed focus sharpened to my lips. "So, if I get you shot with silver and steal your wolf, then you'd kiss me?"

I refused to address the blatant Derek jab and kept the convo on Sam. "Let me clarify, you acted for the greater good."

"Didn't you *just* say 'my life for the pack'?"

"Yes."

"Then..." His gaze bore into me. "What's the difference between us but time?"

"For the greater good, you would have sacrificed Andrea *and* yourself." My voice hitched. "I don't send people I love— "

Sam's eyes flashed. "You loved me?"

I froze. Tender memories of my pre-monster life swirled in my mind. How Sam had always watched out for me at the bar. Hell, he'd put up with my teasing. My thoughts then rolled through my baptism into the monster world. While in the estate, trapped by bloodsuckers, Sam had cared for me through my transition. He had taught me how to fight. *Why* to fight. And between those survival lessons, well, undeniable chemistry had burned between us. The antecedent, lack of trust, had destroyed our relationship. Fearing I'd lose my life trying to save him, Sam had tried to have my memories scrubbed. Well, I'd beaten him to it. I'd had his stripped for the same reason. So, in the end, was it love or fear that we shared?

"Please, answer me." Intensity blazed in his eyes. "Did you love me?"

"I—"

"You're not"—Jimmy's voice boomed from the other side of the doors—"going—"

Sam shoved himself against me, shielding us from the doors. The blast of his body heat triggered a sigh from me. He responded by grabbing my hips, then splaying his fingers to curl around my bottom. I flashed my eyes to Sam's, for two reasons. One—my freaking hormones had screamed to life. Two—Derek. He stood at the open doors while at his feet lay an unconscious Jimmy.

"Let me go," I whispered to Sam.

"Listen to her, Alpha." Derek closed the doors on the gathering crowd. "Or I will act on her behalf."

Sam refused, tightening his grip. Since he wasn't listening, I'd hoped for a better outcome with Derek whose undivided attention was on Sam's hand cupping my ass. "Hunter—"

"His queen is ash," Sam growled. "He has no title."

"I hold title." Derek's gaze returned to mine. "Once more."

"You cannot title a—" When Sam registered the panic in my eyes, his face blanked. "How?"

"I was bitten by a vampire *before* the alpha and—"

Derek signaled to the sealed doors. The crowd couldn't see but they were listening.

I slid my hand down to one of Sam's, then rested it over where I'd been skewered by the troll.

"At the Gathering…you…" Sam pressed his palm against my side. His wide eyes locked with mine as he mouthed, *"You're an unturned."*

I nodded.

Sam curled his fingers against my ribs. "And now *he* holds a title."

Like a match struck above a pool of gasoline, the truth fell from my mouth. "As do you."

"What"—Derek's controlled tone splintered—"title does the alpha hold?"

Tears crawled down my cheeks as I answered, "Guardian of My Body."

Fury blazed in the pits of Derek's eyes. "You do not bear his mark."

"Yet," I whispered.

Derek shook his head. "It will not happen."

Sam released me to turn and face Derek. "Without my mark, the packs will not follow her. They will not rescue her brother. That is why she titled me. Not because—" Sam looked at me. "I will never force the mark."

"You're not." I grabbed Sam's arm. "This is my choice."

"No," Sam snapped. "You choose out of necessity only."

"The visual show we are missing," Nathaniel teased inside my skull. *"I'm surprised you told the truth. By the by, there is a* temporary *dodge to the marking."*

"What is it?" I screamed at his mind. *"Please!"*

"I'd never tell you."

Derek stiffened and his eyes flashed vampire-black.

Sam tried to shove me behind his body, but I dodged. "Wait."

"He went full bloodsucker." Sam grabbed for me again.

"Trust me," I gritted.

"He hurts you, he's dust," Sam warned. "Hear me?"

I nodded and we both set our attention back to Derek. As the blackness retreated from Derek's irises, he moved to stand by the bed.

"Alpha, you will give her your mark." Derek kept his focus on me as he unfastened his cufflinks, then set them on the nightstand. "That is all you will be giving her."

A heady shot of relief buzzed through me. Nathaniel had shared the loophole with Derek. Still, the tension vibrating through Derek's frame while he rolled his shoulders free of his jacket hinted that it wasn't a get-out-of-jail-free card.

Sam narrowed his eyes. "Why are you undressing?"

"Alpha." Derek tugged his tie loose. "Take off your coat and shirt."

Sam pinged his attention between me and Derek.

"Please," I said to Sam. "Listen to him."

"We race the dawn," Derek warned, slipping free from his dress shirt.

Sam shrugged out of his jacket, then tugged off his shirt, revealing the torso of a Greek god. Heat screamed through me with a flashback from the last time the three of us had been in a bedroom together.

"My wolf." Derek held out his hand to me. "The angels await you."

Sam grabbed my arm, keeping me at his side. "What part do you have in this, bloodsucker?"

"Maestro and accompaniment," Derek answered. "Now, mind your tongue, we have ears on us."

Nathaniel's compulsion snapped against my flesh. Behind the doors, he murmured orders, "You hear nothing but your alpha and the Wolf Born's...coupling." He lifted his voice to us. "Proceed."

"I need to be marked as well," Sam said.

Derek's eyes locked with mine. "She will."

"I'm..." I rested my hand over Sam's thundering heart. "Sorry—"

"I willingly took your title." Sam grabbed my hand, brushing his lips against my knuckles. "I fucking want this. *You.* I vow to protect you. I will be by your side day and"—he shifted his attention to Derek—"night."

While the two shirtless men stood in silent challenge, I used the moment to slip from Sam's arms. A ball of nerves twisted my insides as I went to stand in front of Derek.

"Alpha," Derek said, "I will take her blood. You will wait. When it is time, lay your mark." Derek cupped my face between his chilled hands. "His bite will hurt. Use the pain. Let your wolf free to mark the alpha."

Trepidation skirted goosebumps across my skin. "How are you...while we're—"

"I will keep myself from killing the alpha." Derek released me, then grabbed his discarded tie off the bed. "Now, face him."

I turned to Sam.

Derek sank his fingers against my scalp while he gathered my hair away from my neck, slipping the makeshift hair tie around the locks. He whispered in my ear, "The wait is over, my wolf."

My heart revved when Derek slipped the strap off my left shoulder. Sam shifted closer, his attention fastened to my silver bullet scar. Unable to move or think, I existed, trapped between Derek's chilled breath and Sam's heated gaze.

Derek clasped my ribs, leading me backward, then lowered me into his lap as he sat on the bed. The dress acted as a restraint, limiting my mobility. The discomfort became an afterthought when Derek pressed his fingers against the pressure points at my jaw, tipping back my head and baring my neck to his lips.

"Are you certain that you want his mark?" Derek tightened the arm around my ribs, molding my spine to his hard chest.

"Yes," I whispered.

Derek released the blood-bond and feral want vibrated through my blood and bones, pulsing through every part of my being. Arching my back, I bucked against Derek. His grip intensified, squeezing the air from my lungs as a distraction from his next move. As his fangs sank into the side of my throat, pleasure tore through me. Each of his pulls dragged desperate whimpers from my lips.

An animalistic growl snapped my attention forward. Sam's muscles rippled with his deep breaths of restraint. His stare bore into mine. Refusing to look away, I groaned into the fear and desire tumbling and swirling together, edging me toward my climax.

Bracing myself, I dug my nails against Derek's thighs. He growled into the pain while his hips rolled against my ass. The movement of his thrusts increased the pressure of his bite, hurling me into orgasm.

Simultaneously, Derek retracted his fangs and Sam crashed against me. Still riding across the bridge of ecstasy, I surrendered to their attention. Derek restrained me while Sam ran his hot tongue over my collarbone, intensifying my orgasm to the point of pain. When he clamped his teeth onto my exposed shoulder, the link blazed through me, and every nerve ending fired in unison.

The pressure of the bite increased. More intimate than fucking, Sam's energy sank into my being. There was no avoiding or escaping his thoughts and feelings crashing into me, consuming me, demanding that I give him mine in return. Each heartbeat that I ignored the call, agony warned of pending unconsciousness.

Derek loosened his hold while he brushed his lips against my ear. "Let the wolf free."

At Derek's command, my wolf rushed to answer Sam's call. Using her strength, I shoved Sam to the floor, straddling him.

"That's it." He shifted his hips, forcing my legs to spread, and his jeans rubbed against my throbbing center. "Mark me."

The wolf took over my vision, latching her attention to Sam's throat. My gums throbbed when my fangs lengthened. As a growl rumbled from my chest, I pitched forward, sinking my teeth into his neck. Blood filled my mouth and I moaned into its sweetness, yet I refused to swallow, terrified that if I did, I'd forever seal myself into the monster world.

Sam gripped my ass, anchoring me against his erection. "Take—"

"Drink," Derek rumbled somewhere from behind.

Clenching my eyes shut, I obeyed them both. The agony of Sam's mark eased with each gulp of his blood. Pleasure returned. Ravenous, I tore into his flesh and the link pulsed through me, rocketing into Sam.

"Fuck," he roared as he arched against me with his release.

Feverish hunger consumed me. Even when Sam's grip loosened, I stayed locked to his throat. Each of his weakening heartbeats pulsed lust through me. I needed more.

Derek tugged me upward. His blood-covered lips crashed against mine. Tongues tasting and exploring. Hands grabbed, squeezed and clawed. Every breath and movement rushed me closer to release.

"Sing for me." Derek groaned, slipping his fingers under the dress. He traced a slow path up my inner thigh, dragging a moan from me when he reached my core. As he sank into me, he captured my desperate cries with his lips. Masterfully, he retreated and filled me, over and over. Each repetition pushed me right to the edge until he growled against my ear, "You are mine."

My release burned through my veins, ripping a scream from my soul. Derek lowered his mouth to my raw throat, piercing me with his fangs and the world slipped into darkness.

Chapter Nineteen

The screech of a water faucet roused me into consciousness. As the bliss-filled brain fog rolled away, my vision sharpened onto the overhead mirror's crime scene reflection. More blood than the tattered dress hid my nudity while my left shoulder throbbed and oozed from Sam's bite. Even though the wound had bled, it didn't add up to the amount covering me. I palpated the unmarred skin of my throat.

"I healed my bites." Derek stood at the open bathroom door. From my vantage point, the predawn sky hooded his face in shadows, yet I'd a clear view of his blood-smeared torso. Worry nibbled at my mind. Something was off. *Shit.* Everything was off.

I grasped the dress' scrap material over my exposed parts and the jostling movements sent my stomach sloshing. The coppery-ting of Sam's blood lingered in my mouth. Face flushing, cheeks watering, I crawled to the edge of the bed and retched.

Lucky for unlucky Sam, he missed the blood spray. Feet away, unconscious and unmoved from where I'd left him on the floor, he breathed. Thankfully. My bite wasn't neat or dainty. Botched-up puncture marks serrated his jugular while a halo of blood framed his head.

"He'll live." Derek walked toward the bed, tilting his head at the bedroom doors. "They listen."

Outside the room, hushed voices muttered about having to drive corpses around town. Ben's voice drifted in and out. When he spoke, the room fell silent. *Good for him, taking control.*

As I shifted to sit upright, a mystery fluid ran down my back, triggering my body to convulse. I dry-heaved until black spots danced through my vision. Rubbing my runny nose with the back of my bloodstained hand, I groaned. If I sniffed any more blood, I'd pass out—again. Derek caught me in mid-stumble off the bed.

"The wolves will race in here with your struggles," he warned, lifting me into his arms.

To keep a visual on Sam, I twisted in Derek's hold. "They have noses and we're all bathing in gore."

"Markings are bloody." Derek grunted as my knee crushed against his ribs.

Void of all emotion, he carried me off to the bathroom. Even with our half-naked bodies pressed together, there were no stolen caresses or soft murmurs. Dread seeped into my shivering bones. "Are you okay?"

"I am well enough," he said.

At his elusive answer, my mind flipped to panic mode. Before I could form words into a question, Derek closed the bathroom door. Stiffly, he lowered me to my feet in front of a clawfoot tub filled to the brim with water. When he went for the dress' zipper, I tensed.

He dropped his hands. "You tremble as if it is the first time I have witnessed your nudity."

"Outside dreamland, the times when you have seen me naked, I was your prisoner or saving your ass." I turned to face him. "I'd prefer for our *real* first time that I'm not covered in blood."

Derek extinguished the desire blazing with his gaze, leaving me to peer at his emotionless vampire mask. The feelings camouflage meant bad news waited behind his next breath. "We have urgent matters to discuss." And with that, he spun on his heels to face the door.

I scurried out of the dress and sidestepped the tub, heading straight to the walk-in shower. Marinating in blood and bubbles didn't sit well with me.

Still facing the door, Derek asked, "The bath does not please you?

"Thanks, but"—the needle-cold water ejected a gasp from me—"this clean-up needs a deep scrub."

"We have at most minutes."

"I'm listening." While I set to freeing the travel-sized soap, the water warmed. My teeth chattered. Head spinning, I shoved my hands against the wall to keep from falling.

"You will lose your stomach again if the water runs too hot." Disgruntled, I turned the tap to lukewarm while Derek continued, "You appear to assume another attribute of the dark gift."

"That would be?"

"Your response to wolf blood is like a..." He pointed at his head to answer. Werewolf blood turned a vampire blood-crazy. One of the many reasons the two races were hell-bent on destroying the other. "If I had not intervened..."

I set my gaze on the pink-tinged water swirling around my toes. "I will not feed—bite a wolf ever again."

"You may need to."

"Why?"

"In defense, or if you need their energy and are unable to call the link." Derek raked his hands through his disheveled hair. "However, I agree, in the near future, avoid their blood. Until someone can teach you to control the blood-rage."

"Someone? You're the only vampire I know who does not—"

"I do." Derek threaded his fingers, cradling the back of his neck. "If not for our bond, I fear your death would be imminent."

"I trust you—"

"Do not." His voice tightened. "Watching you feed...it took every fraction of my being to pull you away from your feast. It plays across my mind, what if I had let you—"

"You didn't."

"No." He released the back of his neck. "Another regret."

Warning sirens blared in my head while his words looped in my mind. Since I'd opened my eyes, Derek had been hiding something from me. We didn't have the time to play emotional dodgeball. "Another regret," I repeated while vulnerability cleaved at my heart. "Do you regret what happened afterward?"

"Yes." With no hesitation or burning tongue, Derek answered in a one-hundred-percent, grade-A truth. "May I turn around?"

"No." I dove under the spray to hide my tears.

"Fine." He lifted his voice. "Then let us discuss the additional pressing matter—"

"Your regret *is* the pressing matter." I snatched one of the towels hanging from the shower wall. Tucking it around me, I left the shower but kept the water running to mute our voices from the crowd a room over. "Is it me? What changed? You said I was—"

"I took what was not mine," Derek said. "You belong with the alpha."

I belong with you, my soul screamed, but anger ruled my mind and won my voice, "I belong with *no one*."

"I'm turning around," Derek said.

Waiting to see the *regret* on his face, I balled my fists. Instead, second by second, the day called Derek to the grave. Fury radiated through his sunken eyes. "Are you not repulsed?"

"No." Stupid tears slid down my throat. "I'm pissed. Hurt."

"And another regret." He dropped his gaze. "Stay by the alpha. He will be safe at your side and you at his. Have him explain the nuisance of the mark. Let the wolves… No, make them believe…that you—"

A sick part of me enjoyed Derek stumbling on his words as he did to my heart, but the human part of me suffered along with him. "Got it." I forced my words past my clenched throat. "I slept with Sam."

Derek's lips twisted into a sneer. "Go to *him*—" His legs gave out.

Damn me, I caught Derek and eased him to the floor, propping his upper body against the door while I crouched to his eye level. Never had I witnessed a vampire go into their corpus state. Pain contorted his deteriorating body while he kept his focus on me.

"I regret my selfish nature," he rasped.

Mute energy scattered between us as the light faded from his eyes. The water spraying against the shower wall drowned out the faint exhale of his last breath. I scooted closer, brushing his hair away from his sunken eyelids. When I swept my fingertips across his cold, wax-like skin, I flinched. "No." Recovering my anger, I shoved my lips against his ear. "I hope you can hear me. You're an ass. I regret…."

I shook my head. I wouldn't drop to his ditch-and-die-level copout. I'd wait till he was good and undead to release all my regrets and frustration on him. *Or not.* A fae might take me out before Derek regained consciousness. Grabbing him by the ankles, I dragged him in front of the shower, then covered his body with towels. The bedroom sported a huge window. I wouldn't *literally* burn him, either.

Scrubbing the tears from my eyes, I forced my lungs to breathe and my heart to beat. Derek had chosen. I wasn't worth his regrets or the challenge he'd so craved. For once, I welcomed the numbness needling through my body.

Movement outside the bathroom signaled Sam was up. One more settling breath and I lacquered the image of my brother to my mind. I would save Drew. I would kick fae ass. With my mission firmly in place, I slipped through the door, refusing a backward glance.

Inside the bedroom, Sam paced in front of the closed curtains. When I shut the bathroom door, he paused, and like a perfect gentleman, he averted his attention from my towel-clad body.

"How are you?" I asked.

"Good." Sam winced.

"You don't sound it." *Or look it.*

"You heal faster than me." When he swept his fingers across my mangled bite, the link pulsed through my shoulder.

"Whoa."

He dropped his hand. "Sorry."

"Wait." I tentatively brought my fingers to Sam's mark. The link stirred and the wolf flexed through my subconscious, readying for another romp with Sam. Dropping my hand, I shoved back the wolf.

"Yeah, so, the mark…" Sam cleared his throat and a blush burned across his cheeks. "Try not to touch it unless you want—"

"Got it." I eyed my clothes on the nightstand.

"Your sweater, socks and pants are blood-free," Sam said. "The bra and panties aren't. I sent someone for my change of clothes and food for you."

"I'm not hungry." Willing Sam not to look at the puddle of my blood vomit, I flicked my gaze to the bed. "What are we going to do about the clean-up?"

"The bloodsuckers compelled the humans to stay away from this suite and the foyer to the High Limit Room." Sam stretched. "Until our connections can take care of the damages."

"Connections." I made air quotes around the word. "Like the mob?"

He chuckled. "Of the Otherworldly Creature sort."

"Great, another group to worry about. I swear if I find a horse head in my bed—"

In the main room, someone barked a laugh. Sam cut his gaze and voice at the doors. "My clothes should be here any minute." That got the pitter and stomping of feet moving.

I walked over to my salvageable garments. "Do you want to take a shower?"

Sam glanced at his blood-covered chest. "I worried it was yours."

"Sorry." I gestured at the hack job of my mark. "It's like a rabid raccoon—"

"It is perfect." The command in his voice stirred the wolf below my flesh. Sam moved to stand feet away from me. He drew his brows tight together. "Don't think for a minute I regret—"

"You know what? I *am* hungry." I turned away. "I'm gonna dress and see what scraps Andrea and Max left behind."

"What is it?" Sam asked.

I shook my head.

"What is wrong?" Concern filled his voice, "Did I do something—"

"I'm just tired." I forced a smile over my shoulder. "Careful, a dead guy is blocking the shower."

"Thanks for the tip." Sam tilted his head. Smart man—he didn't pry when I referred to Derek as a dead guy. "I'll be quick."

I was mid-slipping my sweater over my head when the bathroom door opened. At least I was facing the window. Goosebumps rose along my exposed skin. Sam's breath hitched and a whole new type of tension rolled into the room.

A knock at the bedroom door caught both our attention.

Sam, wearing a towel tucked around his hips, cracked the door and grabbed clothes from Max's hand. I went to make my exit but remembered I had to act like seeing Sam in the buff was the new norm. I took up pacing by the window.

"We need to head back to the property," Sam said.

I turned around and my breath caught. The towel parted up to Sam's hip, giving a great view of his muscled thigh. He cleared his throat and my gaze shot to his face. A grin popped his dimple to life.

"Yep." I nodded. "When can we leave?"

"As soon as you're ready."

"I am."

His grin widened as his fingers landed on the tucked fold of the towel below his navel. I averted my eyes as it floated to the floor. When the clinking sound of a belt hit my ear, I raised my head.

"Our coats are in the main room." Sam tossed on his shirt. "One of the men will come in for the hunter. They'll bag him up—"

"They will treat his body with respect." My words came out aggressive. "Is that understood?"

"As you command." With a subtle bow, Sam lowered his gaze.

"Good." I waved at him. "You don't need to—"

"I'll acknowledge when I have upset you." Sam ended his eye-bow. "Ready?"

While I came up to his side, a silent war spun through my mind. It had been so long since I had slept with someone, I'd completely forgotten my actions afterward. *Wait.* I'd ditched them. *Oh no.* Karma showed me the ropes today.

As if reading my mind, Sam turned to me. "Just be you." He went to touch my hand but hesitated.

I threaded my fingers with his. "The bet is off."

"Okay." His scent and heartbeat intensified. "Now, just breathe. Let me lead you through this."

"What do you mean?"

The door opened and every werewolf in the room dropped to their knees, placing their fists on the floor.

Sam led us to the center of the room. Ben sat on the sofa, pausing in mid-bite with a bagel. The Keeper, next to him, flipped through channels while munching on a piece of pizza.

Sam dipped his lips to my ear. "When you are ready, tell them to rise."

"You may rise," I said.

The men rose and proceeded to form a line. *Nine.* Nine werewolves stood in front of us.

Ben lowered the bagel to the paper bag rattling on his lap.

"Not us humans." The Keeper slapped a hand on Ben's shoulder. "Keep eating." She shifted her attention between a cartoon and the live monster documentary before her.

Sam spoke again to my ear. "When I permit them, they will each confirm our marks. Ready?"

As I nodded, my heart lodged in my throat.

"Proceed," Sam said to the men.

One by one, the pack took turns eyeballing our marks. After each inspection, Sam nodded to the member while sweat dampened our clasped hands. Maybe it was mine or both of ours. Finally, the last man in line, Max, came up to us. My heart stopped. Though our interactions had been sparse, he knew me the best. Would Max call us out? He tipped his head and moved to stand with the group of men.

Sam lowered his lips again to my ear. "May I address our pack?"

"Yep." I cleared my throat. "Yes."

"We will head back to the property," Sam said. "Jimmy, you will lead. Take three men with you. The next van leaves in five minutes. The last van leaves ten minutes after the first. Keep your phones on."

Jimmy slung a bulky garment bag over his shoulder. "I got the one corpse."

I cringed. Nathaniel wasn't like the other vampires. He was undead and listening. *Good.* I trusted Jimmy-sharpshooter the least. If Jimmy tried anything, Nathaniel would handle it in his own special way.

As Ben approached, he kept his attention on the Keeper chatting up Max. "Here," he whispered, slipping the talisman into my free hand. I raised an eyebrow. Ben had hidden the talisman from the Keeper. When Ben made his way back to the Keeper, I turned to face Sam, who was glaring at Ben.

"He's my steward." I squeezed Sam's hand. "Not a threat."

"We have a lot to talk about on the drive over." Sam's focus shifted to the men emerging from the bedroom, carrying Derek's body concealed in a garment bag. "A whole fucking lot."

Chapter Twenty

Thanks to Sam's strategic planning, the procession to the vans went off without a hitch. Once everyone had filtered into their assigned vehicles, Sam took my hand and led me through the parking garage. When the purr of an engine drew closer, he shifted our course, slipping us between rows of cars until a souped-up SUV stopped in front of us. "This is ours." Sam opened the back door for me.

The driver looked over his shoulder, grinning.

"You were in the second van," I said to Max.

"With other packs in the area, spies, we proceed with caution," Sam answered, sliding in beside me and closing the door. "Get it moving, Delta."

Nodding, Max tapped the gas.

Sam draped his arm around me. His body heat was welcome, but the tension vibrating his biceps—not so much. Still, not even out of the parking garage, the combination of a smooth ride and the whoosh of heat blasting through the air vents lulled me to the cusp of sleep.

"I hate to keep you awake," Sam said, "but we should talk."

"Yeah." I yawned. "We do."

"Some of this stuff is going to be…" Sam kept his eyes on Max, who pretended he wasn't listening to our conversation.

"Unsettling?" I asked.

Sam hugged me tighter against his side, maybe to keep me from jumping out of the car with the news he was about to serve. He drummed his fingers against my upper arm while his free hand caged his knee. "Depends."

Dread slapped me wide awake. Not sure how much more *awful* I could take today, I steeled my spine. "Lay it on me."

"Our marks…" Sam stilled his finger percussion against my arm. "Think of them as an energetic GPS."

"Oh." *Great.* I already suffered a tether with Derek… Now I had one with Sam. "How far is the range?"

"As far as the mind can reach." Sam flicked his attention to the rearview mirror at Max's reflection. "There's more. Our…"

"Relationship?" I prompted.

"Think of it as a marriage to a bodyguard."

I inhaled in a whistle which had Sam shifting against the seat. When his focus was locked and loaded on me, I explained, "Pre-werewolf life, you used to be my bouncer at the bar."

"How'd I do?"

"You shaved your head. I thought it was to hide a receding hairline from the stress."

Max smirked, then schooled his face.

"That good, huh?" Sam grumbled at Max's reflection before cutting his attention back to me. "In all seriousness, anyone within feet of you stresses my wolf."

"I understand." I looked out at the snow flurry sky. "No fist bumps when you are around."

"I will *always* be around." Sam paused, letting that truth sink into my bones. "You will never leave my sight. On the rare occasion I'm not here, the beta will take my place."

"Anything else?"

"During the full moon, our wolves take over."

"Yep." I rolled my eyes back to Sam. "I know that."

He arched his eyebrows. "We are now mates. The moon calls us to—"

"Oh." I swallowed. "Like…that. Okay. So. We have a couple of weeks before—"

As a silent warning, Sam cut his focus to Max.

Stuffing the news that I'd have an uncontrollable desire to rail Sam into my mental to-do list of finding loopholes, I asked, "Can we switch topics?"

"Sure."

"My brother."

Sam tensed.

I angled my body to look Sam dead in the eyes. "The naiads—"

"For fuck's sake." Sam dragged his hand down his face. "*That's* the group of water fae you visited?"

"They confirmed that he's being held captive in the Light realm."

"Naiads are murderous cons." Sam removed his arm around me.

I stretched the seatbelt to its limit, practically sitting on Sam's lap. "I need *you* to trust *me*."

"I do." Sam's heartbeat said otherwise.

"Look." I forced calm into my tone. "Without *your* trust, the wolves won't follow me willingly."

"*You* are the leader of our race."

"By title only. Our race is patriarchy at its finest." Holding his gaze with mine, I pressed my hands against his chest. "I need you."

"You have me." Tenderness shone through Sam's eyes. "But—"

"Just..." I chewed my lip. I needed a plan. *Shit.* "Hear me out."

"I am." Sam brushed a lock of my hair away from my shoulder. Even through my puffy jacket, when his fingers swept over his mark, the link stirred.

Relief zapped through me. "What if you had *physical* proof that my brother is alive?"

Sam drew his brows together. "How?"

"I share the link with every werewolf. Correct?"

He nodded.

"Since he's my brother, Drew has dormant werewolf blood in his veins." I pressed my palms tighter against Sam's chest. "What if I use the link and travel to him through my dreams?"

The SUV cranked to the side of the road.

"Careful," Sam barked at Max, then flashed the same tone at me. "You're not. If the fae found you—"

"*Us.*" I should have stopped twisting Sam's emotions. But Drew's life hung by the thread of false hope I'd spun for Sam. I glanced at my shoulder. "The mark works like a GPS. Could you follow me into my dreams?"

"Yes." Worry dragged the corners of his mouth into a frown. "These are fae we are dealing with. If we're caught in our dreams, I'm not sure what will happen. We'll have no protection."

"We do." I dug into my pocket, then held up the talisman. "This protects against magic attacks."

"Where did you get that?"

"The witness." When I dropped the chain over my head, the feather charm heated against my flesh, sending a hum of magic along my spine. "Please?"

"You had to say that." Sam's expression shifted to one he wore when addressing the pack—Alpha mode. "We go in. Get confirmation. Then leave. Understood?"

"Yes." I curled up against him, threading my fingers with his. "Drew is my brother's name."

Sam rested his cheek against the crown of my head. "I only need yours."

My heart fluttered, yet my soul cried. No matter Derek's fresh rejection, my stupid spirit screamed out for his.

"Delta," Sam said. "Do not wake us."

Max shot his attention to the rearview mirror. "Can this wait until we are with the pack?"

"No," I answered. "They would try to stop us."

The SUV slowed.

"You have fifteen minutes at most," Max said.

Closing my eyes, in my mind, I repeated my brother's name.

* * * *

Dream travel. Not a fan. However, up until now, I'd only attempted it with a psycho werewolf that had wanted me dead. Slowly, the dreamscape formed. I stood, alone, in the center of an endless white corridor. Above, sunlight flickered off the water-suspended ceiling. If the Lord of Light knew of my whereabouts, all he had to do was send the roof crashing down, drowning me. Pressing my back against the wall, I closed my eyes and focused on the tugging sensation within my gut, beckoning me down the hallway.

With the dream cord attached to my brother, I turned my attention to Sam's mark. Energy buzzed through me while something large brushed against my hip. Snapping open my eyes, I stifled my yipe. Sam stood there in his wolf form. Maybe he thought he was more menacing as a beast. *He'd be correct.*

As I took the lead, he took up the rear, like a blast from our bar days. When dealing with drunks and bosses, we worked great as a team. I had started the shit and Sam'd had my back. *Some things never change.*

When the tugging sensation intensified to shooting pain, I clenched my gut, eyeing the wall to my left. With my free hand, I ran my fingers along the smooth stone, searching for a trap door. *Nada.*

Sam tilted his head and I nodded. Drew was on the other side. I kicked my frustration to the water ceiling, triggering the memories of me blowing up the statues. Wiggling my fingers, I squinted at the wall. *Okay, McKay,* I muttered inside my head to the troll-parasite blood. *Let's see how you handle walls.*

Magic heated my fingertips and I pressed the glowing digits against the stone. On contact, the wall dissolved, revealing an entrance to a room cloaked in complete darkness. While the scent of blood and sweat poured into the hallway, a faint heartbeat hit my eardrums. I cut my eyes to Sam. With his ears flat to his head and fur raised, he crouched in preparation for any incoming threats.

As we stepped through the threshold, the talisman heated against my neck, casting a blood-red glow to illuminate the cell. I stopped dead in my tracks while my brain scrambled to comprehend. Along the back wall, pinned there for our viewing, was the unconscious husk of my once vibrant brother.

Thick silver chains stretched his emaciated arms overhead while haggard breaths jerked his skeletal chest. Deep lacerations covered his torso in hellish markings down to the waistband of the grungy jeans hanging from his protruding hip bones.

Sam's deep growl roused me from my stupor.

Shaking my head, I abandoned our agreement for the in-and-out mission and raced to my brother. Blood caked his eyelashes and plastered his hair against his gaunt cheeks. Gently, I cupped his cold face in my hands. "Drew?" The echoes of his name bouncing around the cell triggered his swollen eyelids to crack open. It'd been almost four years since I'd peered into those soft green orbs.

"Tess?" Drew grimaced while he scrambled to get his feet underneath him. "You're here?"

"Kinda," I whispered.

Tears glazed his eyes. "You *are*…alive—"

"Easy. I got you." Blood rolled down my hands against his face. Narrowing my eyes, I peeled back his hair. Terror and rage swelled within me. Someone had hacked off my brother's earlobes. "I'm alive and so are *you*."

"I'm…" He dropped his gaze to my chin. "He'll know. You gotta leave."

"Not without you." When I pulled at the silver eyehook securing the chains, my skin sizzled. Groaning into the pain, I yanked harder.

"He said you're a—"

"Bitch? Yep. Werewolf? Also yes. Still your sister?" To mask the sob clenching my voice, I dropped to a whisper. "Absolutely."

"You're more." Drew's gaze locked with mine. "*Rìbhinn.*"

Sam bit at the back of my coat, dragging me backward.

I twisted free but Drew raised a knee, blocking me from grabbing the eyehook again.

"Get her out of here," he ordered Sam.

"No." I dodged Drew's knee and tossed my arms around his neck. The talisman blazed to life, burning against my chest while its glow intensified, illuminating the geometric markings carved into my brother's abdomen.

Drew curled away from me. "Go."

"I'm going to save—"

"No." Drew shot his attention at Sam. "Don't let her."

"Yes," I snapped, punctuating every word, "I. Will. Save. You."

Drew gasped for breath as his tear-filled eyes met mine. "You're still stub…born—"

I shoved a smile in front of my tears. Drew needed his big sister. He needed hope.

"Go. He comes." Drew pressed his forehead against mine. "Man…ann…." The talisman's glow deepened at my brother's utterances. "Man…annnn. Man…ann. Remember. Manan—"

As the screech of seagulls ricocheted through the cell, Sam raced forward, biting my thigh.

* * * *

I surged awake. In the backseat of the SUV, lying across Sam's lap, I clamored free of his body. Sam jolted into alertness. He trapped me in a bear hug with a vice-like grip. The link stirred between us, and calm rushed through my limbs, stealing my anger.

"No!" I kicked the passenger headrest through the windshield. "You took me away—"

"Stop." Sam growled against my ear. "There was nothing you could have done."

"You don't know that."

"How the fuck would you save him from your dream?" Sam loosened his hold to turn me so I straddled his hips, forcing me to look him in the face. "You're going to poof him away with that fae shit you used back there?"

I flexed my arms in his unmovable grip. Livid to the tenth degree, I jammed my bony knees against his thighs. My struggles revved up Sam's wolf. The beast set his eyes aglow. "Well," I gritted, "now we won't know. Right? Because you intervened."

"Yeah." A more animalistic than human voice rumbled from his chest. "You're my mate."

"I'm no—"

His wolf was so close to the surface. The beast peered at me through Sam's eyes, stirring my wolf. Too pissed, caught off guard, my control slipped, and my wolf flooded my system with lust. I bit my bottom lip, focusing on the pain versus the heat pooling in my belly.

"You are." A mix of relief and fear crossed Sam's face. "You know it. Feel it."

I wouldn't admit how my insides twisted. How the challenge in his voice set my heart to rattling against my ribs. There wasn't a need. His big bad wolf could hear and smell me. Tears burned down my cheeks.

"Christ…" Sam's voice softened. "I'm—"

"Just…" Teardrops splatted onto my thigh as I forced my blurry gaze to the regret filling his eyes. "Let me go."

"I can't." A swallow lodged in his throat while his muscles around and under me shook. "Not in the way you want."

Damn him. Sam had a knack for spotlighting big-picture predicaments. If we succeeded in rescuing my brother, Sam and I were still mated. There was no way to cut ties and run.

"I know." My words came out in a tight whisper. "Until death."

Sam loosened his hold and I scrambled out of the SUV.

Needle-like flurries hit my tear-stained face and my thigh spasmed from Sam's dream bite. Overshadowing the two discomforts was the frigid air scraping against my hands and my chest pulsing from the silver and talisman burns. Pain attacked me from body to soul. Feet away, werewolves, in human and wolf form, surrounded the vehicle. Clenching my jaw, I marched toward the werewolf barricade.

Sam called out, "Let her through."

Two men stepped to the side, allowing me to slip past. Lucky them, because I so wanted to punch something. On rage autopilot, I headed for the cabin. Corbus stood on the porch. Emotionless, he watched me unfold. One more misstep and he'd deem me a wreck. Unfit. Perhaps he'd kill me right on the spot.

Shifting my course, I headed down the driveway toward the woods. There was no need for a glance behind to confirm Sam was following. His mark heated, sending a current of energy along my spine. Not that I'd expect anything less than a ridiculous amount of overprotection—a cluster of wolves surrounded us, thwarting any opportunity for bolting.

"Mate." Sam spoke in a tone reserved for warning rather than a question. "Where are we going?"

I gritted my teeth. It would be expected of me to answer him. "A stroll."

"It's not safe," Sam said.

Knowing Sam was right ticked me off more. I rolled my eyes. "Is anything?"

"The alphas have not confirmed our marks." Sam picked up his pace, closing the distance between us. "If you get abducted by another pack or worse, killed, who will save your brother?"

"No one." My gaze shifted to the sun fighting to pierce through a storm cloud. In the Light realm, what had seemed like a fleeting minute with my brother had stolen hours from us.

"Look." Sam narrowed his eyes at me. "I understand you're pissed."

"Yep." I jabbed a finger at him. "So back off."

"Besides me leaving, which I won't." He drew his brows deeper together. "I don't know how to un-piss you off."

"You can't." I folded my arms around myself. "Just don't make it worse."

"I'll try, but I can't promise."

Inhaling, I drew in Sam's scent. Not a hint of the trademark aroma of fear. Tilting my head, I listened. His heart beat strong and steady. When I detected no deceit, I hugged myself tighter. "That's the most honest thing someone has said to me in days."

"I'll make it my mission to bring honesty to our…" —he paused—"team."

"Team? This isn't football." Anger seeped into my voice, "If it was, then you just blocked your teammate from stealing the ball, my brother, from the opponent, the fae."

"Fine. Shit analogy. Here's some more truth." Sam leaned forward. "What your brother said about being more? He's right. You are a *rìbhinn*. A queen. And when a ruler lets their emotions control their actions, their kingdom falls. People die. There. Is that better?"

"No," I muttered, "not at all. I'm—"

"The Wolf Born, ruler over all werewolves," Sam said. "That makes you the queen."

Grounding myself firmly in my stance, I dug my nails against my ribs. "Well, this *queen* isn't going to sit on a damn throne while people dictate her life."

"No. But I sure as hell won't let you fight alone." Before I could counter, Sam continued, "You said so yourself, till death."

Too tired of pretending to be a badass, the desire to escape won and I turned away from Sam. Feet away, a black wolf stared daggers at me.

Snow crunched underneath Sam's boots as he stepped close enough for his body heat to permeate through my jacket. His tight exhale hit my earlobe. "We will rescue your brother. Together. We will face this fae lord. Together."

Frost nipped at my toes while Sam waited for me to say something. The black wolf stayed, glaring at me. Most likely, it wanted me to run so it could bite me. I sighed a puff of frozen breath. "All right." I turned to face Sam, coming nose to his chest. I tilted my chin to look him in the eyes. "Since I'm queen, I'm in charge. Got it?"

Sam's dimple popped with his deep grin. "You're something."

"The term you used for me, nightly, was 'a pain in my ass'."

"Yeah." Giving me a mock inspection, Sam rubbed his chin. "I can see that. What else did I say about you?"

"Umm…" Heat crept up my neck. "Things."

"Like?" His voice dipped, and my insides tightened. "Did I tell you?"

"Tell me what?"

"How I felt about you?"

My attention locked on Sam's lips while goosebumps marched to attention in remembrance of his breath caressing utterances of how he *felt* about me across my skin. "Nice." My voice came out in a squeak. "I was nice."

"Nice." Sam dipped his mouth to my ear. The stubble on his jaw brushed against my windburn cheek as he spoke, "I might have lost my memory. However, I'm confident *nice* isn't a word I used for you."

"Well." I cleared my throat. "Surprise, you did."

"I call bullshit." Slowly he pulled away, revealing a wicked grin. "I'm glad you have some pleasant memories of me."

A dull ache pulsed at the corners of my mouth. My eyes widened. A real smile stretched across my lips. As discreetly as possible, I forced my facial muscles to relax.

At the edge of the woods, two wolves with full-on snout grins sat underneath a pine tree. Glad they were enjoying themselves at my expense, I settled my attention back on Sam.

"So, conversation rewind." I released my aching arms from their death-grip against my ribs. "I'm in charge. You follow me. Got it?"

That sexy grin on his face widened. "Loud and clear."

"Good." I spun in the direction of my cabin. "First order, I need coffee."

Chapter Twenty-One

A few minutes more in the great and frigid outdoors convinced me that I was ready to face Corbus and the gaggle of alphas. When we approached the cabin, my gut screamed at me to turn and stall.

An unwanted distraction rounded the porch. Nolan. With a scowl plastered on his face, he trudged through the snow toward us. Bitterness nibbled at me. The last words I'd overheard from the beta were the "vampire's whore" comment. Snow clung to his shoulders and his movements were stiff from the battering wind and snow.

"The beta needs to go indoors," I said to Sam.

"Until you're inside, he won't."

"He hates me."

"No. If he did, he'd have shifted into his wolf form." Amusement spread to Sam's guarded smile. "Then he'd not have to talk to his *queen*."

"You had to use that word," I muttered.

"Yes." Sam's voice dipped. "It's adorable the way you blush."

"Glad to entertain you." The dull ache at the corners of my mouth returned.

"Careful." His eyes lit. "A real smile on those lips—"

"Alpha," Nolan said.

"Beta," Sam responded.

I snapped my attention away from Sam's grin to Nolan. Ice clung to his eyebrows and eyelashes. However, there was a raging inferno blazing in his eyes. He pressed his fist to his heart. Nolan's focus tracked to Sam's neck where the edges of my mark peeked from the collar of his jacket. Relief washed over Nolan's face, which he hid with a bow.

"Wolf Born." The emotion he guarded behind his ebony hair curtain spilled into his voice. "Preparations are underway for the alphas' arrival."

Sam brushed his fingers against mine and I grabbed hold. Old fears died hard. Three months ago, these same alphas had tried to imprison me.

Nolan led the way to the cabin. Once at the door, he tapped out a series of knocks.

Ben swung open the door and I slipped inside before he peppered me with questions. While I was gone, the kitchen had been restored. Shiny nails secured the floorboards and a fresh dirt circle surrounded the table.

"The hunter is…" Ben flicked his eyes to the floor underneath the table. Anger prickled up my spine. Ben studied my forced-neutral expression far too long before continuing. "Nathaniel is in the third cabin. The two on loan from the Vampire King are in the witness' cabin. Andrea is—"

"Aaaaaand I!" Her botched attempt at holding the note of a pop ballad echoed down the hallway.

Ben cringed. "She's been in the shower for an hour."

"Singing the whole damn time," Nolan gritted under his breath as he moved into the kitchen.

Sam closed the cabin door. "Are you sure she's human?"

"Yep." My voice hitched.

"Are you completely sure?" Sam quirked an eyebrow. "Because she sounds more like a dying cat."

So close he was to the truth. If the sticky-sweet fear rose off of Ben any more, we were in trouble. Or dead. I cleared my throat and redirected everyone's attention away from the scream-singing fae. "Where is the witness?" I asked Ben.

"He went for a hike," Ben said. He turned away from us to busy himself at the counter. "He'll be back before the ceremony."

While Ben attended to the lineup of coffee mugs and condiments, I shifted my attention to Sam. "What ceremony?"

A spoon clattered against the counter. Ben sucked in a breath while he composed himself, scooping up the utensil.

Nolan cut his eyes at his alpha.

Heat crept up Sam's thick neck. "The alphas need to validate our marks."

No one elaborated.

Sweat gathered at the small of my back. Instead of tossing off my coat, I gripped the damp sleeve openings like a security blanket. "Okay. So the alphas will take turns ogling our marks. Like the pack did at the casino?"

"Yes and no." Sam stared into my eyes, keeping me locked in place. "It's like a wedding."

Ben hid a gasp behind a fake cough.

"Can we talk in private?" Sam asked me.

All the wind had escaped my lungs, so I jerked a nod, then pivoted toward my bedroom. The short trip embellished with the Keeper's background vocals gave me zero chance to chill out. Once inside my room, I moved to the furthest spot away from the door—my bed. *Oh nope.* I rerouted to hang out by my dresser.

Sam closed the door. "Fuck. I'm sorry. I wanted to tell you."

I rested my hip against the dresser. "When is this...ceremony?"

"Sunset. It will be held at the hunting campgrounds down the street."

"Shit." I glanced at my shaking hands. "Humans are there."

"They will be cleared out."

"After the alphas validate our marks, then they will follow your orders?"

The floorboards creaked as Sam moved closer toward me. "*Your* orders."

I nodded at my feet.

"Hey." Sam waited until I looked at him. "You lead. I follow."

"I just want to save my brother."

"We will." He shifted forward, bringing our bodies into kissing range. My mind scrambled. Nerves frayed. The wolf in me wanted me to plant my lips on his. Hell. The human part in me wanted it, too. But... My soul pulled me in the opposite direction toward the floorboards underneath my kitchen table. As if Sam had read my thoughts, he reached out for my hand. The brisk contact of his thumb brushing against my wrist caused his mark to heat. Ripples of energy shivered down my body, pooling low in my belly. "Please. Just give me a chance to prove to you—"

I pressed my free hand to Sam's chest, lowering my focus to his heart slamming against my palm. "We save Drew and then we can figure out..."

"Us," Sam answered.

My mind fixated on Derek's rejection. *You belong to the alpha.* I forced my concentration back on Sam. "Yes."

"Good." Sam's gaze lowered to my mouth and the room jacked up a few hundred degrees. Although he stayed rooted in place, his muscles jumped underneath my hand, eyes darkened to mine. A true apex predator waiting for their prey to succumb. Well, he'd have to wait. A rhythmic tapping hit the bedroom window.

I looked around Sam at the crow perched on the window ledge. When its beady eyes locked with mine, the talisman heated against my skin. Corbus had handed me an identical feather to those of the crow peering at me. "Enjoyed your hike?" I muttered to the bird.

"Tell me that's not the witness," Sam gritted.

"Sorry, but yep." I tugged the glowing talisman from underneath my coat.

Sam's eyes widened. "Why's he in bird form?"

"I don't know." I shrugged. "And we can't ask him."

"This fucking day." Sam growled.

"Hey, look at the bright side." I tucked the talisman underneath my sweater. "It could be Andrea out there serenading us."

"God damn." Sam let his words out in a burst of breath. "You're fucking perfect."

The ghost of my girly-self rose from the grave. I bit my lip to keep my nervous giggle in check. "Hardly."

"For me." Sam locked his glowing eyes with mine. "Now let's figure out what the bird wants."

Thankfully, the dresser still supported my ass because Sam spun the conversation like a carnival ride. As I gathered my composure, he forced open the window. Shards of ice skidded across the floor while snow and wind rushed inside, pelting me in the face. It took the crow a few attempts to perch on the windowsill. Once it landed, the bird disposed of a tuft of gray fur on the ledge.

Keeping his focus locked on the crow, Sam pinched the fur between his fingers and lifted it to his nose. Anger blazed in his eyes, then he held the fluff out to me.

Mint tickled my nose with my inhale. "I haven't smelled this pack member."

"Not pack. Got ourselves a spy," Sam said. "The fucker could have heard anything. If the alphas learn about the vampire alliance—"

The crow tilted its head toward the woods, then flew off, landing in a tree on the outskirts of the forest. When the bird cawed, the talisman heated against my flesh.

"He'll lead me to the spy," I said, tugging off my coat.

"Or he could turn human and just fucking tell us." Sam glared at the bird.

"There's a reason he isn't." I touched Sam's arm to gain his attention back. "And there is a reason why he wants me to follow him."

"That worries me more." A war of emotions played across the crease between Sam's brows. "I don't trust him."

"You trust the alphas?" I asked, slipping free of my boots and socks.

"Hell no."

"I trust Corbus." I drifted my fingers to the talisman. "Yes, he may kill me, but I have this weird gut instinct screaming at me that he wants to help."

"Someone will see you." Sam shifted in front of the window. "Your fur sticks out like blood against the snow."

He had a point. Damn it.

"I'll be careful," I said.

"The pack will feel your Change."

"Distract them with your link." I unfastened my jeans. "I'll be back before—"

"I'll go with you."

"No. You need to keep an eye out in case they send more spies." I brushed my hair away from my shoulder, revealing Sam's mark. "You'll know where I am."

"Yes. And I'll know… I'll feel"—his voice tumbled into a growl—"if you're in trouble. Scared."

"So, you can use the mark to tap into my emotions. Great." I tucked an annoying lock of hair behind my ear. "You left that part off in the car."

"Wasn't at the top of my list when you grabbed my hand and laid your head on my shoulder." He shook his head. "It took everything in me not to drag you into my lap. There. Now you know that too."

Taking a deep breath, I shoved my stupid heart back into my rib cage. Transplanting Drew's battered face into the center of my thoughts, I stared into Sam's tender eyes, which pleaded with me to stay.

"You'll know my feelings and location." I swallowed, forcing my voice not to shake. "Time to walk the talk, Sam. You never let me take care of myself. Always tried to protect me from…me. Let me do this."

Without warning, Sam leaned into me. I braced against the counter, readying for his lips to descend onto mine. As he dipped his head, my heart jumped into my throat. When he avoided my mouth, relief and surprise buzzed through my mind. Feather-light, he pressed his lips against my temple. "Be safe."

I brushed my nose against the crook of his neck and it took everything within me not to deepen my inhale. "Same."

Abruptly, he turned to the window. "On my count of three."

I tore off my sweater.

"One."

I struggled out of the jeans.

"Two."

I dropped to my hands and knees.

"Three."

As Sam sent the link out to the pack, I called the Change. Once the energy ebbed, he moved away from the open window. With not much room for a running start, I crouched and launched through the window. Landing in a roll, I scrambled to my feet, then raced to the woods.

The crow sailed over my head, sweeping and dodging through the barren forest canopy while I struggled to keep pace. I was confident that, if I lost track of the bird, I knew where he was leading me. The hunting campground. At least twenty humans resided there. Trepidation raised the fur on the nape of my neck as memories clawed through the surface of my subconscious, forcing me to replay the image of a body torn apart by werewolves. Tucking my head, I bound through the snow, dragging in the frigid air, willing myself not to hit on the scent of human blood.

A mile from the campground, a blend of werewolf scents and campfire smoke flooded my snout. No hint of blood. *Yet.* My wolf hummed through me, demanding control. She wanted the spy's blood and bone between our fangs.

The crow flew past me, landing yards away on a boulder. In what I imagined was a proceed with caution signal, the bird hopped around and flapped its wings. When the grumblings of a man filtered through the still landscape, I paused in my approach. To test the wind, I raised my head, letting the air hit my wet snout. If the breeze behaved, keeping me downwind, the werewolves would have a harder time catching my scent. Dropping to a crouch, I closed the distance to peek around the massive rock.

In an instant, my wolf stole my vision, surveying the landscape for herself before turning control back to me. The competition excited her and the fur at my haunches rose. No sight or scent of a human within the campground. Nope. Just freaking ground zero for the werewolf packs.

Off to the right, a man rested his back against a tree. Cursing under his breath, he shoved his chin toward his chest. A counterpart with a crossbow draped across his back heaved through the snow toward the man.

"Any word?" Crossbow asked.

The man against the tree lifted his tucked head. Ice and snow hung from his beard and mustache. "Does it look like it?"

Crossbow grunted. "So Lyncourt took the bait?"

Hearing Sam's last name paired with the word 'bait' triggered my adrenaline.

"If he didn't want the ceremony, Lyncourt would've told our alpha to fuck off," Beard Man said. "Lyncourt's not a fool."

"He's a damn idiot for meeting with the alphas."

"Unless it's true." Beard Man cut his glare to Crossbow. "That she's allied with the bloodsuckers."

Shit. They know.

Crossbow spit into the snow. "Serves us right that our queen is a fang banger."

"Don't disrespect." Beard Man pointed a finger toward the campgrounds. "For hundreds of years, we couldn't hold a decent conversation between packs. Within months, twice, she joined the alphas."

"For another suicide mission. Rescuing her brother from the fae."

I dug my claws against the frozen earth. *Who told them about Drew?*

"When are we not killing or dying?" Beard Man kicked the snow from his boot against the tree. "Besides, if she has the bloodsuckers, Lyncourt will convince her to send them to the frontline. The way I see it, let the fae obliterate the fang heads."

"What if she succeeds in taking out this fairy fuck? Think about it." Crossbow jabbed a gloved hand up, ticking off his self-imposed worries on each finger. "She'll control the werewolves, ally the vampires and then what? The fae will follow her too?"

"That's fucked-up," Beard Man answered for us all. "Lyncourt better hold up his end of the deal."

Sam had mentioned nothing about a deal. An anger-infused worry spread through my mind, which I ignored to follow along with the conversation.

"A lot of good that will do," Crossbow said. "The scout felt magic in every one of those cabins. What if there are more of those winged fuckers already ponying up to her?"

"Lyncourt controls the Wolf Born."

"You put too much faith in that bastard. His beta says Lyncourt is infatuated with her. He told *his* pack to follow *her* orders." A phone buzzed inside Crossbow's coat. "About time."

I cut a glance to the crow which had its beady eyes locked on me.

"Here," Crossbow said into the phone.

An old geezer's voice responded, "A call came in that a wolf is heading toward the grounds."

"Our scout came back." Crossbow set his attention to Beard Man. "We are all counted for."

"I know." The geezer expelled an annoyed breath. "Be on the lookout for one of Lyncourt's wolves."

"Shit," Beard Man muttered. His eyes flickered as he sent out his link. Energy buzzed around me before returning to the man. He growled at Crossbow, "The wolf is here."

Crossbow tossed his phone to Beard Man, then hauled his weapon over his shoulder, securing an arrow ready to kill.

Making it my mission to not get caught or shot, I raced toward our cabins. As the crow sailed overhead, taking the lead, my mind reeled. *Sam's secret deal. Nolan's a snitch.*

Stopping our progress, two wolves blocked our path. Before they caught sight of us, the crow took a sharp turn, leading us deeper into the woods, and away from our cabins to the caverns, an area I avoided because of hidden deathtraps. A canopy of snow covered the gaps between rocks, and one wrong step meant a free fall to an early grave. While I shot a glance skyward, the bird dodged invisible obstacles as a cue for me to mirror his flight path.

As the ground sloped upward, I dug my claws against the ice beneath the snow. We made it to the waterfalls. The crow took a sharp turn, disappearing behind a ledge. Cautiously, I followed. Maybe it was his way of offing me. Death by frozen waterfall. As the thought left my mind, the ground disappeared underneath my claws.

In a fluid movement, human Corbus draped me over his shoulder. To avoid the hundred-foot drop, I decided against squirming out of his hold. The ledge tapered to a mere foot space which he maneuvered with ease. Also impressive—when Corbus shifted between forms, he kept his clothing intact.

As he slipped into an opening between the cliff and waterfall, icicles scraped against my ducked head. Carefully, he set me down. Shaking myself from the hum of his magic, I scanned the cave of ice and stone. Corbus had been here. Recently. His scent permeated the cavern. In the center, a well-used fire pit held the remains of charcoal logs. Along one of the ice-covered walls sat a sleeping bag and a fair amount of camping equipment. I rode on a huge hunch that he had sheltered here for a while. On the other side of the cave, a tarp covered a pile of firewood and a large fur pelt. *Perfect.*

"I came here to talk," Corbus said. "Stay wolf—" The link bounced off the cave walls as I shifted into my human form. Lowering his gaze, he continued, "So you are not tempted to ask questions."

"I'll be careful." Wrapping the bearskin pelt around me, I inhaled its earthy scent. *Interesting.* Magic hummed along the hide. My inspection was cut short by the ice-covered ground biting against my feet. I hurried over to the sleeping bag, tucking the pelt under my bottom while shoving my freezing toes inside the sack. "I see why you moved next door."

"I will be happy to return to the forest." Corbus set to tending the fire pit. Instantly, flames danced our shadows across the cave. "What did you gather from your survey of the camp?"

"I didn't notice any humans."

Tension slipped from his shoulders. "It is good that you care for the humans."

"Always will."

"Perhaps." His voice took on a somber tone. "What else did you observe?"

"Nolan slipping the packs information."

"Perhaps."

"*Perhaps,*" I grumbled. "I don't like these non-answers."

Removing the pocketknife from his jeans, Corbus took a seat across from me. For a show, a warning, or just because, he left the weapon balancing on his knee. "What else?"

"Sam has a deal of some sort…" I let my words trail, hoping Corbus would provide any information. Nope. He just nodded. I smirked at his refusal.

"What else?"

"They believe that fae are helping us."

Corbus poked a stick at the fire. "Are they?"

"I don't know what you are." How I wanted to ask Corbus about his origin. Clearly, he wasn't giving it freely. Worry nibbled at the back of my skull. Corbus had to have seen Andrea. Had the Keeper's cover failed? If so, why didn't he leave? My attention landed on the pocketknife resting on his knee. I tucked the bearskin tighter around me.

"Your observations gained important information. However, you avoid bringing voice to the great truth." Corbus cut his eyes to me. "The wolves are wise to fear you."

"I know. I mean." I gestured at my shivering body. "I'm such a badass."

"The moon is smaller than the Earth. Yet, it is by the moon's delicate balance that she refrains from flooding the lands with her tides." Corbus paused. "Balance is a ruler's true power."

"I don't want to be a ruler," I snapped. "I just want to save my brother."

"I witnessed your attempt." Corbus' gaze lowered to my neck.

"The talisman..." Surprised it had survived through my Changes, I touched the feather charm resting against my breasts.

"When you embraced your brother, what happened?"

"It burned me." I denied Corbus the opportunity to pause and reflect. "It was warning us that the fae was heading our way." My breath squeezed from my clenching throat. "I touched Drew *before* I hugged him, and it did not burn me. He is alive. He is...good."

Corbus returned his attention to the fire. "Perhaps."

"You can have this back." I yanked at the unbreaking chain. Huffing, I spun it around to find that the clasp had disappeared. Unable to remove the talisman, I sighed.

"It's stubborn like you." A smile pulled at the corners of Corbus' mouth.

"Look, if you're not going to help or kill me, I need to get back to the pack."

"I do not want to kill you, Wolf Born. However, I cannot outright help you. You need to forge your own path."

"Yeah." I ran my finger through a puddle of melting ice. "If you hadn't noticed, I suck at that too."

"I've had a bird's eye view." His chuckle echoed through the cave.

"To further your amusement..." I shot him a glare. "How about giving me a hint for where to go next."

"You know." Corbus nodded. "*I* just needed to make sure."

Shaking my head, I stood. "Well, this has been...awkward."

"I will offer you advice." All warmth slipped from his expression and foreboding layered his voice. "You must let your hunter go."

"I don't have a choice." I swallowed. "He goes to Hector after I save my brother. You must have zoned out eavesdropping on that part of my meeting with the Vampire King."

"As long as you wore the talisman, I witnessed all."

"Umm…oh." Fear blended with relief because I hadn't had the talisman on when I'd met with the Keeper or while I had been sandwiched between Derek and Sam.

"Before sunrise." Corbus rolled his focus up to me. "I did take a flight to the casino."

My relief nosedived into embarrassment.

"The hunter's actions this morning—"

"No. Please." I smacked my forehead with the heel of my hand. "I get it. You *witnessed* everything."

"His rejection was meant to protect you."

"Protection." I smirked. "How chivalrous."

"If you become consumed by his affections—"

"Derek wants nothing from me. He made that truth crystal-clear." I pointed at my mouth. "His tongue didn't burst into flames."

"Proof he means to protect you. Now, you need to protect him. Let him go."

"You and Nathaniel just don't get it." I balled the bearskin in my trembling fingers. How clear did it need to be for supernatural beings to understand? "Derek is free. I don't own him."

"Your soul does." Corbus' eyes cut to mine. "You love—"

"Monsters don't get to love," I whispered. "They get their souls torn apart and burned to ashes." My body vibrated with rage. I clenched my eyes shut, caging the stream of tears. Not that I had expected anything less than a tragedy. When it came to me, love, in any complexity, meant someone ended up dead. Period.

Scrubbing the tears from my eyes, I rolled my shoulders. One shaky breath in and one tight exhale out.

Corbus moved to stand in front of me. He wasn't ready to let go of the conversation, "Derek will not be able to fight his desires much longer. You need to be the stronger one."

Staring into Corbus' eyes without reaching for a half-truth or avoidance, I gave him my undeniable certainty. "I don't know if I can be."

"If the hunter claims you—"

My mind flicked to the memory of the elevator where Derek had used that term while branding kisses to my skin. "Claim." I made it a statement but hoped Corbus saw the question in my eyes.

"When a vampire shares their soul, completing the blood-bond." Corbus paused. "You cannot be turned. If Derek attempts, he will lose control and kill you. The wolves will die. Having no use for your brother, the fae will kill him. Everyone you fight for, love… Everyone who depends on you…will perish."

"Derek will keep his soul to himself." I paused, letting my words permeate *my* soul. "I promise."

Corbus expelled a heavy breath. "This realm will hold you to that promise."

In a blur of movement, Corbus was holding the spine of an ebony dagger against my chest. *Where did he pull it from?* Not a clue. But there it was. A quick thrust upward would send its point through my skull. While flame reflections spun and twisted within his eyes, no movement or breath passed between us.

Finally, he broke the stillness with his voice. "Keep the balance." When his fingers slipped from around the hilt of the dagger, he used his free hand to gather mine, which grasped the bearskin. Then he placed the hilt of the blade into my sweaty palm. My attention flicked to the dagger. A faint hum of magic ran from the weapon through my hand. Corbus took a step backward. "The blade is raw iron."

"Hmm. Iron and vampires," I muttered to myself. "I *really* need to read that Otherworldly Creatures book."

"Indeed." Corbus reached down and grabbed the pocketknife, tucking it into his jeans. "*Fae* have the aversion to raw iron."

"This is… Wait." The pieces clicked into place. "This will take out the Lord of Light."

Corbus flicked his gaze down and up.

"I could kiss you." Even though our relationship fit somewhere between friendzone and killzone, a blush warmed Corbus' cheeks. "Relax. It's a figure of speech. Thank—"

He pressed a finger to his lips. "Thank me, and you will owe me."

I answered with a nod.

Corbus extinguished the fire, plunging the cave into darkness. Once more he stepped up to me and his magic skirted the space between us. "Place the dagger inside," he said, handing me a coarse fabric pouch. "Do not show it to anyone. Not even the alpha. If word reached the wrong ears…"

"I lose the advantage." I maneuvered the satchel over my shoulder and placed the weapon inside. The cloth muted the magic of the dagger, relieving the tingling in my fingertips. "We need to head back."

"You cannot change forms while holding the dagger." Corbus grabbed my forearms, guiding me against his body. As magic raced through me, gravity flipped its axis and my feet lifted from the earth. Corbus rested his chin against the top of my head. "Do not move."

Chapter Twenty-Two

Unlike when Nathaniel had mashed our atoms into a scrambled ball of pain while he moved us through space, Corbus just blinked us to point B—my bedroom. Collecting my bearings, I landed my focus on the bed where the Keeper sat polishing her toenails. She flicked her eyes over us, mouth gaping.

Corbus loosened his grip. His attention was fully set on the imposter human. Like two gunslingers from the Old West, they stared at each other. Thankfully, the dagger remained tucked in its pouch underneath the bearskin, hidden from the Keeper's view and away from Corbus' hands. Eighties music filtered from the speaker on my dresser, embellishing the awkwardness of the whole situation.

"This"—I patted Corbus' chest—"is the witness."

"I'm Andrea." The Keeper ticked her chin at me. "Bearskin girl's friend. I know about the Otherworldly crap. You can go on out of here with your magic, witness."

The thunder of footsteps toward the room did nothing to sway their mutual scrutiny. Sam's mark heated, tipping off who was coming. He burst through the door. At the lack of proximity between Corbus and me, Sam tensed.

"I'm okay." I moved a step backward to my dresser, discreetly shoving the dagger into my sock drawer while keeping my attention on Sam. "Are you?"

Balling his fists to his side, Sam gave me a sharp nod.

"Good." I cut a glance at Corbus and the Keeper, still locked in an eyeball battle. "We need to talk. Andrea, can you—"

"I'm not botching my nails." She waved at me. "Talk around me."

"Clearly, you've been hanging out with Nathaniel," I grumbled at the Keeper, who was painting her pinky toe. "It appears his self-entitlement has rubbed off on you."

She smirked.

"Bloodsuckers have a way of poisoning minds." Sam leveled his attention at Corbus. "Like the fae."

And that was my cue. I needed to move further away from Corbus but not toward Sam. Since the Keeper wasn't moving her ass, I plopped my butt on the mattress next to her, causing the paintbrush to drag a line of red across the outside arch of her foot.

Corbus took up my prior position, standing next to the dresser. I sent a prayer up that he'd not grab the dagger and attack the Keeper now sniffing the bearskin.

She wrinkled her nose. "Where have you been?"

A lighter set of footsteps raced toward the room. Ben poked his head through the doorway. "Tes—" He cleared his throat to hide his accident of almost using my name. "Wolf Born," he continued. "Are you okay?"

I patted the sliver of mattress beside me. Ben shuffled past the two men and plopped down. Once more, the brush ran over the Keeper's foot. She screwed on the nail polish top and huffed.

"I'm still not leaving." She knocked her shoulder against mine before resting her back on the wall. "The last time you were naked in a room with pretty men, I was left watching cartoons with the steward."

A heartbeat passed as I took stock of my feelings. Wearing only the bearskin while Andrea recapped the marking shenanigans, I felt…unfazed. *Shit.* I needed a break from the monster world ASAP.

"Since we are mostly all here," I said before anyone else got a word in, "the packs know about my alliance with the vampires as well as my brother's rescue mission because we have a spy. Second." I stared at Sam reeling from my first bit of news. "What is this *deal* they are talking about?"

Ben sucked in a breath. The Keeper vibrated with excitement. Corbus, well, he witnessed. Sam's jaw ticked.

"Well?" I prompted.

"Do you know who the spy is?" Sam asked.

"I have a damn good idea. I'll share with you later."

"Umm." Ben shoved his glasses up on the bridge of his nose. "Why not now?"

"Werewolves have impeccable hearing," I said. "This gives the spy a chance to come clean before action is taken against them."

The Keeper whistled. "Oh, she's pissed."

"Let me clear the air about the deal." Sam shifted his weight. "After the alphas confirm our marks, I agreed to take you to a secure location. A place free of vampires and fae."

Ben rested his hand on my kneecap. Once he realized it was bare, his cheeks flushed yet he kept his hand in place. "I worked the deal."

I tugged my kneecap free. "What?"

"There are major loopholes," Ben offered. "For one, you choose the place. Also, you can come and go as you please. With the alpha of course." As if he were a creepy salesman selling me some timeshare scheme, Ben's voice lifted. " Like you've been."

"Have been?" I stared Ben dead in the eyes.

Ben's heartbeat increased. Fear poured from his pores. When he darted his eyes toward Sam, I scrambled to my feet.

"Mate." Sam tossed the link into his voice, causing my knees to buckle and my ass to hit the mattress. "Two days after the Gathering, I learned of your location. I've been waiting to reintroduce myself."

"Well, some habits die hard," I snapped. When confusion crossed Sam's expression, I clarified, "You've been stalking me."

"Protecting you." Sam stepped further into the room, blocking my view of Corbus. "Every alpha this side of the continent has been hunting you. I've kept your whereabouts hidden." Apology flooded Sam's eyes and words. "Giving you space and time to adjust to your—"

"Monsterhood?" I snapped. The Keeper grabbed my hand and squeezed it, startling me. The action choked me up. So much like Andrea. I swallowed and redirected my anger at Sam. "So, I've never been…free."

"Did you feel trapped?" he asked.

"No."

"Good." He gave a curt nod. "Then I did something right."

I spared a glance at Ben. A trickle of sweat ran from his temple. Could I even trust my best friend? "It was you. Wasn't it? You told him where we were."

"Yes." Although in escape mode, Ben stayed by my side. "I was terrified some other monsters would kill you, so I called the alpha. I made sure he wouldn't interfere and he held to his word—"

"You should have talked to me."

"Like I did? Hundreds of times? You *chose* not to hear me." Tears brimmed in Ben's eyes. "So, I *chose* to shut up, because I knew you would leave...*me*."

Still holding the Keeper's hand, I hooked my free arm around the back of Ben's head, running my fingers through his shaggy hair. "I will never leave you." I pressed my forehead to his. "Hear me?"

He nodded his forehead against mine. While waves of exhaustion rolled off his spine, I shifted to glance at his protruding vertebrae. Ben had always had a lithe frame, but these past few days had reduced him to a bag of bones. I released him from our embrace. He blinked red-rimmed eyes at me. As I smoothed a lock of Ben's hair behind his ear, my attention landed on the angry puncture marks at his neck. I glanced up at Sam and flicked my focus to the bite on Ben's neck, silently asking why Ben had not healed.

"Steward"—Sam kept his eyes to mine as he asked—"how many times have you been bitten by the same vampire?"

Ben pinched his brows. "I'm not sure."

"Twice," I answered. "That I know of."

Ben's eyes bulged. "What does that mean?"

Corbus shifted closer to Ben. "If the same vampire feeds from you three times and you drink their blood, when you die, you will become the undead."

"I..." Ben blanched. "I feel...dizzy—"

He passed out. As Ben went lax, I freed my hand from the Keeper's to guide his head into my lap. *How did I miss the signs?* I gnashed my teeth. *Because I worried only about me. My needs. My wants.*

"The vampire is feeding off his energy," Corbus said.

Nathaniel... Rage blazed through me when I thought the bloodsucker's name. If Ben died—*No.* I glanced at Sam but hoped that Corbus would answer my question. "How do we help my steward?"

"He needs rest, nourishment." Corbus paused until I looked at him. "And magic."

"Well, I don't do the magic stuff," the Keeper piped in. "But I'll watch over the steward while you attend your werewolf thing. And someone needs to go shopping for *real* food. None of this boxed crap you have here."

Sam nodded. "Make a list, I'll send out a group."

"Righty-o." The Keeper patted my shoulder as she stood. "Also, I request that the tea-sipping hottie be our guard."

Sam cocked an eyebrow at me.

I mouthed, *"Max."*

While the Keeper exited the bedroom, Sam's attention flicked to the talisman as he helped me lift Ben off my lap. "You can Change with that?"

"Yep." When I eased off the bed, I tucked the bearskin tight around me. "We need to chat about the packs."

"Too many ears are on us," Sam said. "I'll grab some paper, you can—"

Magic prickled in the air and Corbus' eyes turned opaque. "No one will hear your conversation."

"That trick would have been useful earlier," Sam grumbled.

"When humans are involved, rules can be… altered," Corbus said, looking at Ben.

"The ceremony is some type of bait," I said, staring at Sam.

"I know." Sam grunted. "Figured someone's stupid and wants to challenge me. *They* chose the hunting campground for the location."

"Yeah, that's where all their packs are hanging out. We'll have the ceremony." I nodded. "But it will take place at the bowling alley."

"That'll be a blood bath." Sam folded his arms across his chest. "Those bloodsuckers are in the cellar."

"They have a blood supply waiting when they rise," I said. "And they must obey me or be incinerated by their king."

"They can turn his words," Sam warned.

"The vampires fear their king," Corbus said. "He desires the Wolf Born. They will not rise against her this night."

"Jesus." Sam raked his hands through his hair. "How does the witness know that?"

I pointed at the talisman. "It's like a looking glass."

"Nothing like a nosy fae." Sam rubbed his temples. "Speaking of noses. The alphas will smell the bloodsuckers."

"The packs already know about the vampires." I shifted my attention fully to Corbus. "Time I show my teeth. Own my title. Prove that I will not cower to vampires or werewolves."

"Wise," Corbus said. "Work through any disagreements and hostilities tonight before you confront the Lord of Light."

"Yeah." Sam smirked. "I don't trust *any* of them."

I stared at Sam. "We said nothing about trust."

"Fine." He studied me. "What about the humans?"

"They'll be safe," I said. "Our pack and some of the vampires will patrol the town."

Corbus nodded at my idea.

Sam just stared at me.

"What?" I asked.

"Tonight, in front of the alphas, we will be recognized as mates."

It was my turn to offer a blank stare. I dug my fingers deeper into the bearskin.

"The hunter—"

"Will be in attendance." I locked my eyes with Sam's. "The hunter will uphold his title, or I will release him."

In one stride, Sam loomed over me. Thank all the stars that Corbus remained with us because there was no denying my wolf's intentions toward Sam. Lust screamed through me, zipping along to his mark. Sam's attention flew to my shoulder then landed back on my face.

"I'll make the change in arrangements." His voice dropped into a rumble, fritzing my libido. "I suggest you rest." Before I could respond, he dipped his head, brushing his nose against my temple. The heat of his breath undid me. My vision blurred. My nerves scattered. He curved his lips into a grin against my cheek. "While you can."

Chapter Twenty-Three

The crimson sunset spilled through my bedroom window, spotlighting Ben, who was fast asleep. For the umpteenth time, I smoothed his hair at his temples, while outside, the vans sat idling.

"I'll be back before morning." I leaned over and placed a kiss on his forehead. A wisp of chilled breath sputtered from his cracked lips, hitting against my throat. I drew away to stare once more at his sunken features. If it hadn't been for his shallow breathing, he would have appeared…dead. "You get better. Okay?"

"He'll make it," the Keeper said from the doorway. She shoved up the worn sleeves of one of my T-shirts and pinned me with an amused look. "If he holds on like your outdated wardrobe."

"If—*after*—I live through this, we'll go clothes shopping for you."

A wary half-grin lit her face. "Dare I say you like me around, Wolf Born?"

"Yes." Why lie? Try to rationalize it? The truth was I did. She brought a sense of female comradery. "That means you stay safe," I said, tightening my bootlaces for the third time.

"No worries there." The Keeper rested her shoulder against the doorframe. "I got that hottie as a guard."

Reluctantly, I stepped across the dirt circle. Even with Corbus' protection ring, and an incognito fae and a werewolf as protection, I worried about leaving Ben.

The Keeper took up walking around me. "Yeah, *we're* going shopping. Who goes to a mating ceremony in jeans and an old-ass sweater?"

"It's the new trend in Otherworldly apparel." For show, I did a spin. Ending my turn, I met Sam's shit-eating grin.

Once more he had dressed to grace some rustic outdoors ad. Boots, jeans and a burgundy sweater clung to his muscular chest. Seriously, a man should not be that attractive. There had to be a universal law against it. My mind scrambled as he held out my coat to me. "Ready?"

"Call me for anything," I said to the Keeper. "I mean it."

"Have her home and happy by sunrise." She wiggled her finger at Sam. "Or I'll kill you."

"She's kidding," I squeaked.

Sam's dimple popped as he gave the Keeper a nod. "Yes, ma'am."

I gave Ben one last glance before shoving on my coat. Tugging my hair free, I looked at Sam. "Let's go lay down some order."

On the ride over to the bowling alley, Sam caught me up on what to expect from the werewolves. Basically, a whole lot of patriarchal bullshit. While Nathaniel, tucked away in the garment bag and rolling around in the trunk, blabbered to my mind, updating me on how we would reveal the vampires to the alphas.

For my brother's sake, I kept silent and gazed out of the window, hoping to catch a glimpse of Corbus flying ahead of the caravan.

"Shit." Jimmy grunted as the SUV pulled hard to the left. "Hold on."

My heart rocketed against my ribs while my seatbelt tightened. Since Max had stayed behind as a guard, sharpshooter Jimmy was our chauffeur.

"Before the Lord of Light tears you apart, this buffoon might very well kill you," Nathaniel muttered as Jimmy corrected with a sharp turn.

"You'd be lucky, because once all this is over, you're re-dead, Blondy."

"Blondy?" Nathaniel chuckled in my skull. *"That's not what Benjamin calls me."*

"You almost killed him. Are killing him – "

"You're the one killing him. Even with your pathetic mental barrier up, you still draw on his energy. Very rude of you." Nathaniel paused. *"I, at least, said thank you, after I fed on him."*

Before I could spin and flog Nathaniel, Sam patted my knee. He nodded at the nighttime sky. "The vampires will wake soon. We're going to park and let them feed. We'll still be at the location before the alphas."

"Nathaniel." I paused to control the growl in my voice. "Tell the vampires not to harm my wolves."

Sam tightened his fingers against my kneecap. "I like how that sounds."

A blast of Nathaniel's compulsion tore through and out of the car.

"That's not like any bloodsucker mindfuck I've felt before." Jimmy growled.

Nathaniel sat up, then sliced a claw down the middle of the garment bag. He peeked his head through and eyeballed Jimmy.

"What the fuck—" Jimmy slammed the brakes, sending the SUV fishtailing.

"Delta." Sam blasted the alpha link at Jimmy. "Release the brakes. Now."

Jimmy cranked the SUV, steering to the side of the road. "He's not dead-looking!"

"Nor are you…yet." Nathaniel failed at removing the tremor in his voice. "I'll take my leave."

When Nathaniel disappeared, Sam said to Jimmy, "Drive."

I passed the rest of the drive counting my jacked-up heartbeats. Jimmy parked across the street from the bowling alley. Muted by the snowfall, a streetlight cast a dim glow against the ridged silhouette of the building. Thankfully, Nathaniel's prior pyrotechnics had kept the humans away. Maybe Corbus had had a hand in the missing locals as well. I rode on the hunch after his comment about Otherworldly rules that could alter when it came to humans. Pretty sure he was also behind the lack of *people* at the hunting campgrounds. Speaking of Corbus, a black dot perched atop the brick building's roof.

To conserve heat, I huddled against Sam. Luckily freezing temps didn't faze vampires. Before we pulled up, they'd cleared out and hidden downwind. Once I gave Nathaniel the signal, the vampires would enter the building, blocking all exits from the werewolves.

Movement at the entrance caught my attention. Nolan, along with two other pack members, coordinated the check-in process for the alphas while most of our pack patrolled the town. Every monster was in their manipulated positions…but Sam and me.

The link stirred, setting Sam's eyes aglow. "The alphas are all in. Ready?"

Nope. With my mind spinning, I stared at my paling reflection in the window.

"Hey." Sam grabbed my hand, waiting until I turned to him. "We face them *all* together."

Vaguely, I nodded.

Jimmy opened the vehicle's door and if not for Sam still holding my hand to help me exit, I'd have lost my footing against the icy sidewalk. Observing my near-spill, emotionless, Nolan waited in front of the doorway with a gold rope hanging from his loose-held fist. As we climbed the steps, Sam lifted our clasped hands to Nolan, who threaded the satin coil around our fists. Nolan's heartbeat ticked normally. No scent of fear. Maybe he wasn't the spy. Surely, he'd give off some kinda shady vibe, because he didn't hide his dislike for me. Once we were good and fastened, Nolan cut his eyes to mine. "May the link forever remain."

"Beta," Sam said, "announce us."

Nolan turned and pushed open the doors. "Presenting the Wolf Born and her mate."

Sam escorted us around to greet each alpha and their accompanying beta. There wasn't enough room for all the visiting pack members. Fine by me. The fewer, the merrier. Not that the extra hundreds of men were not being 'watched over'—we had a few of our wolves and vampires patrolling at the hunting campground. I tucked my free hand into my coat pocket. Sam and I were underdressed. Smartly. These pompous assholes were about to learn they couldn't run on ice wearing dress shoes.

After the obligatory mingling, Sam led us past the bowling lanes and into the reception area. What an attack on the senses. The odor of smoke and mildew permeated from the walls and floor of the room. Overhead, a rusty disco ball hung from the water-stained ceiling, casting a disjointed spectrum of light across the rows of tables covered in white paper tablecloths. Red Solo cups, filled with boxed wine, acted as place markers. To keep from laughing at the setup—my life—I bit my lip.

With his free hand, Sam rubbed his nose, hiding his chuckle. "Is this the wedding you always dreamed of?"

"Everything but the missing DJ."

"Jimmy could sing some country for you."

My laugh escaped.

Sam grinned at me. "I know you hate that twangy stuff."

I froze. "How do you know that?"

Beyond the room's heady stench of alphas and mold, the sweetness of fear wafted from Sam. "Your steward gave me some pointers."

"When?"

"Since I found you." Sam's pulse revved against my wrist. "Every day."

Warmth crept through my face. Annoyed with the girly reaction, I flicked my attention at the werewolves flooding into the room as I muttered, "Didja ask what my favorite color is?"

"Storm-cloud gray." Sam escorted me toward the table against the back wall. He flicked his eyes to mine. "My favorite is emerald green."

I blinked at him. *Why did he have to be so…Sam?* A man my family would've loved to have sat down and shown all my embarrassing preteen photos to, someone for me to *really* marry.

"What's wrong?" Sam asked.

Everything. "So you get my goldfish's name too?"

"Free Willy, which you poured down the storm drain because you thought it was mean, keeping it trapped inside a bowl." Sam lowered his gaze to our bound hands. "Shit."

"Sorry." I turned to face him. "There's not a drain big enough for me to send you down. You're stuck with me."

"Good." His eyes darkened. "I want to know *everything* about you." The rawness of Sam's voice pitched my pulse to race in tandem with his. My gaze fell to Sam's lips moving once more. "I want…"

"What?" I whispered.

"I want to kiss you." He leaned in with his breath skimming across his mark, then he dragged in my scent. "And you want me to."

Driving the tension skyward, a metal rhythmic clanking of chairs ricocheted through the room while encouraging shouts erupted. Yet all noise disappeared into a muffled echo, drowned out by the roaring of my heart. Physically, no doubt I wanted Sam to kiss me. But my treacherous memories replayed the elevator lip-lock with Derek until his last image echoed in my skull. He regretted…me.

Meeting Sam's heated gaze, I cemented myself in the present moment and said, "What are you waiting for?"

Sam brought our bound hands to rest on his pounding chest. Gathering me even closer, he ran his free hand to the small of my back, splaying his fingers across my hip. Anticipation vibrated through my body as I hooked my free arm around the back of his neck, drawing his mouth down to mine. A growl shook his chest and he tightened his hand against my hip. He rolled his tongue against mine, teasing. My skin flushed and shivered at his restraint. Before he devoured me in front of the alphas, Sam broke the kiss.

A smile curved his lips and my stomach plummeted. The implications left my brain reeling. I enjoyed kissing Sam. It felt right. Good. *But…* As if he had read my thoughts, Sam pulled me back in, adamant to steal my heart with his kiss.

"That is enough," Derek said.

"He's early," Sam muttered, keeping us locked in our embrace.

No matter the ninety-eight werewolves surrounding him, Derek fastened his attention on me. Dressed in his signature suit, he put the alphas to shame. Not just with his looks, but through the confidence and power he exuded.

"Caution, brothers," Sam warned. "This was the Vampire Queen's Hunter."

As growls vibrated through the room and the men's lips rose over their elongated fangs, no one dared move against Derek. The tracking and slaying of werewolves had brought him notorious recognition amongst both races. No werewolf Derek had hunted survived. Except for one…me. From the intensity of Derek's stare, perhaps he was about to perfect his kill score.

An alpha rose from his seat. "She *is* allied with the vampires."

Sam held me firm, brushing his lips against my ear. "Call them."

"Now," I sent Nathaniel.

Silence answered.

And my panic answered the silence.

Sam inhaled. "What's wrong?"

"Not answering," I whispered.

"Fine. We'll do this ourselves." A deep breath fanned my cheek as Sam called the link from our pack, blasting it out to the room toward the alphas and betas.

The sudden draw on my energy rocked me against Sam's chest.

Derek took a step closer.

"Nathaniel?" I sent. *"Where are you?"*

"Enjoying the view." Nathaniel paused and all teasing dispersed from his voice. *"Time to prove to the wolves that* you *are in control. Not the alpha. Not us brilliantly powerful vampires. You, she-beast."*

I brushed my fingers against Sam's neck. When my fingertips touched my mark, energy pulsed between us. Sam snapped his focus to me. Holding his glowing eyes with mine, I opened my emotions to him, hoping he would pick up on the I-got-this vibes over the oh-shit ones.

He relinquished control of the link while he dropped his hand from my hip, allowing me to face out toward the room to Derek, whose attention leveled on Sam's and my bound hands.

Derek raised his eyes to mine. "Show them."

He became my focal point while the link rushed through me. Though my control was not as flawless as Sam's, I unleashed the power on the alphas, forcing them to their knees. When the betas pulled away from the walls, I used the link to hold them in their places. Instantly, a sea of glowing eyes stared in awe and horror at me. Sam, having not much of a choice, being attached at the hand, moved with me as I walked into the center of the room.

When Derek came to stand on my left, foreign energy buzzed around the room, followed by a series of inhales from the werewolves. Different than the rich-maddening scent of Derek, the tilled earth stench of vampires filtered around us.

Inhales overshadowed the frantic mutterings of the werewolves.

"Bloodsuckers," someone growled. "I smell them everywhere."

Sam tensed and Derek narrowed his eyes. Before I lost further control of the situation, I shot another blast of the link toward the alphas. Once more, the room fell silent.

"You will *all* listen to me," I said. "Tomorrow, we, wolves and vampires, face the fae, together."

"I'd rather die than fight alongside a bloodsucker." An old geezer of an alpha spit on the floor. Oh, I recognized him. Before my first Change, he had been the ringleader that had rallied for my imprisonment and death. *Some monsters never change.*

Sam cut his eyes to mine. He'd warned that some alphas might die tonight for refusing my petition. I planned for that not to be the case. "Who is his beta?" I asked the room.

Beard Man, from the camping grounds, stepped forward.

"Stand next to your alpha." I paused while Beard Man moved into position. "Alpha," I said to the geezer. "You are relieved of your title."

He outright cackled. "That's not how it works, girl."

"He must die," Sam said. "The beta must drink his blood."

"No." *Shit. Now what?* Answering my anxiety, my wolf stirred, taking control of my vision. Through her eyes, she revealed the threads of energy drifting from the alphas to their betas. Zeroing in on the link attaching the old geezer to his beta, I sent a blast of my energy, severing their link.

"Well." Sam schooled his expression, although fear drifted from his pores. "That works, too."

The geezer's face bleached. "What have you done?"

Beard Man fell to his knees, clawing at his heart. "She destroyed our link."

I let the link rise between me and Sam. He tensed at my side, then narrowed his eyes at the two men. "Holy shit," he whispered. "I can *see* their links."

"Make him an alpha," I said to Sam.

Still viewing through my wolf's eyes, Sam took up the beta's broken link, binding it to himself. "Run your pack with trust, respect and integrity," Sam said to Beard Man.

"Till the moon takes me." Beard Man touched his forehead to the ground.

Sam then sent the restored link to Beard Man. "Rise, Alpha Khyber."

Khyber, Beard Man, rose on shaky legs.

The geezer wept, clawing at the floor. "I'll kill—"

Khyber grabbed the geezer by his throat, lifting him to his tiptoes. "You are a lone wolf. You have a day before we hunt you down."

The geezer shot another glare at me before stumbling away.

I took back control from my wolf, sending her to my subconscious. "Does anyone else want to relinquish their packs to their betas?"

The rest of the alphas remained silent.

"Show them *all*," Derek prompted, ticking his chin at the window, where two vampires with their black-pit eyes leered at me.

"Mark my word," Nathaniel sent. *"The vampire guards are Hector's spies. Terrify them into submission. They must fear you more than their king... Good luck with that."*

Me—scare a vampire? "Not possible," I whispered.

Sam cut a glance at me. His jaw knotted the slightest before he turned his attention to Derek. "What is your *new* title, vampire?"

"I am the Wolf Born's hunter." Derek's voice brushed against my bones. "My blood for

her blood, until my eternal night."

"Saved by your lover. Or should I say, lovers?" Nathaniel teased as he appeared next to Derek. "The hunter's title is legitimate." Nathaniel opened his mouth, revealing his unburnt tongue to the room. "Now show yourselves."

A cluster of vampires materialized, surrounding our group.

Still under the restraint of my link, fear poured from the werewolves. I drew my energy back, allowing them some movement to defend themselves should a vampire attack. As Sam's mark hummed against my skin, he took over the link. I squeezed his hand. Having a mating bond had its perks in times of dire straits. He would handle the werewolves while I dealt with the vampires.

"Hunter," I said to Derek. "Tell them what I am."

"The Wolf Born is an unturned vampire," Derek answered.

"I witnessed her death," Nathaniel said. "Afterward, she bested the Vampire Queen. Thus this unturned outranks us all." Nathaniel gave Derek a curt nod.

"As the Wolf Born's hunter, I demand you pledge your loyalties to her by a blood-promise—"

"Wait—" Panic stole my voice.

"They will only spill their blood at your feet," Derek said before returning his focus to the vampires. "Or else they will be given their final death."

The vampires flicked their attention at one another. In unison they went to their knees, drawing claws across their wrists. Blood splattered on the floor, forming a circle around us.

Derek drew a claw across his wrists. Refusing to acknowledge Sam, Derek stepped in front of me. He flicked his gaze at my fist and I uncurled my fingers. With his gashed wrist hand, Derek took hold, lacing our fingers. "I blood-promise loyalty to the Wolf Born."

As blood slid between our palms, he gestured to the kneeling vampires. Each took turns standing and repeating the blood-promise. After the last vampire, Derek nodded to me.

I returned a nod, then addressed the vampires. "All werewolves are mine and are under my protection." I cut my attention to the wolves before continuing, "Do not harm them unless one attacks you."

After each vampire nodded, I looked at each alpha and beta and said, "Do not harm the vampires unless one attacks you."

The room fell silent. I glanced at Sam. He nodded. I glanced at Derek. He nodded. We did it. *I'm coming, Drew,* I sent out to my brother.

"Now that we are all bosom brothers"—Nathaniel grabbed a cup—"can we finish this mating ceremony?"

Chapter Twenty-Four

When Derek released my hand, Nolan was quick to take his place with a wet towel, washing the blood away. I focused on Nolan and not the fact that Derek had left without so much as a glance.

Sam spoke to Nolan. "The pack is silent."

"In town, there has been no human activity." Nolan kept his attention on the task of scrubbing my hand clean of Derek. "The vampires have been…helpful with patrolling."

"And the campgrounds?" Sam asked.

A spark lit Nolan's eyes. "While the alphas are away…."

Sam and Nolan recited together, "The packs play."

I cleared my throat. "Any word from home?"

"No change." Nolan raised his eyes to mine. "I'm sorry."

I sucked in a breath. There should have been some improvement in Ben's condition. Using the uncomfortable pause, Nolan tipped his head, released my hand and returned to patrolling the room.

Sam squeezed our joined hands. "He's not worse."

Nodding, I glared at Nathaniel, who was chumming it up with the newly appointed alpha, Khyber. Back in the car, the vampire hadn't been twisting his words. *It's me. I'm killing Ben.* As I stared daggers at Nathaniel, goosebumps raced up my spine. Discreetly, I glanced over my shoulder, meeting Derek's intense stare. When our eyes met, he glanced away. With hurt fronting as anger blazing in my gut, I snapped my head forward, catching Sam's attention.

He lifted our bound hands, placing a kiss across my knuckles. "You can order him away."

A blush heated my face. "Gotta get used to you being able to read my feelings."

"No need to." Sam lowered our hands. "Your heart races."

"Oh." I chewed my lip.

"I'll never invade your private emotions without permission." Sam straightened and surveyed the room. "What I will do is show you mine. Constantly. There will be no confusion. You will know." He paused, locking his stare with mine. "I want you—"

The glowing reflection of the talisman filled Sam's eyes. Before I could react, a man's shout tore through the bowling alley, cut short by a thunderous crash.

Nathaniel appeared at my side with his black-mirrored gaze pinned to the sealed doors of the room. "It's the fae."

"How?" Derek stood behind me. "They cannot cross without permission."

"I know the laws," Nathaniel snapped.

As the doors opened, a cloud of vampire ash drifted inside the room. Sam used his claws to free our hands from the rope. "Take her," he said to Nathaniel.

"That is not necessary." The Lord of Light dipped his head to enter the room. Beyond his flowing robes, the bowling lanes were visible through his transparent body. "I've come to pay my respects to the mated couple."

"He's not really here," I sent Nathaniel.

"He doesn't need to be to eliminate everyone in this room. Warn them."

"Stand guard," I said to the wolves and vampires.

A grin stretched across the fae's lips. "How this human realm enchants me. Light and Dark Otherworldly Creatures breaking words together."

"Yep," I said. "And you're not invited."

"Do not entice him," Nathaniel sent.

"Betrayer of Kin." The Lord of Light cooed. "Of all places, this is where you came to wallow?"

Nathaniel just stared at the fae.

"As for invitations…" The Lord of Light returned his full attention to me. He lifted his pinky finger, nicking it with the nail of his thumb. A blue droplet boiled to the surface, perching on the tip of his finger, wobbling as he spoke. "With stolen blood, you entered my realm. *Uninvited.*"

"Korrigan blood cannot pierce the Light realm," Nathaniel whispered.

"No. It cannot," the Lord of Light said, watching the droplet roll down his finger. "Yet, that she did."

Nathaniel's black-mirrored eyes shifted to me. "By Hell and Heaven, who is your father?"

"Dead," the Lord of Light answered. "No matter her origins, all must be granted permission to my kingdom. Since she was not, I settled my grievance. Her brother paid in teeth."

Sam shifted in front of me. "You said you came to offer respect."

"Indeed." The fae let the droplet splatter against the floor.

The blood turned and rolled over itself, morphing into three massive humanoids. While their heads brushed the ceiling, each monster stretched two pairs of arms ending in razor-like talons. Below their blue flesh, muscles popped and flexed as they turned to face the fae.

"Wolf Born," the Lord of Light said. "Tomorrow, when the sun touches the earth, you will return the stolen blood. Until then, here are my respects. Spare the alphas and vampires." The fae's eyes held mine. "Kill the betas."

The monsters attacked the men along the walls.

"Alphas, shield," Sam ordered.

Derek signaled to the vampires. "Attack."

Nathaniel ensnared my arm, keeping me in place. "Stay by the alpha. He gave mercy *only* to alphas and vampires."

A monster grabbed Khyber by his arm. As the wet snap of bone and his wail hit my ears, the twistedness of the Lord of Light's command struck. Just the alphas' *lives* were to be spared.

Nathaniel attacked an incoming monster while Sam and Derek shoved me between their bodies. My attention darted to Nolan flanking Sam. I hooked my fingers underneath the talisman burning against my flesh, yanking at the unbreaking chain.

"Witness," I screamed.

A monster loomed toward Nolan, lashing out its talons. Once more, I ripped at the chain, and the talisman gave way. I raced to Nolan, shoving it around his neck. A sphere of light threw back the monster…only too late. Blood coated my hands as I tucked Nolan's arm underneath my shoulder to support him.

Sam tore over to us, then grabbed Nolan from me. "Get to the center."

"No." Energy pulsed through my hands and I shot my attention to my glowing fingertips. "I can help."

Sam's focus shifted to a target behind me. "Take her away."

I whirled around, knocking Derek's protective hands away from me. Calling on the korrigan's blood within me, I charged the closest monster, driving my claws into its spiny back, surging my power into the beast. An eruption of light surrounded its writhing body. As I drove another current of energy at it, the creature exploded, tossing me against a wall.

Forcing air into my lungs, I struggled to my feet. Rage fueled me as I charged the nearest monster. Catapulting myself onto its back, I pierced both sides of the beast's neck with my claws. While it thrashed around, I summoned the energy, driving it into the monster. Not waiting for the sphere of light, I released a second blast and the explosion hurled me against the blood-slick floor.

Across the room, the Lord of Light's blood-splattered face hardened. My attention raced to the alphas and vampires working together, shielding the handful of surviving betas from the remaining creature. I blinked. The damn thing was growing. Body parts from the two monsters I'd exploded slithered across the floor, joining with the creature.

Sam raced to my side with blood pouring from a gash across his face. My lungs didn't work correctly to attempt to speak so I jabbed a finger at Derek and Nathaniel distracting the monster, taking turns attacking, then fleeing as they had done with the Keeper's stone men. Sam nodded and joined the vampires.

The creature spun. Dodging a blow, Sam narrowly missed its talon. I took his place slicing at the creature's throat. One of its four arms ensnared my hair, dragging me up the length of its body. When I was face-level, I drove my claws into its eye socket and the beast threw back an arm, readying a blow aimed at my head.

"Stop," the Lord of Light bellowed.

The monster froze.

"You cannot kill the golem," the Lord of Light spoke at me. "Hand over the remaining betas."

"No," I wheezed.

"Wolf Born," Nathaniel whispered to my mind, *"do it. Or you will have no one left to face him in the flesh."*

I spared a glance at the shield of battered alphas and vampires protecting a handful of betas. Expressions mixed with fear and acceptance graced their faces. Nolan stumbled to his feet, ripped off the talisman and tossed it to the floor, then shoved his way through the circle.

"For the good of the pack," Nolan screamed.

The monster dropped me to charge Nolan.

Clamoring to my feet, I drew on the energy. Only this time, it came racing from the ground and the air, igniting an inferno within me. My body lit up, blazing with energy which I aimed at the creature. A blast of light engulfed the beast mid-strike, incinerating it into thin air.

As the light dimmed, the stench of seared flesh layered the ozone. In front of me, alive, Nolan crumbled against the wall. Blisters covered his face and exposed skin from the energy I had used. Thankfully, unconsciousness claimed him.

I flashed my attention to the wall that the Lord of Light had occupied. It sat empty of his goading presence.

Derek approached, holding out his tattered suit jacket. Glancing at my shivering, naked body, I took the jacket and wrapped it around myself. However, with the blood-soaked fabric pressing against my skin, I almost preferred to be stark naked. Instead of disrobing, I turned, taking stock of the room.

Any other moment in time, seeing vampires aiding the werewolves and vice versa happening all around me would have been a cause to celebrate.

The crunching of glass underfoot snapped my head toward the doorway. Corbus moved into the room. Not a wrinkle on his clothing or drop of blood. Anger filled my parched throat. Tears burned down my cheeks. Instead of screaming, I stared at Corbus and sobbed. Derek gathered me into his arms, supporting my weight to keep me upright.

"This is not just a rescue mission," Corbus said to the room. "This is a war. He now knows your weaknesses and strengths."

"Not every strength," I whispered.

"Wolf Born." Nathaniel cut his attention back to Corbus, then the vampire's voice slipped into my mind. *"Now is not the time to reveal the Keeper."*

"You need to leave this place," Corbus said to me. "You bit his pride. He may send his magic again."

Derek squeezed my forearms as he asked Sam, "What assistance do you need with the injured?"

More tears leaked from my eyes. Derek couldn't care less about the werewolves, but he asked because he knew that I did.

Sam walked over to my right side. Unable to move from sheer exhaustion, I shuddered a breath of relief. The angry gash across his face had stopped bleeding. He had all his appendages, and the burning distaste for Derek, Sam kept under wraps. "I will stay to help the wounded. No one will be left behind." He leveled his eyes at Nathaniel creeping around to my left side. "Take her home. Guard her."

"You don't order me, alpha." Nathaniel folded his arms across the mangled talon marks scoring his chest. "Furthermore, she incinerated the golems. She can guard herself."

"Nathaniel." Derek's voice vibrated against my chest. "Take her home."

"Fine," Nathaniel grumbled. "I cannot move you both. The distance taxes me in my current…state."

Derek slowly moved me away from his chest, forcing me to lift my gaze to his. "I'll stay and aid the alphas."

"I, too, will watch over your warriors, Wolf Born," Corbus said. "Be ready at dawn. We have much to prepare."

With that, the vampires passed me off and Nathaniel crushed me against his body, pulling the shadows around us.

Chapter Twenty-Five

In prime Nathaniel fashion, he dropped me on the floor of Ben's bedroom. Against the glow of Ben's desk lamp, Nathaniel's vampire eyes consumed the blue of his irises. His fangs peeked from his thin lips.

"Leav—" Before the word left my lips, he disappeared.

Good timing, too, because footfalls thundered toward the room. Together, the Keeper and Max burst through the door. One look at me and Max knocked his shoulder against the frame.

"You're alive," the Keeper said. "That's good."

Max's jaw dropped but only air exited. Like most people, monsters, Andrea left many speechless. The Keeper would've made Andrea proud.

My eyes shot open. "Ben."

"Sleeping in your room," Max said. "He's okay."

"Yep. He's less goth-looking." The Andrea impersonator extraordinaire walked into the room. Grabbing a blanket off Ben's bed, she then draped it around me. "We got the call you would be here." She beat Max again to the chase. "The alpha filled us in. He said we're to stay in the cabin until he returns..."

Her words went mute against the flashback of the night running on repeat. *So many dead. My fault.* Another wave of stifled cries rocked my body.

Max lowered to his knees, then crawled over to me. My wolf instinct took over, recognizing the submissive display, I held an arm out, pulling him into an embrace. The pack link stirred around us and Sam's mark heated. A man of his word, he did not barge into my feelings, but gave me a subtle reminder that he was available through his mark.

"So." The Keeper arched her eyebrow. "Can I join the werewolf pile?"

I motioned her over and she snuggled against my free side. We all sat there through a series of heartbeats until the tearstains dried tight to my cheeks.

The Keeper patted my forearm and stood. "Do you know how many have gone against him?"

I shook my head.

"How does a human know about this fae?" Max asked, shifting to face the door. He rested his back against mine.

"Thousands." The Keeper ignored Max. "But Wolf Queen, minus her clothes, has faced him twice. Badass."

Max's phone rang and he stood. I turned around at the uptick of his heartbeat. Max shoved the phone against his ear. "Hello."

Sam's muted voice drifted through the room. "Is the vampire there?"

Max's brow creased. "No."

A pause, then Sam said, "Let me speak to her."

I took the phone from Max, pressing it to my ear.

Having heard the exchange of the phone, or the sound of my breath, Sam said, "Hey," followed by an awkward pause, perhaps unsure of how to address me, blended also by fear-fueled exhaustion, he cleared his throat and continued, "I need to help the alphas reestablish order among their packs."

"How many did we lose?" I asked.

"Thirty-nine."

The room tilted. *I did this… I killed them.*

"I'll be using the link a lot. I don't want to drain you. If you need me, reach out. Otherwise, I'm going to buffer our link." His mark tingled, then lay silent against my skin. I rubbed the mark, testing the hum of Sam's energy below.

"Damn." His breath caught, and his voice rolled into a rumble. "You got my attention. Good. You need me, you know how to reach me. I'll be back before sunrise."

"Be safe," I said.

"You too." He disconnected the call.

I handed the phone back to Max. "It's going to be the four of us for a while."

"Good." The Keeper dragged me to my feet. "Now go wash up. We'll get some food cooking."

The two flirted mercilessly in the kitchen while I showered. If not for the soap, I would probably have gotten a nose full of pheromones. By the time I had dressed, their voices had fallen silent. However, their heartbeats did enough talking for them.

Clearing my throat, loudly, I hoped to alert them that I was on my way. Nothing changed. I rolled my eyes and shoved open the door. Confused, I tilted my head, pinning my hearing toward the now-closed bedroom doors. One steady heartbeat inside my bedroom and two excited hearts beat inside Ben's. Yet, in the kitchen, a knife clicked against a chopping board. Inhaling, I froze.

In stealth mode, I crept to the kitchen, taking in the view. My breath hitched. Dressed in jeans and a flannel shirt with sleeves shoved up his muscular forearms, Derek diced a blend of vegetables into a boiling pot of water. My brain dragged up the memories of his rejection, playing it on loop. *Good.* I let the anger burn through me. *People died because of me.* I deserved his dismissal.

"Thought vampires were allergic to garlic."

He turned his profile to me, lips tugging into a half-grin. "An old wives' tale."

"What about the aversion to common threads?"

His brow creased, and I flicked my finger at his half-buttoned shirt.

"I've worn worse," he said.

I chewed the inside of my cheek. I could have stared stupidly at him forever, but the past events swirled through my mind. A soft moan from Ben's bedroom sent my lips flat.

Derek's grin deepened. "Just a touch of compulsion for them to give in to their wants."

"The Keeper said she'd kill us if anyone used magic on her."

"I used it only on the wolf. They'll be occupied—"

"I have ears." I raised my hands in front of my face. "I don't need the playbook."

Another moan.

I groaned. "They're supposed to be watching over Ben."

"The witness laid a circle of protection around the bed. No harm will befall your steward."

Careful not to disturb the new dirt ring around the kitchen, I took a seat. Propping my elbow on the table, I rested my chin against my palm, quirking an eyebrow at Derek. "So, I'm safe now, too."

Derek shifted his attention to the ring and smirked. "From harm."

"Why are you here?"

He moved to the sink with his focus seemingly set on the snowstorm outside the window.

"All I need to do is touch the mark—"

"I'm your hunter," he said. "You can order me away as you see fit. No need to bring your *mate* running."

"Kinda bitter there."

"No." The sink groaned under his clenched fingers. *"Furious."*

The heat in that single word had me fake-studying the table's wood grain pattern to keep my deceitful hormones in line.

Derek, holding his culinary delight, moved to the edge of the circle. "You'll need to let me in."

Too tired to banter, I ran my foot through the ring and Derek settled in the chair next to mine. *For fuck's sake.* He could wreck me alone with his damn knee brushing against mine.

He slid the bowl of pasta in front of me.

"Thanks. But I'm not hungry—" My stomach rumbled, ratting me out, so I grabbed up the fork. *Just eat. Then kick him out.* My stare connected with Derek sitting back in the chair, arms tucked across his chest. "You're going to sit there and watch me?"

"I like watching you."

Camouflaging my sputter, I shoved a bite into my mouth, and my moan joined the Keeper's. Closing my eyes, I savored the flavors of my first home-cooked meal in months. After my second bite, I dragged open my eyes. "You missed your calling."

Derek brandished a real smile, one that warmed the seriousness in his eyes. Even the tips of his fangs appeared less menacing, startling me, because if he wasn't trying to kill or seduce me, I'd never seen a genuine smile. His gaze lowered to my mouth. And there it was, desire hotter than the chili pepper in his sauce. Ignoring the fluttering of my heart, I set to eating, and Derek rose to his feet, making himself busy cleaning up.

Polishing off the bowl, I sat back, sighing. "To think, this is what I have been missing."

"Indeed." He took the empty bowl. "Having me serve you in *every* way."

Delirious if he were hinting or teasing, I crossed my legs while Corbus popped into my thoughts. *Balance.* Well, Derek was doing a fine job balancing his demeanor. Another sigh came from the bedroom, and I slapped my hands on the table. Before I went crazy, I needed all the sex and desire out of the cabin. "Come tomorrow," I said, "whatever the outcome, you'll be free of me."

The bowl shattered into the sink. "Don't."

"You're the one—"

"What I said was to protect you."

I shoved to my feet. "I don't need your protection."

"Tonight, you proved that you do." He spun to face me. "That you are still…"

"Still what?"

He stalked toward me. "Good."

"Good?" I countered his steps until my back pressed against the door. "Because of me, thirty-nine betas are dead."

"You put your life at risk to save them—"

"If I hadn't broken into the Light realm, they would *all* be alive."

"Wrong." Derek paused a foot away from me. "The fae would have found a reason—"

"I *am* the reason." A sob wrecked my voice. "Because of me, people die."

"No." Emotion blazed within his determined stare. "You are not a monstrous being."

"I'm a fucking werewolf, Derek."

"Have you directly killed anyone?" He raised a finger, adding, "Stone men and golems are not living."

I gashed my teeth. "No."

"Last night when you lost control, I wanted you to tear into the alpha. Watch as his life slipped past your lips—"

"You stopped me."

"Yes. If I did not, this innocence, goodness, you possess would have been marred. Your fight. Your drive. Your essence is rooted in this purity." He stepped up against me, running his hands up my forearms, burning a path of desire to where he rested his fingertips against the junctures of my throat. "Let me protect your innocence."

My pulse hammered against his chilled fingertips. "I'm not some virginal maiden needing a rescue. "

"I agree." Derek tipped his head, grazing his lips against my temple. "From your dreams, I have experienced your mastery of coupling," he rumbled.

Mouth dry, knees trembling, I reached for words, "That's—"

"Tomorrow, let me be your death dealer." He placed a finger against my lips, silencing my protest. "Tonight, let me love you."

Our eyes connected while the plea and reserve of his request still lingered in his touch against my lips. Blood roared inside my ears, stomach tightened, and sweat dampened the hair at my temples, while I fought the urge to lick his finger. My evident desire was on full display to the predator. However, he made no advancement. He could've released the blood-bond. Devoured me with his mouth. Yet he refused to decide for me.

"Yes," I whispered.

Derek crashed against me. When he claimed my lips, I released my frustration and want on him.

"Yes," he groaned. "Give me everything." Without breaking our kiss, he slipped an arm around the small of my back and reached for the door handle with the other. As his tongue rolled across mine, he ushered us outside.

When the snow bit at my bare feet, I whimpered against his mouth.

"Hold on to me," he breathed, hiking my legs to hug around his hips. The landscape blurred with his speed. Flawless, Derek navigated the forest, only slowing the pace when just the sound of my heartbeat and breath surrounded us. Wrapping my arms around his neck, I dragged my nose across his neck, inhaling him. As I traced my teeth across his collarbone, a growl vibrated from his throat.

Derek rocked us to a halt against a tree. Breath exploded from my lungs as he hoisted me upward, raising his lips to my jugular. The force of his want buffered any discomfort from the frozen bark digging against my back, driving my desire to searing need. He replaced his lips with his fangs, dragging my heart into my throat.

His voice shook against my skin. "I'll claim you right here."

"Wait," I moaned. "Can't claim me."

Derek stilled. "Oh, my wolf." He ran his lips along my throat, pressing his words to my skin, driving me to insanity. "The Gods themselves could not stop me from giving you my soul."

"Corbus will kill me." I pulled away, taking a moment to collect my bearings. Soft falling snow drifted through the forest canopy, reflecting the moonlight and illuminating the determination etched within Derek's face.

"Then my blood will not pass your lips." His finger trailed down my temple. "My name, your song of raptures, will."

Relief left me in a rush of breath, curling upward to tangle with my body heat.

Derek's brows drew tight. "You'll freeze."

I dragged his face to mine. "Do I feel cold to you?"

"No."

"Then keep my mind off the elements." I tipped my chin skyward, baring my neck to his waiting mouth, and he pierced me with his fangs. Pain raked my nerves, pulsing me to the edge of orgasm. As he pulled harder at my vein, his lips, warmed by my blood, sucked at my skin. I grasped the back of his head, groaning as heat and pressure built between my legs. At the brink of my release, he withdrew, capturing the blood trickling down my neck, then he grazed his tongue over the bite. Forcing sound into my voice, I stammered, "More—"

He slanted his mouth to mine, and the taste of my blood paralyzed me with sensory overload. I broke the kiss, shoving the sweater over my head and groaning from the sting of ice melting against my back. Clenching my thighs around his waist, I made fast work of removing his shirt, moaning as my breaths and flesh crashed against his.

In frenzied passion, he sank us to the ground. Rolling me beneath him, he pinned my arms taut overhead. The snow melted underneath my feverish body while he worshipped my ribs with his mouth. I bucked against his hips as he dragged his fangs across the side of my breast. With no warning, he sank them into my flesh and a release blazed through me, tearing a scream from my soul.

The scent of his blood called me back to the earth. When I lifted my fingers, blood rolled to my palm. In the throes of my climax, I'd scored my nails across his shoulders. My gums pulsed. Hunger tumbled with desire. Straining my head from the ground, I darted my tongue to my wrist which Derek captured.

He pinned my knuckles to the frozen ground, then ate me with his heated gaze. "Do not taste my blood, unless you are ready to accept my soul."

Need flooded my system and I arched to claim his hungry mouth. He used my thrust upward to tug my jeans free while kissing his way down the center of my breasts. Without breaking the connection between my flesh and his mouth, he removed the rest of our clothing.

"Please—"

My begging was cut short when he pressed his fingers against my core, stroking me to the edge again. A master, attuned to my nearing release, Derek withdrew, allowing his tongue to continue the blessed torture, lapping at my navel.

"I will taste every part of you." He nibbled and explored my hip bone. "I will kiss your soul." Tugging my hips upward, he ran his tongue over my center. I raked his hair through my fingers, moaning as stars shot through my vision. He teased me to a frenzy, denying me what I craved.

"Derek—" I panted. "I need…"

Bringing his body to hover over me, he removed the stray hairs sticking to my face. "What does my wolf need?"

"You," I breathed.

He pressed a soft kiss to my lips. "You have *always* had me." The brisk pause allowed me to steal a glance between our naked bodies. A slight tremor consumed his taunt frame. "I—" His voice caught. "I cannot lose you."

"Right now, you have me." I traced his jaw with my index finger. "We have us."

His mouth crashed against mine. Desperation. Need. Hands and lips moved in synchronicity, only pausing as I hooked my ankles around his hips, guiding him. Holding his gaze with mine, Derek drove forward. Heart shattered and soul taken, I screamed his name. Surrendering to his possession, I caged his face between my hands, capturing his lust-filled stare as his thrusts spiraled me closer to release.

"You are mine," he groaned, filling me deeper.

I drove my hips to match his rhythm, refusing to go over the edge without him, I tightened my grip, dragging his face closer. "Derek," I growled against his lips. "*You* are *mine*."

He came undone, taking his pleasure by driving harder into me. As he swelled, stretching me to the point of delicious pain, I sent my screams down his throat. While my orgasm crashed through me, a growl tore from Derek and he filled me with his release. He rolled his hips, carrying us to the end of our climaxes. When he pressed his lips to my throbbing temple, my heart fluttered. Refusing to remove my legs from around him, I kissed his shoulder as our deep pants froze in the air.

Above us, the twilight sky warned of the approaching dawn. Closing my eyes against the glaring reminder of what was to happen today, I ran my fingers through Derek's damp hair, holding him tight to me. Sighing, I relished in his weight grounding me in the moment. Yet, with each passing heartbeat, thoughts clawed their way to the surface. A kaleidoscope of obligations turning and swirling together, until they collided into one central thought.

Pressing my lips to Derek's neck, I sealed my silent pledge. No matter the cruelty and cost, to keep everyone alive, I would give the Lord of Light exactly what he desired.

Chapter Twenty-Six

Dizzy and blissfully fatigued from Derek's attention, I swayed in getting to my feet, knocking against him. The moss-covered earth held some of our body heat, keeping my feet semi-warm. As for my other parts…I cursed and shivered, scanning the snow for my discarded clothing. Even though Derek wrapped his arms around me, the effects of the pending day already drew warmth from his body.

"If the sun did not chase us, I'd make you mine again," he rumbled against my lips.

I cracked a smile, and a gust of wind tore it away. "I need to Change—"

"I can carry you back." His embrace tightened. "Let me hold you a little longer."

"We're out of time." I brushed my nose against the crook of his neck. "You need to get to the cabin. I need to find Corbus and avoid…"

Derek pressed a kiss to the opposite shoulder of Sam's mark. "After tomorrow—"

Before Derek could convince the Devil that all was well, I gripped the back of his head, kissing him deeply. Only when my lungs screamed for breath did I let go. "You will go to Hector."

Derek caged my face in his hands, holding me prisoner in the depths of his eyes. "I have existed through centuries laden with death, misery and mundaneness. I accepted this pantomime as my existence until a single spark set me aflame." My vision tunneled. A literal spark had shot between us when we first touched as a human and a grumpy vampire. Seeing my recognition, Derek continued, "Within that moment, my soul recognized its mate. And yours did, too. Their screams cannot be ignored."

"We need to." Tears spilled from my eyes, rolling across his thumbs which caressed my cheeks.

"No." He tangled his fingers in my hair. "I do not care who or what I need to kill. I refuse to lose you." A shudder of chilled breath passed his lips as he stared into my eyes. "I love you."

My heart plummeted. Fear danced up my ribs. If anything was sure in this world, it was when someone loved me, they died. "Please don't."

"Too late." Keeping his gaze on mine, Derek drew my wrists to his lips, placing his words at my pulse. "My blood for your blood, until my eternal night."

The instant he released me, I made the Change. Not sparing a glance behind, I raced to the cave. The only being I trusted with my plan was Corbus. Without the talisman, I'd hope to find something in his cave that might summon Corbus to me versus heading to the cabin where I'd face everyone.

Props to me for not falling to my death while weaving along the cavern passage. Ahead, the glow of a fire flickered from the cave, sparking my hope. Until I drew in the frozen air carrying the stench of earthworms.

"I can smell you, too, she-beast," Nathaniel said.

Crouching, I peeked inside. Nathaniel, in his tattered suit, sat crossed-legged in front of a roaring fire at the farthest point from the entrance. Pinched between his fingers, a piece of paper browned over the hungry flames. I took a closer look…he held a photo. Four silhouettes came into focus.

I called the Change, taking my human form. "Give it to me."

His blue eyes locked onto me, tipping his chin at the pile of clothes at the entrance. "Dress. I may spew."

Keeping my attention on the photo, I shoved on my go-to sweater and sweatpants while red flags waved across my thoughts. Nathaniel had gone back to the cabin and grabbed *my* clothes. He had known that I needed them. Also, he knew where I would be, and he held the only photo of my family over the fire. Yet, more than any of those alarming facts, another screamed front and center. "Ben?"

"Is delicious." Nathaniel flashed a smile, showcasing his fangs.

"If you hurt him—"

"Benjamin talks in his sleep." Nathaniel lowered the photo to an eager flame, curling the corner. "He loves you."

"Like a sister." I scanned the cave for anything to toss at Nathaniel.

"Tsk-tsk." He clicked his tongue. "You think I did not safeguard myself?"

"The sun will be up soon."

He motioned with his free hand at the daylight-secured cave.

Threatening, I hovered my fingers over Sam's mark. "I'll call—"

"Oh, please." Nathaniel chuckled. "I'll delight in watching the alpha's adoration sour as he scents Derek all over you."

I took a step, which Nathaniel countered by lowering the photo closer to the fire. I froze.

"Are you calling my bluff?" he asked.

"No." Pain gnawed up my ankles from the snow licking at my toes. In an act of cease-fire, I held out my hands. Pressing my back against the cave, I slipped inside further. "I can't smell Ben on you." I swallowed. "Where is he?"

Nathaniel squinted at me. "Where you left him. Alone. Vulnerable."

"He's protected by Corbus' magic and—"

"A horny imposter and her bedded wolf. Yes, they were doing a fine job keeping Benjamin safe."

Safe. Nathaniel cared. Hope for my plan flourished. I forced my heartbeat to slow. I needed to get my photo from the fanged asshole and send him back to the cabin. "Why are you here?"

"To burn a secret." He rattled the picture in his hand.

Sweat trickled down the small of my back. "What secret?"

"The man in this photograph, is he your father?"

When I fisted my hands around the sleeves of my sweater, my hesitance triggered Nathanial to lower the photo closer to the fire.

"Yes," I snapped.

He blinked at me. "You are certain."

"Yes."

"Your mother wasn't a harlot?"

"No," I growled.

Sighing, Nathaniel tapped the photo against his lips. "A human. I could have sworn you used a glimmer of Dark magic tonight."

"A glimmer?" I tilted my head. "I incinerated that thing."

"True. A speck." He paused, glancing at the picture. "Dark magic is the sun compared to the candle of Light magic."

As interesting as the Light and Dark magic mumbo-jumbo was, I needed to distract Nathaniel from the photo bubbling over the flames while simultaneously extracting information if he knew the whereabouts of Corbus. "How did you find this place?"

"Followed the witness."

"Where is he?"

"Not here." Nathaniel pursed his lips, eyes beaming. "He was also spared witnessing your carnal excursion."

"Did *you* witness everything?"

"Enough." Nathaniel eyed me. "Should you tempt fate again, Derek will lay claim and the witness will kill you."

"Maybe."

Nathaniel scrunched his brows. "Perhaps Derek drained too much blood, or you are truly daft. A refresher, you die, and all the werewolves will as well."

It was my turn to grin. "Perhaps."

Nathaniel's eyes flicked to the photo between his fingers. The gears of his clever mind turned through his eyes. "Hm. If your brother is living, he carries the blood of the wolves as well. Should you die, the hounds still live. However, I cannot let you."

"What?"

"The vampire who just professed his love to you." Nathaniel's voice hollowed. "The one you left like a coward. Him. He is the reason. You owe me my favor."

"Derek would be free."

"No, he goes to Hector."

I folded my arms. "There is a loophole."

With his free hand, Nathaniel cupped his ear. "Better go on with it before I move you back to the cabin. The alpha is worried for you. You haven't reached out to him, and no one has seen Derek—"

"Fine." I'd planned to share my idea only with Corbus. But if I didn't key in Nathaniel he'd ruin my single chance at saving both my brother and Derek. "Hector's terms were, after and then, as in, *after,* the vampires aid me with my meeting, *then,* Derek goes to Hector. So, the vampires will not attend the meeting. That includes you and Derek. I'll not have Hector use you two vampires as a loophole against my loophole."

"Interesting. Feasible. Yet"—Nathaniel dangled the photo a fraction closer to the flames—"without us, you will die facing the fae."

"Possibly, and Hector's punishment still becomes obsolete. Derek will be free." I stepped closer. "You would have Ben too."

"Why would I want the human?"

"You have feelings for Ben." I jabbed up a finger. "Not saying they are healthy. But you did not kill him or turn him." I chewed my lip, running Ben's reactions through my mind when it came to Nathaniel. "And he has some for you."

Nathaniel's lip twitched.

"For so long, all Ben and I had was each other," I said. "After this is over, it will never be safe for Ben to go back to the non-monster world. A werewolf, vampire or the Keeper could kill him for what he knows. Besides, Ben thrives in this Otherworldly Creature stuff. He will need your protection, Nathaniel. He will need…you."

Nathaniel sat in silence with his eyes locked on the photo. "Let me tell you why I am called the Betrayer of Kin." He moved his free hand down by his hip and out of view, as he spoke, "To be freed from the Dark realm, I allowed my own blooded family to perish. No matter their cries and pleas, I shed not one tear or lost a heartbeat. Forever and always, I will act in my *own* self-interest. Now, as for you…" Nathaniel lifted his hand. Smoke rolled from his fist which grasped Corbus' dagger.

My heart dropped. "Please—"

"You need to brush up on your hiding skills," he said with a twisted grin. "Should this dagger fall, it would shatter. Raw iron is so hard to come by and your meeting is only hours away." His focus flicked to the photo as he stood. "Yet your heart races more for this crumbled photograph. I ponder."

"Stop—"

Nathaniel raised the photo over the fire. "Sleeping with Derek was selfish." He raised the dagger over the ground. "Taking the alpha's mark for the greater good was selfless. Selfless, the dagger. Selfish, the photograph. Where do your interests truly lie, she-beast?"

Without warning, he released both.

I dove, stretching my hand to catch the dagger a breath from hitting the ground. My attention locked onto the flames devouring my family's photograph. Memories tore free, carrying the echoes from the car crash, tires screeching clashed with screams, filling the cavern. Closing my eyes, I curled into a ball, keeping my rage and wolf below the flesh. Nathaniel would not win. A vibration ran up my hand that grasped the dagger. Energy hummed around me.

I cracked open my eyes to a pair of boots. Slowly, my gaze crawled up the man's body, landing on a pair of opaque eyes.

Corbus' brow creased. "You burn."

Smoke drifted from my fist where it clenched the dagger. Sitting up, I set the blade to balance on my sweatpants while I wagged my hand. Oddly enough, there was not a hint of pain. When I flipped my palm over, only the figure-eight scar from my silver chain encounter marred my skin.

"It is true." Nathaniel clapped his hands. His eyes locked on the now glowing dagger sitting on my lap. "Write that in the Otherworldly book, witness. Dylan's daughter lives."

We both turned to look at Nathaniel.

"How do you know my father's name?"

Nathaniel's grin deepened.

With each passing second, the dagger's glow intensified. Symbols appeared down its spine. I snapped up my head. "These markings—"

"You can see them?" Corbus crouched to my eye level.

"They're like the ones carved into my brother's chest." Careful with directing my question, I cut my eyes to Nathaniel. "What do they mean?"

"They are runes used to bind magic," Corbus answered.

"That makes no sense. Except for the dormant werewolf blood, my brother has no magic." I placed the dagger on the ground. Once off my body, the blade's glow and symbols vanished. "Wait. The last time I touched the dagger, it only gave off a pulsing sensation. No symbols. No glowing."

"When I gave the dagger to you, I thought the touch of magic was mine." Corbus reached inside his pocket and pulled out the talisman. "You were wearing the amulet. The dagger's magic was buffered."

"I don't want—" Magic pressed against me. When I glanced down, the talisman rested around my neck—"it back."

"It chose you," Corbus said. "It no longer listens to me."

Nathaniel shoved his knuckles to his mouth, muttering at me, "I warned you about accepting fae gifts. They take on a life of their own."

"Magic"—I thumbed the feather charm—"from the korrigan's blood. That's why the dagger glows."

Nathaniel laughed. When Corbus looked at the giddy vampire, Nathaniel ceased. His lips tugged over his fangs as he dropped some Otherworldly Creature knowledge on me, "Korrigans were not fae. The vile creatures were fleas. They were the fae's spies into the human realm and in return, they took fae blood as payment."

"Wolf Born." Corbus took a seat across from me. "Do you know about your father?"

"Apparently not."

"Iron reacts to fae blood," Corbus said.

My mind raced. "My mother carried werewolf blood and my father was—"

"You made the *iron* dagger glow." Nathaniel sighed. "Your father was fae."

"I figured it out," I grumbled at him. "Just needed to process."

"You do not have time to muse," he said.

"Why didn't they tell me?" I whispered to myself. "Why did they lie?"

"Did you ask them if they were not human?" Corbus asked.

"No." I tucked my knees to my chest. "Not the type of question a person asks their family."

"Then they did not lie to you." Corbus nodded. "They did it to protect you."

"Wonderful job that did," I muttered.

"I did not recognize Dylan's human form," Nathaniel said. "We served the same fae court. I preferred his company the most before he abandoned us for the Human realm, getting himself killed."

"Now that's a nightmare." I shook my head. "My father was friends with you."

"On the contrary." Nathaniel scoffed. "We hated each other. He had a way with words. Mesmerizing. A true gift. One which you do not possess."

A gust of wind curled into the cave, causing the flames to sputter. Nothing remained of the photo of my secret-hiding family. Living our best fake lives in our perfect suburban home—my eyes widened. "I had a dream that the Lord of Light met with my dad."

"A dream"—Nathaniel slid his back down the wall, resting his bottom on the floor, he daintily crossed his legs at the ankles—"is not reality."

"This was different." I eyed him. "More like a memory."

"When did you have this dream?" he asked.

"After I was shot with the silver bullet."

"A near-death, fevered illusion." Nathaniel laced his hands behind his head. "This should be interesting."

"In the dream, Drew and I were little, and the Lord of Light came to our house." I returned my focus to Corbus, who sat patient, giving no hints about what or how he felt. "The fae told my father the guard stirs."

"Precious." Nathaniel smirked. "Dylan filled his spawns' heads with nighttime myths about supreme beings guarding the realms."

"Dad never read fairytales to us." I glared at Nathaniel. "He read poetry."

Nathaniel mocked wiping a tear from his eye.

"Anything else you remember?" Corbus asked.

Running the dream memory through my head, the proverbial lightbulb moment struck. I asked Nathaniel, "What does 'denounce' mean to the fae?"

"To give up your magic," he answered.

"When does a fae come into their magic?"

"There is no set timeline." Nathaniel cocked his head at me. "Given your finger pyrotechnics, last night, I'd presume you are at the cusp of coming into yours."

"She is," Corbus said.

"How do I stop it?" I asked Nathaniel.

"You do not," Corbus answered.

"She-beast." Nathaniel leaned forward, resting his hands under his chin. "What did the fae say about denouncing?"

"My brother and I needed to denounce ourselves before we came into our power, or we would be exterminated."

Corbus stared into my eyes. "Tonight, the Lord of Light means for you to denounce yourself. He will take your power into himself. You must not give the fae your blood."

I shoved to my feet. "If I don't, then Drew dies."

"If the runes mark your brother's body" —Corbus waited until I looked him back in the eyes—"your brother already gave his blood to the Lord of Light. He denounced his magic. Your brother is lost."

"No," I whispered. "I will save him."

Neither of them responded.

The groaning wind and crackling fire filled the space around us while Corbus just sat there. His attention was on me, yet his gaze rested somewhere in the distance. Nathaniel stayed chilling against the cavern wall, probably waiting for Corbus to kill me.

I snagged up the dagger. No glowing or symbols proved Corbus' observation about the talisman being a buffer to my…power. Just when I had started getting used to going furry. Even coming to terms with the whole unturned vampire bit. Now what? Would I sprout wings? Throw glitter at people? Not that I needed to worry, because I planned on busting into that Light realm then denouncing myself to save my brother. Drew for my blood and my blood only. "Nathaniel, take me to the cabin."

Nathaniel rose to his feet. "You do not order—"

"There's minutes before the sun rises. We go now"—I paused, waiting for him to focus on the bribe about to come out of my mouth—"and you can watch as I tell Sam about Derek."

Nathaniel's eyes widened with jubilation. "Oh, bless my un-beating heart, get over here."

Corbus stood, blocking my path to Nathaniel. "You mean to drive away the alpha just as you did your hunter. You cannot go alone."

Keeping my mouth from falling open, I chewed the inside of my cheek. Maybe Corbus was a mind reader, too.

"Excuse me," Nathaniel chimed in. "Where is the dog going alone?"

"To the Light realm," I answered.

"You cannot take the dagger through your dreams," Nathaniel said.

"How did you cross through?" I asked.

"You *do* want to die," Nathaniel quipped. His voice filtered into my mind, *"Any body of water. Touch it and say...."*

"Say what?" I sent.

Nathaniel looked at Corbus. "She truly means to."

"Look." I shoved the dagger into the waistband of my sweats. "There is no way I'm inviting that asshole into our realm. And there is no way I'm letting anyone else die because of me. So, by myself, I am going to save Drew. If you two won't tell me how to get into that Light realm, I'll find someone who will."

Corbus extended his hand to me. "I will show you what will happen if you rescue your brother."

"Caution." Nathaniel walked around the fire toward me. "Like all fae, his actions are self-serving."

"The witness is neutral," I said.

"No fae is allowed neutrality." Nathaniel rolled his eyes. "You choose a side or die. The witness hasn't divulged which side he supports. The power he possesses leads me to tip his favor to the Dark."

My attention rested on Corbus' extended hand. "When I touched the dagger, it reacted Nathaniel, it reacted to you, too. But it does not react to the witness. When he first gave me the dagger, no smoke. No glowing or symbols came from his touch."

"She-beast…" Nathaniel shifted in front of me. "What is your scattered mind proposing?"

"My father's poems centered around four guardian angels who watched over the world, tasked with keeping order." I stared into Nathaniel's baby-blue eyes. "If the balance was disturbed, the perpetrator who upset the harmony was slain by one of the angels."

"Careful." Nathaniel's Adam's apple quivered. "I wish you to breathe long enough to wreck the alpha's heart."

"The witness is not fae." I glanced around Nathaniel's trembling shoulder to stare at Corbus. His eyes lit with amusement. "You are a *Tuath Dé*. One of the four guards."

He didn't confirm or deny it. Instead, Corbus beckoned me with his fingers. "Come and see what happens should you free your brother."

Wagering the implications of not taking Corbus' offer, I looked at Nathaniel. "I need as many one-ups as possible on the fae," I said to the scowling vampire. Chewing my lip, I grabbed Corbus' hand. Magic pulsed between our palms, followed by an explosion of light that engulfed the cave, forcing our hands apart.

When I lost contact with Corbus, the threads of reality plummeted into Hell. Blinded by the magic, I froze in place while smoke filled my lungs and screams pierced my eardrums. My vulnerability presented someone with the opportunity to grab me from behind, snagging their forearm around my shoulders. With my arms crushed to my sides, the person pinned my back to their chest. From the boney build and height difference, I knew it wasn't Corbus or Nathaniel.

As my vision cleared, a scene of destruction and death materialized. Held hostage in the middle of the burning hunting campground, I scanned the battlefield for Corbus. Piles of torn-apart werewolves littered the ground while vampire dust thickened the air. Below my feet, streams of blood melted the snow, rolling toward the frozen lake. I glanced at the freckled arm around my shoulder then spun to face my captor.

The talisman burned against my skin as I peered into my brother's hollow eyes. Before I could speak, Drew pressed a blade against my neck and whispered, "I'll kill you. He'll make…me."

While metal bit at my jugular, I forced courage into my voice. "Drew, you're stronger than him—"

"I'm not…" His gaze hardened. "*You.*"

"You'll be free. Soon. Just hold on a little longer." Tears ran with the blood racing down my throat while I summoned the magic within me. Pressing my palms against Drew's chest, I drove the light into his body, freeing myself of the vision. The nightmarish scene disappeared, and the cavern came into focus. Nathaniel stood where my brother had been. Shock filled the bloodsucker's eyes.

"You reek of death," he whispered.

"She now knows," Corbus said. I whirled around, setting my fury on him. Sadness consumed his usually blank features. "Your brother is not stronger than the Lord of Light."

Warm wetness rolled down my trembling neck. When I inhaled, a familiar metallic scent flooded my nose. Gripping the edges of my sweater, I refused to wipe the blood away. "I will save my brother." My stupid voice hitched. Straightening my spine, I snapped on my pseudo-ruler's persona. "While I am doing so, witness, keep everyone else safe."

Corbus placed a fist to his heart. "I will protect the Human realm."

Not trusting my voice, I nodded.

"You need to prepare," he said. "I will meet you at the lake."

"What lake?" Nathaniel demanded.

"The hunting campgrounds," I answered. "That's where I enter."

"I cannot aid her within the Light realm," Corbus said to Nathaniel.

"I am expelled." Nathaniel cut his attention to me. "I set foot inside, and I am incinerated."

"Then she goes into the Light realm ill prepared." Corbus walked toward the dying fire.

"*That's* the one thing I am good at," I said.

Both men stared at me.

So, I added, "I'm always winging it."

Corbus puffed his cheeks with a stifled breath as he continued to the fire.

As the flames ignited upward, my reflexes took over and I grabbed Nathaniel by the wrists, yanking him away. While I squinted at the fire, no heat hit against my face. Unfazed as well, Corbus walked into the flames, disappearing as the fire imploded.

"You will deny the Keeper her revenge," Nathaniel said. "She is in the same predicament as me."

Blinking at the wisps of smoke coiling from the charcoal logs, I nodded. "Then I have two more Otherworldly Creatures' hearts to break. Take me back."

Nathaniel folded his arms around me, giving me a bit of a squeeze. Perhaps I imagined the embrace more hug-like than his regular detestable grasp. As he drew the shadows around us, he grumbled against my ear. "You are a fool."

Chapter Twenty-Seven

We materialized inside the hallway of my cabin. Avoiding the predawn glow spilling through the kitchen window, Nathaniel released me and stayed against the wall. When I tuned in to my hearing, only Ben's steady heartbeat filtered from my bedroom. Outside, trucks idled, and pack members held heated conversations. As I spun to face the front door, panic strangled my throat. Underneath the kitchen table, the floorboards sat undisturbed.

Not wanting to draw attention to us, I sent to Nathaniel, *"Where is Derek?"*

"Not the faintest idea." Nathaniel's focus tipped in the direction of my bedroom. To Ben.

"Derek must follow my orders. Right?"

"Yes. But…" Reluctant, Nathaniel tore his attention away from my bedroom to stare at me. *"Did you say, 'slumber beneath the floorboards of my kitchen'?"*

"Well…no." I sighed. *"I said he needed to go to the cabin."*

Nathaniel shrugged. *"Then you left a vast breadth for manipulating your orders."*

"Can you find him?"

Footfalls thundered up the porch.

"Not now." Nathaniel switched to talking, giving the approaching werewolf a hint about who was in the cabin. "I need to take shelter."

The front door swung open. Nolan braced against the doorframe. His heavy breaths tightened a blood-soaked bandage wrapped around his throat. Turning his attention to Nathaniel, Nolan growled, "She bleeds."

"I'm fine." Slapping a hand over the nearly healed scratch, I shifted in front of Nathaniel, blocking him from the ticked-off werewolf. "Where is—"

Outside, the Keeper screamed.

I raced for the door. Countering me, Nolan used his mass to barricade my exit. "You must stay here."

"Move," I gritted.

"No." Nolan's jaw knotted. "You don't need to see—"

"What?"

"The delta must be punished."

I shoved the link through my voice, "I *command* you to move."

When my energy forced him to obey, the sticky-sweet scent of fear rolled off Nolan. As I barged out to the porch, the frigid air burned my lungs, causing me to sputter in pain. With the subzero temperatures and near whiteout conditions, if the pack and Keeper didn't get inside soon, people would die.

Squinting against the blizzard in disbelief, I hesitated a second to make sense of the action in front of me. A pack member blocked the Keeper attempting to get to Max, who was tied to a tree. Sam stood to the side, aiming a gun at Max.

I released the link and the wave of energy plowed into the pack members. Every werewolf crumbled to their knees. Sam turned to look at me. Relief flooded through his mark as he struggled to his feet.

"Drop the gun," I ordered.

Sam engaged the safety, then tossed it to the ground. Ignoring the snow stabbing at my bare feet, I raced down the steps.

"You better fucking control them," the Keeper snapped at me while yanking at the knots holding Max in place. "Or else."

When I stopped next to Sam, he engulfed me in a rib-crushing hug. His wolf flooded my senses while mine crashed through me. When I was caught off guard by how natural and good it felt, Sam managed to move faster than me, his freezing hands cupping my face. Sam's eyes set aglow. "You're bleeding."

"I'm okay." I kept authority in my tone. "Why were you pointing a gun at him?"

"The delta left you unprotected," Sam growled.

I cut my focus to Max. His wide eyes latched to mine. I shot my attention back to Sam. "Let him go."

"No." Sam matched the heat in my words. "He swore, on his life, to protect you. He failed."

"He did protect me." I leaned into Sam, putting him off balance so he released my face to keep from stumbling backward. "I waited until he was occupied and then I left. Me. So, if anyone is to be punished, it's me."

Sam's limbs tensed. "He is also the spy."

I couldn't believe it. I shifted my attention back to Max shaking his head.

"It wasn't me," Max pleaded.

Deep down in my bone marrow, I believed him. "It wasn't Max."

"We have proof," Sam said. "Yesterday, there were calls made from his cellphone. We retrieved the excommunicated alpha's phone at the campgrounds, confirming they were in communication." Sam lowered his attention to the gun. "I'm sorry, but it is our law."

"No." I dug my nails against his arm. "Not anymore."

"Laws cannot change." Below my nails, Sam's arm flexed. Making a fist, he had given a silent signal. Movement from my peripheral vision, pulled my attention away from Sam to Jimmy aiming a crossbow at Max.

"It wasn't the delta," Ben shouted. He stumbled onto the porch, bracing against the snow-covered banister. He wheezed, "It...was me."

"You little shit." The Keeper struggled her way through the snow toward the porch.

"Release the delta," I said to Jimmy.

"The delta failed to protect you." Sam shoved his face toward mine, forcing me to look at him in the glowing eyeballs. "No matter if you snuck out. It is the law. You are my mate. You cannot be alone. Ever."

I popped open my mouth to confess I wasn't alone until the pack had encroached on us. The confession would wait for when we were alone.

Misinterpreting my silence as understanding, Sam continued, "That means the delta will be punished."

"You don't have to kill him."

"No." Sam lowered his voice. "And I wasn't planning to."

I blinked. "You had a gun."

"A shot to the kneecap. He'd heal in a couple of weeks." Sam moved closer, muttering against my ear, "But you had to go and pull rank on me. Now, we have some major damage control to deal with."

"Let me talk to my steward, then I'll fix whatever monster law I broke to keep people from being maimed." I pulled away to look Sam square in his wind-burned face. "Until then, no more guns or crossbows aimed at pack members. Got it?"

He gave a curt nod.

I pivoted back to the cabin. As Nathaniel blocked the Keeper's advancement to the porch, the rising sun blistered and burned his exposed skin. Simultaneously, Nolan denied a frantic Ben from reentering the cabin while I marched up the steps. Grabbing Ben by the collar of his sweat-drenched T-shirt, I raised an eyebrow at Nolan, who tipped his chin and stepped away from the door.

While I dragged Ben inside the cabin, Sam followed, pausing to give orders to Nolan, "Take the delta to the third cabin. Everyone is to take shelter."

Nathaniel abandoned his sparring with the Keeper, taking up pursuit behind us. Preaching every cuss word combo, the Keeper barged her way between Sam and Nathaniel. We all filed into my bedroom.

Nathaniel tossed the comforter over the curtain rod, then tucked himself inside the narrow closet. Sam stood at the bedroom door, holding the Keeper by the forearm, restraining her from attacking Ben, who I forced to plop on the bed. The frame bounced and he winced. Not trusting my strength around him, I moved to stand by the dresser.

Sweat beaded at Ben's hairline as his wide-eyed stare bounced between the unfavorable ratio of three livid to one smitten monster. Since Nathaniel was no longer on fire, he hadn't taken his focus off Ben. I huffed at the vampire. The corner of his charred lip pulled into a grin. Shaking my head, I set my frustration on the spy.

"Why?" I asked Ben.

He sucked in a gulp of air, puffing out his narrow chest. "As your steward, I wanted to make sure you had titled the strongest alpha. One with the resources to protect you and who would also be open to working with the vampires. From those discussions with the other alphas, Sam still *is* the only match."

"The steward was acting on behalf of her interests," Nathaniel stated. "From this testimony, I see no cause for punishment."

"Agreed," Sam said.

"Agreed," the Keeper muttered.

Sam peered down at her.

"Err, I mean, what a dick move, but it isn't a reason to drown him." She winked at me, then glared at Sam. "Let me go."

"Behave," he warned, releasing her.

"Wolf Born," Ben prompted me. "What is your verdict?"

"Wait." I folded my arms. "Is this a trial?"

"Andrea does not count." Ben shared a look with me. Oh, the Keeper counted, but for the sake of hiding her identity from Sam, Ben added the clause. "The two Otherworldly Creatures cast their votes. However, me being your steward, in the end, it is your ultimate ruling what happens to me."

"No punishment for my steward," I said.

The room fell silent of words, however, tension still buzzed off Ben. "Tess—"

"She is a queen," Sam warned. "Address her as such."

"Ben is my family," I retorted. "He can call me whatever he wants."

"There is more, I wish to come clean about." Ben's voice tightened. "With you…alone."

"No," the three monsters said.

I nodded for Ben to keep going.

"Fine." Ben swallowed. He set his full attention on me. "I've been spying as well on the alpha. Listening to his calls. His conversations. Watching him."

Sam tensed.

"Go on," I said to Ben.

"I wanted to make sure that he would accept your relationship with the hunter." Gripping the edges of the mattress, Ben flicked his attention at Sam. "And he doesn't."

I cut a weary glance at Sam before I slumped against the dresser. The dagger pressed against my hip. And there it would stay. I wouldn't part from the weapon until it was embedded in the Lord of Light's chest. "Alpha, the hunter is missing. Would you know his location?"

"The last time I saw the bloodsucker was at the campgrounds." Through clenched teeth, Sam added, "I am sure you have seen him since."

I nodded.

"He was here. You left with…him." Sam's gaze hardened. "You were alone with him. You—"

"I was there," Nathaniel cut in. "She did not sleep with the hunter."

Shocked, we both snapped our attention to the vampire with his mouth open, showing his unburning tongue. His voice wormed into my mind. "*Sleep has so many meanings these days.*"

I jabbed a finger at Nathaniel. "He's twisting—"

The bloodsucker cut me off, "To protect your life, Alpha, she will try to convince you that she did, hoping you will leave her." Nathaniel's gaze shifted to the Keeper. "She means to go to the Light realm and face the fae by herself."

She leered at me. "The fuck you will."

Sam shoved away from the door. In one stride, he towered over me. "We go together. We save your brother. Together." Sam's eyes blazed and his voice deepened in warning, "Understood, Mate?"

Gritting my teeth, I met the challenge in his eyes. How quickly my plan had frayed at the seams. Desperate, I lashed out, "I'm not your mate. Derek—"

A growl vibrated from Sam's chest. He snapped his focus to Nathaniel. "I accept. I owe you a favor."

"Done," Nathaniel said.

I spun to face Nathaniel. "What?"

"That's what I was trying to get at," Ben mumbled to me. "There was a deal being discussed between the alpha and Nathaniel. Only, the alpha hadn't committed to it until now."

"Fool," the Keeper muttered at Sam.

"What was it?" I asked Ben.

"After the meeting with the fae, Nathaniel would turn your hunter over to the Vampire Council."

"Derek already belongs to the head of the Vampire Council. After the meeting with the fae, the hunter must leave to serve the king." Gripping the sides of my head, I glared at Sam. "You owe Nathaniel for *nothing*."

Dramatically, Nathaniel sighed. "If you stopped living in your world of secrets, the alpha would have known." Nathaniel goaded, "Alas, you do, and now the alpha owes me a favor."

The scent of fear oozed from Sam's pores.

"What was the favor?" I whispered.

Sam just stared at me.

"The next full moon…" Ben's voice trailed off. "Umm, you see, the alpha agreed to—"

"Conceive a child," Sam answered.

The Keeper shook her head at Nathaniel. "That's very fae of you."

"Oh, I want nothing of their spawn." Nathaniel smirked. "Only to relish in her bitterness and woes."

Black dots ate at my vision as my heart dropped to my toes. *Let Nathaniel think he won.* Knowing full well that I'd not live to see the next full moon, I'd deny Nathaniel Sam's favor. I reaffirmed my decision, for in the end, Derek would be free, and my brother would be safe and alive. *I win.*

Ben stood.

"I'm fine." A full-out sob rose from my chest and I snapped my teeth around it, keeping it from exploding past my lips. I waited until I trusted my voice not to wobble. "I just need space."

Tears burned down my cheeks while I stumbled out of the bedroom and almost smacked into Nolan's chest. *Great.* Unable to avoid him physically, I focused past Nolan's rigid frame. Inside the kitchen and living room, pack members sheltering from the storm sat on the floor, staring slack-jawed at me. They had heard everything. Outside, the wind howled, and snow pelted the windows. There was no escape. *Nope.* Trapped, I faced all their silent judgments.

"Rise," Nolan said. The pack clambered to their feet while Nolan set his attention on me. "May I speak?"

Too tired to protest, I just nodded.

He lowered his gaze to my chin as he spoke, "You took our alpha as your mate, strengthening our pack. You saved my life. You broke law to protect a pack member. You risk your life to save *our* brother from the fae. You are *my* queen. I stand with you." He raised his eyes to mine, placing a fist on his chest. "My life for *yours.*"

Oh, my tears ran in streams now. After our rocky introduction to the betas' slaughtering hours ago, there Nolan stood unwavering with admiration flooding his voice. He had destroyed the scales of favor, unifying the entire pack with his public display of support. I placed a trembling fist at my heart. Staring into my beta's gunmetal-gray eyes, I said, "My life for the pack."

Each pack member raised a fist to their chest and recited as a choir, "My life for yours."

The muted responses of pack members in the other cabins echoed.

"My life for the pack," I repeated.

I let my hand slip. Everyone else stayed at attention, waiting. I nodded at the pack, and they moved to their prior floor-side positions. Catching the fall of tears on my sleeve, I searched for a distraction, and the bronze frame over the fireplace caught my attention. Well, I'd not sit and wait for sunset. Storming into the living room, I stepped over pack members' legs on my way to the county map.

Glaring at my distorted reflection within the glass cover, I tore the map from the chimney, then marched to the kitchen. Busting the frame over my knee, I retrieved the yellowed map, slapping it on the table.

Nolan rounded the table to stand next to me. I pointed at the hunting campground's lake. "This is where the fae will try to enter our realm."

Nolan nodded. "What does our queen need?"

"The packs will flank the sides of the campgrounds while the vampires form a barricade in front of the lake. Many of them can use shadows as cover. Perhaps the fae will miscalculate our numbers." I flicked my eyes to the Keeper, who came up to my right side, slipping an arm around my waist.

Using her free index finger, she drew an arch at the back half of the lake. "The naiads will strike here."

Nolan's eyebrows shot to his forehead. "You're human."

She winked. "I have friends."

In an attempt to keep Nolan from asking more questions, I pointed at the town. "The witness will protect the humans."

"Is he strong enough?" the Keeper asked.

I nodded then returned my attention to Nolan. "Before this storm gets worse, we need to head there."

"I'm riding with you." The Keeper squeezed me before letting go. "I'll get your clothes ready. You're not facing the fae in sweats. Although that would be an epic sight, you kicking his ass in peasant attire."

"I'm coming too." Ben peeked his head out of my bedroom.

I chewed my lip. The advantages of him coming outweighed the disadvantages. "Bundle up. I need you to teach me all you can about fae protocols on the way over."

"Beta." Sam approached from behind. "Get the word to the packs."

"I'll grab the book," Ben said as he slipped away.

When he was out of hearing range, I gained the courage to look at Sam. "Before sunset, I want my steward away from the campgrounds."

Chapter Twenty-Eight

If there was a minor chance for my survival, I pledged that Jimmy would never to the ever-est-ever chauffeur for me again. Because of the deteriorating weather conditions and his lack of offensive driving skills, a typical fifteen-minute drive to the hunting campgrounds took almost an hour.

In the backseat, wedged between Ben grabbing the oh-shit handle while hyperventilating against the window and the Keeper fussing with my hair, I dipped into my memories. Imminent death approached, yet my focus drifted to Derek. He had to be okay since my heart kept beating and no weird sixth sense hinted that he was in trouble. Because of our blood-bond, Derek explained his death would be insufferable to me. As I reaffirmed my decision to save my brother, my stomach twisted. Derek would survive my death. I'd order him to.

"There." The Keeper draped the intricate braid over my shoulder. "Now. No touching, I spent my morning perfecting the skill from the YouTube." She narrowed her brows. "But it is not a tube. Instead, videos of chickens wearing hats morph into ones of braiding hair. Next thing you know, you've lost an hour. It runs on fae time."

"Is this chick for real?" Jimmy cut a look at Sam in the passenger seat.

In response, Sam grunted as he sent texts on one phone while talking into another propped against his shoulder. The whole trip he communicated with the packs while avoiding me. *Smart.*

The vehicle slid to a stop and Nathaniel, in his garment bag, knocked against the back of my seat. "Once this truce is over," he muttered, "the driver will be underneath my teeth."

Jimmy glanced at me through the rearview mirror. "Can you order him to shut up?"

"Nope." I made air quotes. "I don't have that power."

"Correct," Nathaniel said.

Jimmy shook his head and exited the vehicle.

"So many…" Ben peered out of the foggy window, dropping his hands to the Otherworldly Creatures book balanced on his thighs. "And they're all…."

"Yep. All werewolves," the Keeper answered. "Just the two of us humans. Could be only one soon."

Ben sucked in a breath. "I didn't know they would blame Max."

"You used his phone," she gritted.

"If he left his phone outside *my* bedroom, where you were getting it on, I could have deleted—"

"Stop." I glared at them both. "Max will not be punished. Right, Alpha?"

Sam let his sigh fog the windshield. "We have a lot to discuss after tonight."

Nathaniel chuckled.

"It's two hours to sunset," I warned. "Hope you're comfortable back there."

"You mean to leave me here?" Nathaniel asked. "My body will freeze. Come nightfall, I will be useless."

"Damn." I let my evident nonconcern filter through my voice. "That super sucks."

All bickering ceased when a pack member opened Sam's door. As I leaned over the Keeper to open ours, she flicked her gaze at me. "Get used to the hospitality, queen. They must hold doors. Guard you. Wait for you to address their existence. You deny them any of these, and they can be punished. Tonight, you need all their beating hearts loyal and ready to die for you."

"The vampires too," Ben added. "This is not the time to challenge rules."

"In simplistic terms," Nathaniel said, "the vampires sent by the king are beneath your standing. Do not directly acknowledge them. Only speak to your hunter. Be very precise in your orders. Don't be a fool forfeiting our laws. Last night, your reckless attack on the golems worried them—"

"Worried?" The Keeper snapped her head at the garment bag. "After she risked her life to save the betas and singlehanded destroyed the golems, the hunter told me—"

I grabbed her by the arm. "When did you talk to Derek?"

"Before." A blush crept through her cheeks. "Max and I—"

Sam opened our door.

Minus Nathaniel, we exited and huddled together. I was not at all dressed for the elements, but better off than the damn skirt the Keeper had tried to bribe me into. No. I'd let my attire further insult the Lord of Light, with me showing up in my sneakers, jeans, worn sweater, jacket and an iron dagger.

I motioned Jimmy over. "Let Nathaniel chill for a bit before he joins us."

Jimmy's lips tugged into a half-grin while he pressed his fist to his heart. "Yes, my queen."

Once Sam moved to my side, our pack escorted us into the camp's dining hall. Inside, a couple of hundred men cleaned weapons while others shoveled food into their mouths. When everyone stopped what they were doing to stand, I let go of my fear that the packs were still divided when it came to the mission. In unison, they thumped fists to hearts and raised their voices, "My life for you."

"Mine for the pack," I responded. The Keeper arched her eyebrow, giving me a silent cue. "Carry on," I added.

With that, the men returned to their activities.

"I'm never going to get used to that," Ben whispered.

Instead of countering him with, "In a matter of hours you won't have to," I caught the attention of one of the men. "My steward needs to eat."

Ben's glasses slid down his nose as he stared at me. Shoving the book against his chest, smartly, he refused to protest out loud.

I patted his shoulder. "You will return to my side once your stomach stops growling."

Pressing his lips flat, Ben followed the man.

"Wolf Born," Sam said, holding his hand out to me. Staring at the appendage, unable to bear touching him, I linked my arm with the Keeper's, dragging her tight to my side. I nodded at Sam to lead the way.

In the center of the room sat a huge circular table. All the alphas stood by waiting for us. In their winter gear, each wore a different-colored band wrapped around their forearm. When I drew closer to the table, I understood why. Colored markers, coordinating with each of the alpha's bands, peppered a large map of the campgrounds.

"Most will fight in human form." Khyber, with his arm in a sling, stepped forward. "A quarter of each pack will shift along with the able betas."

I looked at Sam. "Are they well enough?"

"They will be ready come nightfall."

Khyber gave a wary glance at the other alphas.

Crap. Not even ten minutes, and I had pulled a no-no by interrupting an alpha.

"Say something." The Keeper rubbed her forehead. "About the map."

I turned to Sam. "Walk me through the defensive tactics."

Sam spent the next few minutes going over and fine-tuning the coordinates. The Keeper stood at my side, holding my hand, and squeezing when something needed correction.

"Did you get all that?" I sent Nathaniel.

"Yes. I will communicate with the vampires. Now. Bring me – oh, the reckless driver is here. He is singing. Tear me asunder and spread my ashes to the four corners of the earth."

Rubbing my nose, I hid my grin. The ghost of a smile faded. Through a dusty skylight, the sun punctured a storm cloud, spotlighting the table. As the talisman warmed my skin, the shadow of a crow flew over the map. My next meeting had arrived.

"I am going to take a tour of the lake." I faced the Keeper, whose attention fastened to the map. "Andrea, will you join?"

Her dark eyes rose to lock with mine. "This is really going down."

I nodded.

"I am honored to be a part, Wolf Born."

Sam moved to my side, tipping his head in the direction of the front doors. "While there is a break in the weather, we should head out."

"Agreed," I said. "Lead the way."

As we passed by the men cleaning weapons, the glint of copper caught my attention, and I paused by a man loading the odd-colored pistol.

"May I borrow that?" I asked.

"My queen." The man engaged the safety, then offered me the weapon.

Sam gave me a questionable look.

"I've had three months of practice." I dropped the gun into my coat pocket. "I'm a decent marksman."

Once outside, my heart kicked against my ribcage. Behind the thinning storm clouds, the sun descended toward the horizon. Magic hummed around me, raising goosebumps across my skin.

The Keeper grabbed my hand. "Do you feel—"

A commotion arose from the direction of the lake. Men raced toward the campgrounds. The standard greeting was forfeited. The men formed a barricade around us, nailing home the deadly progression of the situation.

"The lake is glowing," one of the men said. His face paled. "Beneath the ice…there were so many…eyes."

"He is here," the Keeper whispered to me. "He cannot cross without your invitation. We are safe to survey the lake from a distance."

"Last night," Sam said, "he sent those things without an invite."

She shrugged. "The queen has done nothing to warrant an attack today."

To get Sam's focus off the Keeper dropping her fae knowledge, I pointed at the binoculars around the messenger's neck. "Can I have those?"

"My queen." Kneeling, the man gave them over to me.

"Now"—I hung the binoculars around my neck—"all of you go inside."

Sam cut a look at me, so I clarified, "Andrea and the alphas, please stay with me."

The men trotted inside while Sam and Khyber turned away from me, muttering about surveying tactics. Ignoring them in return, I pulled the Keeper along, trudging through the snow to where I had first scouted the camp as a wolf.

"You have to follow the laws," she grunted.

"Is there one about me walking away from conversations?"

"Well…no."

"Good." We stopped next to the boulder. "Keep a lookout for me?"

"For things that can snap my human neck?" She sighed and plopped her back against the stone. "Sure. I'll be the werewolf's lookout."

I cleared the ten-foot landing. Not prepared for the layer of ice beneath the snow, I flailed my arms to correct my balance and a hand encircled my forearm, keeping me upright.

"His army cannot cross," Corbus said. "However, they can lure your wolves to the lake and drown them."

When I turned to face him, my breath hitched. A bear pawprint, drawn in charcoal, covered his face while he wore the bearskin draped across his shoulders. Although impressive in his attire, what lay beneath rendered me stupefied. Magic emanated from his body in a pulsing glow. He'd kicked his human disguise curbside. Corbus was magic itself.

"Oh shit." The Keeper belly-flopped onto the boulder. I tugged her up, pulling her to my side. Breath exploded from her lips. "He's…not fae."

"Nope," I answered.

Sam joined us. As there was not much room, we stood shoulder touching shoulder. No need for binoculars. Like a lightbulb, the lake glowed while its layers of ice cracked.

"The packs will keep the humans away," Sam said.

"Okay." I crossed my arms and glanced at Sam. "But who protects the wolves?"

"For now, they are safe," Corbus said. "When the battle begins, it will be difficult to watch over them all."

"The fae's army numbers compare to the stars in the sky." The Keeper shivered next to me. "Much blood will be spilled."

"They will not cross," I affirmed.

"He will use your brother." The Keeper's voice shook. "And if the torturing does not work, he will send his magic through. The Lord of Light will turn your wolves against each other. You."

Sam growled. "That will not happen."

"Alpha." Corbus glanced at Sam. "Before last night, have you fought against the fae?"

"No," Sam said.

"Heed your human friend's warning, Wolf Born." Corbus paused, his eyes fixed on the glowing lake. "You have a thousand werewolves and a handful of vampires. Your numbers are weak. There is still time—"

"I will save my brother." I skimmed my fingers against the hilt of the concealed dagger. In the distance, seagulls screamed. As I sucked in a breath, salt-layered air stung my nose. "Tell the packs, no more talking outside," I said to Sam. "Nathaniel said magic affects our wolf forms less. Have the patrollers shift."

Sam glanced over the edge of the boulder, nodding to Khyber, who radioed the order to the packs.

"Smart," the Keeper whispered. With her attention fused to the lake, she didn't notice that a soft glow illuminated beneath her skin. To hide the light from the men, I tossed the coat hood over her head. Minutes from the meeting and all I needed was for Corbus to abandon us and the Keeper to destroy the earth because she turned into a human glowstick, revealing her fae identity.

"Alpha!" Jimmy bolted up the hill toward us. "There are a shit-ton of vehicles heading our way."

"Which direction?" Sam asked.

"From the casino," Jimmy answered.

The Keeper shook her head, hinting the vehicles weren't carrying naiads.

Corbus tensed. Magic brushed my arms as his eyes flicked opaque.

Khyber's radio crackled. An urgent voice mumbled, and Khyber relayed the message. "Caravans are heading from *all* directions."

I shoved the binoculars to my eyes. Across the lake, the first cluster of vehicles appeared. On the leading vehicle's driver-side door sat a gold emblem of two snakes intertwined. All blood drained from my face and pooled in my frantic heart. "It's the Vampire King."

"No." Corbus' eyes returned to normal. "It is the entire Vampire Council and their entourages."

"Thousands of bloodsuckers," Sam growled.

Nathaniel's voice swirled in my mind. *"This is not good."*

"It has begun." Corbus turned to face me. "In this final hour, you must choose between loyalty and love. Before acting, listen to your heart and soul."

"What do you—" Before the last word left my mouth, Corbus disappeared.

Overhead, the air grew dense with magic and the talisman burned against my skin. Storm clouds rushed to cover the sun, pitching the sky into early twilight.

"Formations," Sam ordered.

I dropped the binoculars. My mind scrambled to remember the map. The werewolves inside the dining hall would shift. Once they Changed, the alphas would use their links to control the wolves from attacking anyone outdoors.

Khyber screamed into the radio, "Barricade the hall."

"No—" I gasped. "Ben. He's in the dining hall."

"I'll get him." Jimmy took off.

The Keeper released my arm, and Sam missed grabbing me as I launched off the boulder. Within a few strides, I blazed past Jimmy. Closer to the dining hall, the camp swarmed with men moving into their positions, protecting the wolves in transition. Two alphas pushed the doors to shut, and I dove through, landing in a roll.

The wet cracking of bones combined with the pungent scent of hormones pumping through the werewolves' systems triggered my wolf to fight for control of my body. Shoving her down, I scanned the dimly lit room. Ben must have hit the lights. Only the twilight sky illuminated the hall.

Underneath the center table, Ben huddled, clutching the book to his chest. Not wanting to draw attention to us, I pressed a finger to my lips.

With the men more than halfway through their Changes, using my link could kill or leave them weakened and unable to defend themselves and others. The only option left me sneaking through the room. Each of my steps echoed my thundering heartbeats. Within minutes, hundreds of wolves would see us as food. A foot away, Ben scurried from underneath the table. To keep him from bolting, I grabbed his forearms.

"Tess—" He gasped. "You came back for me."

"I'll always—" I sucked the lie back into my lungs. No. *Always,* wasn't an option after tonight. "Listen, I need you to trust me."

A violent nod bounced Ben's glasses to the tip of his nose.

"Remember when I went wolf and almost—"

Ben gripped the book tighter to his chest. "Are they going to eat me?"

"No. Maybe. Shit." I took a deep breath. "Don't look at them. Try to stay calm. When we get outside, you climb a tree."

I turned to face the room. The only way out required an agonizing walk to the front doors. Ben curled his hand against my shoulder, transporting me back to the staircase of my family home, huddling with Drew, where we had first laid eyes on the Lord of Light. Shaking the memory from my mind, I led Ben through the room.

Snarls rose around us. Feet from the doors, I brushed my fingertips against Sam's mark, sending the link to him. Instantly, the doors opened. While we slipped out, someone shut the doors and the alphas circled the dining hall, preparing to release their links at the wolves.

While a cluster of men surrounded the two of us, Ben's legs buckled, and he plopped into the snow. Currently safe, I turned my focus to scanning for a car. Ben needed to leave. Now. At the edge of the woods, Sam raced toward us, only to be cut off by the Vampire Council's caravan.

"Stay down," I warned Ben.

He nodded in my direction. His foggy glasses protected him from the terror filling my eyes. Time had run out. Speeding Ben away to safety wasn't an option.

"Arms," Sam shouted over the engines. "Protect your queen."

Nathaniel appeared at my side. "Warn your wolves not to attack."

"Stand guard," I ordered the men.

Fluidly, every other man faced away, leaving half the weapons aimed at Nathaniel and the others toward the vehicles. To be able to shoot and fight, the men shifted their stances far enough apart, sparing me glimpses of the cars. Human drivers with compulsion-glazed eyes manned the wheels of the sleek SUVs. Windows tinted to blend with the doors deterred glancing inside. Yards away, the vehicle flaunting the intertwined snake emblem pulled to a stop.

"What could Hector want?" I sent Nathaniel.

"A deal with the fae. Sell you out. Imprison you..."

While Nathaniel listed all the torture-filled possibilities, like a compass seeking north, my thoughts centered on Derek.

"Your attention span is that of a gnat." Nathaniel sighed. *"Indulge me in your mind's urgent affairs."*

"With the clouds blocking the sun, would Derek be awake?"

Nathaniel's jaw dropped. *"You have a fae lord waiting to attack. Wolves mid-transition at your back, and the entire Vampire Council at your door, yet, you want to know if Derek is awake?"*

"I multitask."

Nathaniel's cheeks puffed with his exaggerated breath. *"Unlikely, Derek wouldn't. It is not true night. Only a council member would have the power to rise this soon."*

In unison, the human chauffeurs exited the vehicles, and moved to the back driver's side doors, pausing with their hands at the handles. Ever vigilant, the werewolves aimed their guns, waiting for me to give an order. The driver of the Vampire King's vehicle opened the door.

The angle of the car door hindered a direct view of the Vampire King. While I forced myself to stand tall, anticipation for Hector's grand entrance constricted my throat.

"Tell your guards to part so that I may gaze upon you or I will dissolve our alliance," Hector warned.

"Allow me a visual of the Vampire King," I said to the werewolves.

The guards moved inches.

"Steward, allow me to handle this...interaction," Nathaniel said to Ben, still sitting on the ground. "You are needed to stay focused on the task at hand."

Ben gawked up at me and I nodded. He forced his face back into the book. I shot a look across the way toward Sam. He gave me a slight nod. I took it that meant he would wait for my order to attack.

Nathaniel stepped forward, then bowed to the Vampire King. When Nathaniel rose, he asked, "What is the meaning of the council's…presence?"

"They are my enforcers." Hector's violet-eyed stare burned through me. "Wolf Born, you will forgo this meeting." Before I could counter, he continued, "Should you defy me, the hunter will meet his eternal night." Hector snapped his fingers and the human driver reached inside the vehicle, then tugged Derek's lifeless body out, dropping him to the ground.

"Don't." Nathaniel blocked me with vampire speed. "The king will kill the hunter before you take a single step."

"True," Hector said. The weight of that word crushed my heart. "I will not allow you to throw yourself at the whims of this fae lord. You are a gift of unimaginable…possibilities."

Nathaniel tensed. "She is a foolish disaster."

"She *is* power." Hector ignored Nathaniel and kept his focus on me. "I give you the highest regard using your unturned nature to title the hunter and then flip the loyalties of my guards."

Blankly, I stared at the king as the memory of me titling Derek spun through my mind. He had taken my blood before we had met with Hector. The king had then consumed Derek's. Hector knew I was unturned through Derek's blood. I flicked my gaze down to the snow-covered ground as my memory landed on the Lord of Light tasting my blood, then claiming I was a disgrace to the bloodlines. Fisting my hands, I raised my gaze back to the Vampire King. Through Derek's blood, Hector must have known that I was part…fae.

Hector grinned at me. "I could gaze into your eyes for eternity. Such expression. I trust them more than a vampire's tongue." He drew his attention to Derek's body. "Blood."

"The king outwitted me," Nathaniel gasped. "He planned this interception all along. He means to use the council *and* the wolves to keep you from the meeting." Nathaniel grabbed my forearm and his emotionless mask frayed at the corner of his eyes. "He knows what you *truly* are."

"Save your hunter." Hector reached out his hand. "Come with me, Wolf Born. Our reign begins tonight." Time slammed to a halt while images of my brother and Derek tangled in my frantic thoughts. "Little ruler." Hector's fury-laced voice claimed my attention. "You have forgotten my lesson regarding risks. May this one strike your heart—"

Blood sputtered from Hector's lips. He gazed down at the claws protruding from his chest.

I froze, locking my eyes on the assailant behind Hector. Derek. When Hector attempted to escape, Derek drove his fangs into the king's throat. With each violent gulp Derek took, a foreign energy pulsed around him. Hector ceased struggling. His skin cracked and paled.

"No," Nathaniel whispered. He released me. "Now Derek will never be free from the vampires…either."

Derek kept his eyes to mine as he dropped the king's ash-like body to the ground.

While my brain fired off the flight response through my nervous system, by order from my soul, I moved toward Derek.

"Let me through," I ordered.

When the werewolf barricade parted, I stopped dead in my tracks. The foreign power now exuded from Derek.

"I went to the king this morning," Derek said. "I offered him my eternal servitude if he supported you. He refused."

"Hunter." Nathaniel moved to stand by me. "You committed an atrocity."

Derek turned to nod at the vehicles. When the drivers opened the doors for the council members, they emerged with their attention concentrated on Derek. Waiting.

"No one is to attack or kill a werewolf." Derek continued, "Protect the alphas." He tilted his head and his gaze slid over the black band around Sam's forearm. "They have colored wrappings on their arms."

Without protest, the vampires dispersed.

"Why are they listening to you?" I whispered.

"My wolf needed an army." Derek leveled his heated stare at me. "This is how we win."

"He bested Hector. Drank his blood," Nathaniel answered. "Derek now leads the Vampire Council. He is the king."

"I am your servant." Derek closed the distance between us. Tears raced down my cheeks. He could have died. He still could. Derek caged the sides of my face, branding my lips with a searing kiss. His words rushed against my mouth. "Let me serve you."

Squeezing my eyes tight, I pulled away. "The Lord of Light cannot cross our realm. I need to go to him. I'm—"

"Going with me." The rage in Sam's voice screamed goosebumps up my spine. "Remove your hands from my queen. "

In response, Derek raised his hands in a mock surrender while his mouth tugged into a devilish grin. Leaning into me, he grazed his lips along my jawline. "No one. No law. No fate. Will keep me from you." He pressed a kiss to my tear-stained cheek. "Now, let us save your brother."

Chapter Twenty-Nine

Magic burned across my skin.

Derek's attention lowered to the glowing talisman and he dragged me tight to his body.

"Incoming," someone shouted.

Overhead, a car-sized fireball exploded against the dining hall. The werewolf barricade constricted around us as another torpedo blazed across the sky, hitting the building.

"Open the doors," Sam ordered. "Get the wolves out."

Beneath Derek's protective arm, I caught sight of Ben, still in the snow, flipping through the damn book. Not trusting the werewolf barricade to hold, I slipped free of Derek to scramble over to Ben. When I grabbed him, magic hummed against my fingertips while a glowing orb of protection spanned from Ben's ring, encircling us.

"Don't worry about me," Ben said. "The ring protects against magic attacks."

"Not from werewolves and vampires," I gritted. Tossing my body over him, I shielded Ben from the wolves racing to escape the fire-engulfed building.

"Alphas, control your wolves," Sam shouted.

Threads of energy crisscrossed around us, attaching alphas to their packs. Still, members in their wolf forms continued racing toward the lake. As for the men surrounding us, every guard shifted to face outward. Forming an additional barrier, Derek took up behind us, Nathaniel remained at my side and Sam moved in front. I dragged Ben tight to me while the guards marched away from the raging fire, causing us to mirror their direction. From the wind blasting plumes of smoke at us, killing visibility to mere feet, only growls and screams hinted at what lay past the werewolf barricade.

Sam spun to face me. "The links are weakening."

"The wolves will run to their deaths," Nathaniel warned. "Alpha, join your link to hold them away from the lake."

Instantly, Sam released our link and the drawing of my energy sent me knocking against Ben. While I recovered my footing, the Keeper barged her way through the werewolf barricade.

"We"—she gasped for breath—"need to...negotiate the—"

"Let me." Ben dusted the snow off the book. He thumbed through the pages, skimming. "Negotiations must be addressed prior to a meeting. Also, no direct action may take place until the agreed-upon time."

I jabbed a finger at the burning building. "*That* is a fucking direct action."

"The *Lord of Light* cannot attack." The Keeper paused, catching her breath. "That's his army testing yours."

"We cannot retaliate," Ben added. "We must wait for the meeting. Sunset. That's about..." Ben cranked his head to the smoke-filled sky. "Shit."

"We have a quarter-hour," Derek said. "Most of the vampires will awaken in time. Those who do not, we will use as a second wave."

"Same." The Keeper held my attention letting her piercing gaze finish the sentence. The naiads were currently unavailable.

"We might not have until sunset." Tension vibrated through Sam's body. "The alphas are draining their links keeping the packs from falling to the fae's magic."

"I'll use mine," I said.

"No." Sam cut his glowing eyes to mine. "You are not facing that thing weakened."

"The council will aid the packs," Derek said. The black pits of his pupils consumed his eyes while the foreign power rolled from his body, caressing against me, tugging at my very soul.

"Derek is sharing his strength with the council members," Nathaniel muttered to my mind. *"Risky. They could turn on him. Or slaughter the packs. Perhaps both."*

"Derek won't let that happen," I sent Nathaniel.

"As I have said, with a handful of wasted breaths, you are his final death."

I clenched my jaw. Refocusing on the group, I said, "King and Alpha. Both werewolves and vampires will follow my orders." I pinned Sam with a look and he pressed a fist to his heart. Nodding, I prayed for his safety and that he really meant his genuflection. I turned my attention to the Keeper, raising an eyebrow, hoping she got the hint that the naiads were part of the message as well. When she answered with a thumb's up, I settled my attention onto Derek's black-pit eyes.

"My wolf." He shifted to stand in front of me. "I am your servant until my eternal night."

Selfishly, I took the span of a heartbeat to engrave this moment into my memory. From the gravel in his voice to the command of his presence, a fierceness emanated from Derek, one begotten not from violence but by love. My mind spun, lips moved to form words yet… I'd rather he lived than admit what my soul screamed at me. Tearing my focus from Derek, I headed toward the lake.

"Wait." Ben trotted in front of me. "Remember, you don't talk directly to the Lord of Light. It is all passed through me."

"Correct." Nathaniel moved to stand next to Ben. "I will aid the steward with wording questions."

"If any word should twist," Derek spoke at Nathaniel, "and my wolf comes to harm, you will meet your final death."

Nathaniel bowed. "You have my word, king. Tonight, no harm will befall the Wolf Born from my actions or words." When Nathaniel rose, his gaze flicked to Ben. "Steward, we will lead the way."

Once more, my attention locked on Ben clutching the book to his chest. He shivered against the wind, but his attitude morphed. He exuded his reporter persona, ready and eager to diverge into a war of wits.

The closer we came to the lake, the more magic constricted around us. Clenching my fists at my side, I focused on my nails biting into my palms versus the fae's power, until Jimmy, hauling ass up the hill, provided a greater distraction.

Sam surged in front of us, blasting Jimmy with the alpha link. With his eyes glowing and claws bared at his sides, Jimmy came to a hard stop. The stench of sweat and fear poured from his body. One wrong movement or word, and Jimmy's wolf would force his Change. Terror-laced sweat dripped down my temples. How many werewolves had already succumbed to their wolves, possibly attacking the vampires?

"Report," Sam said to Jimmy.

In a voice more animalistic than human, Jimmy answered, "The vampires are helping the alphas hold off the packs from entering the lake." Cringing, he gripped the side of his head. "The fae are skull-fucking us, calling us to the lake. And there's this huge-ass bear. It's just standing there. Glowing." Jimmy cut his attention over his shoulder. "The thing is twelve feet tall."

"The witness," Nathaniel sent me. *"He is only here to watch the events. Or kill you. Hopefully, both – "*

Another fireball blazed across the sky, striking a tree behind us. The Keeper grabbed my hand, dragging me in a run toward the lake. "Should you acquire the Lord of Light's true name, use it."

"True name? Like in Rumpelstiltskin?"

"Yep," she said. "Names hold power. That's why they use titles. Or nicknames, or — "

As we drew closer to the lake, the bear's head came into view. I tugged the Keeper to a stop and our party clambered to a halt.

"See?" Jimmy jabbed a claw at the bear. "Huge-ass motherfucker."

The bear's glowing opaque eyes locked with mine before he returned to his vigilance at the lake. Feet away from the water's edge, vampires drove back werewolves, while within the lake stood a vast army of humanoid creatures.

"We cannot stall any longer," Nathaniel shouted at me. "Look."

A council member screamed as a group of wolves tore into them. With the vampire down, werewolves raced through the opening and continued toward the lake. Awaiting creatures met the wolves, ensnaring them and dragging them beneath the icy waves. As blood decorated the glowing lake, screams and howls rang against my eardrums. When I raced forward, a blast of magic rushed from the lake, knocking everyone but the bear off their feet.

No sound or movement crossed the landscape until the lake parted, morphing into a hallway. Within the pearly-white pathway, the Lord of Light drifted toward us. Unable to breach the shore, he stood at the edge. Cautiously, everyone rose to their feet. The bear angled its snout toward the lake as a cue for me to move.

"He has slain thousands of armies, and you still stand. It enrages him." The Keeper threaded her fingers with mine, tugging me down to whisper in my ear, "By my blood rite, I open the doors to the Realm of Light."

I pulled away to look her in the eyes.

"That is what a fae says to enter the realm." She tapped her glowing fingers on my knuckles. A soft illumination emanated from my skin. "I knew there was more to you, Wolf Queen. Dare I say…kin?" She released my hand. "Now. Head high. Feelings locked away, so you come back to your realm…alive."

"Be safe." My voice tightened. "And stay alive too."

With a nod, she fell back behind the werewolf guards.

While my precise steps carried me to the shore, within the towering waves, the fae's legion watched on, waiting to consume our world.

"Greetings, Wolf Born." A smile tugged at the Lord of Light's lips while he gestured at our scattered army. "Did you wish to fight?"

Posed with the open book, Ben moved forward. His jaw trembled as he took in the sight of the twelve-foot toga-clad being. "The Wolf Born addresses your presence. We move to the negotiations. Since the Lord of Light requested the meeting, he will proceed."

"A human." Glee filled the fae's voice. Spreading his arms, he bowed, shooting his focus at the bear. "*Tuath Dé*. I acknowledge you and look forward to crossing into your guarded realm."

Corbus released a growl that vibrated the ground beneath our feet.

The Lord of Light chuckled. "I warned your father, Wolf Born. They wake. I have no negotiations. You will give back what you have stolen."

Sam steeled his spine next to me, while Derek moved behind my right shoulder. The fae tracked both men. "Long rule the *new* Vampire King. Alpha, I fear, tonight, your time is ended—"

"The Lord of Light"—Ben shoved authority into his voice, cutting off the fae—"agrees to the Wolf Born's negotiations." Ben pointed at words on a page. "You spoke out of turn, forfeiting a counter."

"Pray tell what the little queen wishes?" The fae snapped his fingers, and the water parted further, revealing my brother suspended between two golems while a third pressed the point of a sword against Drew's throat.

Nathaniel muttered something at Ben.

Ben shook his head, spinning to face me with his rage before answering the Lord of Light, "The Wolf Born will give her blood in exchange for her brother's life and his freedom to return to the Human realm. She will do so within the Light realm."

The fae steepled his fingers under his pointed chin. "You *truly* think you can best me?"

I remained silent.

"Very well." He grinned. "The sun touches the horizon. Come, Wolf Born. If you know how to open the doors to my kingdom."

Ben turned to me. "Do you?"

Nathaniel shook his head. "She does not—"

"Are the negotiations over?" I asked Ben.

"Yes," he answered.

I nodded at Derek. Power rose from him, swelling around us as vampires poured out of the woods, surrounding the lake. Once they were in place, magic buzzed across my skin. Thousands of naiads rose from the waves, forming another barrier within the lake. At the slight tremor at the corners of the Lord of Light's eyes as he took in our reinforcements, relief crashed through me.

I slipped my hand into my coat pocket, touching the gun as I stepped to the edge of the lake. "By my blood rite, I open the doors to the Realm of Light."

Magic crackled around us and an outline of two massive, transparent doors appeared. As they opened, thousands of creatures gathered within the vast stretching hallway. Some cast wary glances at the Lord of Light, while others tensed, ready to tear me apart.

Ben hooked his arm around my neck, knocking his forehead against mine. "Please rethink this."

"I have." I brushed a kiss on his tear-stained cheek. Tightening my grip on the concealed weapon, I pulled away to stare past Ben's cracked glasses and into his wide eyes. "Keep next to Nathaniel."

Once more, I faced the doors to the Light realm.

"Tess, no," my brother shouted. "He'll kill you. He'll kill you all—"

The golem pressed the sword's tip into Drew's neck.

Sam shifted in front of me. "I will go first—"

"No." I tore my attention away from my brother. "I am going alone."

"I won't allow you," Sam growled.

"I was afraid of that." I disengaged the safety, and the soft click grabbed Sam's attention. "We heal within a few weeks, right?" I asked, raising the gun at Sam.

"We are a team—" Sam's focus landed on my legs. Before he tackled me, I squeezed the trigger. As Sam crumbled to the ground, gripping the wound at his blown-apart kneecap, he shouted at Derek, "Don't let her go."

I released the link, knocking the werewolf guards to their knees, and kept them from reaching me, while I pointed the gun at Derek.

"A bullet won't stop me." His voice sent my adrenaline into overdrive. "Nothing will."

"You serve me," I said.

"For eternity." He stepped closer.

I countered his advancement. "I order you to protect this realm."

He took another step. "And your army will."

"With you leading it." I raised the gun to his heart. "Do not take another step…hunter." He froze when I reverted to his title. Hurt flashed across the blood-bond, which he locked down and masked with his emotionless façade. Before I lost the courage, I continued, "No matter what happens to me, I order you to remain undead."

"A true queen." His eyes burned with fury. "To sentence such torture."

Derek's words dug into my heart as I turned and slipped through the doors. Once I was across the threshold, magic crashed against me, stealing the air from my lungs. Still, I pressed onward. The magic within my veins raced to escape only to be denied, blocked by the talisman. To keep from screaming, I bit my tongue.

The metallic taste of blood stirred my wolf and she tore through me, demanding control. Only her fight intensified the sensation of being burned from the inside out. The magic focused on her presence, attacking the wolf. In a clash of screams and howls, I crumbled to my knees, speckling the marble floor with blood.

"Behold." The Lord of Light's sandals came to rest in front of my quivering fingertips. "Her blood is not pure. The stolen magic fights to escape her useless body." Wildly, I scanned for the gun. Taking note, the fae cackled. "No human weapon may cross our realm."

As I rose to my knees, the talisman seared against my chest and light exploded behind my eyes, threatening to splinter my skull. Realization prickled along my nerve endings. It wasn't my magic attacking me—it was the Lord of Light. I yanked on the feather charm, snapping the chain and the talisman clattered against the floor, shattering into pieces.

"What shall you do now, little queen?" the fae cooed. "Without your *Tuath Dé* trinket to protect you?"

Not wanting to faceplant, but *really* wanting to piss off the fae, I struggled to my feet. Fighting for my balance, I looked into his putrid, sea-moss-colored eyes. "Save my brother."

A choir of gasps and mumbles echoed through the hall. The corners of the fae's eyes pinched as he set a glare at the spectators. When silence stole their mutterings, he spoke at me. "You are an abomination."

Snarky replies bubbled to my lips, yet my focus streamlined to Drew, suspended between the golems with a sword cutting into his throat. Along with a mouthful of blood, I swallowed the comebacks and whispered, "Release my brother."

The Lord of Light snapped his fingers and a golem, balancing a four-foot-long golden sword between its four arms, stepped forward.

"Tess—" Drew groaned. "Don't give him your blood."

"She will." The Lord of Light took the golem's offering. The fae raised the sword to his lips, pressing a kiss to its shiny façade while he peered at me. "Honor my curiosity before I release your brother. Why did you shoot the alpha?"

I jutted my chin up, meeting the amusement in the fae's eyes with the rage in mine. "To save him from you."

"Alas, the alpha is not safe." The Lord of Light pointed the sword in the direction of the doors. "With your blood, I will enter the Human realm. I will enslave the wolves. My army will kill the *Tuath Dé* and I shall rule both realms. I will then set my worlds upon the Dark realm." His power-drunk gaze fell on me. "I will be unstoppable."

"Unstoppable? You're not the first Otherworldly Creature to make that statement." With the back of my knuckles, I wiped a bead of blood from the corner of my lips. "And with my horrible luck, you won't be the last."

A grin stretched across his serrated teeth. "While you still draw breath, I will cut that mouth from your body."

"He can't take your blood by force," Drew called out.

The Lord of Light disappeared and reappeared behind me, resting the sword across my shoulders.

Only able to shift my gaze to my brother, in a similarly compromising position of a sword to the throat, I skirted my fingers past the hem of my coat, slipping beneath, and into the harness holding the dagger. Without the talisman as a buffer, the blade's magic hummed against my fingertips. Not wanting to draw attention, I hovered my hand over the dagger, waiting. I needed the Lord of Light distracted. Currently, his entire focus was fixed on me.

"Answer me, one last question, before you give back what you have stolen." His acrid breath scraped against my earlobe. "Do you love your brother? Or are you loyal to him? They are not the same. As you proved with the alpha. No hesitation when you shot him. That was not love. No. That was loyalty to keep him safe. Yet with the Vampire King, there was cruelty that only comes from the betrayal of love."

"Like you even know what love is," I gritted.

"I *witnessed* it on a beach." The fae raked his ice-cold tongue along my throat. "The night your mother and father died."

"Don't listen to him," Drew screamed.

My brother's voice went mute against the memory of the car crash plowing into my mind. Instead of watching the flames consume the vehicle from the cliff edge, I viewed it from a different perspective...my father's. At his feet, Drew cradled my mother, who struggled to breathe, while across the beach, among the burning wreckage, lay my lifeless body. I was unable to look away. The fae's voice echoed inside my head, *"Your father called out to me. He begged me to save you."* The Lord of Light tucked a strand of my hair behind my ear, leaving my neck bare to the sword. The gesture pulled me from my memory, rooting me into the present. My attention locked with Drew's eyes, glazed with angry tears.

"Stop," Drew screamed. "He's fucking lying—"

The golem slid the sword against Drew's throat. Still, he continued to mouth words at me but only what filtered from the fae's lips mattered. "In return for my aid, your father gave me your brother."

Drew went still. His jaw clenched.

"So indeed, I know what love is," the fae murmured. "As I dragged your brother into my realm, within his eyes, love died to birth hate."

"No," I whispered.

"That is not the sweetest part," the fae said.

"Please," Drew said. "Don't—"

"Your brother denounced himself, in exchange for revenge—"

"I *never* asked you to slaughter my parents," Drew hissed.

"Son of Dylan." The Lord of Light stepped us closer to Drew. "Stare into her eyes and tell her you did not welcome your father's death."

Drew refused to look at me. Instead, his hate blazed through his stare, locked on the fae.

The Lord of Light tapped my shoulder with the blade. "I used this very sword to stab your mother through her heart, and then I severed your father's head."

Guilt washed through Drew's gaunt face.

"Drew," I whispered. "He killed them. Not you. You are innocent. Look at—"

"Son of Dylan, you will bear the fruition of your revenge." The fae brought us another step closer to Drew. "You will fulfill your duty."

Warning bells blared in my head and I grab the dagger.

"It is true, Tess. I denounced myself for revenge." Drew's gaze locked with mine before he cut his attention back to the fae. "On *you*."

As I raised the dagger, the Lord of Light countered, snatching my hand and forcing me to hold the dagger mid-strike. The fae's laughter shook against my spine. "Your hostile actions forfeited the negotiations." The Lord of Light angled my hand brandishing the glowing dagger toward Drew. "You will gift me, once more, the hate within your brother's eyes as you take his life."

I slammed my heel against the fae's toes while lengthening the claws of my free hand, slicing them down his thigh. With a vice-like grip, he buffered my attack, keeping me tight to his chest while pressing the sword against my windpipe. "I will destroy all you love—"

Energy screamed through me, threatening to tear my heart from my chest as it fastened to me. Behind us, the doors groaned open. A roar of the spectators' gasps crashed around us while fear seized my body, forcing me to rely on the fae to keep me standing.

"How is this possible?" the fae seethed, nicking the sword against my neck as he jerked me around to face the doors.

"We are blood bound," Derek answered. "Her blood runs through my veins, allowing me to open the doors to the Light realm. You permitted her into your realm, therefore, through her blood, I am a welcomed guest." Derek's attention fastened to the sword at my throat. "I offer you a trade."

"No," I snapped.

The Lord of Light grabbed my hair, tugging my neck to the side, then pressing the sword at my jugular. "Speak, Vampire King."

"You desire power. Rule both wolf and vampire—"

"Speak clearly, king." The sword bit at my throat. "By her actions, I have a right to take her life."

"Let the Wolf Born and her brother leave this realm, alive and without further harm." Derek lifted his eyes to mine. "Take my blood instead."

"I accept," the Lord of Light said.

"No—" My plea was cut short as the Lord of Light ripped the dagger out of my hand, shattering the weapon against the floor. Then he disappeared.

The Lord of Light appeared behind Derek.

When Derek's eyes locked with mine, the fae drew the sword across Derek's throat.

"*Manannán,*" Drew screamed.

Magic raced from the Lord of Light and his flesh thinned, sucking to his bones. He screamed as his mummified hands quivered, dropping the sword at Derek's throat.

The Keeper's voice echoed inside my head. *"Manannán is the Lord of Light's name!"*

Drew screamed around the sword at his throat, "Manan—"

"Silence his tongue," the Lord of Light shouted at the golem.

"*Manannán*," I screamed.

Another blast of magic tore from the Lord of Light and the golems exploded. Beneath my feet, the shards of the dagger glowed. As I grabbed the largest piece, magic blazed against my flesh. Spinning to my feet, I froze.

The fae drove the sword into my brother's chest.

Again, I screamed, "*Manannán*."

The fae crumpled to his knees.

Drew pulled the sword from his chest. As blood poured from the wound he clutched with one hand, he dragged the sword across the floor toward the fae.

Derek appeared behind the Lord of Light, grasping the back of his hair, then bared the fae's neck to me.

While the Lord of Light's eyes blurred, he spat his blood and words at me. "You do not win. You cannot—"

Drew's blood-slick hand covered mine. Together, we drove the splinter into the fae's throat. At the dagger's contact, a blinding light engulfed the hall. When it dimmed, in the Lord of Light's place knelt a stone statue of the fae with the splinter embedded in the marble.

Behind the statue, Derek stood with a crescent wound pouring blood from his neck. He caged the gaping slice at his throat. Eyes to mine, he mouthed, *Your brother.*

I spun to Drew, who was lying on the floor.

Of the thousands of onlookers now crowding around us, no one moved against me or to aid me. They just watched as I gathered Drew into my lap. Blood and air bubbled from his chest. Uselessly, I cupped the wound, trying to hold his life in place.

"Tess…" Drew reached his hand toward my face, brushing his cold fingers against my tears. "You're… gonna…be—"

The light slipped from his eyes, and a scream tore from my throat. Gasping for breath, I clutched Drew to me. As warmth left his lifeless body, my heart turned numb. I lowered my brother's head to rest against the marble floor.

A soft thud echoed through the hall and I spun around. Derek lay in a pool of his blood.

"No," I screamed.

Unable to get my feet underneath me fast enough, I crawled to Derek, gathering him to me as I dragged a claw across my wrist, forcing my blood to his mouth which spilled past his unresponsive lips. Beneath us, the pool of his blood turned to ash. Panic stilled my heart. Sobs wracked my body as the hue of Derek's skin turned ashen.

"No. No." I gashed my wrist against his fangs. The flesh of his lips cracked. I reached within myself, searching for the blood-bond. Silence greeted me. The rush of my breath stirred specks of ash from his cheek. "No! Don't. Please. I need you." I buried my face against his hair, whispering, "I love you."

Pain sliced through my wrist and the blood-bond roared to life. Derek entwined his fingers through my hair, cradling my head to keep me in place. His eyes flicked open to meet mine. Hungrily, he pulled at my vein. My heart struggled to pump blood. Lungs fought for breath. As my eyelashes sealed, he broke from my wrist to capture my lips, breathing life into my soul.

When I forced my eyes open, searing love stared back at me from the depths of Derek's gaze. He rumbled against my mouth. "My blood for your blood, un—"

I stole his words, finishing them with my own, "Until *our* eternal night."

Epilogue

A week later

The empire-silhouette emerald gown molded to my chest and cascaded into a flowing skirt. The dress's accenting golden beadwork cut spectrums across my empty bedroom each time I moved. Once more, Nathaniel had outdone himself. Not that I'd admit it to the bloodsucker. He still held a high ranking on my shitlist.

"This is *really* happening," I mumbled, settling in front of the dresser. Eyeballing myself in the mirror, I swallowed my panic to mix with the army of anticipation butterflies fluttering through my insides.

Knuckles wrapped against the doorframe, and in rushed Ben, looking all dapper in his tailored tux. "You forgot—"

"I'm wearing a floor-length dress and satin slippers. That's as far as this dress-up goes." I pursed my lips at the thing suspended between Ben's hands. "No way am I wearing a—"

"Crown and go time." The Keeper, in a skintight, cocktail number paired with heels that could be deemed as weapons for where we were heading, burst into the bedroom. She took the white-gold crown from Ben, swinging it around her index finger. "We're late. I'm hungry."

In a stall tactic, I thumbed the gold chain around my neck, careful not to reveal the hidden pendant beneath the dress bodice. The bauble had cost me a hefty favor to the Keeper. She had become my permanent, *human* guest. Cocking an eyebrow at Andrea's smirk, I was pretty sure I benefited more from the trade than the Keeper. She had said it was a charity favor, stating I needed a tutor in all things fae.

Sparing a weary glance at my nightstand showcasing the engraved invitation, more like a summons, to the Light realm, I sighed. Nothing like penciling death opportunities on the to-do calendar. Thanks to the disintegration of the Light fae hierarchy, during the Spring Equinox, my court had to travel to the Light realm for a competition to name a new Lord or Lady of Light. Thankfully, that was months away. Unfortunately, there were a plethora of life-ending opportunities awaiting before then, like meeting with the Vampire Council next Tuesday. At least tonight, all seemed…copasetic.

The Keeper strolled behind me, toying with the beaded cap sleeves of my dress. "Nice cleavage, queenie. You're gonna distract the Vampire King during his coronation."

I chewed my lip. Our regal titles had kept us occupied with formalities and obligations to our kingdoms. It had been a week since seeing Derek in the flesh... In my dreams, well, that was exactly an hour ago.

Ben's phone chirped. Scanning the text, he threw authority into his voice, "The caravan is waiting. The ceremony begins in three hours. Crown. Now."

"We can forgo," Nolan, my escort, grumbled, resting his shoulder against the doorframe, fidgeting with his emerald cufflinks. "Gladly. I'll send word to the alpha."

Guilt nibbled at my gut. Sam's gunshot injury prevented him from traveling...and willingly talking to the perpetrator. When I came back to our realm, physically unharmed, toting the Lord of Light's sword and a posse of naiads bearing witness that I had defeated the fae, saving our world from an attack, the packs had unanimously agreed that me shooting Sam was an act done to save our race, not to solely hurt my mate.

The Keeper was right—a little fear allowed the head to rest. For the first time, I didn't worry about some covert werewolf operation that had me kidnapped and marched into some dungeon to rot. Regardless, *I* feared time. Sam and I had two weeks until the full moon to find a solution to the ixnay on the baby predicament. Even though I had the best investigative steward on the hunt for how to retract owing a vampire a favor or a loophole, each day, each hour we met with defeat, my dread grew.

Magic ran along my spine as the next spectator made their way into the crowded bedroom. Since snowflakes kept falling from the never-ending storm, my invitation to Corbus had remained.

"Your turn"—the Keeper relinquished the crown to Corbus—"angel man."

Currently, the *Tuath Dé* spent his days guzzling coffee while splitting his focus between running me ragged with magic lessons and holding a silent vigil for something or someone. As persistent as I might've been, I'd yet to pull the mystery threat out of him. He assured me that I'd know when I needed to.

"Balance, Wolf Born." Corbus set the delicate but heavy crown on top of my head. "Enjoy the night. Your lessons await you at dawn."

A final glance in the mirror and my breath caught in my throat. Corbus stepped away, cloaking his expression within the shadows. The Keeper beamed at my reflection. Ben wiped a tear from the corner of his eye. Nolan paused in fussing with the cufflinks, heartbeat revving to life. He swept a fist to his chest. "My life for yours."

Outside, pack members repeated the beta's words while others, in their wolf form, howled. When their echoes drifted up to the twilight sky, I rose with wobbly knees. Careful not to have the crown fall off my head, I dipped my chin at Nolan, and pledged, "Mine for the pack."

* * * *

A little over three hours later, we arrived. A congregation of tux-clad vampires waited outside for our caravan. Practicing some deep breathing exercises, I reminded myself that tonight, I entered the vampire estate through the front door as a guest and not as the prisoner who had escaped through a busted window almost four months ago.

When the SUV door opened, Nathaniel peered inside at me. "Late as usual." Offering me his hand, he helped me out of the car. My gaze locked on the pendant resting on the lapel of Nathaniel's tux. A white-gold ring encircled the howling profile of a wolf with an emerald for its eye. Nathaniel took note, flicking the emblem with his fingers. "The king's wolf," he grumbled. "In a sense, I must wear *you* on my sleeve for the rest of my nights."

The display of Derek's devotion sent heat to warm my cheeks and tighten my belly. Nathaniel pointed at my racing heart. "I preferred its dance to the ballad of terror." The bloodsucker rolled his gaze to the sky and switched to whining at my mind. *"I'm damned to serve the rest of my life, watching him fawn over you."*

"Better than being turned over to the fae," I sent. *"Or, you could regain your freedom by taking back the favor Sam owes you."*

"That *is the reason I chose to serve Derek versus a poetic death from the fae."* Nathaniel smiled. *"Two weeks. I cannot wait for the drama to commence."*

"Two weeks." I returned a sweet smile. *"Better think on that. You'll be serving a very, very pissed-off king."*

"I have served much worse." Nathaniel moved to let Nolan through. *"Try not to die before the full moon."*

"My queen," Nolan said, offering me his arm. Once I slipped my arm through his, he said, "I could tear him apart."

"I appreciate the offer, but..."—I patted his knuckles with my free hand while casting a look at Ben, whose eyes were latched to Nathaniel—"we need him."

"When he's done being useful"—Nolan guided me up the steps and through the massive double doors—"just say the word."

Once inside the estate, the fresh aroma of night jasmine filled the air around us, masking the scent of vampire and adding another flush of color to my cheeks. Since my return from the Light realm, my base scent had changed. The Keeper believed it was part of me coming into my fae power.

Nolan's deep inhale echoed around the empty foyer adorned with night jasmine. Vines ran along the grand staircase banisters and petals dressed the crimson floor runner leading to the sealed glass doors of the ballroom. "It smells like…you," he whispered.

"Hush." Nathaniel appeared at the doors. "No more words until the king addresses you."

While our pack filtered into the estate, Ben's heart rate spiked. There wasn't a need for me to order protection—they surrounded us.

The Keeper giggled. "Oh, the fun to be had."

I shot her a look, then gave Ben a reassuring smile, before nodding to Nathaniel.

When the doors opened, my heart dropped to my toes. Every vampire stood, lining both sides of the floor runner leading to an elevated stage showcasing a massive, vacant throne.

As Nolan escorted me down the aisle, I scouted for the empty seats or a sign directing us to the werewolf section. *Nada.*

"My wolf." Derek's voice vibrated through my body. He appeared in front of the throne, dressed in a tux fit for…well, a king. The emerald eye on his wolf pendant shimmered in the chandelier's soft glow as he opened his arms, directing my pack members to take up the empty spaces between the vampires. Time stopped when Derek's eyes met mine. Love and desire burned us both into stillness.

Nolan squeezed my hand, snapping me back into motion. I raised my focus to the crown encircling

Derek's dark locks, the masculine counterpart to the one teetering on my head.

Slowing, Nolan ushered us to the stage. There weren't any seats. "What do we do?" I gritted.

"Stay alive," he muttered.

As Derek descended the steps of the stage, his gaze flicked to Nolan's arm linked with mine. With a nod to my beta, I released my hold. Immediately, Nolan stepped behind my right shoulder while Ben moved to my left. Up front, the Keeper squeezed in between Nathaniel and a pack member.

Standing before Derek, I stifled a nervous giggle. He quirked his eyebrow in amusement. How I wished we could talk through the blood-bond because I'd share my observation. We looked like a nightmare prom king and queen. Slowly, he took my hand, brushing a kiss against my knuckles. All joking aside, when his eyes locked with mine, raw admiration filled my heart as he lowered to his knees.

Every vampire followed his cue. When Nolan took a knee, the werewolves followed suit.

"My honored guest, welcome." When Derek rose, everyone followed. Some vampires cast not-so-nice-nice looks at me. After thousands of years of murdering each other, it would take a lot of charm and muscle to make things work between werewolves and vampires.

"Sorry, we were late." I flicked my gaze at his crown. "Did we miss...."

Derek's lips curved into a smile. "We're just beginning."

When he turned to lead me up the steps to the throne, I let my feet drag. "You didn't say anything about me being front and center."

"You are my moon." He brushed his lips against my ear. "*My* center."

What could a hotblooded werewolf say to that, but just nod and follow? He escorted me up the steps and guided me to stand on his right side. Giving me a wink, he then spoke to the crowd. "Proceed."

Two council members approached. One held a golden goblet. Each took turns cutting their wrists, allowing their blood to spill into the chalice. They raised the cup toward Derek and chanted, "My blood for yours." Then they passed the goblet to the next pair of council members. After the last group, Nathaniel appeared on Derek's left side and offered the filled chalice.

Derek raised the goblet and turned to me. "Their blood for me. My blood for you."

As he drank, his gaze held mine. Once he gave the empty chalice to Nathaniel, the room erupted into cheers. "Long rule the Vampire King."

When I took a quick check-in with my group, Nolan looked about to vomit. Make that all the pack members and Ben too. The Keeper bounced on her heels, giving me a thumb's up.

Derek threaded his hand with mine. Lowering his lips to my ear, he whispered, "I have something for you."

"This is your coronation." I quirked an eyebrow. "I'm the one bearing gifts tonight."

A spark of curiosity filled his eyes. "Beneath that dress?"

"Umm." My voice squeaked. "Kinda."

His grin deepened, revealing the tips of his bloodstained fangs. "Close your eyes, and do not open them until I tell you."

I gave a reassuring look to Nolan. Ben mumbled something at our beta. Neither the vampires nor werewolves were happy about our relationship. With a clenched jaw, Nolan gave a curt nod. I glanced at Derek then sealed my eyes while he drew the shadows around us.

From the wind hitting my cheeks, the scent of pine and the soft crunch of stone underfoot, I knew we were in the courtyard. Derek shifted his hold, moving to my back. His hands rested on my hips while his chin brushed against my temple. "Open."

My heart truly did stop. Underneath the half-moon stood a marble statue of my brother. In his hand was a sword, while beneath his feet lay the Lord of Light's head. I forced my legs closer. Tears brimmed my eyes as I read the bronze placard.

Slánaitheoir ár Ríochta

"What does it mean?" I asked.

"Savior of our realm."

As I burst into tears, Derek held me, whispering in a foreign tongue against the crown of my head. Once I recovered my voice, I mumbled against his shoulder, "Thank you."

"It is a pale gesture." He squeezed me tighter. "Compared to what you have given me."

I drew away from Derek's chest to gaze upon my brother's image. "Nothing will ever compare to this." I tugged the chain out from the dress, almost knocking the crown off my head in the process. "But I'll have you know, I had to trade a favor to a fae to acquire this."

"No." Worry slipped into Derek's voice. "What was the favor?"

"Allow her to live with me." I pulled away to look him in the eyes. "And she likes country music."

He grinned. "If a queen subjects herself to daily torture, then this gift shall make the Gods weep with jealousy."

Instead of giving him the gift, my lust and love demanded that I jump Derek. "You have to be so damn hot."

He furrowed his brows.

I answered his confusion. "It means you're attractive. Now, gorgeous king, hold out your hand."

He obeyed, and I placed the chain in his palm. He suspended the penny between us. When he dropped the chain over his head, letting the pendant rest against his chest, he returned a heated gaze to me. "You are my blood." His voice trembled and deepened. "My love. My soul." Gathering me into an embrace that made me forget to breathe, he claimed my lips.

Too soon, the orchestra sounded the first notes to an aria, calling me back. My exhale swirled in the air around us. "We should return to your coronation."

Derek hooked a finger underneath a sleeve of my dress, exposing my shoulder, where he placed a kiss. "Let them celebrate."

"Ummm." Lust clouded my mind as I forced reasoning into my words. "They'll be scheming. Plotting—"

He slipped the other sleeve free from my shoulder, running his lips across the exposed skin, then kissed a path along my throat. "A certain *Tuath Dé* gave his word all will behave this night."

"Corbus." I hummed. "I owe him all the coffee."

Derek's chuckle sent goosebumps racing across my flesh. After a moment, he pulled away to stare into my eyes. "Tonight, we are free to rule how we choose."

"Then…" I looped my arms around his neck. "What is your desire, my king?"

Derek grabbed a hold of the backs of my thighs, lifting me to wrap my legs around his waist. "I am going to worship my queen until sunrise."

Want to see more like this?
Here's a taster for you to enjoy!

Grave Concerns:
Grave Robbing and Other Hobbies
Jayce Carter

Excerpt

I wished a floating, nearly headless body at three in the morning were an unusual thing for me, but this was the fourth time this one had visited me in as many weeks.

A squinty gaze at my watch made me groan. *At least she's punctual.*

"Avenge me!" the apparition demanded in an over-the-top ghostly voice.

I pushed myself upright to offer an annoyed look. "Don't pull that scary crap with me, Melinda. I'm not some kid trying to contact spirits at a sleepover."

The spirit shimmered then crossed her arms and gave me the same dirty look back. *Ghosts have the worst attitude.* "Well, if you did what I wanted the first time I asked, I wouldn't have to keep bothering you."

"You want me to kill a teenager."

"He killed me. How is that not a fair reaction?"

"You ran a red light because you were trying to get your caramel macchiato to mix while complaining the barista didn't make it right. Can't really blame him for that."

She pursed her lips as though she'd blown out a huge sigh, but with her being incorporeal, no actual air escaped. "If he hadn't been driving, it would have been fine. Isn't this your job? To make things right? You were given this gift for a reason."

"I don't know why I was given this *gift,* but I know I won't be using it to murder innocent teenagers."

"Can I talk to someone above you? Like your boss?"

I groaned and rubbed my eyes as it became clear I wasn't going to be getting back to sleep any time soon. "Did you really just ask to speak to my manager? Look, if you can find whoever is responsible for me, please, be my guest and speak to them. While you're at it, tell them I'd like to quit."

Melinda jammed a bony finger at me. "Do you know who I am?"

"Someone who has ruined my sleep for four weeks."

"And I'll keep doing it until you agree to help."

The threat was good, as far as threats went. Most ghosts tried to scare me into doing what they wanted, but after a person had seen as much as I had, those tactics fell flat. The worst an apparition could do was annoy me until they lost their hold on this world and went to the afterlife. A poltergeist could do some damage, but they were few and far between, luckily.

Melinda's outline had already lost its sharpness. She'd dimmed until she was more of a shimmer than a clear picture. Another week—maybe two—and she'd drift to a whisper, then to nothing.

"And I'll keep ignoring you until you're no longer in this realm."

An entitled huff came from her. "Look at me! I can't believe I'm sitting here being ignored by some short, frumpy girl with bad hair."

I considered pointing out that my hair didn't normally look quite so wild, but she *had* woken me up in the middle of the night.

"Make peace with what happened," I told her as I rolled over, my back to her. "Because I'm not going to help you."

The bed didn't sink, but an electric feeling that said she'd neared ran along my back. "It wasn't supposed to happen like this," she whispered, some of that sureness missing. "I wasn't supposed to die like this."

"Well, that's how it always goes. Everyone thinks *their* death will be some great sacrifice, some noble leap, but that isn't what it is."

"Harrison already moved his mistress into our home."

Okay, so I wasn't entirely jaded, because an ache ran through my chest at that. Being dead sucked, I was sure, but being forgotten so quickly? Replaced? *Far worse.*

"The world keeps moving. If there's one thing I've learned, it's that no matter what, no matter who dies or how, the world doesn't stop for any of us."

"Then what's the point? Why does any of it matter if as soon as we're gone, it all goes away?"

I cuddled into the warmth of my bed, unsure what to tell her. She wanted to be reassured. She wanted me to tell her there was some great plan, that at the end of the day everything, made sense. I would have loved to tell her that because I'd love to hear it—to believe it.

The reality was that despite having spent my life surrounded by death, I had no stunning pieces of wisdom about it. I didn't know why we were all here, or what the great purpose was, or why any of it meant a damn thing.

Instead, I told her the only thing I could. "Make your peace, Melinda, because you don't want to end up where you'll go if you don't."

She wailed, the screeching of a soul that few could hear and even fewer could survive. It made my ears want to bleed, so I grabbed my headphones and cranked up the music to cover it.

She'd be gone soon, since she only ever stayed for twenty minutes or so. I'd done this long enough to know which ones would cross over and which ones who would get stuck. Melinda?

She'd get stuck. She'd cling and try to bargain until the last moment, when she faded to nothing and ended up in purgatory. Even I didn't like to think about that, about the place I'd glimpsed a handful of times that sent a creeping, gnawing terror through me.

The deep bass and rhythmic drumming drowned out her wailing, and I fell back to sleep. Eventually.

* * * *

A banging on my door at ten at night made me grit my teeth.

Really? Last night Melinda kept me up and now this?

Did the universe have a personal vendetta against my sleep? It didn't matter who was there, I couldn't be blamed for whatever I did. Even if it was the hottest stripper-gram I'd ever seen, I'd tell him to take his G-string on home and let me rest.

Dicks were nice and all, but at thirty-five, I'd realized sleep mattered more. Finding a willing cock was far easier than managing a full eight hours.

When I pulled open the front door, a dark-haired man stood there, his suit impeccable and his hands folded behind him like some regal prince.

It took a moment for me to realize I'd seen him before. We hadn't ever spoken, but he'd been into the small occult store I spent time at. I doubted he'd noticed me—I didn't tend to be the sort of person others spent a lot of time caring about. The sharp points of his fangs also told me exactly *what* he was.

"Ava Harlin?" he said, voice smooth and careful, my name a question. Maybe he didn't remember he'd seen me before? "My name is Kase, and I am here at the behest of Lord Raymond Colter."

And that was about the time I realized my night was going to get much, much worse, because Raymond Colter led the local vampire coven.

I'd avoided most of the supernatural world by treading along the outskirts like a mouse avoiding the trap. Others like myself—those who walked the line between human and supernatural—tended to leap right into a world they weren't equipped for. Humans playing the games of immortals never went well for the human.

They ended up dead, which was a fate I'd rather avoid for as long as possible.

"What exactly does he want?"

Kase lifted one of his perfectly manicured eyebrows. "That isn't for me to ask, and I'd suggest you not ask, either. All I know is that he sent me to collect you."

I groaned, wishing Melinda would come back. She wasn't great company, but it had to be better than vampires. The few I'd run into were always insufferable bores who thought far too much of themselves.

"Let me get dressed," I muttered. Arguing with vampires was, in general, a bad idea.

"There isn't time."

I waved down at myself—my pink fluffy bath robe with cartoon penises on it over a pair of boy shorts and a tank top—both with a quip about books being better than boys. "I'm not well versed with vampire etiquette, but I'm thinking this might not be the best outfit to go meeting royalty, huh?"

Kase traced his gaze down my body impassively, a look so uninterested it offended. Sure, fucking a dead guy wasn't my idea of a good time, but he could at least look as though I were slightly more appetizing than spoiled meat.

Though, at the same time…using 'appetizing' when talking about a vampire was probably a poor choice of terms.

"He won't care. He made it clear time is of the essence, so this way." Kase held his hand out toward a dark car parked in front of my house, someone else in the driver's seat.

There wasn't really a way to refuse that was there? I was pretty sure if I pushed any further, I'd end up gagged and tied, and while that might be wonderfully fun on my days off, I just didn't think this vampire was a fan of safewords.

So instead, I followed his lead.

He sat up front with the driver, leaving me in the back alone.

Faint whispers rattled through the cab, and I did my best to ignore them. They were the echoes of ghosts who followed vampires around. When I'd still been young and full of optimism, I'd thought they were the whispers of the souls from the vampires themselves. Eventually I'd realized the truth—they were the whispers of their *victims*. Why those whispers never went away, I didn't understand. They just kept growing into a chorus that followed the vampire everywhere, even though only I heard it.

The presence of so many whispers in the car said the two up front were not vampires I should trust. *Like anything that eats people should be trusted.* I'd sooner turn my back on a man-eating tiger than a vampire.

The ride didn't take long, and the stretches of empty road in the barren night reminded me of how isolated the desert was. Why so many vampires would choose to settle in a place with so much sun and heat never made much sense to me, but then again, no one asked for my opinion.

The car pulled past large iron gates, and the house before us didn't fit the area at all. Instead of a Spanish style—all flat stucco walls and clay roofs—this house was an old Victorian mansion with peaked roofs and oval windows near the top. A large porch sat at the front, the wood aged as though the place had been there for centuries.

Maybe it had. Who knew the truth when it came to immortals?

Kase opened my door, and I ignored the way the pebbles of the driveway dug into the bottom of my fuzzy slippers. My absurd outfit might have bothered me, but there was a benefit to looking weak and ridiculous.

It was easy to play the part of a medium when I had to, to pretend my abilities were on par with fortune tellers at fairs and the stay-at-home-moms who sold love potions along with MLM leggings. Safer, too, since *those* people were never seen as a threat. What I was, I didn't know, but I didn't need anyone else taking an interest in it—or me.

Inside the house, a young man offered to take my robe as though it were a jacket.

Keeping covered seemed a good idea, so I waved him off. No reason to walk into a room full of blood drinkers looking like a buffet.

I followed Kase not up the staircase but down. Beneath the first level, the already impressive mansion spread out into more rooms and areas than I could count.

It made sense, though. Being underground helped them conduct business even when the sun was up and reduced the chance of attack or danger. It had to suck to know only a curtain stood between someone and a fiery end.

Inside the final set of doors—two large ones that reached from floor to ceiling and were adorned with gold and jewels—was a place that made me rethink the entire thing.

Vampires stood on either side of a center aisle, the floor shiny black stone except for a middle strip of red tile. At the end of the walkway were several seats on two different levels of stage, most on the lower level, and on the upper level, just one.

Dense shadows twisted around the throne, as though a layer of living darkness surrounded the chair. I sensed *something* from those shadows, but I couldn't tell what they were. If they had ever been spirits, it had been so long ago that they were nothing but glimmers of what they had been.

And on the throne? A vampire who made my skin crawl and all my warnings go off like an old car the owner hoped would keep limping forward. He had long, straight black hair and dark skin. Flat and empty red-rimmed eyes met mine.

The older a vampire got, the less human they appeared and acted. It was as though they stopped remembering how to be human. All that showed in the absolute stillness of the one in the throne, the way he didn't even blink.

"Ms. Harlin?"

I gulped and nodded. The whole idea of not showing fear before predators sounded like great advice until facing off against one.

"Thank you for coming. I wish to hire you."

Well…that wasn't what I expected…

I tried to play dumb, to pretend we were talking about my boring day job selling life insurance. "I'm afraid I don't do policies for the undead since you don't really…die."

Colter tilted his head, as though unused to having to tell anyone something twice. Then again, as ruler of a coven, he probably never did. "I require your *other* set of skills."

Well fuck. I supposed that answered if they knew about me, didn't it? I'd thought I'd kept that side of me under wraps, but clearly, I hadn't done a good enough job.

"What did you need?"

"I need you to speak to the spirit of someone recently deceased."

Not a difficult task, nor an unusual one for those who knew my powers. Though… "I can't talk to vampires who have died." I frowned. "I mean, dead-dead. Like, deader than you are."

And that was not the best example of self-preservation I'd ever heard.

Still, if Colter was offended, he didn't show it. "No. Not a vampire." *Good.* The last thing I needed was to explain how vampires didn't have souls anymore, thus couldn't be summoned. That was the sort of thing they might take offense to, and offending things that could kill me was dumb. For beings with such hard skin, I'd found vampires to be exceptionally sensitive. "I need you to speak with the most recent person a vampire killed."

Less good.

I shuffled my fluffy slippers along the tile to buy time. Turning down the leader of a vampire coven was a good way to waste all that staying alive I'd done, but getting involved with the mess of a vampire who had been killing people—and the whole 'most recent person he killed' was a very bad way to put it—wasn't a great idea either.

"Murder victims are notoriously difficult to summon—" I started, trying for my best 'oh, I wish I could, really' tone.

Colter's eyes flashed red, the rim expanding until the entire iris turned ruby and bright. "You will do as I ask, and I will pay you well for your time. If you refuse, you will be lucky if a medium can find what is left of *your* soul when we finish with you. Now, let us try this again. I have a job for you."

My gulp was harsh against my bone-dry throat, but really, there was only one answer.

I plastered on a smile I didn't feel and stuck my hands into the pockets of my penis robe. "Sounds great. Just give me a shovel and point me in the direction of the corpse."

I wish fewer of my nights led to graverobbing.

About the Author

When not writing stories, where the villain and heroine fall madly in love, I can be found daydreaming, singing all the 80's songs, drinking copious amounts of coffee, reading books in headstand, protecting wildlife, and advocating for students with disabilities.

MJ Klipfel loves to hear from readers. You can find her contact information, website details and author profile page at https://www.totallybound.com

TOTALLY
BOUND
Home of Erotic Romance

www.ingramcontent.com/pod-product-compliance
Lightning Source LLC
Chambersburg PA
CBHW022145010726
47493CB00002B/345

9781802505474